D1105998

# THREE SUPERNATURAL NOVELS OF THE VICTORIAN PERIOD

# THE HAUNTED HOTEL
*by Wilkie Collins*

# THE HAUNTED HOUSE
# AT LATCHFORD
*by Mrs. J.H. Riddell*

# THE LOST STRADIVARIUS
*by J. Meade Falkner*

# THREE SUPERNATURAL NOVELS OF THE VICTORIAN PERIOD

Edited by
E.F. Bleiler

DOVER PUBLICATIONS, INC.
NEW YORK

Published in Canada by General Publishing Company, Ltd., 30 Lesmill Road, Don Mills, Toronto, Ontario.
Published in the United Kingdom by Constable and Company, Ltd., 10 Orange Street, London WC 2.

*Three Supernatural Novels of the Victorian Period* is a new selection of three unabridged works, first published by Dover Publications, Inc., in 1975. The novels were originally published as follows:

*The Haunted Hotel: A Mystery of Modern Venice,* in *Belgravia* magazine, London, 1879; the present text reprinted from the 1889 Chatto & Windus edition, London.

*The Haunted House at Latchford* (original title: *Fairy Water*), as *Routledge's Christmas Annual,* London, 1873; the present text reprinted from the 1878 George Routledge and Sons edition, London.

*The Lost Stradivarius,* Blackwoods, Edinburgh & London, 1895; the present text reprinted from the 1896 D. Appleton and Company edition, New York.

*International Standard Book Number: 0-486-22571-2*
*Library of Congress Catalog Card Number: 74-82204*

Manufactured in the United States of America
Dover Publications, Inc.
180 Varick Street
New York, N. Y. 10014

# *CONTENTS*

# INTRODUCTION to the DOVER EDITION

Around 9:30 on the evening of Tuesday, April 4, 1939, a manuscript was held up for auction at Parke Bernet in New York. "Lot Number 119," the auctioneer intoned. "Manuscript of *The Haunted Hotel* by Wilkie Collins." What else the auctioneer said we now have no way of knowing, nor what the response of the audience was. But the audience must have been very largely indifferent, since the manuscript was sold for only $100, a very low price. To cite another lot for comparison, a comparable manuscript by Trollope, *The Vicar of Bullhampton*, went for almost ten times as much as the Collins novel.

The reason is probably that Wilkie Collins had not yet emerged from the decline in reputation that had beset him even during his lifetime, and had overtaken his works in the first part of the twentieth century. There simply was very little interest in Collins, and even little biographical information about him. Today, of course, Collins's unique qualities are recognized, and it is possible to say far more about him than could have been known in 1900 or 1925 or even 1939.

William Wilkie Collins (1824-1889), the foremost figure in the mid-Victorian detective literature, was the son of William Collins the Royal Academician. The family circle of the Collinses consisted largely of painters of the day—Wilkie, Allston, Constable—and Wilkie Collins acquired not only some painterly skill but also the habit of writing painterly prose: scenes that could be described like a genre painting.

After several years of apprenticeship to a tea merchant and a brief fling at the law, Wilkie Collins eventually settled into a living as a freelance writer. A very social man, he had a large circle of literary acquaintances, and it was not long before he became closely associated with the official pre-Raphaelite movement, and through this, in 1851, the circle of Charles Dickens. This contact, which soon blossomed into close friendship, structured the main areas of Collins's life, and indeed, had repercussions on

Dickens. After contributing to Dickens's *Household Words* anonymously for several years, Collins joined the staff in 1856 as a subeditor. When Dickens abandoned *Household Words* and founded *All the Year Round*, Collins stayed with him until 1861, by which time Collins found it more profitable to write independently. He continued to collaborate with Dickens occasionally, acted in Dickens's amateur theatrical group, and wrote certain of the plays which they performed, the most important being *The Frozen Deep*.

Collins first burst into fame with *The Woman in White*, which appeared in *All the Year Round* in 1859-60. This established him as one of the leading writers of his day. A succession of other works, *No Name* (1862) and *Armadale* (1866), intervened between this and his second major work, *The Moonstone*, which also appeared in *All the Year Round*, in 1868. This was Collins's high point. He continued to write prolifically after *The Moonstone*, but his work deteriorated greatly. Physical illness, premature aging, and drugs possibly account for this decline: he suffered greatly from a metabolic disorder, and to kill the pain he consumed enormous quantities of laudanum, to the point where his mental balance was sometimes affected. He died in 1889, much older than his 65 years might indicate. His work included 25 novels, more than 30 short stories and novelettes, more than a dozen plays, and much miscellaneous journalism. His range of writing was wide: historical novels, sentimental novels, comic novels, and propagandistic social novels. Best of all, of course, were his mystery novels, where he set a new standard for clearness of conception, complexity of development, and quality.

Most of the Victorian novelists of importance practiced the ghost story at one time or another, and Collins was no exception. His ghost stories were not as many in number, nor as significant, as those by the specialists, but they still amount to a small volume. Indeed, his first published story, "The Last Stage Coachman" (1843), was a supernatural allegory about railroads, in the manner of Dickens. Other ghost stories are scattered throughout his nearly four decades of writing: "Mad Monkton," "Blow Up with the Brig!," "The Clergyman's Confession," "Percy and the Prophet," "The Ghost's Touch," "The Magic Spectacles," "My Black Mirror," and "The Dream-Woman." Most of these are short, only "Mad Monkton" and the final version of "The Dream-Woman" being fully developed.

Collins also embodied many supernatural elements in work that is not basically supernatural. *The Two Destinies* embodies the notion of the Corsican brothers, linked fates and telepathy. The long novel *Armadale* is based on the working out of a prophetic dream, and there are hints of the supernatural in *The Dead Secret* and *The Moonstone*.

*The Haunted Hotel*, however, is the only lengthy work of Wilkie Collins's in which the supernatural plays more than a transitory part and is central to the story. Traditional and unexceptional in its concept of the supernatural, it shows the typical Collins originality in other ways.

Collins started to work on *The Haunted Hotel* in February 1878. His physical condition was poor, for his metabolic disorder was at one of its cyclical highs, and had settled in his eyes. At times he was nearly totally blind, and had to stay in darkened rooms. One of his friends refers to his eyes at this time as two distended bags of blood. At certain stages during the composition of *The Haunted Hotel* Collins was unable to write, and was forced to dictate to Lizzie Graves Bartley (sometimes known as Harriette), the daughter by her previous marriage of his mistress Caroline Graves. Parts of the surviving manuscript are in Lizzie's hand.

Dosing himself with colchicum and laudanum, he worked steadily on his story, presumably expanding, as was his usual practice, an extremely detailed scenario that went down to the level of conversations. Venice he knew quite well from several Italian trips. The source of the story, however, is not known precisely, but it incorporates an idea that he had gained from a French collection of factual crimes and had used earlier: falsification of a death for financial fraud. This idea seems to have interested him. It was one of the key points to *The Woman in White*, it will be remembered, and it was the theme of his last, weak novel, *Blind Love* (1889), which he did not live to finish. Once the central idea had been established he presumably used the same system that he used in his other work: find characters, let the characters develop the incidents, begin the story at the beginning.

*The Haunted Hotel* appeared serially in *Belgravia*, that home of much fine mystery fiction, in 1879, and was then published in book form. It seems to have been reasonably popular in Great Britain—for the decline came later—but it was somewhat disappointing financially. It had been Collins's practice to sell advance sheets of his works to Harper's in New York, thereby enabling Harper's to anticipate the pirated editions that were sure to follow. (There was no copyright protection for British authors at that time.) But Harper's rejected the story. We do not know why. Possibly they had suffered losses with Collins's previous fiction; possibly they had been unsuccessful because of the pirates; or perhaps they simply did not like the story. In any case *The Haunted Hotel* was not officially published in the United States, an authorized Canadian edition doing little to fill the gap. This may be the reason that it has never been well known or easily available in America.

*The Haunted Hotel* is not on a level with Collins's big three (*The Woman in White, Armadale, The Moonstone*), for obviously the scope (despite some prolixity), complexity, and vigor of the major novels are not present. But it may be called the last flash of sustained good storytelling in Collins's life. The personalities are well imagined, the atmosphere is well maintained, the local color is successful, and there are many of the ingenious little idea-plays that make his better work inimitable.

In the 1920's, when Walter de la Mare, S. M. Ellis, and T. S. Eliot led the modern revival of Wilkie Collins, Eliot, in his essay "Wilkie Collins and Charles Dickens," commented about *The Haunted Hotel:*

What makes it better than a mere readable second-rate ghost story is the fact that fatality in this story is no longer merely a wire jerking

the figures. The principal character, the fatal woman, is herself ob-
sessed by the idea of fatality . . . she therefore compels the coinci-
dences to come, feeling that she is compelled to compel them . . .

Eliot further adds about Collins's work in general, "It has the immense
merit of being never dull . . . there is no contemporary novelist who could
not learn something from Collins in the art of interesting and exciting the
reader." It is still true, over forty years later.

## II

During her long and productive literary lifetime Mrs. Charlotte E. Riddell
(1832-1906) enjoyed two reputations, reputations that one would not
expect to find associated in the same person.

Her first reputation stemmed from the fact that she wrote *George Geith
of Fen Court* (1864), which was originally published under the pseudonym
G. Trafford. It was a revolutionary book, in a small way, since it was the
first serious novel of any merit to consider the business life a suitable topic
for a novel. Geith, who was a connection of a noble house (later revealed
as a direct heir), decamped to the City and became an accountant and
broker simply because he liked the work. This was something of a break-
through in the Victorian novel, for writers usually avoided anything that
explained a livelihood. Dickens, it will be remembered, described Scrooge
as a moneylender and a broker, but said nothing about his business. As for
the lesser writers, a modern reader could come away from them with the
impression that taking a job, to the British aristocracy and middle classes,
was a fate worse than death, infinitely more reprehensible than murdering
one's fellow heirs or swindling them out of their patrimonies. The result of
*George Geith of Fen Court* was that Mrs. Riddell was labeled the chron-
icler of business. A practicality and solidity on finances infuse much of her
other work.

Supernaturalism, surprisingly enough, formed her second reputation,
and the same solidity characterizes her ghost novels as her business novels.
Her supernatural fiction was an expected feature of Christmas annuals,
such as *London Society, Routledge's Christmas Annual*, and *The London
Illustrated News*. It is no exaggeration to say that she is the leading female
writer of ghost stories between Ann Radcliffe and Mrs. Shelley and the
Edwardians May Sinclair and Edith Wharton. During her lifetime she had
only three rivals: Mary Braddon, Rhoda Broughton, and Amelia B. Edwards. Miss Braddon wrote a fair amount of supernatural fiction, but was
more successful in the area of mystery; Miss Broughton wrote several fine
stories, but concentrated more on lively psycho-social novels; and Miss
Edwards eventually immersed herself in ancient Egypt via the Egypt Exploration Fund, of which she was Secretary.

Charlotte Riddell (née Cowan) was born in Carrickfergus, Ireland,
where her father was High Sheriff for Antrim. He died when she was

young, and the depressed family circumstances caused her to go to London, where she tried to earn a living by writing. Small success in the first few years was followed by gradual acceptance in the publishing world, and eventually recognition with *George Geith of Fen Court* in 1864. In 1857 she had married Joseph H. Riddell, an engineer by profession; her marriage was happy, but like many another Victorian female novelist, she discovered that her husband, instead of being a breadwinner, was a liability whose financial ineptnesses she had to correct. When Riddell died in 1880, Mrs. Riddell felt honor bound to pay off his debts, and used her income, during her declining years, for this purpose. As a result she died in poverty. She is said to have been amiable, gentle, pleasant, and intelligent.

Mrs. Riddell wrote four supernatural novels: *The Uninhabited House* (1875), which was republished in *Five Victorian Ghost Novels* (Dover, 1971), *The Haunted River* (1877), *The Disappearance of Mr. Jeremiah Redworth* (1878), and *Fairy Water* (1873), which is reprinted here. She also wrote many supernatural short stories, which on the whole are stronger than the novels. Her finest work is *Weird Stories* (1885), which has also been reprinted under the title *Weird Tales*. It contains six excellent, moderately long stories. Her other work is scattered in Victorian periodicals, sometimes picked up in her short-story collections along with general fiction.

Her work at its best is almost a type specimen of a Victorian novel: careful, well planned, clearly (if prosaically) written, with skillful characterization and good plotting. Her concept of the supernatural is typical of the period: it was simply a story to be told for entertainment. Her storemes, too, were those of her period: a ghost is a personality fragment that remains either to convey information or to seek justice or revenge. Within this limitation of range and depth, Mrs. Riddell's work is sometimes quite good.

*The Haunted House at Latchford* was first published under the title *Fairy Water* as *Routledge's Christmas Annual* for 1873. It was reprinted by Routledge in book form in 1878, and later by Chatto & Windus. An extremely scarce book, it is not recorded in American libraries, and only two or three copies are known in Great Britain.

It is a typical example of Victorian double-plotting, with a social-psychological plot running parallel to the mystery and supernaturalism. The influence of Wilkie Collins is apparent in the characterizations and the style, but the haunted house itself has a couple of unusual touches. A rather common motive, however, is to be found in the strange will, which sets up the circumstances for the novel. This was before the days of female liberation in Great Britain, of course, and such wills delighted the novelists of the day, serving as the springboard for all sorts of shenanigans. Similar wills turn up in the work of Miss Braddon, Mrs. Henry Wood, and LeFanu.

## I I I

If Mrs. J. H. Riddell had two reputations, John Meade Falkner (1858-1932), the author of *The Lost Stradivarius*, led a very paradoxical double life. He was not a professional writer like Collins or Mrs. Riddell. By inclination he was an antiquarian, one of the foremost authorities on paleography and medieval ritual. He was saturated in church lore, and one might have expected him to have earned his bread as a university don or churchman. Instead, by occupation, he was a merchant of death, for many years the chairman of Armstrong, Whitworth and Co., Ltd., then the largest British munitions manufacturer.

Falkner's entry into the arms business came about by chance. After graduating from Oxford with high honors, he became tutor to the children of Anthony Noble, at that time one of the partners of Armstrong. Very able, remarkably affable, Falkner gradually assumed work beyond tutoring, and when the Noble boys outgrew him, Falkner became official secretary to Noble, and from there eventually rose to the chairmanship of the firm.

Falkner traveled extensively, and received many decorations from foreign governments. Although no details, obviously, are available, he presumably undertook the undercover skulduggery necessary to obtain large munitions orders. But Falkner does not seem to have been too effective in his control of Armstrong-Whitworth, which suffered heavily after World War I, and was eventually absorbed by Vickers. As a result, after his retirement, Falkner was regarded with bitterness by his colleagues. His necrologist referred to him as occupying a "position to which he can hardly be called a success." One can guess that he was another Sir Limpidus.

J. M. Falkner the antiquarian, however, was never really bothered much by Armstrong-Whitworth. While still in the business, he became associated with the University of Durham and became honorary librarian. After his retirement, he was awarded a fellowship at Oxford, where he was highly regarded for his scholarship. Biographical notices characterize him as a very pleasant man, but fantastically rigid in his daily habits. In his later years he seems to have lost some contact with reality, and romanticized entertainingly about his exploits. While it would probably be too strong to say that he became a psychopathic liar, his listeners often had to take his statements with a grain of salt. He was extremely tall, very stooped in his later years, rugged of features, face "almost deliquescent" in his old age.

The literary output of J. M. Falkner was not large. Apart from some poetry, he wrote two county guidebooks, a county history, a short story, and three novels. Even today, his guidebooks are highly regarded for their antiquarian resourcefulness and their excellent writing, the Oxfordshire book being particularly useful for one wandering about the countryside. His three novels are *The Lost Stradivarius* (1895), *Moonfleet* (1898), and *The Nebuly Coat* (1903). *Moonfleet*, which was made into a motion picture not many years ago, is an excellent juvenile adventure story, which has been called the finest sister-work to *Treasure Island* and *Kidnapped*. It conveys a period atmosphere quite well, and it is exciting reading. *The Nebuly Coat*, on the other hand, is probably modeled after Hardy. Besides revealing Falkner's passionate interest in architecture, it is a curious mixture of sophisticated narrative form, neo-Gothic alienation plot, naturalism, and antiquarian lore. Certain critics regard it as his best work; others, myself included, consider it much the poorest of his three novels, impossibly dull.

*The Lost Stradivarius* (1895) is a novel with considerable reputation. Although the first edition is a scarce and valuable book, other editions have been in print intermittently since publication. It was particularly popular in America around the turn of the century. Besides drawing on the work of Vernon Lee for background, probably, it shows obvious influences from Bulwer Lytton's *Strange Story* for the structure of ceremonial magic. As a part of the late nineteenth-century efflorescence of supernatural fiction, however, it shows a loosening of the concept of the ghostly. A haunting is now an active principle, not simply a personality fragment.

Cosmic evil plays an important part in *The Lost Stradivarius*. The Evil Principle is not simply a whimsical being who escorts an adventurer. Instead, it is a power that can be approached via ceremonial magic. Summoning such a power may result in a mystical experience of Evil, the so-called *visio malefica*, which parallels the traditional mystical union. In fiction this idea has not been used very often in premodern works, although there are a few outstanding examples: Bulwer Lytton's *Dweller at the Threshold*, which Bulwer apparently understood in terms of psychology; *The Master of the Day of Judgment* by the Hungarian author Leo Perutz, and his *Virgin's Brand*, both of which are concerned with such experiences set off by chemical means—a true anticipation of modern hallucinogens—while Gerald Bullett's short story "The Street of the Eye" is concerned with the older theological aspects of the Wrath of God. Falkner's novel differs from all these in conveying a period charm that has made it, despite some awkwardnesses, a favorite minor novel for generations of readers.

E. F. BLEILER

New York, 1974

# THE HAUNTED HOTEL

## A MYSTERY OF MODERN VENICE

by *Wilkie Collins*

WITH 3 ILLUSTRATIONS BY ARTHUR HOPKINS

# THE FIRST PART

## CHAPTER I

In the year 1860, the reputation of Doctor Wybrow as a London physician reached its highest point. It was reported on good authority that he was in receipt of one of the largest incomes derived from the practice of medicine in modern times.

One afternoon, towards the close of the London season, the Doctor had just taken his luncheon after a specially hard morning's work in his consulting-room, and with a formidable list of visits to patients at their own houses to fill up the rest of his day—when the servant announced that a lady wished to speak to him.

'Who is she?' the Doctor asked. 'A stranger?'

'Yes, sir.'

'I see no strangers out of consulting-hours. Tell her what the hours are, and send her away.'

'I have told her, sir.'

'Well?'

'And she won't go.'

'Won't go?' The Doctor smiled as he repeated the words. He was a humourist in his way; and there was an absurd side to the situation which rather amused him. 'Has this obstinate lady given you her name?' he inquired.

'No, sir. She refused to give any name—she said she wouldn't keep you five minutes, and the matter was too important to wait till to-morrow. There she is in the consulting-room; and how to get her out again is more than I know.'

Doctor Wybrow considered for a moment. His knowledge of women (professionally speaking) rested on the ripe experience of more than thirty years; he had met with them in all their varieties—especially the variety which knows nothing of the value of time, and never hesitates at sheltering itself behind the privileges of its sex. A glance at his watch informed him that he must soon begin his rounds among the patients who were waiting for him at their own houses. He decided forthwith on taking the only wise course that was open under the circumstances. In other words, he decided on taking to flight.

'Is the carriage at the door?' he asked.

'Yes, sir.'

'Very well. Open the house-door for me without making any noise, and leave the lady in undisturbed possession of the consulting-room. When she gets tired of waiting, you know what to tell her. If she asks when I am expected to return, say that I dine at my club, and spend the evening at the theatre. Now then, softly, Thomas! If your shoes creak, I am a lost man.'

He noiselessly led the way into the hall, followed by the servant on tip-toe.

Did the lady in the consulting-room suspect him? or did Thomas's shoes creak, and was her sense of hearing unusually keen? Whatever the explanation may be, the event that actually happened was beyond all doubt. Exactly as Doctor Wybrow passed his consulting-room, the door opened—the lady appeared on the threshold—and laid her hand on his arm.

'I entreat you, sir, not to go away without letting me speak to you first.'

The accent was foreign; the tone was low and firm. Her fingers closed gently, and yet resolutely, on the Doctor's arm.

Neither her language nor her action had the slightest effect in inclining him to grant her request. The influence that instantly stopped him, on the way to his carriage, was the silent influence of her face. The startling contrast between the corpse-like pallor of her complexion and the overpowering life and light, the glittering metallic brightness in her large black eyes, held him literally spell-bound. She was dressed in dark colours, with perfect taste; she was of middle height, and (apparently) of middle age—say a year or two over thirty. Her lower features—the nose, mouth, and chin—possessed the fineness and delicacy of form which is oftener seen among women of foreign races than among women of English birth. She was unquestionably a handsome person—with the one serious drawback of her ghastly complexion, and with the less noticeable defect of a total want of tenderness in the expression of her eyes. Apart from his first emotion of surprise, the feeling she produced in the Doctor may be described as an overpowering feeling of professional curiosity. The case might prove to be something entirely new in his professional experience. 'It looks like it,' he thought; 'and it's worth waiting for.'

She perceived that she she had produced a strong impression of some kind upon him, and dropped her hold on his arm.

'You have comforted many miserable women in your time,' she said. 'Comfort one more, to-day.'

Without waiting to be answered, she led the way back into the room.

The Doctor followed her, and closed the door. He placed her in the patients' chair, opposite the windows. Even in London the sun, on that summer afternoon, was dazzlingly bright. The radiant light flowed in on her. Her eyes met it unflinchingly, with the steely steadiness of the eyes of an eagle. The smooth pallor of her unwrinkled skin looked more fearfully white than ever. For the first time, for many a long year past, the Doctor felt his pulse quicken its beat in the presence of a patient.

Having possessed herself of his attention, she appeared, strangely enough, to have nothing to say to him. A curious apathy seemed to have taken possession of this resolute woman. Forced to speak first, the Doctor merely inquired, in the conventional phrase, what he could do for her.

The sound of his voice seemed to rouse her. Still looking straight at the light, she said abruptly: 'I have a painful question to ask.'

'What is it?'

Her eyes travelled slowly from the window to the Doctor's face. Without the slightest outward appearance of agitation, she put the 'painful question' in these extraordinary words:

'I want to know, if you please, whether I am in danger of going mad?'

Some men might have been amused, and some might have been alarmed. Doctor Wybrow was only conscious of a sense of disappointment. Was this the rare case that he had anticipated, judging rashly by appearances? Was the new patient only a hypochondriacal woman, whose malady was a disordered stomach and whose misfortune was a weak brain? 'Why do you come to *me*?' he asked sharply. 'Why don't you consult a doctor whose special employment is the treatment of the insane?'

She had her answer ready on the instant.

'I don't go to a doctor of that sort,' she said, 'for the very reason that he *is* a specialist: he has the fatal habit of judging everybody by lines and rules of his own laying down. I come to *you*, because my case is outside of all lines and rules, and because you are famous in your profession for the discovery of mysteries in disease. Are you satisfied?'

He was more than satisfied—his first idea had been the right idea, after all. Besides, she was correctly informed as to his professional position. The capacity which had raised him to fame and fortune was his capacity (unrivalled among his brethren) for the discovery of remote disease.

'I am at your disposal,' he answered. 'Let me try if I can find out what is the matter with you.'

He put his medical questions. They were promptly and plainly answered; and they led to no other conclusion than that the strange lady was, mentally and physically, in excellent health. Not satisfied with questions, he carefully examined the great organs of life. Neither his hand nor his stethoscope could discover anything that was amiss. With the admirable patience and devotion to his art which had distinguished him from the time when he was a student, he still subjected her to one test after another. The result was always the same. Not only was there no tendency to brain disease—there was not even a perceptible derangement of the nervous system. 'I can find nothing the matter with you,' he said. 'I can't even account for the extraordinary pallor of your complexion. You completely puzzle me.'

'The pallor of my complexion is nothing,' she answered a little impatiently. 'In my early life I had a narrow escape from death by poisoning. I have never had a complexion since—and my skin is so delicate, I cannot paint without producing a hideous rash. But that is of no importance. I wanted your opinion given positively. I believed in you, and you have disappointed me.' Her head dropped on her breast. 'And so it ends!' she said to herself bitterly.

The Doctor's sympathies were touched. Perhaps it might be more correct to say that his professional pride was a little hurt. 'It may end in the right way yet,' he remarked, 'if you choose to help me.'

She looked up again with flashing eyes, 'Speak plainly,' she said. 'How can I help you?'

'Plainly, madam, you come to me as an enigma, and you leave me to make the right guess by the unaided efforts of my art. My art will do much, but not all. For example, something must have occurred—something quite unconnected with the state of your bodily health—to frighten you about yourself, or you would never have come here to consult me. Is that true?'

She clasped her hands in her lap. 'That is true!' she said eagerly. 'I begin to believe in you again.'

'Very well. You can't expect me to find out the moral cause which has alarmed you. I can positively discover that there is no physical cause of alarm; and (unless you admit me to your confidence) I can do no more.'

She rose, and took a turn in the room. 'Suppose I tell you?' she said. 'But, mind, I shall mention no names!'

'There is no need to mention names. The facts are all I want.'

'The facts are nothing,' she rejoined. 'I have only my own impressions to confess—and you will very likely think me a fanciful fool when you hear what they are. No matter. I will do my best to content you—I will begin with the facts that you want. Take my word for it, *they* won't do much to help you.'

She sat down again. In the plainest possible words, she began the strangest and wildest confession that had ever reached the Doctor's ears.

## CHAPTER II

'It is one fact, sir, that I am a widow,' she said. 'It is another fact, that I am going to be married again.'

There she paused, and smiled at some thought that occurred to her. Doctor Wybrow was not favourably impressed by her smile—there was something at once sad and cruel in it. It came slowly, and it went away suddenly. He began to doubt whether he had been wise in acting on his first impression. His mind reverted to the commonplace patients and the discoverable maladies that were waiting for him, with a certain tender regret.

The lady went on.

'My approaching marriage,' she said, 'has one embarrassing circumstance connected with it. The gentleman whose wife I am to be, was engaged to another lady when he happened to meet with me, abroad: that lady, mind, being of his own blood and family, related to him as his cousin. I have innocently robbed her of her lover, and destroyed her prospects in life. Innocently, I say—because he told me nothing of his engagement until after I had accepted him. When we next met in England —and when there was danger, no doubt, of the affair coming to my knowledge—he told me the truth. I was naturally indignant. He had his excuse ready; he showed me a letter from the lady herself, releasing him from his engagement. A more noble, a more high-minded letter, I never read in my life. I cried over it—I who have no tears in me for sorrows of my own! If the letter had left him any hope of being forgiven, I would have positively refused to marry him. But the firmness of it—without anger, without a word of reproach, with heartfelt wishes even for his happiness—the firmness of it, I say, left him no hope. He appealed to my compassion; he appealed to his love for me. You know what women are. I too was soft-hearted—I said, Very well: yes! In a week more (I tremble as I think of it) we are to be married.'

She did really tremble—she was obliged to pause and compose herself, before she could go on. The Doctor, waiting for more facts, began to fear that he stood committed to a long story. 'Forgive me for reminding you that I have suffering persons waiting to see me,' he said. 'The sooner you can come to the point, the better for my patients and for me.'

The strange smile—at once so sad and so cruel—showed itself again on the lady's lips. 'Every word I have said is to the point,' she answered. 'You will see it yourself in a moment more.'

She resumed her narrative.

'Yesterday—you need fear no long story, sir; only yesterday—I was among the visitors at one of your English luncheon parties. A lady, a perfect stranger to me, came in late—after we had left the table, and had retired to the drawing-room. She happened to take a chair near me; and we were presented to each other. I knew her by name, as she knew me. It was the woman whom I had robbed of her lover, the woman who had written the noble letter. Now listen! You were impatient with me for not interesting you in what I said just now. I said it to satisfy your mind that I had no enmity of feeling towards the lady, on my side. I admired her, I felt for her—I had no cause to reproach myself. This is very important, as you will

presently see. On her side, I have reason to be assured that the circumstances had been truly explained to her, and that she understood I was in
no way to blame. Now, knowing all these necessary things as you do,
explain to me, if you can, why, when I rose and met that woman's eyes
looking at me, I turned cold from head to foot, and shuddered, and
shivered, and knew what a deadly panic of fear was, for the first time in
my life.'

The Doctor began to feel interested at last.

'Was there anything remarkable in the lady's personal appearance?' he
asked.

'Nothing whatever!' was the vehement reply. 'Here is the true description of her: –The ordinary English lady; the clear cold blue eyes, the fine
rosy complexion, the inanimately polite manner, the large good-humoured
mouth, the too plump cheeks and chin: these, and nothing more.'

'Was there anything in her expression, when you first looked at her,
that took you by surprise?'

'There was natural curiosity to see the woman who had been preferred
to her; and perhaps some astonishment also, not to see a more engaging
and more beautiful person; both those feelings restrained within the limits
of good breeding, and both not lasting for more than a few moments–so
far as I could see. I say, "so far," because the horrible agitation that she
communicated to me disturbed my judgment. If I could have got to the
door, I would have run out of the room, she frightened me so! I was not
even able to stand up–I sank back in my chair; I stared horror-struck at
the calm blue eyes that were only looking at me with a gentle surprise. To
say they affected me like the eyes of a serpent is to say nothing. I felt her
soul in them, looking into mine–looking, if such a thing can be, unconsciously to her own mortal self. I tell you my impression, in all its horror
and in all its folly! That woman is destined (without knowing it herself) to
be the evil genius of my life. Her innocent eyes saw hidden capabilities of
wickedness in me that I was not aware of myself, until I felt them stirring
under her look. If I commit faults in my life to come–if I am even guilty
of crimes–she will bring the retribution, without (as I firmly believe) any
conscious exercise of her own will. In one indescribable moment I felt all
this–and I suppose my face showed it. The good artless creature was
inspired by a sort of gentle alarm for me. "I am afraid the heat of the
room is too much for you; will you try my smelling bottle?" I heard her
say those kind words; and I remember nothing else–I fainted. When I
recovered my senses, the company had all gone; only the lady of the house
was with me. For the moment I could say nothing to her; the dreadful
impression that I have tried to describe to you came back to me with the
coming back of my life. As soon I could speak, I implored her to tell me
the whole truth about the woman whom I had supplanted. You see, I had
a faint hope that her good character might not really be deserved, that her
noble letter was a skilful piece of hypocrisy–in short, that she secretly
hated me, and was cunning enough to hide it. No! the lady had been her

friend from her girlhood, was as familiar with her as if they had been sisters—knew her positively to be as good, as innocent, as incapable of hating anybody, as the greatest saint that ever lived. My one last hope, that I had only felt an ordinary forewarning of danger in the presence of an ordinary enemy, was a hope destroyed for ever. There was one more effort I could make, and I made it. I went next to the man whom I am to marry. I implored him to release me from my promise. He refused. I declared I would break my engagement. He showed me letters from his sisters, letters from his brothers, and his dear friends—all entreating him to think again before he made me his wife; all repeating reports of me in Paris, Vienna, and London, which are so many vile lies. "If you refuse to marry me," he said, "you admit that these reports are true—you admit that you are afraid to face society in the character of my wife." What could I answer? There was no contradicting him—he was plainly right: if I persisted in my refusal, the utter destruction of my reputation would be the result. I consented to let the wedding take place as we had arranged it—and left him. The night has passed. I am here, with my fixed conviction—that innocent woman is ordained to have a fatal influence over my life. I am here with my one question to put, to the one man who can answer it. For the last time, sir, what am I—a demon who has seen the avenging angel? or only a poor mad woman, misled by the delusion of a deranged mind?'

Doctor Wybrow rose from his chair, determined to close the interview.

He was strongly and painfully impressed by what he had heard. The longer he had listened to her, the more irresistibly the conviction of the woman's wickedness had forced itself on him. He tried vainly to think of her as a person to be pitied—a person with a morbidly sensitive imagination, conscious of the capacities for evil which lie dormant in us all, and striving earnestly to open her heart to the counter-influence of her own better nature; the effort was beyond him. A perverse instinct in him said, as if in words, Beware how you believe in her!

'I have already given you my opinion,' he said. 'There is no sign of your intellect being deranged, or being likely to be deranged, that medical science can discover—as *I* understand it. As for the impressions you have confided to me, I can only say that yours is a case (as I venture to think) for spiritual rather than for medical advice. Of one thing be assured: what you have said to me in this room shall not pass out of it. Your confession is safe in my keeping.'

She heard him, with a certain dogged resignation, to the end.

'Is that all?' she asked.

'That is all,' he answered.

She put a little paper packet of money on the table. 'Thank you, sir. There is your fee.'

With those words she rose. Her wild black eyes looked upward, with an expression of despair so defiant and so horrible in its silent agony that the Doctor turned away his head, unable to endure the sight of it. The bare idea of taking anything from her—not money only, but anything even that she had touched—suddenly revolted him. Still without looking at her, he said, 'Take it back; I don't want my fee.'

She neither heeded nor heard him. Still looking upward, she said slowly to herself, 'Let the end come. I have done with the struggle: I submit.'

She drew her veil over her face, bowed to the Doctor, and left the room.

He rang the bell, and followed her into the hall. As the servant closed the door on her, a sudden impulse of curiosity—utterly unworthy of him, and at the same time utterly irresistible—sprang up in the Doctor's mind. Blushing like a boy, he said to the servant, 'Follow her home, and find out her name.' For one moment the man looked at his master, doubting if his own ears had not deceived him. Doctor Wybrow looked back at him in silence. The submissive servant knew what that silence meant—he took his hat and hurried into the street.

The Doctor went back to the consulting-room. A sudden revulsion of feeling swept over his mind. Had the woman left an infection of wickedness in the house, and had he caught it? What devil had possessed him to degrade himself in the eyes of his own servant? He had behaved infamously—he had asked an honest man, a man who had served him faithfully for years, to turn spy! Stung by the bare thought of it, he ran out into the hall again, and opened the door. The servant had disappeared; it was too late to call him back. But one refuge from his contempt for himself was now open to him—the refuge of work. He got into his carriage and went his rounds among his patients.

If the famous physician could have shaken his own reputation, he would have done it that afternoon. Never before had he made himself so little welcome at the bedside. Never before had he put off until to-morrow the prescription which ought to have been written, the opinion which ought to have been given, to-day. He went home earlier than usual—unutterably dissatisfied with himself.

The servant had returned. Dr. Wybrow was ashamed to question him. The man reported the result of his errand, without waiting to be asked.

'The lady's name is the Countess Narona. She lives at ——'

Without waiting to hear where she lived, the Doctor acknowledged the all-important discovery of her name by a silent bend of the head, and entered his consulting-room. The fee that he had vainly refused still lay in its little white paper covering on the table. He sealed it up in an envelope; addressed it to the 'Poor-box' of the nearest police-court; and, calling the servant in, directed him to take it to the magistrate the next morning. Faithful to his duties, the servant waited to ask the customary question, 'Do you dine at home to-day, sir?'

After a moment's hesitation he said, 'No: I shall dine at the club.'

The most easily deteriorated of all the moral qualities is the quality called 'conscience.' In one state of a man's mind, his conscience is the severest judge that can pass sentence on him. In another state, he and his conscience are on the best possible terms with each other in the comfortable capacity of accomplices. When Doctor Wybrow left his house for the second time, he did not even attempt to conceal from himself that his sole object, in dining at the club, was to hear what the world said of the Countess Narona.

# CHAPTER III

There was a time when a man in search of the pleasures of gossip sought the society of ladies. The man knows better now. He goes to the smoking-room of his club.

Doctor Wybrow lit his cigar, and looked round him at his brethren in social conclave assembled. The room was well filled; but the flow of talk was still languid. The Doctor innocently applied the stimulant that was wanted. When he inquired if anybody knew the Countess Narona, he was answered by something like a shout of astonishment. Never (the conclave agreed) had such an absurd question been asked before! Every human creature, with the slightest claim to a place in society, knew the Countess Narona. An adventuress with a European reputation of the blackest possible colour—such was the general description of the woman with the deathlike complexion and the glittering eyes.

Descending to particulars, each member of the club contributed his own little stock of scandal to the memoirs of the Countess. It was doubtful whether she was really, what she called herself, a Dalmatian lady. It was doubtful whether she had ever been married to the Count whose widow she assumed to be. It was doubtful whether the man who accompanied her in her travels (under the name of Baron Rivar, and in the character of her brother) was her brother at all. Report pointed to the Baron as a gambler at every 'table' on the Continent. Report whispered that his so-called sister had narrowly escaped being implicated in a famous trial for poisoning at Vienna—that she had been known at Milan as a spy in the interests of Austria—that her 'apartment' in Paris had been denounced to the police as nothing less than a private gambling-house—and that her present appearance in England was the natural result of the discovery. Only one member of the assembly in the smoking-room took the part of this much-abused woman, and declared that her character had been most cruelly and most unjustly assailed. But as the man was a lawyer, his interference went for nothing: it was naturally attributed to the spirit of contradiction inherent in his profession. He was asked derisively what he thought of the circumstances under which the Countess had become engaged to be married; and he made the characteristic answer, that he thought the circumstances highly creditable to both parties, and that he looked on the lady's future husband as a most enviable man.

Hearing this, the Doctor raised another shout of astonishment by inquiring the name of the gentleman whom the Countess was about to marry.

His friends in the smoking-room decided unanimously that the celebrated physician must be a second 'Rip-van-Winkle,' and that he had just awakened from a supernatural sleep of twenty years. It was all very well to say that he was devoted to his profession, and that he had neither time nor inclination to pick up fragments of gossip at dinner-parties and balls. A man who did not know that the Countess Narona had borrowed money at Homburg of no less a person than Lord Montbarry, and had then deluded him into making her a proposal of marriage, was a man who had probably never heard of Lord Montbarry himself. The younger members of the club, humouring the joke, sent a waiter for the 'Peerage'; and read aloud the memoir of the nobleman in question, for the Doctor's benefit—with illustrative morsels of information interpolated by themselves.

'Herbert John Westwick. First Baron Montbarry, of Montbarry, King's County, Ireland. Created a Peer for distinguished military services in India. Born, 1812. Forty-eight years old, Doctor, at the present time. Not married. Will be married next week, Doctor, to the delightful creature we have been talking about. Heir presumptive, his lordship's next brother, Stephen Robert, married to Ella, youngest daughter of the Reverend Silas Marden, Rector of Runnigate, and has issue, three daughters. Younger brothers of his lordship, Francis and Henry, unmarried. Sisters of his lordship, Lady Barville, married to Sir Theodore Barville, Bart.; and Anne, widow of the late Peter Norbury, Esq., of Norbury Cross. Bear his lordship's relations well in mind, Doctor. Three brothers Westwick, Stephen, Francis, and Henry; and two sisters, Lady Barville and Mrs. Norbury. Not one of the five will be present at the marriage; and not one of the five will leave a stone unturned to stop it, if the Countess will only give them a chance. Add to these hostile members of the family another offended relative not mentioned in the 'Peerage,' a young lady ——'

A sudden outburst of protest in more than one part of the room stopped the coming disclosure, and released the Doctor from further persecution.

'Don't mention the poor girl's name; it's too bad to make a joke of that part of the business; she has behaved nobly under shameful provocation; there is but one excuse for Montbarry—he is either a madman or a fool.' In these terms the protest expressed itself on all sides. Speaking confidentially to his next neighbour, the Doctor discovered that the lady referred to was already known to him (through the Countess's confession) as the lady deserted by Lord Montbarry. Her name was Agnes Lockwood. She was described as being the superior of the Countess in personal attraction, and as being also by some years the younger woman of the two. Making all allowance for the follies that men committed every day in their relations with women, Montbarry's delusion was still the most monstrous delusion on record. In this expression of opinion every man present agreed—the lawyer even included. Not one of them could call to mind the innumerable instances in which the sexual influence has proved irresistible in the persons of women without even the pretension to beauty. The very members of the club whom the Countess (in spite of her personal disadvantages) could have most easily fascinated, if she had thought it worth her while, were the members who wondered most loudly at Montbarry's choice of a wife.

While the topic of the Countess's marriage was still the one topic of conversation, a member of the club entered the smoking-room whose appearance instantly produced a dead silence. Doctor Wybrow's next neighbour whispered to him, 'Montbarry's brother—Henry Westwick!'

The new-comer looked round him slowly, with a bitter smile.

'You are all talking of my brother,' he said. 'Don't mind me. Not one of you can despise him more heartily than I do. Go on, gentlemen—go on!'

But one man present took the speaker at his word. That man was the lawyer who had already undertaken the defence of the Countess.

'I stand alone in my opinion,' he said, 'and I am not ashamed of repeating it in anybody's hearing. I consider the Countess Narona to be a cruelly-treated woman. Why shouldn't she be Lord Montbarry's wife? Who can say she has a mercenary motive in marrying him?'

Montbarry's brother turned sharply on the speaker. '*I* say it!' he answered.

The reply might have shaken some men. The lawyer stood on his ground as firmly as ever.

'I believe I am right,' he rejoined, 'in stating that his lordship's income is not more than sufficient to support his station in life; also that it is an income derived almost entirely from landed property in Ireland, every acre of which is entailed.'

Montbarry's brother made a sign, admitting that he had no objection to offer so far.

'If his lordship dies first,' the lawyer proceeded, 'I have been informed that the only provision he can make for his widow consists in a rent-charge on the property of no more than four hundred a year. His retiring pension and allowances, it is well known, die with him. Four hundred a year is therefore all that he can leave to the Countess, if he leaves her a widow.'

'Four hundred a year is *not* all,' was the reply to this. 'My brother has insured his life for ten thousand pounds; and he has settled the whole of it on the Countess, in the event of his death.'

This announcement produced a strong sensation. Men looked at each other, and repeated the three startling words, 'Ten thousand pounds!' Driven fairly to the wall, the lawyer made a last effort to defend his position.

'May I ask who made that settlement a condition of the marriage?' he said. 'Surely it was not the Countess herself?'

Henry Westwick answered, 'It was the Countess's brother'; and added, 'which comes to the same thing.'

After that, there was no more to be said—so long, at least, as Mont-barry's brother was present. The talk flowed into other channels; and the Doctor went home.

But his morbid curiosity about the Countess was not set at rest yet. In his leisure moments he found himself wondering whether Lord Mont-barry's family would succeed in stopping the marriage after all. And more than this, he was conscious of a growing desire to see the infatuated man himself. Every day during the brief interval before the wedding, he looked in at the club, on the chance of hearing some news. Nothing had hap-pened, so far as the club knew. The Countess's position was secure; Mont-barry's resolution to be her husband was unshaken. They were both Ro-man Catholics, and they were to be married at the chapel in Spanish Place. So much the Doctor discovered about them—and no more.

On the day of the wedding, after a feeble struggle with himself, he actually sacrificed his patients and their guineas, and slipped away secretly to see the marriage. To the end of his life, he was angry with anybody who reminded him of what he had done on that day!

The wedding was strictly private. A close carriage stood at the church door; a few people, mostly of the lower class, and mostly old women, were scattered about the interior of the building. Here and there Doctor Wy-brow detected the faces of some of his brethren of the club, attracted by curiosity, like himself. Four persons only stood before the altar—the bride and bridegroom and their two witnesses. One of these last was an elderly woman, who might have been the Countess's companion or maid; the other was undoubtedly her brother, Baron Rivar. The bridal party (the bride herself included) wore their ordinary morning costume. Lord Mont-barry, personally viewed, was a middle-aged military man of the ordinary type: nothing in the least remarkable distinguished him either in face or figure. Baron Rivar, again, in his way was another conventional representa-tive of another well-known type. One sees his finely-pointed moustache, his bold eyes, his crisply-curling hair, and his dashing carriage of the head, repeated hundreds of times over on the Boulevards of Paris. The only noteworthy point about him was of the negative sort—he was not in the least like his sister. Even the officiating priest was only a harmless, humble-looking old man, who went through his duties resignedly, and felt visible rheumatic difficulties every time he bent his knees. The one remarkable person, the Countess herself, only raised her veil at the beginning of the ceremony, and presented nothing in her plain dress that was worth a second look. Never, on the face of it, was there a less interesting and less romantic marriage than this. From time to time the Doctor glanced round at the door or up at the galleries, vaguely anticipating the appearance of some protesting stranger, in possession of some terrible secret, commis-sioned to forbid the progress of the service. Nothing in the shape of an event occurred—nothing extraordinary, nothing dramatic. Bound fast to-gether as man and wife, the two disappeared, followed by their witnesses, to sign the registers; and still Doctor Wybrow waited, and still he cherished the obstinate hope that something worth seeing must certainly happen yet.

The interval passed, and the married couple, returning to the church, walked together down the nave to the door. Doctor Wybrow drew back as they approached. To his confusion and surprise, the Countess discovered him. He heard her say to her husband, 'One moment; I see a friend.' Lord Montbarry bowed and waited. She stepped up to the Doctor, took his hand, and wrung it hard. He felt her overpowering black eyes looking at him through her veil. 'One step more, you see, on the way to the end!' She whispered those strange words, and returned to her husband. Before the Doctor could recover himself and follow her, Lord and Lady Montbarry had stepped into their carriage, and had driven away.

Outside the church door stood the three or four members of the club who, like Doctor Wybrow, had watched the ceremony out of curiosity. Near them was the bride's brother, waiting alone. He was evidently bent on seeing the man whom his sister had spoken to, in broad daylight. His bold eyes rested on the Doctor's face, with a momentary flash of suspicion in them. The cloud suddenly cleared away; the Baron smiled with charming courtesy, lifted his hat to his sister's friend, and walked off.

The members constituted themselves into a club conclave on the church steps. They began with the Baron. 'Damned ill-looking rascal!' They went on with Montbarry. 'Is he going to take that horrid woman with him to Ireland?' 'Not he! he can't face the tenantry; they know about Agnes Lockwood.' 'Well, but where *is* he going?' 'To Scotland.' 'Does *she* like that?' 'It's only for a fortnight; they come back to London, and go abroad.' 'And they will never return to England, eh?' 'Who can tell? Did you see how she looked at Montbarry, when she had to lift her veil at the beginning of the service? In his place, I should have bolted. Did *you* see her, Doctor?' By this time, Doctor Wybrow had remembered his patients, and had heard enough of the club gossip. He followed the example of Baron Rivar, and walked off.

'One step more, you see, on the way to the end,' he repeated to himself, on his way home. 'What end?'

# CHAPTER IV

On the day of the marriage Agnes Lockwood sat alone in the little drawing-room of her London lodgings, burning the letters which had been written to her by Montbarry in the bygone time.

The Countess's maliciously smart description of her, addressed to Doctor Wybrow, had not even hinted at the charm that most distinguished Agnes—the artless expression of goodness and purity which instantly attracted everyone who approached her. She looked by many years younger than she really was. With her fair complexion and her shy manner, it seemed only natural to speak of her as 'a girl,' although she was now really advancing towards thirty years of age. She lived alone with an old nurse devoted to her, on a modest little income which was just enough to support the two. There were none of the ordinary signs of grief in her face, as she slowly tore the letters of her false lover in two, and threw the pieces into the small fire which had been lit to consume them. Unhappily for herself, she was one of those women who feel too deeply to find relief in tears. Pale and quiet, with cold trembling fingers, she destroyed the letters one by one without daring to read them again. She had torn the last of the series, and was still shrinking from throwing it after the rest into the swiftly destroying flame, when the old nurse came in, and asked if she would see 'Master Henry,'—meaning that youngest member of the Westwick family, who had publicly declared his contempt for his brother in the smoking-room of the club.

Agnes hesitated. A faint tinge of colour stole over her face.

There had been a long past time when Henry Westwick had owned that he loved her. She had made her confession to him, acknowledging that her heart was given to his eldest brother. He had submitted to his disappointment; and they had met thenceforth as cousins and friends. Never before had she associated the idea of him with embarrassing recollections. But now, on the very day when his brother's marriage to another woman had consummated his brother's treason towards her, there was something vaguely repellent in the prospect of seeing him. The old nurse (who remembered them both in their cradles) observed her hesitation; and sympathising of course with the man, put in a timely word for Henry. 'He says, he's going away, my dear; and he only wants to shake hands, and say good-bye.' This plain statement of the case had its effect. Agnes decided on receiving her cousin.

He entered the room so rapidly that he surprised her in the act of throwing the fragments of Montbarry's last letter into the fire. She hurriedly spoke first.

'You are leaving London very suddenly, Henry. Is it business? or pleasure?'

Instead of answering her, he pointed to the flaming letter, and to some black ashes of burnt paper lying lightly in the lower part of the fireplace.

'Are you burning letters?'

'Yes.'

'*His* letters?'

'Yes.'

He took her hand gently. 'I had no idea I was intruding on you, at a time when you must wish to be alone. Forgive me, Agnes—I shall see you when I return.'

She signed to him, with a faint smile, to take a chair.

'We have known one another since we were children,' she said. 'Why should I feel a foolish pride about myself in your presence? why should I have any secrets from you? I sent back all your brother's gifts to me some time ago. I have been advised to do more, to keep nothing that can remind me of him—in short, to burn his letters. I have taken the advice; but I own I shrank a little from destroying the last of the letters. No—not because it was the last, but because it had this in it.' She opened her hand, and showed him a lock of Montbarry's hair, tied with a morsel of golden cord. 'Well! well! let it go with the rest.'

She dropped it into the flame. For a while, she stood with her back to Henry, leaning on the mantel-piece, and looking into the fire. He took the chair to which she had pointed, with a strange contradiction of expression in his face: the tears were in his eyes, while the brows above were knit close in an angry frown. He muttered to himself, 'Damn him!'

She rallied her courage, and looked at him again when she spoke. 'Well, Henry, and why are you going away?'

'I am out of spirits, Agnes, and I want a change.'

She paused before she spoke again. His face told her plainly that he was thinking of *her* when he made that reply. She was grateful to him, but her mind was not with him: her mind was still with the man who had deserted her. She turned round again to the fire.

'Is it true,' she asked, after a long silence, 'that they have been married to-day?'

He answered ungraciously in the one necessary word:—'Yes.'

'Did you go to the church?'

He resented the question with an expression of indignant surprise. 'Go to the church?' he repeated. 'I would as soon go to ——' He checked himself there. 'How can you ask?' he added in lower tones. 'I have never spoken to Montbarry, I have not even seen him, since he treated you like the scoundrel and the fool that he is.'

She looked at him suddenly, without saying a word. He understood her, and begged her pardon. But he was still angry. 'The reckoning comes to some men,' he said, 'even in this world. He will live to rue the day when he married that woman!'

Agnes took a chair by his side, and looked at him with a gentle surprise.

'Is it quite reasonable to be so angry with her, because your brother preferred her to me?' she asked.

Henry turned on her sharply. 'Do *you* defend the Countess, of all the people in the world?'

'Why not?' Agnes answered. 'I know nothing against her. On the only occasion when we met, she appeared to be a singularly timid, nervous person, looking dreadfully ill; and *being* indeed so ill that she fainted under the heat of my room. Why should we not do her justice? We know that she was innocent of any intention to wrong me; we know that she was not aware of my engagement ——'

Henry lifted his hand impatiently, and stopped her. 'There is such a thing as being *too* just and *too* forgiving!' he interposed. 'I can't bear to hear you talk in that patient way, after the scandalously cruel manner in which you have been treated. Try to forget them both, Agnes. I wish to God I could help you to do it!'

Agnes laid her hand on his arm. 'You are very good to me, Henry; but you don't quite understand me. I was thinking of myself and my trouble in quite a different way, when you came in. I was wondering whether anything which has so entirely filled my heart, and so absorbed all that is best and truest in me, as my feeling for your brother, can really pass away as if it had never existed. I have destroyed the last visible things that remind me of him. In this world I shall see him no more. But is the tie that once bound us, completely broken? Am I as entirely parted from the good and evil fortune of his life as if we had never met and never loved? What do *you* think, Henry? I can hardly believe it.'

'If you could bring the retribution on him that he has deserved,' Henry Westwick answered sternly, 'I might be inclined to agree with you.'

As that reply passed his lips, the old nurse appeared again at the door, announcing another visitor.

'I'm sorry to disturb you, my dear. But here is little Mrs. Ferrari wanting to know when she may say a few words to you.'

Agnes turned to Henry, before she replied. 'You remember Emily Bidwell, my favourite pupil years ago at the village school, and afterwards my maid? She left me, to marry an Italian courier, named Ferrari—and I am afraid it has not turned out very well. Do you mind my having her in here for a minute or two?'

Henry rose to take his leave. 'I should be glad to see Emily again at any other time,' he said. 'But it is best that I should go now. My mind is disturbed, Agnes; I might say things to you, if I stayed here any longer, which—which are better not said now. I shall cross the Channel by the mail to-night, and see how a few weeks' change will help me.' He took her hand. 'Is there anything in the world that I can do for you?' he asked very earnestly. She thanked him, and tried to release her hand. He held it with a tremulous lingering grasp. 'God bless you, Agnes!' he said in faltering tones, with his eyes on the ground. Her face flushed again, and the next instant turned paler than ever; she knew his heart as well as he knew it himself—she was too distressed to speak. He lifted her hand to his lips, kissed it fervently, and, without looking at her again, left the room. The nurse hobbled after him to the head of the stairs: she had not forgotten the time when the younger brother had been the unsuccessful rival of the elder for the hand of Agnes. 'Don't be down-hearted, Master Henry,' whispered the old woman, with the unscrupulous common sense of persons in the lower rank of life. 'Try her again, when you come back!'

Left alone for a few moments, Agnes took a turn in the room, trying to compose herself. She paused before a little water-colour drawing on the wall, which had belonged to her mother: it was her own portrait when she was a child. 'How much happier we should be,' she thought to herself sadly, 'if we never grew up!'

The courier's wife was shown in—a little meek melancholy woman, with white eyelashes, and watery eyes, who curtseyed deferentially and was troubled with a small chronic cough. Agnes shook hands with her kindly. 'Well, Emily, what can I do for you?'

The courier's wife made rather a strange answer: 'I'm afraid to tell you, Miss.'

'Is it such a very difficult favour to grant? Sit down, and let me hear how you are going on. Perhaps the petition will slip out while we are talking. How does your husband behave to you?'

Emily's light grey eyes looked more watery than ever. She shook her head and sighed resignedly. 'I have no positive complaint to make against him, Miss. But I'm afraid he doesn't care about me; and he seems to take no interest in his home—I may almost say he's tired of his home. It might be better for both of us, Miss, if he went travelling for a while—not to mention the money, which is beginning to be wanted sadly.' She put her handkerchief to her eyes, and sighed again more resignedly than ever.

'I don't quite understand,' said Agnes. 'I thought your husband had an engagement to take some ladies to Switzerland and Italy?'

'That was his ill-luck, Miss. One of the ladies fell ill—and the others wouldn't go without her. They paid him a month's salary as compensation. But they had engaged him for the autumn and winter—and the loss is serious.'

'I am sorry to hear it, Emily. Let us hope he will soon have another chance.'

'It's not his turn, Miss, to be recommended when the next applications come to the couriers' office. You see, there are so many of them out of employment just now. If he could be privately recommended ——' She stopped, and left the unfinished sentence to speak for itself.

Agnes understood her directly. 'You want my recommendation,' she rejoined. 'Why couldn't you say so at once?'

Emily blushed. 'It would be such a chance for my husband,' she answered confusedly. 'A letter, inquiring for a good courier (a six months' engagement, Miss!) came to the office this morning. It's another man's turn to be chosen—and the secretary will recommend him. If my husband could only send his testimonials by the same post—with just a word in your name, Miss—it might turn the scale, as they say. A private recommendation between gentlefolks goes so far.' She stopped again, and sighed again, and looked down at the carpet, as if she had some private reason for feeling a little ashamed of herself.

Agnes began to be rather weary of the persistent tone of mystery in which her visitor spoke. 'If you want my interest with any friend of mine,' she said, 'why can't you tell me the name?'

The courier's wife began to cry. 'I'm ashamed to tell you, Miss.'

For the first time, Agnes spoke sharply. 'Nonsense, Emily! Tell me the name directly—or drop the subject—whichever you like best.'

Emily made a last desperate effort. She wrung her handkerchief hard in her lap, and let off the name as if she had been letting off a loaded gun:—'Lord Montbarry!'

Agnes rose and looked at her.

'You have disappointed me,' she said very quietly, but with a look which the courier's wife had never seen in her face before. 'Knowing what you know, you ought to be aware that it is impossible for me to communicate with Lord Montbarry. I always supposed you had some delicacy of feeling. I am sorry to find that I have been mistaken.'

Weak as she was, Emily had spirit enough to feel the reproof. She walked in her meek noiseless way to the door. 'I beg your pardon, Miss. I am not quite so bad as you think me. But I beg your pardon, all the same.'

She opened the door. Agnes called her back. There was something in the woman's apology that appealed irresistibly to her just and generous nature. 'Come,' she said; 'we must not part in this way. Let me not misunderstand you. What *is* it that you expected me to do?'

Emily was wise enough to answer this time without any reserve. 'My husband will send his testimonials, Miss, to Lord Montbarry in Scotland. I only wanted you to let him say in his letter that his wife has been known to you since she was a child, and that you feel some little interest in his welfare on that account. I don't ask it now, Miss. You have made me understand that I was wrong.'

Had she really been wrong? Past remembrances, as well as present troubles, pleaded powerfully with Agnes for the courier's wife. 'It seems only a small favour to ask,' she said, speaking under the impulse of kindness which was the strongest impulse in her nature. 'But I am not sure that I ought to allow my name to be mentioned in your husband's letter. Let me hear again exactly what he wishes to say.' Emily repeated the words— and then offered one of those suggestions, which have a special value of their own to persons unaccustomed to the use of their pens. 'Suppose you try, Miss, how it looks in writing?' Childish as the idea was, Agnes tried the experiment. 'If I let you mention me,' she said, 'we must at least decide what you are to say.' She wrote the words in the briefest and plainest form:—'I venture to state that my wife has been known from her childhood to Miss Agnes Lockwood, who feels some little interest in my welfare on that account.' Reduced to this one sentence, there was surely nothing in the reference to her name which implied that Agnes had permitted it, or that she was even aware of it. After a last struggle with herself, she handed the written paper to Emily. 'Your husband must copy it exactly, without altering anything,' she stipulated. 'On that condition, I grant your request.' Emily was not only thankful—she was really touched. Agnes hurried the little woman out of the room. 'Don't give me time to repent and take it back again,' she said. Emily vanished.

'Is the tie that once bound us completely broken? Am I as entirely parted from the good and evil fortune of his life as if we had never met and never loved?' Agnes looked at the clock on the mantel-piece. Not ten minutes since, those serious questions had been on her lips. It almost shocked her to think of the common-place manner in which they had already met with their reply. The mail of that night would appeal once more to Montbarry's remembrance of her—in the choice of a servant.

Two days later, the post brought a few grateful lines from Emily. Her husband had got the place. Ferrari was engaged, for six months certain, as Lord Montbarry's courier.

# THE SECOND PART

## CHAPTER V

After only one week of travelling in Scotland, my lord and my lady returned unexpectedly to London. Introduced to the mountains and lakes of the Highlands, her ladyship positively declined to improve her acquaintance with them. When she was asked for her reason, she answered with a Roman brevity, 'I have seen Switzerland.'

For a week more, the newly-married couple remained in London, in the strictest retirement. On one day in that week the nurse returned in a state of most uncustomary excitement from an errand on which Agnes had sent her. Passing the door of a fashionable dentist, she had met Lord Montbarry himself just leaving the house. The good woman's report described him, with malicious pleasure, as looking wretchedly ill. 'His cheeks are getting hollow, my dear, and his beard is turning grey. I hope the dentist hurt him!'

Knowing how heartily her faithful old servant hated the man who had deserted her, Agnes made due allowance for a large infusion of exaggeration in the picture presented to her. The main impression produced on her mind was an impression of nervous uneasiness. If she trusted herself in the streets by daylight while Lord Montbarry remained in London, how could she be sure that his next chance-meeting might not be a meeting with herself? She waited at home, privately ashamed of her own undignified conduct, for the next two days. On the third day the fashionable intelligence of the newspapers announced the departure of Lord and Lady Montbarry for Paris, on their way to Italy.

Mrs. Ferrari, calling the same evening, informed Agnes that her husband had left her with all reasonable expression of conjugal kindness; his temper being improved by the prospect of going abroad. But one other servant accompanied the travellers—Lady Montbarry's maid, rather a silent, unsociable woman, so far as Emily had heard. Her ladyship's brother, Baron Rivar, was already on the Continent. It had been arranged that he was to meet his sister and her husband at Rome.

One by one the dull weeks succeeded each other in the life of Agnes. She faced her position with admirable courage, seeing her friends, keeping herself occupied in her leisure hours with reading and drawing, leaving no means untried of diverting her mind from the melancholy remembrance of the past. But she had loved too faithfully, she had been wounded too deeply, to feel in any adequate degree the influence of the moral remedies which she employed. Persons who met with her in the ordinary relations of life, deceived by her outward serenity of manner, agreed that 'Miss Lockwood seemed to be getting over her disappointment.' But an old friend and school companion who happened to see her during a brief visit to London, was inexpressibly distressed by the change that she detected in Agnes. This lady was Mrs. Westwick, the wife of that brother of Lord Montbarry who came next to him in age, and who was described in the 'Peerage' as presumptive heir to the title. He was then away, looking after his interests in some mining property which he possessed in America. Mrs. Westwick insisted on taking Agnes back with her to her home in Ireland. 'Come and keep me company while my husband is away. My three little girls will make you their playfellow, and the only stranger you will meet is the governess, whom I answer for your liking beforehand. Pack up your things, and I will call for you to-morrow on my way to the train.' In those hearty terms the invitation was given. Agnes thankfully accepted it. For three happy months she lived under the roof of her friend. The girls hung round her in tears at her departure; the youngest of them wanted to go back with Agnes to London. Half in jest, half in earnest, she said to her old friend at parting, 'If your governess leaves you, keep the place open for me.' Mrs. Westwick laughed. The wiser children took it seriously, and promised to let Agnes know.

On the very day when Miss Lockwood returned to London, she was recalled to those associations with the past which she was most anxious to forget. After the first kissings and greetings were over, the old nurse (who had been left in charge at the lodgings) had some startling information to communicate, derived from the courier's wife.

'Here has been little Mrs. Ferrari, my dear, in a dreadful state of mind, inquiring when you would be back. Her husband has left Lord Montbarry, without a word of warning—and nobody knows what has become of him.'

Agnes looked at her in astonishment. 'Are you sure of what you are saying?' she asked.

The nurse was quite sure. 'Why, Lord bless you! the news comes from the couriers' office in Golden Square—from the secretary, Miss Agnes, the secretary himself!' Hearing this, Agnes began to feel alarmed as well as surprised. It was still early in the evening. She at once sent a message to Mrs. Ferrari, to say that she had returned.

In an hour more the courier's wife appeared, in a state of agitation which it was not easy to control. Her narrative, when she was at last able to speak connectedly, entirely confirmed the nurse's report of it.

After hearing from her husband with tolerable regularity from Paris, Rome, and Venice, Emily had twice written to him afterwards—and had received no reply. Feeling uneasy, she had gone to the office in Golden Square, to inquire if he had been heard of there. The post of the morning had brought a letter to the secretary from a courier then at Venice. It contained startling news of Ferrari. His wife had been allowed to take a copy of it, which she now handed to Agnes to read.

The writer stated that he had recently arrived in Venice. He had previously heard that Ferrari was with Lord and Lady Montbarry, at one of the old Venetian palaces which they had hired for a term. Being a friend of Ferrari, he had gone to pay him a visit. Ringing at the door that opened on the canal, and failing to make anyone hear him, he had gone round to a side entrance opening on one of the narrow lanes of Venice. Here, standing at the door (as if she was waiting for him to try that way next), he found a pale woman with magnificent dark eyes, who proved to be no other than Lady Montbarry herself.

She asked, in Italian, what he wanted. He answered that he wanted to see the courier Ferrari, if it was quite convenient. She at once informed him that Ferrari had left the palace, without assigning any reason, and without even leaving an address at which his monthly salary (then due to him) could be paid. Amazed at this reply, the courier inquired if any person had offended Ferrari, or quarrelled with him. The lady answered, 'To my knowledge, certainly not. I am Lady Montbarry; and I can positively assure you that Ferrari was treated with the greatest kindness in this house. We are as much astonished as you are at his extraordinary disappearance. If you should hear of him, pray let us know, so that we may at least pay him the money which is due.'

After one or two more questions (quite readily answered) relating to the date and the time of day at which Ferrari had left the palace, the courier took his leave.

He at once entered on the necessary investigations—without the slightest result so far as Ferrari was concerned. Nobody had seen him. Nobody appeared to have been taken into his confidence. Nobody knew anything (that is to say, anything of the slightest importance) even about persons so distinguished as Lord and Lady Montbarry. It was reported that her ladyship's English maid had left her, before the disappearance of Ferrari, to return to her relatives in her own country, and that Lady Montbarry had taken no steps to supply her place. His lordship was described as being in delicate health. He lived in the strictest retirement—nobody was admitted to him, not even his own countrymen. A stupid old woman was discovered who did the housework at the palace, arriving in the morning and going away again at night. She had never seen the lost courier—she had never even seen Lord Montbarry, who was then confined to his room. Her ladyship, 'a most gracious and adorable mistress,' was in constant attendance on her noble husband. There was no other servant then in the house (so far as the old woman knew) but herself. The meals were sent in from a restaurant. My lord, it was said, disliked strangers. My lord's brother-in-law, the Baron, was generally shut up in a remote part of the palace, occupied (the gracious mistress said) with experiments in chemistry. The experiments sometimes made a nasty smell. A doctor had latterly been called in to his lordship—an Italian doctor, long resident in Venice. Inquiries being addressed to this gentleman (a physician of undoubted capacity and respectability), it turned out that he also had never seen Ferrari, having been summoned to the palace (as his memorandum book showed) at a date subsequent to the courier's disappearance. The doctor described Lord Montbarry's malady as bronchitis. So far, there was no reason to feel any anxiety, though the attack was a sharp one. If alarming symptoms should appear, he had arranged with her ladyship to call in another physician. For the rest, it was impossible to speak too highly of my lady; night and day, she was at her lord's bedside.

With these particulars began and ended the discoveries made by Ferrari's courier-friend. The police were on the look-out for the lost man—and that was the only hope which could be held forth for the present, to Ferrari's wife.

'What do you think of it, Miss?' the poor woman asked eagerly. 'What would you advise me to do?'

Agnes was at a loss how to answer her; it was an effort even to listen to what Emily was saying. The references in the courier's letter to Montbarry—the report of his illness, the melancholy picture of his secluded life—had reopened the old wound. She was not even thinking of the lost Ferrari; her mind was at Venice, by the sick man's bedside.

'I hardly know what to say,' she answered. 'I have had no experience in serious matters of this kind.'

'Do you think it would help you, Miss, if you read my husband's letters to me? There are only three of them—they won't take long to read.'

Agnes compassionately read the letters.

They were not written in a very tender tone. 'Dear Emily,' and 'Yours affectionately'—these conventional phrases, were the only phrases of endearment which they contained. In the first letter, Lord Montbarry was not very favourably spoken of:—'We leave Paris to-morrow. I don't much like my lord. He is proud and cold, and, between ourselves, stingy in money matters. I have had to dispute such trifles as a few centimes in the hotel bill; and twice already, some sharp remarks have passed between the newly-married couple, in consequence of her ladyship's freedom in purchasing pretty tempting things at the shops in Paris. "I can't afford it; you must keep to your allowance." She has had to hear those words already. For my part, I like her. She has the nice, easy foreign manners—*she* talks to me as if I was a human being like herself."

The second letter was dated from Rome.

'My lord's caprices' (Ferrari wrote) 'have kept us perpetually on the move. He is becoming incurably restless. I suspect he is uneasy in his mind. Painful recollections, I should say—I find him constantly reading old letters, when her ladyship is not present. We were to have stopped at Genoa, but he hurried us on. The same thing at Florence. Here, at Rome, my lady insists on resting. Her brother has met us at this place. There has been a quarrel already (the lady's maid tells me) between my lord and the Baron. The latter wanted to borrow money of the former. His lordship refused in language which offended Baron Rivar. My lady pacified them, and made them shake hands.'

The third, and last letter, was from Venice.

'More of my lord's economy! Instead of staying at the hotel, we have hired a damp, mouldy, rambling old palace. My lady insists on having the best suites of rooms wherever we go—and the palace comes cheaper for a two months' term. My lord tried to get it for longer; he says the quiet of Venice is good for his nerves. But a foreign speculator has secured the palace, and is going to turn it into an hotel. The Baron is still with us, and there have been more disagreements about money matters. I don't like the Baron—and I don't find the attractions of my lady grow on me. She was much nicer before the Baron joined us. My lord is a punctual paymaster; it's a matter of honour with him; he hates parting with his money, but he does it because he has given his word. I receive my salary regularly at the end of each month—not a franc extra, though I have done many things which are not part of a courier's proper work. Fancy the Baron trying to borrow money of *me*! he is an inveterate gambler. I didn't believe it when my lady's maid first told me so—but I have seen enough since to satisfy me that she was right. I have seen other things besides, which—well! which don't increase my respect for my lady and the Baron. The maid says she means to give warning to leave. She is a respectable British female, and doesn't take things quite so easily as I do. It is a dull life here. No going into company—no company at home—not a creature sees my lord—not even the consul, or the banker. When he goes out, he goes alone, and generally towards nightfall. Indoors, he shuts himself up in his own room with his books, and sees as little of his wife and the Baron as possible. I fancy things are coming to a crisis here. If my lord's suspicions are once awakened, the consequences will be terrible. Under certain provocations, the noble Montbarry is a man who would stick at nothing. However, the pay is good—and I can't afford to talk of leaving the place, like my lady's maid.'

Agnes handed back the letters—so suggestive of the penalty paid already for his own infatuation by the man who had deserted her!—with feelings of shame and distress, which made her no fit counsellor for the helpless woman who depended on her advice.

'The one thing I can suggest,' she said, after first speaking some kind words of comfort and hope, 'is that we should consult a person of greater experience than ours. Suppose I write and ask my lawyer (who is also my friend and trustee) to come and advise us to-morrow after his business hours?'

Emily eagerly and gratefully accepted the suggestion. An hour was arranged for the meeting on the next day; the correspondence was left under the care of Agnes; and the courier's wife took her leave.

Weary and heartsick, Agnes lay down on the sofa, to rest and compose herself. The careful nurse brought in a reviving cup of tea. Her quaint gossip about herself and her occupations while Agnes had been away, acted as a relief to her mistress's overburdened mind. They were still talking quietly, when they were startled by a loud knock at the house door. Hurried footsteps ascended the stairs. The door of the sitting-room was thrown open violently; the courier's wife rushed in like a mad woman. 'He's dead! they've murdered him!' Those wild words were all she could say. She dropped on her knees at the foot of the sofa—held out her hand with something clasped in it—and fell back in a swoon.

The nurse, signing to Agnes to open the window, took the necessary measures to restore the fainting woman. 'What's this?' she exclaimed. 'Here's a letter in her hand. See what it is, Miss.'

The open envelope was addressed (evidently in a feigned hand-writing) to 'Mrs. Ferrari.' The post-mark was 'Venice.' The contents of the envelope were a sheet of foreign note-paper, and a folded enclosure.

On the note-paper, one line only was written. It was again in a feigned handwriting, and it contained these words:

*'To console you for the loss of your husband.'*

Agnes opened the enclosure next.

It was a Bank of England note for a thousand pounds.

## CHAPTER VI

The next day, the friend and legal adviser of Agnes Lockwood, Mr. Troy, called on her by appointment in the evening.

Mrs. Ferrari—still persisting in the conviction of her husband's death—had sufficiently recovered to be present at the consultation. Assisted by Agnes, she told the lawyer the little that was known relating to Ferrari's disappearance, and then produced the correspondence connected with that event. Mr. Troy read (first) the three letters addressed by Ferrari to his wife; (secondly) the letter written by Ferrari's courier-friend, describing his visit to the palace and his interview with Lady Montbarry; and (thirdly) the one line of anonymous writing which had accompanied the extraordinary gift of a thousand pounds to Ferrari's wife.

Well known, at a later period, as the lawyer who acted for Lady Lydiard, in the case of theft, generally described as the case of 'My Lady's

Money,' Mr. Troy was not only a man of learning and experience in his profession—he was also a man who had seen something of society at home and abroad. He possessed a keen eye for character, a quaint humour, and a kindly nature which had not been deteriorated even by a lawyer's professional experience of mankind. With all these personal advantages, it is a question, nevertheless, whether he was the fittest adviser whom Agnes could have chosen under the circumstances. Little Mrs. Ferrari, with many domestic merits, was an essentially commonplace woman. Mr. Troy was the last person living who was likely to attract her sympathies—he was the exact opposite of a commonplace man.

'She looks very ill, poor thing!' In these words the lawyer opened the business of the evening, referring to Mrs. Ferrari as unceremoniously as if she had been out of the room.

'She has suffered a terrible shock,' Agnes answered.

Mr. Troy turned to Mrs. Ferrari, and looked at her again, with the interest due to the victim of a shock. He drummed absently with his fingers on the table. At last he spoke to her.

'My good lady, you don't really believe that your husband is dead?'

Mrs. Ferrari put her handkerchief to her eyes. The word 'dead' was ineffectual to express her feelings. 'Murdered!' she said sternly, behind her handkerchief.

'Why? And by whom?' Mr. Troy asked.

Mrs. Ferrari seemed to have some difficulty in answering. 'You have read my husband's letters, sir,' she began. 'I believe he discovered ——' She got as far as that, and there she stopped.

'What did he discover?'

There are limits to human patience—even the patience of a bereaved wife. This cool question irritated Mrs. Ferrari into expressing herself plainly at last.

'He discovered Lady Montbarry and the Baron!' she answered, with a burst of hysterical vehemence. 'The Baron is no more that vile woman's brother than I am. The wickedness of those two wretches came to my poor dear husband's knowledge. The lady's maid left her place on account of it. If Ferrari had gone away too, he would have been alive at this moment. They have killed him. I say they have killed him, to prevent it from getting to Lord Montbarry's ears.' So, in short sharp sentences, and in louder and louder accents, Mrs. Ferrari stated *her* opinion of the case.

Still keeping his own view in reserve, Mr. Troy listened with an expression of satirical approval.

'Very strongly stated, Mrs. Ferrari,' he said. 'You build up your sentences well; you clinch your conclusions in a workmanlike manner. If you had been a man, you would have made a good lawyer—you would have taken juries by the scruff of their necks. Complete the case, my good lady—complete the case. Tell us next who sent you this letter, enclosing the bank-note. The "two wretches" who murdered Mr. Ferrari would hardly put their hands in their pockets and send you a thousand pounds.

Who is it—eh? I see the post-mark on the letter is "Venice." Have you any friend in that interesting city, with a large heart, and a purse to correspond, who has been let into the secret and who wishes to console you anonymously?'

It was not easy to reply to this. Mrs. Ferrari began to feel the first inward approaches of something like hatred towards Mr. Troy. 'I don't understand you, sir,' she answered. 'I don't think this is a joking matter.'

Agnes interfered, for the first time. She drew her chair a little nearer to her legal counsellor and friend.

'What is the most probable explanation, in your opinion?' she asked.

'I shall offend Mrs. Ferrari if I tell you,' Mr. Troy answered.

'No, sir, you won't!' cried Mrs. Ferrari, hating Mr. Troy undisguisedly by this time.

The lawyer leaned back in his chair. 'Very well,' he said, in his most good-humoured manner. 'Let's have it out. Observe, madam, I don't dispute your view of the position of affairs at the palace in Venice. You have your husband's letters to justify you; and you have also the significant fact that Lady Montbarry's maid did really leave the house. We will say, then, that Lord Montbarry has presumably been made the victim of a foul wrong—that Mr. Ferrari was the first to find it out—and that the guilty persons had reason to fear, not only that he would acquaint Lord Montbarry with his discovery, but that he would be a principal witness against them if the scandal was made public in a court of law. Now mark! Admitting all this, I draw a totally different conclusion from the conclusion at which you have arrived. Here is your husband left in this miserable household of three, under very awkward circumstances for *him*. What does he do? But for the bank-note and the written message sent to you with it, I should say that he had wisely withdrawn himself from association with a disgraceful discovery and exposure, by taking secretly to flight. The money modifies this view—unfavourably so far as Mr. Ferrari is concerned. I still believe he is keeping out of the way. But I now say he is *paid* for keeping out of the way—and that bank-note there on the table is the price of his absence, sent by the guilty persons to his wife.'

Mrs. Ferrari's watery grey eyes brightened suddenly; Mrs. Ferrari's dull drab-coloured complexion became enlivened by a glow of brilliant red.

'It's false!' she cried. 'It's a burning shame to speak of my husband in that way!'

'I told you I should offend you!' said Mr. Troy.

Agnes interposed once more—in the interests of peace. She took the offended wife's hand; she appealed to the lawyer to reconsider that side of his theory which reflected harshly on Ferrari. While she was still speaking, the servant interrupted her by entering the room with a visiting-card. It was the card of Henry Westwick; and there was an ominous request written on it in pencil. 'I bring bad news. Let me see you for a minute downstairs.' Agnes immediately left the room.

Alone with Mrs. Ferrari, Mr. Troy permitted his natural kindness of heart to show itself on the surface at last. He tried to make his peace with the courier's wife.

'You have every claim, my good soul, to resent a reflection cast upon your husband,' he began. 'I may even say that I respect you for speaking so warmly in his defence. At the same time, remember, that I am bound, in such a serious matter as this, to tell you what is really in my mind. I can have no intention of offending you, seeing that I am a total stranger to you and to Mr. Ferrari. A thousand pounds is a large sum of money; and a poor man may excusably be tempted by it to do nothing worse than to keep out of the way for a while. My only interest, acting on your behalf, is to get at the truth. If you will give me time, I see no reason to despair of finding your husband yet.'

Ferrari's wife listened, without being convinced: her narrow little mind, filled to its extreme capacity by her unfavourable opinion of Mr. Troy, had no room left for the process of correcting its first impression. 'I am much obliged to you, sir,' was all she said. Her eyes were more communicative—her eyes added, in *their* language, 'You may say what you please; I will never forgive you to my dying day.'

Mr. Troy gave it up. He composedly wheeled his chair around, put his hands in his pockets, and looked out of window.

After an interval of silence, the drawing-room door was opened.

Mr. Troy wheeled round again briskly to the table, expecting to see Agnes. To his surprise there appeared, in her place, a perfect stranger to him—a gentleman, in the prime of life, with a marked expression of pain and embarrassment on his handsome face. He looked at Mr. Troy, and bowed gravely.

'I am so unfortunate as to have brought news to Miss Agnes Lockwood which has greatly distressed her,' he said. 'She has retired to her room. I am requested to make her excuses, and to speak to you in her place.'

Having introduced himself in those terms, he noticed Mrs. Ferrari, and held out his hand to her kindly. 'It is some years since we last met, Emily,' he said. 'I am afraid you have almost forgotten the "Master Henry" of old times.' Emily, in some little confusion, made her acknowledgments, and begged to know if she could be of any use to Miss Lockwood. 'The old nurse is with her,' Henry answered; 'they will be better left together.' He turned once more to Mr. Troy. 'I ought to tell you,' he said, 'that my name is Henry Westwick. I am the younger brother of the late Lord Montbarry.'

"The *late* Lord Montbarry!' Mr. Troy exclaimed.

'My brother died at Venice yesterday evening. There is the telegram.' With that startling answer, he handed the paper to Mr. Troy.

The message was in these words:

'Lady Montbarry, Venice. To Stephen Robert Westwick, Newbury's Hotel, London. It is useless to take the journey. Lord Montbarry died of bronchitis, at 8.40 this evening. All needful details by post.'

'Was this expected, sir?' the lawyer asked.

'I cannot say that it has taken us entirely by surprise,' Henry answered. 'My brother Stephen (who is now the head of the family) received a telegram three days since, informing him that alarming symptoms had declared themselves, and that a second physician had been called in. He telegraphed back to say that he had left Ireland for London, on his way to Venice, and to direct that any further message might be sent to his hotel. The reply came in a second telegram. It announced that Lord Montbarry was in a state of insensibility, and that, in his brief intervals of consciousness, he recognised nobody. My brother was advised to wait in London for later information. The third telegram is now in your hands. That is all I know, up to the present time.'

Happening to look at the courier's wife, Mr. Troy was struck by the expression of blank fear which showed itself in the woman's face.

'Mrs. Ferrari,' he said, 'have you heard what Mr. Westwick has just told me?'

'Every word of it, sir.'

'Have you any questions to ask?'

'No, sir.'

'You seem to be alarmed,' the lawyer persisted. 'Is it still about your husband?'

'I shall never see my husband again, sir. I have thought so all along, as you know. I feel sure of it now.'

'Sure of it, after what you have just heard?'

'Yes, sir.'

'Can you tell me why?'

'No, sir. It's a feeling I have. I can't tell why.'

'Oh, a feeling?' Mr. Troy repeated, in a tone of compassionate contempt. 'When it comes to feelings, my good soul ——!' He left the sentence unfinished, and rose to take his leave of Mr. Westwick. The truth is, he began to feel puzzled himself, and he did not choose to let Mrs. Ferrari see it. 'Accept the expression of my sympathy, sir,' he said to Mr. Westwick politely. 'I wish you good evening.'

Henry turned to Mrs. Ferrari as the lawyer closed the door. 'I have heard of your trouble, Emily, from Miss Lockwood. Is there anything I can do to help you?'

'Nothing, sir, thank you. Perhaps, I had better go home after what has happened? I will call to-morrow, and see if I can be of any use to Miss Agnes. I am very sorry for her.' She stole away, with her formal curtsey, her noiseless step, and her obstinate resolution to take the gloomiest view of her husband's case.

Henry Westwick looked round him in the solitude of the little drawing-room. There was nothing to keep him in the house, and yet he lingered in it. It was something to be even near Agnes—to see the things belonging to her that were scattered about the room. There, in the corner, was her chair, with her embroidery on the work-table by its side. On the little easel near the window was her last drawing, not quite finished yet. The book she had been reading lay on the sofa, with her tiny pencil-case in it to mark the place at which she had left off. One after another, he looked at the objects that reminded him of the woman whom he loved—took them up tenderly—and laid them down again with a sigh. Ah, how far, how unattainably far from him, she was still! 'She will never forget Montbarry,' he thought to himself as he took up his hat to go. 'Not one of us feels his death as she feels it. Miserable, miserable wretch—how she loved him!'

In the street, as Henry closed the house-door, he was stopped by a passing acquaintance—a wearisome inquisitive man—doubly unwelcome to him, at that moment. 'Sad news, Westwick, this about your brother. Rather an unexpected death, wasn't it? We never heard at the club that Montbarry's lungs were weak. What will the insurance offices do?'

Henry started; he had never thought of his brother's life insurance. What could the offices do but pay? A death by bronchitis, certified by two physicians, was surely the least disputable of all deaths. 'I wish you hadn't put that question into my head!' he broke out irritably. 'Ah!' said his friend, 'you think the widow will get the money? So do I! so do I!'

## CHAPTER VII

Some days later, the insurance offices (two in number) received the formal announcement of Lord Montbarry's death, from her ladyship's London solicitors. The sum insured in each office was five thousand pounds—on which one year's premium only had been paid. In the face of such a pecuniary emergency as this, the Directors thought it desirable to consider their position. The medical advisers of the two offices, who had recommended the insurance of Lord Montbarry's life, were called into council over their own reports. The result excited some interest among persons connected with the business of life insurance. Without absolutely declining to pay the money, the two offices (acting in concert) decided on sending a commission of inquiry to Venice, 'for the purpose of obtaining further information.'

Mr. Troy received the earliest intelligence of what was going on. He wrote at once to communicate his news to Agnes; adding, what he considered to be a valuable hint, in these words:

'You are intimately acquainted, I know, with Lady Barville, the late Lord Montbarry's eldest sister. The solicitors employed by her husband are also the solicitors to one of the two insurance offices. There may possibly be something in the report of the commission of inquiry touching on Ferrari's disappearance. Ordinary persons would not be permitted, of course, to see such a document. But a sister of the late lord is so near a relative as to be an exception to general rules. If Sir Theodore Barville puts it on that footing, the lawyers, even if they do not allow his wife to look at the report, will at least answer any discreet questions she may ask referring to it. Let me hear what you think of this suggestion, at your earliest convenience.'

The reply was received by return of post. Agnes declined to avail herself of Mr. Troy's proposal.

'My interference, innocent as it was,' she wrote, 'has already been productive of such deplorable results, that I cannot and dare not stir any further in the case of Ferrari. If I had not consented to let that unfortunate man refer to me by name, the late Lord Montbarry would never have engaged him, and his wife would have been spared the misery and suspense from which she is suffering now. I would not even look at the report to which you allude if it was placed in my hands—I have heard more than enough already of that hideous life in the palace at Venice. If Mrs. Ferrari chooses to address herself to Lady Barville (with your assistance), that is of course quite another thing. But, even in this case, I must make it a positive condition that my name shall not be mentioned. Forgive me, dear Mr. Troy! I am very unhappy, and very unreasonable—but I am only a woman, and you must not expect too much from me.'

Foiled in this direction, the lawyer next advised making the attempt to discover the present address of Lady Montbarry's English maid. This excellent suggestion had one drawback: it could only be carried out by spending money—and there was no money to spend. Mrs. Ferrari shrank from the bare idea of making any use of the thousand-pound note. It had been deposited in the safe keeping of a bank. If it was even mentioned in her hearing, she shuddered and referred to it, with melodramatic fervour, as 'my husband's blood-money!'

So, under stress of circumstances, the attempt to solve the mystery of Ferrari's disappearance was suspended for a while.

It was the last month of the year 1860. The commission of inquiry was already at work; having begun its investigations on December 6. On the 10th, the term for which the late Lord Montbarry had hired the Venetian palace, expired. News by telegram reached the insurance offices that Lady Montbarry had been advised by her lawyers to leave for London with as little delay as possible. Baron Rivar, it was believed, would accompany her to England, but would not remain in that country, unless his services were absolutely required by her ladyship. The Baron, 'well known as an enthusiastic student of chemistry,' had heard of certain recent discoveries in connection with that science in the United States, and was anxious to investigate them personally.

These items of news, collected by Mr. Troy, were duly communicated to Mrs. Ferrari, whose anxiety about her husband made her a frequent, a too frequent, visitor at the lawyer's office. She attempted to relate what she had heard to her good friend and protectress. Agnes steadily refused to listen, and positively forbade any further conversation relating to Lord

Montbarry's wife, now that Lord Montbarry was no more. 'You have Mr. Troy to advise you,' she said; 'and you are welcome to what little money I can spare, if money is wanted. All I ask in return is that you will not distress me. I am trying to separate myself from remembrances ——' her voice faltered; she paused to control herself—'from remembrances,' she resumed, 'which are sadder than ever since I have heard of Lord Montbarry's death. Help me by your silence to recover my spirits, if I can. Let me hear nothing more, until I can rejoice with you that your husband is found.'

Time advanced to the 13th of the month; and more information of the interesting sort reached Mr. Troy. The labours of the insurance commission had come to an end—the report had been received from Venice on that day.

## CHAPTER VIII

On the 14th the Directors and their legal advisers met for the reading of the report, with closed doors. These were the terms in which the Commissioners related the results of their inquiry:

'*Private and confidential.*

'We have the honour to inform our Directors that we arrived in Venice on December 6, 1860. On the same day we proceeded to the palace inhabited by Lord Montbarry at the time of his last illness and death.

'We were received with all possible courtesy by Lady Montbarry's brother, Baron Rivar. "My sister was her husband's only attendant throughout his illness," the Baron informed us. "She is overwhelmed by grief and fatigue—or she would have been here to receive you personally. What are your wishes, gentlemen? and what can I do for you in her ladyship's place?"

'In accordance with our instructions, we answered that the death and burial of Lord Montbarry abroad made it desirable to obtain more complete information relating to his illness, and to the circumstances which had attended it, than could be conveyed in writing. We explained that the law provided for the lapse of a certain interval of time before the payment of the sum assured, and we expressed our wish to conduct the inquiry with the most respectful consideration for her ladyship's feelings, and for the convenience of any other members of the family inhabiting the house.

'To this the Baron replied, "I am the only member of the family living here, and I and the palace are entirely at your disposal." From first to last we found this gentleman perfectly straighforward, and most amiably willing to assist us.

'With the one exception of her ladyship's room, we went over the whole of the palace the same day. It is an immense place only partially furnished. The first floor and part of the second floor were the portions of it that had been inhabited by Lord Montbarry and the members of the household. We saw the bedchamber, at one extremity of the palace, in which his lordship died, and the small room communicating with it, which he used as a study. Next to this was a large apartment or hall, the doors of which he habitually kept locked, his object being (as we were informed) to pursue his studies uninterruptedly in perfect solitude. On the other side of the large hall were the bedchamber occupied by her ladyship, and the dressing-room in which the maid slept previous to her departure for England. Beyond these were the dining and reception rooms, opening into an antechamber, which gave access to the grand staircase of the palace.

'The only inhabited rooms on the second floor were the sitting-room and bedroom occupied by Baron Rivar, and another room at some distance from it, which had been the bedroom of the courier Ferrari.

'The rooms on the third floor and on the basement were completely unfurnished, and in a condition of great neglect. We inquired if there was anything to be seen below the basement—and we were at once informed that there were vaults beneath, which we were at perfect liberty to visit.

'We went down, so as to leave no part of the palace unexplored. The vaults were, it was believed, used as dungeons in the old times—say, some centuries since. Air and light were only partially admitted to these dismal places by two long shafts of winding construction, which communicated with the back yard of the palace, and the openings of which, high above the ground, were protected by iron gratings. The stone stairs leading down into the vaults could be closed at will by a heavy trap-door in the back hall, which we found open. The Baron himself led the way down the stairs. We remarked that it might be awkward if that trap-door fell down and closed the opening behind us. The Baron smiled at the idea. "Don't be alarmed, gentlemen," he said; "the door is safe. I had an interest in seeing to it myself, when we first inhabited the palace. My favourite study is the study of experimental chemistry—and my workshop, since we have been in Venice, is down here."

'These last words explained a curious smell in the vaults, which we noticed the moment we entered them. We can only describe the smell by saying that it was of a twofold sort—faintly aromatic, as it were, in its first effect, but with some after-odour very sickening in our nostrils. The Baron's furnaces and retorts, and other things, were all there to speak for themselves, together with some packages of chemicals, having the name and address of the person who had supplied them plainly visible on their labels. "Not a pleasant place for study," Baron Rivar observed, "but my sister is timid. She has a horror of chemical smells and explosions—and she has banished me to these lower regions, so that my experiments may neither be smelt nor heard." He held out his hands, on which we had noticed that he wore gloves in the house. "Accidents will happen sometimes," he said, "no matter how careful a man may be. I burnt my hands severely in trying a new combination the other day, and they are only recovering now."

'We mention these otherwise unimportant incidents, in order to show that our exploration of the palace was not impeded by any attempt at concealment. We were even admitted to her ladyship's own room—on a subsequent occasion, when she went out to take the air. Our instructions recommended us to examine his lordship's residence, because the extreme privacy of his life at Venice, and the remarkable departure of the only two servants in the house, might have some suspicious connection with the nature of his death. We found nothing to justify suspicion.

'As to his lordship's retired way of life, we have conversed on the subject with the consul and the banker—the only two strangers who held any communication with him. He called once at the bank to obtain money on his letter of credit, and excused himself from accepting an invitation to visit the banker at his private residence, on the ground of delicate health. His lordship wrote to the same effect on sending his card to the consul, to excuse himself from personally returning that gentleman's visit to the palace. We have seen the letter, and we beg to offer the following copy of it. "Many years passed in India have injured my constitution. I have ceased to go into society; the one occupation of my life now is the study of Oriental literature. The air of Italy is better for me than the air of England, or I should never have left home. Pray accept the apologies of a student and an invalid. The active part of my life is at an end." The self-seclusion of his lordship seems to us to be explained in these brief lines. We have not, however, on that account spared our inquiries in other directions. Nothing to excite a suspicion of anything wrong has come to our knowledge.

'As to the departure of the lady's maid, we have seen the woman's receipt for her wages, in which it is expressly stated that she left Lady Montbarry's service because she disliked the Continent, and wished to get back to her own country. This is not an uncommon result of taking English servants to foreign parts. Lady Montbarry has informed us that she abstained from engaging another maid in consequence of the extreme dislike which his lordship expressed to having strangers in the house, in the state of his health at that time.

'The disappearance of the courier Ferrari is, in itself, unquestionably a suspicious circumstance. Neither her ladyship nor the Baron can explain it; and no investigation that we could make has thrown the smallest light on this event, or has justified us in associating it, directly or indirectly, with the object of our inquiry. We have even gone the length of examining the portmanteau which Ferrari left behind him. It contains nothing but clothes and linen—no money, and not even a scrap of paper in the pockets of the clothes. The portmanteau remains in charge of the police.

'We have also found opportunities of speaking privately to the old woman who attends to the rooms occupied by her ladyship and the Baron. She was recommended to fill this situation by the keeper of the restaurant who has supplied the meals to the family throughout the period of their residence at the palace. Her character is most favourably spoken of. Unfortunately, her limited intelligence makes her of no value as a witness. We were patient and careful in questioning her, and we found her perfectly willing to answer us; but we could elicit nothing which is worth including in the present report.

'On the second day of our inquiries, we had the honour of an interview with Lady Montbarry. Her ladyship looked miserably worn and ill, and seemed to be quite at a loss to understand what we wanted with her. Baron Rivar, who introduced us, explained the nature of our errand in Venice, and took pains to assure her that it was a purely formal duty on which we were engaged. Having satisfied her ladyship on this point, he discreetly left the room.

'The questions which we addressed to Lady Montbarry related mainly, of course, to his lordship's illness. The answers, given with great nervousness of manner, but without the slightest appearance of reserve, informed us of the facts that follow:

'Lord Montbarry had been out of order for some time past—nervous and irritable. He first complained of having taken cold on November 13 last; he passed a wakeful and feverish night, and remained in bed the next day. Her ladyship proposed sending for medical advice. He refused to allow her to do this, saying that he could quite easily be his own doctor in such a trifling matter as a cold. Some hot lemonade was made at his request, with a view to producing perspiration. Lady Montbarry's maid having left her at that time, the courier Ferrari (then the only servant in the house) went out to buy the lemons. Her ladyship made the drink with her own hands. It was successful in producing perspiration—and Lord Montbarry had some hours of sleep afterwards. Later in the day, having need of Ferrari's services, Lady Montbarry rang for him. The bell was not answered. Baron Rivar searched for the man, in the palace and out of it, in vain. From that time forth not a trace of Ferrari could be discovered. This happened on November 14.

'On the night of the 14th, the feverish symptoms accompanying his lordship's cold returned. They were in part perhaps attributable to the annoyance and alarm caused by Ferrari's mysterious disappearance. It had been impossible to conceal the circumstance, as his lordship rang repeatedly for the courier; insisting that the man should relieve Lady Montbarry and the Baron by taking their places during the night at his bedside.

'On the 15th (the day on which the old woman first came to do the housework), his lordship complained of sore throat, and of a feeling of oppression on the chest. On this day, and again on the 16th, her ladyship and the Baron entreated him to see a doctor. He still refused. "I don't want strange faces about me; my cold will run its course, in spite of the doctor,"—that was his answer. On the 17th he was so much worse that it was decided to send for medical help whether he liked it or not. Baron Rivar, after inquiry at the consul's, secured the services of Doctor Bruno, well known as an eminent physician in Venice; with the additional recommendation of having resided in England, and having made himself acquainted with English forms of medical practice.

'Thus far our account of his lordship's illness has been derived from statements made by Lady Montbarry. The narrative will now be most fitly continued in the language of the doctor's own report, herewith subjoined.

' "My medical diary informs me that I first saw the English Lord Montbarry, on November 17. He was suffering from a sharp attack of bronchitis. Some precious time had been lost, through his obstinate objection to the presence of a medical man at his bedside. Generally speaking, he appeared to be in a delicate state of health. His nervous system was out of order—he was at once timid and contradictory. When I spoke to him in English, he answered in Italian; and when I tried him in Italian, he went back to English. It mattered little—the malady had already made such progress that he could only speak a few words at a time, and those in a whisper.

' "I at once applied the necessary remedies. Copies of my prescriptions (with translation into English) accompany the present statement, and are left to speak for themselves.

' "For the next three days I was in constant attendance on my patient. He answered to the remedies employed—improving slowly, but decidedly. I could conscientiously assure Lady Montbarry that no danger was to be apprehended thus far. She was indeed a most devoted wife. I vainly endeavoured to induce her to accept the services of a competent nurse; she would allow nobody to attend on her husband but herself. Night and day this estimable woman was at his bedside. In her brief intervals of repose, her brother watched the sick man in her place. This brother was, I must say, very good company, in the intervals when we had time for a little talk. He dabbled in chemistry, down in the horrid under-water vaults of the palace; and he wanted to show me some of his experiments. I have enough of chemistry in writing prescriptions—and I declined. He took it quite good-humouredly.

' "I am straying away from my subject. Let me return to the sick lord.

' "Up to the 20th, then, things went well enough. I was quite unprepared for the disastrous change that showed itself, when I paid Lord Montbarry my morning visit on the 21st. He had relapsed, and seriously relapsed. Examining him to discover the cause, I found symptoms of pneumonia—that is to say, in unmedical language, inflammation of the substance of the lungs. He breathed with difficulty, and was only partially able to relieve himself by coughing. I made the strictest inquiries, and was assured that his medicine had been administered as carefully as usual, and that he had not been exposed to any changes of temperature. It was with great reluctance that I added to Lady Montbarry's distress; but I felt bound, when she suggested a consultation with another physician, to own that I too thought there was really need for it.

' "Her ladyship instructed me to spare no expense, and to get the best medical opinion in Italy. The best opinion was happily within our reach. The first and foremost of Italian physicians is Torello of Padua. I sent a special messenger for the great man. He arrived on the evening of the 21st, and confirmed my opinion that pneumonia had set in, and that our patient's life was in danger. I told him what my treatment of the case had been, and he approved of it in every particular. He made some valuable suggestions, and (at Lady Montbarry's express request) he consented to defer his return to Padua until the following morning.

' "We both saw the patient at intervals in the course of the night. The disease, steadily advancing, set our utmost resistance at defiance. In the morning Doctor Torello took his leave. 'I can be of no further use,' he said to me. 'The man is past all help—and he ought to know it.'

' "Later in the day I warned my lord, as gently as I could, that his time had come. I am informed that there are serious reasons for my stating what passed between us on this occasion, in detail, and without any reserve. I comply with the request.

' "Lord Montbarry received the intelligence of his approaching death with becoming composure, but with a certain doubt. He signed to me to put my ear to his mouth. He whispered faintly, 'Are you sure?' It was no time to deceive him; I said, 'Positively sure.' He waited a little, gasping for breath, and then he whispered again, 'Feel under my pillow.' I found under his pillow a letter, sealed and stamped, ready for the post. His next words were just audible and no more—'Post it yourself.' I answered, of course, that I would do so—and I did post the letter with my own hand. I looked at the address. It was directed to a lady in London. The street I cannot remember. The name I can perfectly recall: it was an Italian name —'Mrs. Ferrari.'

' "That night my lord nearly died of asphyxia. I got him through it for the time; and his eyes showed that he understood me when I told him, the next morning, that I had posted the letter. This was his last effort of consciousness. When I saw him again he was sunk in apathy. He lingered in a state of insensibility, supported by stimulants, until the 25th, and died (unconscious to the last) on the evening of that day.

' "As to the cause of his death, it seems (if I may be excused for saying so) simply absurd to ask the question. Bronchitis, terminating in pneumonia—there is no more doubt that this, and this only, was the malady of which he expired, than that two and two make four. Doctor Torello's own note of the case is added here to a duplicate of my certificate, in order (as I am informed) to satisfy some English offices in which his lordship's life was insured. The English offices must have been founded by that celebrated saint and doubter, mentioned in the New Testament, whose name was Thomas!"

'Doctor Bruno's evidence ends here.

'Reverting for a moment to our inquiries addressed to Lady Montbarry, we have to report that she can give us no information on the subject of the letter which the doctor posted at Lord Montbarry's request. When his lordship wrote it? what it contained? why he kept it a secret from Lady Montbarry (and from the Baron also); and why he should write at all to the wife of his courier? these are questions to which we find it simply impossible to obtain any replies. It seems even useless to say that the matter is open to suspicion. Suspicion implies conjecture of some kind—and the letter under my lord's pillow baffles all conjecture. Application to Mrs. Ferrari may perhaps clear up the mystery. Her residence in London will be easily discovered at the Italian Couriers' Office, Golden Square.

'Having arrived at the close of the present report, we have now to draw your attention to the conclusion which is justified by the results of our investigation.

'The plain question before our Directors and ourselves appears to be this: Has the inquiry revealed any extraordinary circumstances which render the death of Lord Montbarry open to suspicion? The inquiry has revealed extraordinary circumstances beyond all doubt—such as the disappearance of Ferrari, the remarkable absence of the customary establishment of servants in the house, and the mysterious letter which his lordship asked the doctor to post. But where is the proof that any one of these circumstances is associated—suspiciously and directly associated—with the only event which concerns us, the event of Lord Montbarry's death? In the absence of any such proof, and in the face of the evidence of two eminent physicians, it is impossible to dispute the statement on the certificate that his lordship died a natural death. We are bound, therefore, to report, that there are no valid grounds for refusing the payment of the sum for which the late Lord Montbarry's life was assured.

'We shall send these lines to you by the post of to-morrow, December 10; leaving time to receive your further instructions (if any), in reply to our telegram of this evening announcing the conclusion of the inquiry.'

## CHAPTER IX

'Now, my good creature, whatever you have to say to me, out with it at once! I don't want to hurry you needlessly; but these are business hours, and I have other people's affairs to attend to besides yours.'

Addressing Ferrari's wife, with his usual blunt good-humour, in these terms, Mr. Troy registered the lapse of time by a glance at the watch on his desk, and then waited to hear what his client had to say to him.

'It's something more, sir, about the letter with the thousand-pound note,' Mrs. Ferrari began. 'I have found out who sent it to me.'

Mr. Troy started. 'This is news indeed!' he said. 'Who sent you the letter?'

'Lord Montbarry sent it, sir.'

It was not easy to take Mr. Troy by surprise. But Mrs. Ferrari threw him completely off his balance. For a while he could only look at her in silent surprise. 'Nonsense!' he said, as soon as he had recovered himself. 'There is some mistake—it can't be!'

'There is no mistake,' Mrs. Ferrari rejoined, in her most positive manner. 'Two gentlemen from the insurance offices called on me this morning, to see the letter. They were completely puzzled—especially when they heard of the bank-note inside. But they know who sent the letter. His lordship's doctor in Venice posted it at his lordship's request. Go to the gentlemen yourself, sir, if you don't believe me. They were polite enough to ask if I could account for Lord Montbarry's writing to me and sending me the money. I gave them my opinion directly—I said it was like his lordship's kindness.'

'Like his lordship's kindness?' Mr. Troy repeated, in blank amazement.

'Yes, sir! Lord Montbarry knew me, like all the other members of his family, when I was at school on the estate in Ireland. If he could have done it, he would have protected my poor dear husband. But he was helpless himself in the hands of my lady and the Baron—and the only kind thing he could do was to provide for me in my widowhood, like the true nobleman he was!'

'A very pretty explanation!' said Mr. Troy. 'What did your visitors from the insurance offices think of it?'

'They asked if I had any proof of my husband's death.'

'And what did you say?'

'I said, "I give you better than proof, gentlemen; I give you my positive opinion." '

'That satisfied them, of course?'

'They didn't say so in words, sir. They looked at each other—and wished me good-morning.'

'Well, Mrs. Ferrari, unless you have some more extraordinary news for me, I think I shall wish you good-morning too. I can take a note of your information (very startling information, I own); and, in the absence of proof, I can do no more.'

'I can provide you with proof, sir—if that is all you want,' said Mrs. Ferrari, with great dignity. 'I only wish to know, first, whether the law justifies me in doing it. You may have seen in the fashionable intelligence of the newspapers, that Lady Montbarry has arrived in London, at Newbury's Hotel. I propose to go and see her.'

'The deuce you do! May I ask for what purpose?'

Mrs. Ferrari answered in a mysterious whisper. 'For the purpose of catching her in a trap! I shan't send in my name—I shall announce myself as a person on business, and the first words I say to her will be these: "I come, my lady, to acknowledge the receipt of the money sent to Ferrari's widow." Ah! you may well start, Mr. Troy! It almost takes *you* off your guard, doesn't it? Make your mind easy, sir; I shall find the proof that everybody asks me for in her guilty face. Let her only change colour by the shadow of a shade—let her eyes only drop for half an instant—I shall discover her! The one thing I want to know is, does the law permit it?'

'The law permits it,' Mr. Troy answered gravely; 'but whether her lady-ship will permit it, is quite another question. Have you really courage enough, Mrs. Ferrari, to carry out this notable scheme of yours? You have been described to me, by Miss Lockwood, as rather a nervous, timid sort of person—and, if I may trust my own observation, I should say you justify the description.'

'If you had lived in the country, sir, instead of living in London,' Mrs. Ferrari replied, 'you would sometimes have seen even a sheep turn on a dog. I am far from saying that I am a bold woman—quite the reverse. But when I stand in that wretch's presence, and think of my murdered hus-band, the one of us two who is likely to be frightened is not *me*. I am going there now, sir. You shall hear how it ends. I wish you good-morning.'

With those brave words the courier's wife gathered her mantle about her, and walked out of the room.

Mr. Troy smiled—not satirically, but compassionately. 'The little sim-pleton!' he thought to himself. 'If half of what they say of Lady Mont-barry is true, Mrs. Ferrari and her trap have but a poor prospect before them. I wonder how it will end?'

All Mr. Troy's experience failed to forewarn him of how it *did* end.

## CHAPTER X

In the mean time, Mrs. Ferrari held to her resolution. She went straight from Mr. Troy's office to Newbury's Hotel.

Lady Montbarry was at home, and alone. But the authorities of the hotel hesitated to disturb her when they found that the visitor declined to mention her name. Her ladyship's new maid happened to cross the hall while the matter was still in debate. She was a Frenchwoman, and, on being appealed to, she settled the question in the swift, easy, rational French way. 'Madame's appearance was perfectly respectable. Madame might have reasons for not mentioning her name which Miladi might ap-prove. In any case, there being no orders forbidding the introduction of a strange lady, the matter clearly rested between Madame and Miladi. Would Madame, therefore, be good enough to follow Miladi's maid up the stairs?'

In spite of her resolution, Mrs. Ferrari's heart beat as if it would burst out of her bosom, when her conductress led her into an ante-room, and knocked at a door opening into a room beyond. But it is remarkable that persons of sensitively-nervous organisation are the very persons who are capable of forcing themselves (apparently by the exercise of a spasmodic effort of will) into the performance of acts of the most audacious courage. A low, grave voice from the inner room said, 'Come in.' The maid, opening the door, announced, 'A person to see you, Miladi, on business,' and immediately retired. In the one instant while these events passed, timid little Mrs. Ferrari mastered her own throbbing heart; stepped over the threshold, conscious of her clammy hands, dry lips, and burning head; and stood in the presence of Lord Montbarry's widow, to all outward appearance as supremely self-possessed as her ladyship herself.

It was still early in the afternoon, but the light in the room was dim. The blinds were drawn down. Lady Montbarry sat with her back to the windows, as if even the subdued daylight were disagreeable to her. She had altered sadly for the worse in her personal appearance, since the memorable day when Doctor Wybrow had seen her in his consulting-room. Her beauty was gone—her face had fallen away to mere skin and bone; the contrast between her ghastly complexion and her steely glittering black eyes was more startling than ever. Robed in dismal black, relieved only by the brilliant whiteness of her widow's cap—reclining in a panther-like suppleness of attitude on a little green sofa—she looked at the stranger who had intruded on her, with a moment's languid curiosity, then dropped her eyes again to the hand-screen which she held between her face and the fire. 'I don't know you,' she said. 'What do you want with me?'

Mrs. Ferrari tried to answer. Her first burst of courage had already worn itself out. The bold words that she had determined to speak were living words still in her mind, but they died on her lips.

There was a moment of silence. Lady Montbarry looked round again at the speechless stranger. 'Are you deaf?' she asked. There was another pause. Lady Montbarry quietly looked back again at the screen, and put another question. 'Do you want money?'

'Money!' That one word roused the sinking spirit of the courier's wife. She recovered her courage; she found her voice. 'Look at me, my lady, if you please,' she said, with a sudden outbreak of audacity.

Lady Montbarry looked round for the third time. The fatal words passed Mrs. Ferrari's lips.

'I come, my lady, to acknowledge the receipt of the money sent to Ferrari's widow.'

Lady Montbarry's glittering black eyes rested with steady attention on the woman who had addressed her in those terms. Not the faintest expression of confusion or alarm, not even a momentary flutter of interest stirred the deadly stillness of her face. She reposed as quietly, she held the screen as composedly, as ever. The test had been tried, and had utterly failed.

There was another silence. Lady Montbarry considered with herself. The smile that came slowly and went away suddenly—the smile at once so sad and so cruel—showed itself on her thin lips. She lifted her screen, and pointed with it to a seat at the farther end of the room. 'Be so good as to take that chair,' she said.

Helpless under her first bewildering sense of failure—not knowing what to say or what to do next—Mrs. Ferrari mechanically obeyed. Lady Montbarry, rising on the sofa for the first time, watched her with undisguised scrutiny as she crossed the room—then sank back into a reclining position once more. 'No,' she said to herself, 'the woman walks steadily; she is not intoxicated—the only other possibility is that she may be mad.'

She had spoken loud enough to be heard. Stung by the insult, Mrs. Ferrari instantly answered her: 'I am no more drunk or mad than you are!'

'No?' said Lady Montbarry. 'Then you are only insolent? The ignorant English mind (I have observed) is apt to be insolent in the exercise of unrestrained English liberty. This is very noticeable to us foreigners among you people in the streets. Of course I can't be insolent to you, in return. I hardly know what to say to you. My maid was imprudent in admitting you so easily to my room. I suppose your respectable appearance misled her. I wonder who you are? You mentioned the name of a courier who left us very strangely. Was he married by any chance? Are you his wife? And do you know where he is?'

Mrs. Ferrari's indignation burst its way through all restraints. She advanced to the sofa; she feared nothing, in the fervour and rage of her reply.

'I am his widow—and you know it, you wicked woman! Ah! it was an evil hour when Miss Lockwood recommended my husband to be his lordship's courier ——!'

Before she could add another word, Lady Montbarry sprang from the sofa with the stealthy suddenness of a cat—seized her by both shoulders—and shook her with the strength and frenzy of a madwoman. 'You lie! you lie! you lie!' She dropped her hold at the third repetition of the accusation, and threw up her hands wildly with a gesture of despair. 'Oh, Jesu Maria! is it possible?' she cried. '*Can* the courier have come to me through that woman?' She turned like lightning on Mrs. Ferrari, and stopped her as she was escaping from the room. 'Stay here, you fool—stay here, and answer me! If you cry out, as sure as the heavens are above you, I'll strangle you with my own hands. Sit down again—and fear nothing. Wretch! It is I who am frightened—frightened out of my senses. Confess that you lied, when you used Miss Lockwood's name just now! No! I don't believe you on your oath; I will believe nobody but Miss Lockwood herself. Where does she live? Tell me that, you noxious stinging little insect—and you may go.' Terrified as she was, Mrs. Ferrari hesitated. Lady Montbarry lifted her hands threateningly, with the long, lean, yellow-white fingers outspread and crooked at the tips. Mrs. Ferrari shrank at the sight of them, and gave the address. Lady Montbarry pointed contemptuously to the door—then changed her mind. 'No! not yet! you will tell Miss Lockwood what has happened, and she may refuse to see me. I will go there at once, and you shall go with me. As far as the house—not inside of it. Sit down again. I am going to ring for my maid. Turn your back to the door—your cowardly face is not fit to be seen!'

She rang the bell. The maid appeared.

*'You lie! You lie!'*

'My cloak and bonnet—instantly!'

The maid produced the cloak and bonnet from the bedroom.

'A cab at the door—before I can count ten!'

The maid vanished. Lady Montbarry surveyed herself in the glass, and wheeled round again, with her cat-like suddenness, to Mrs. Ferrari.

'I look more than half dead already, don't I?' she said with a grim outburst of irony. 'Give me your arm.'

She took Mrs. Ferrari's arm, and left the room. 'You have nothing to fear, so long as you obey,' she whispered, on the way downstairs. 'You leave me at Miss Lockwood's door, and never see me again.'

In the hall they were met by the landlady of the hotel. Lady Montbarry graciously presented her companion. 'My good friend Mrs. Ferrari; I am so glad to have seen her.' The landlady accompanied them to the door. The cab was waiting. 'Get in first, good Mrs. Ferrari,' said her ladyship; 'and tell the man where to go.'

They were driven away. Lady Montbarry's variable humour changed again. With a low groan of misery, she threw herself back in the cab. Lost in her own dark thoughts, as careless of the woman whom she had bent to her iron will as if no such person sat by her side, she preserved a sinister silence, until they reached the house where Miss Lockwood lodged. In an instant, she roused herself to action. She opened the door of the cab, and closed it again on Mrs. Ferrari, before the driver could get off his box.

'Take that lady a mile farther on her way home!' she said, as she paid the man his fare. The next moment she had knocked at the house-door. 'Is Miss Lockwood at home?' 'Yes, ma'am.' She stepped over the threshold— the door closed on her.

'Which way, ma'am?' asked the driver of the cab.

Mrs. Ferrari put her hand to her head, and tried to collect her thoughts. Could she leave her friend and benefactress helpless at Lady Montbarry's mercy? She was still vainly endeavouring to decide on the course that she ought to follow—when a gentleman, stopping at Miss Lockwood's door, happened to look towards the cab-window, and saw her.

'Are you going to call on Miss Agnes too?' he asked.

It was Henry Westwick. Mrs. Ferrari clasped her hands in gratitude as she recognised him.

'Go in, sir!' she cried. 'Go in, directly. That dreadful woman is with Miss Agnes. Go and protect her!'

'What woman?' Henry asked.

The answer literally struck him speechless. With amazement and indignation in his face, he looked at Mrs. Ferrari as she pronounced the hated name of 'Lady Montbarry.' 'I'll see to it,' was all he said. He knocked at the house-door; and he too, in his turn, was let in.

# CHAPTER XI

'Lady Montbarry, Miss.'

Agnes was writing a letter, when the servant astonished her by announcing the visitor's name. Her first impulse was to refuse to see the woman who had intruded on her. But Lady Montbarry had taken care to follow close on the servant's heels. Before Agnes could speak, she had entered the room.

'I beg to apologise for my intrusion, Miss Lockwood. I have a question to ask you, in which I am very much interested. No one can answer me but yourself.' In low hesitating tones, with her glittering black eyes bent modestly on the ground, Lady Montbarry opened the interview in those words.

Without answering, Agnes pointed to a chair. She could do this, and, for the time, she could do no more. All that she had read of the hidden and sinister life in the palace at Venice; all that she had heard of Montbarry's melancholy death and burial in a foreign land; all that she knew of the mystery of Ferrari's disappearance, rushed into her mind, when the black-robed figure confronted her, standing just inside the door. The strange conduct of Lady Montbarry added a new perplexity to the doubts and misgivings that troubled her. There stood the adventuress whose character had left its mark on society all over Europe—the Fury who had terrified Mrs. Ferrari at the hotel—inconceivably transformed into a timid, shrinking woman! Lady Montbarry had not once ventured to look at Agnes, since she had made her way into the room. Advancing to take the chair that had been pointed out to her, she hesitated, put her hand on the rail to support herself, and still remained standing. 'Please give me a moment to compose myself,' she said faintly. Her head sank on her bosom: she stood before Agnes like a conscious culprit before a merciless judge.

The silence that followed was, literally, the silence of fear on both sides. In the midst of it, the door was opened once more—and Henry Westwick appeared.

He looked at Lady Montbarry with a moment's steady attention—bowed to her with formal politeness—and passed on in silence. At the sight of her husband's brother, the sinking spirit of the woman sprang to life again. Her drooping figure became erect. Her eyes met Westwick's look, brightly defiant. She returned his bow with an icy smile of contempt.

Henry crossed the room to Agnes.

'Is Lady Montbarry here by your invitation?' he asked quietly.

'No.'

'Do you wish to see her?'

'It is very painful to me to see her.'

He turned and looked at his sister-in-law. 'Do you hear that?' he asked coldly.

'I hear it,' she answered, more coldly still.

'Your visit is, to say the least of it, ill-timed.'

'Your interference is, to say the least of it, out of place.'

With that retort, Lady Montbarry approached Agnes. The presence of Henry Westwick seemed at once to relieve and embolden her. 'Permit me to ask my question, Miss Lockwood,' she said, with graceful courtesy. 'It is nothing to embarrass you. When the courier Ferrari applied to my late husband for employment, did you ——' Her resolution failed her, before she could say more. She sank trembling into the nearest chair, and, after a moment's struggle, composed herself again. 'Did you permit Ferrari,' she resumed, 'to make sure of being chosen for our courier by using your name?'

Agnes did not reply with her customary directness. Trifling as it was, the reference to Montbarry, proceeding from *that* woman of all others, confused and agitated her.

'I have known Ferrari's wife for many years,' she began. 'And I take an interest ——'

Lady Montbarry abruptly lifted her hands with a gesture of entreaty. 'Ah, Miss Lockwood, don't waste time by talking of his wife! Answer my plain question, plainly!'

'Let me answer her,' Henry whispered. 'I will undertake to speak plainly enough.'

Agnes refused by a gesture. Lady Montbarry's interruption had roused her sense of what was due to herself. She resumed her reply in plainer terms.

'When Ferrari wrote to the late Lord Montbarry,' she said, 'he did certainly mention my name.'

Even now, she had innocently failed to see the object which her visitor had in view. Lady Montbarry's impatience became ungovernable. She started to her feet, and advanced to Agnes.

'Was it with your knowledge and permission that Ferrari used your name?' she asked. 'The whole soul of my question is in *that*. For God's sake answer me—Yes, or No!'

'Yes.'

That one word struck Lady Montbarry as a blow might have struck her. The fierce life that had animated her face the instant before, faded out of it suddenly, and left her like a woman turned to stone. She stood, mechanically confronting Agnes, with a stillness so wrapt and perfect that not even the breath she drew was perceptible to the two persons who were looking at her.

Henry spoke to her roughly. 'Rouse yourself,' he said. 'You have received your answer.'

She looked round at him. 'I have received my Sentence,' she rejoined— and turned slowly to leave the room.

To Henry's astonishment, Agnes stopped her. 'Wait a moment, Lady Montbarry. I have something to ask on my side. You have spoken of Ferrari. I wish to speak of him too.'

Lady Montbarry bent her head in silence. Her hand trembled as she took out her handkerchief, and passed it over her forehead. Agnes detected the trembling, and shrank back a step. 'Is the subject painful to you?' she asked timidly.

Still silent, Lady Montbarry invited her by a wave of the hand to go on. Henry approached, attentively watching his sister-in-law. Agnes went on.

'No trace of Ferrari has been discovered in England,' she said. 'Have you any news of him? And will you tell me (if you have heard anything), in mercy to his wife?'

Lady Montbarry's thin lips suddenly relaxed into their sad and cruel smile.

'Why do you ask *me* about the lost courier?' she said. 'You will know what has become of him, Miss Lockwood, when the time is ripe for it.'

Agnes started. 'I don't understand you,' she said. 'How shall I know? Will some one tell me?'

'Some one will tell you.'

Henry could keep silence no longer. 'Perhaps, your ladyship may be the person?' he interrupted with ironical politeness.

She answered him with contemptuous ease. 'You may be right, Mr. Westwick. One day or another, I may be the person who tells Miss Lockwood what has become of Ferrari, if — —' She stopped; with her eyes fixed on Agnes.

'If what?' Henry asked.

'If Miss Lockwood forces me to it.'

Agnes listened in astonishment. 'Force you to it?' she repeated. 'How can I do that? Do you mean to say my will is stronger than yours?'

'Do *you* mean to say that the candle doesn't burn the moth, when the moth flies into it?' Lady Montbarry rejoined. 'Have you ever heard of such a thing as the fascination of terror? I am drawn to you by a fascination of terror. I have no right to visit you, I have no wish to visit you: you are my enemy. For the first time in my life, against my own will, I submit to my enemy. See! I am waiting because you told me to wait—and the fear of you (I swear it!) creeps through me while I stand here. Oh, don't let me excite your curiosity or your pity! Follow the example of Mr. Westwick. Be hard and brutal and unforgiving, like him. Grant me my release. Tell me to go.'

The frank and simple nature of Agnes could discover but one intelligible meaning in this strange outbreak.

'You are mistaken in thinking me your enemy,' she said. 'The wrong you did me when you gave your hand to Lord Montbarry was not intentionally done. I forgave you my sufferings in his lifetime. I forgive you even more freely now that he has gone.'

Henry heard her with mingled emotions of admiration and distress. 'Say no more!' he exclaimed. 'You are too good to her; she is not worthy of it.'

The interruption passed unheeded by Lady Montbarry. The simple words in which Agnes had replied seemed to have absorbed the whole attention of this strangely-changeable woman. As she listened, her face settled slowly into an expression of hard and tearless sorrow. There was a marked change in her voice when she spoke next. It expressed that last worst resignation which has done with hope.

'You good innocent creature,' she said, 'what does your amiable forgiveness matter? What are your poor little wrongs, in the reckoning for greater wrongs which is demanded of me? I am not trying to frighten you, I am only miserable about myself. Do you know what it is to have a firm presentiment of calamity that is coming to you—and yet to hope that your own positive conviction will not prove true? When I first met you, before my marriage, and first felt your influence over me, I had that hope. It was a starveling sort of hope that lived a lingering life in me until to-day. *You* struck it dead, when you answered my question about Ferrari.'

'How have I destroyed your hopes?' Agnes asked. 'What connection is there between my permitting Ferrari to use my name to Lord Montbarry, and the strange and dreadful things you are saying to me now?'

'The time is near, Miss Lockwood, when you will discover that for yourself. In the mean while, you shall know what my fear of you is, in the plainest words I can find. On the day when I took your hero from you and blighted your life—I am firmly persuaded of it!—you were made the instrument of the retribution that my sins of many years had deserved. Oh, such things have happened before to-day! One person has, before now, been the means of innocently ripening the growth of evil in another. You have done that already—and you have more to do yet. You have still to bring me to the day of discovery, and to the punishment that is my doom. We shall meet again—here in England, or there in Venice where my husband died— and meet for the last time.'

In spite of her better sense, in spite of her natural superiority to superstitions of all kinds, Agnes was impressed by the terrible earnestness with which those words were spoken. She turned pale as she looked at Henry. 'Do *you* understand her?' she asked.

'Nothing is easier than to understand her,' he replied contemptuously. 'She knows what has become of Ferrari; and she is confusing you in a cloud of nonsense, because she daren't own the truth. Let her go!'

If a dog had been under one of the chairs, and had barked, Lady Montbarry could not have proceeded more impenetrably with the last words she had to say to Agnes.

'Advise your interesting Mrs. Ferrari to wait a little longer,' she said. '*You* will know what has become of her husband, and you will tell her. There will be nothing to alarm you. Some trifling event will bring us together the next time—as trifling, I dare say, as the engagement of Ferrari. Sad nonsense, Mr. Westwick, is it not? But you make allowances for women; we all talk nonsense. Good morning, Miss Lockwood.'

She opened the door—suddenly, as if she was afraid of being called back for the second time—and left them.


# CHAPTER XII


'Do you think she is mad?' Agnes asked.

'I think she is simply wicked. False, superstitious, inveterately cruel—but not mad. I believe her main motive in coming here was to enjoy the luxury of frightening you.'

'She *has* frightened me. I am ashamed to own it—but so it is.'

Henry looked at her, hesitated for a moment, and seated himself on the sofa by her side.

'I am very anxious about you, Agnes,' he said. 'But for the fortunate chance which led me to call here to-day—who knows what that vile woman might not have said or done, if she had found you alone? My dear, you are leading a sadly unprotected solitary life. I don't like to think of it; I want to see it changed—especially after what has happened to-day. No! no! it is useless to tell me that you have your old nurse. She is too old; she is not in your rank of life—there is no sufficient protection in the companionship of such a person for a lady in your position. Don't mistake me, Agnes! what I say, I say in the sincerity of my devotion to you.' He paused, and took her hand. She made a feeble effort to withdraw it—and yielded. 'Will the day never come,' he pleaded, 'when the privilege of protecting you may be mine? when you will be the pride and joy of my life, as long as my life lasts?' He pressed her hand gently. She made no reply. The colour came and went on her face; her eyes were turned away from him. 'Have I been so unhappy as to offend you?' he asked.

She answered that—she said, almost in a whisper, 'No.'

'Have I distressed you?'

'You have made me think of the sad days that are gone.' She said no more; she only tried to withdraw her hand from his for the second time. He still held it; he lifted it to his lips.

'Can I never make you think of other days than those—of the happier days to come? Or, if you must think of the time that is passed, can you not look back to the time when I first loved you?'

She sighed as he put the question. 'Spare me Henry,' she answered sadly. 'Say no more!'

The colour again rose in her cheeks; her hand trembled in his. She looked lovely, with her eyes cast down and her bosom heaving gently. At that moment he would have given everything he had in the world to take her in his arms and kiss her. Some mysterious sympathy, passing from his hand to hers, seemed to tell her what was in his mind. She snatched her hand away, and suddenly looked up at him. The tears were in her eyes. She said nothing; she let her eyes speak for her. They warned him—without anger, without unkindness—but still they warned him to press her no further that day.

'Only tell me that I am forgiven,' he said, as he rose from the sofa.

'Yes,' she answered quietly, 'you are forgiven.'

'I have not lowered myself in your estimation, Agnes?'

'Oh, no!'

'Do you wish me to leave you?'

She rose, in her turn, from the sofa, and walked to her writing-table before she replied. The unfinished letter which she had been writing when Lady Montbarry interrupted her, lay open on the blotting-book. As she looked at the letter, and then looked at Henry, the smile that charmed everybody showed itself in her face.

'You must not go just yet,' she said: 'I have something to tell you. I hardly know how to express it. The shortest way perhaps will be to let you find it out for yourself. You have been speaking of my lonely unprotected life here. It is not a very happy life, Henry—I own that.' She paused, observing the growing anxiety of his expression as he looked at her, with a shy satisfaction that perplexed him. 'Do you know that I have anticipated your idea?' she went on. 'I am going to make a great change in my life—if your brother Stephen and his wife will only consent to it.' She opened the desk of the writing-table while she spoke, took a letter out, and handed it to Henry.

He received it from her mechanically. Vague doubts, which he hardly understood himself, kept him silent. It was impossible that the 'change in her life' of which she had spoken could mean that she was about to be married—and yet he was conscious of a perfectly unreasonable reluctance to open the letter. Their eyes met; she smiled again. 'Look at the address,' she said. 'You ought to know the handwriting—but I dare say you don't.'

He looked at the address. It was in the large, irregular, uncertain writing of a child. He opened the letter instantly.

'Dear Aunt Agnes,—Our governess is going away. She has had money left to her, and a house of her own. We have had cake and wine to drink her health. You promised to be our governess if we wanted another. We want you. Mamma knows nothing about this. Please come before Mamma can get another governess. Your loving Lucy, who writes this. Clara and Blanche have tried to write too. But they are too young to do it. They blot the paper.'

'Your eldest niece,' Agnes explained, as Henry looked at her in amazement. 'The children used to call me aunt when I was staying with their mother in Ireland, in the autumn. The three girls were my inseparable companions—they are the most charming children I know. It is quite true that I offered to be their governess, if they ever wanted one, on the day when I left them to return to London. I was writing to propose it to their mother, just before you came.'

'Not seriously!' Henry exclaimed.

Agnes placed her unfinished letter in his hand. Enough of it had been written to show that she did seriously propose to enter the household of Mr. and Mrs. Stephen Westwick as governess to their children! Henry's bewilderment was not to be expressed in words.

'They won't believe you are in earnest,' he said.

'Why not?' Agnes asked quietly.

'You are my brother Stephen's cousin; you are his wife's old friend.'

'All the more reason, Henry, for trusting me with the charge of their children.'

'But you are their equal; you are not obliged to get your living by teaching. There is something absurd in your entering their service as a governess!'

'What is there absurd in it? The children love me; the mother loves me; the father has shown me innumerable instances of his true friendship and regard. I am the very woman for the place—and, as to my education, I must have completely forgotten it indeed, if I am not fit to teach three children the eldest of whom is only eleven years old. You say I am their equal. Are there no other women who serve as governesses, and who are the equals of the persons whom they serve? Besides, I don't know that I *am* their equal. Have I not heard that your brother Stephen was the next heir to the title? Will he not be the new lord? Never mind answering me! We won't dispute whether I am right or wrong in turning governess—we will wait the event. I am weary of my lonely useless existence here, and eager to make my life more happy and more useful, in the household of all others in which I should like most to have a place. If you will look again, you will see that I have these personal considerations still to urge before I finish my letter. You don't know your brother and his wife as well as I do, if you doubt their answer. I believe they have courage enough and heart enough to say Yes.'

Henry submitted without being convinced.

He was a man who disliked all eccentric departures from custom and routine; and he felt especially suspicious of the change proposed in the life of Agnes. With new interests to occupy her mind, she might be less favourably disposed to listen to him, on the next occasion when he urged his suit. The influence of the 'lonely useless existence' of which she complained, was distinctly an influence in his favour. While her heart was empty, her heart was accessible. But with his nieces in full possession of it, the clouds of doubt overshadowed his prospects. He knew the sex well enough to keep these purely selfish perplexities to himself. The waiting policy was especially the policy to pursue with a woman as sensitive as Agnes. If he once offended her delicacy he was lost. For the moment he wisely controlled himself and changed the subject.

'My little niece's letter has had an effect,' he said, 'which the child never contemplated in writing it. She has just reminded me of one of the objects that I had in calling on you to-day.'

Agnes looked at the child's letter. 'How does Lucy do that?' she asked.

'Lucy's governess is not the only lucky person who has had money left her,' Henry answered. 'Is your old nurse in the house?'

'You don't mean to say that nurse has got a legacy?'

'She has got a hundred pounds. Send for her, Agnes, while I show you the letter.'

He took a handful of letters from his pocket, and looked through them, while Agnes rang the bell. Returning to him, she noticed a printed letter among the rest, which lay open on the table. It was a 'prospectus,' and the title of it was 'Palace Hotel Company of Venice (Limited).' The two words, 'Palace' and 'Venice,' instantly recalled her mind to the unwelcome visit of Lady Montbarry. 'What is that?' she asked, pointing to the title.

Henry suspended his search, and glanced at the prospectus. 'A really promising speculation,' he said. 'Large hotels always pay well, if they are well managed. I know the man who is appointed to be manager of this hotel when it is opened to the public; and I have such entire confidence in him that I have become one of the shareholders of the Company.'

The reply did not appear to satisfy Agnes. 'Why is the hotel called the "Palace Hotel"?' she inquired.

Henry looked at her, and at once penetrated her motive for asking the question. 'Yes,' he said, 'it *is* the palace that Montbarry hired at Venice; and it has been purchased by the Company to be changed into an hotel.'

Agnes turned away in silence, and took a chair at the farther end of the room. Henry had disappointed her. His income as a younger son stood in need, as she well knew, of all the additions that he could make to it by successful speculation. But she was unreasonable enough, nevertheless, to disapprove of his attempting to make money already out of the house in which his brother had died. Incapable of understanding this purely sentimental view of a plain matter of business, Henry returned to his papers, in some perplexity at the sudden change in the manner of Agnes towards him. Just as he found the letter of which he was in search, the nurse made her appearance. He glanced at Agnes, expecting that she would speak first. She never even looked up when the nurse came in. It was left to Henry to tell the old woman why the bell had summoned her to the drawing-room.

'Well, nurse,' he said, 'you have had a windfall of luck. You have had a legacy left you of a hundred pounds.'

The nurse showed no outward signs of exultation. She waited a little to get the announcement of the legacy well settled in her mind—and then she said quietly, 'Master Henry, who gives me that money, if you please?'

'My late brother, Lord Montbarry, gives it to you.' (Agnes instantly looked up, interested in the matter for the first time. Henry went on.) 'His will leaves legacies to the surviving old servants of the family. There is a letter from his lawyers, authorising you to apply to them for the money.'

In every class of society, gratitude is the rarest of all human virtues. In the nurse's class it is extremely rare. Her opinion of the man who had deceived and deserted her mistress remained the same opinion still, perfectly undisturbed by the passing circumstance of the legacy.

'I wonder who reminded my lord of the old servants?' she said. 'He would never have heart enough to remember them himself!'

Agnes suddenly interposed. Nature, always abhorring monotony, institutes reserves of temper as elements in the composition of the gentlest women living. Even Agnes could, on rare occasions, be angry. The nurse's view of Montbarry's character seemed to have provoked her beyond endurance.

'If you have any sense of shame in you,' she broke out, 'you ought to be ashamed of what you have just said! Your ingratitude disgusts me. I leave you to speak with her, Henry—*you* won't mind it!' With this significant intimation that he too had dropped out of his customary place in her good opinion, she left the room.

The nurse received the smart reproof administered to her with every appearance of feeling rather amused by it than not. When the door had closed, this female philosopher winked at Henry.

'There's a power of obstinacy in young women,' she remarked. 'Miss Agnes wouldn't give my lord up as a bad one, even when he jilted her. And now she's sweet on him after he's dead. Say a word against him, and she fires up as you see. All obstinacy! It will wear out with time. Stick to her, Master Henry—stick to her!'

'She doesn't seem to have offended you,' said Henry.

'*She*?' the nurse repeated in amazement—'she offend me? I like her in her tantrums; it reminds me of her when she was a baby. Lord bless you! when I go to bid her good-night, she'll give me a big kiss, poor dear—and say, Nurse, I didn't mean it! About this money, Master Henry? If I was younger I should spend it in dress and jewellery. But I'm too old for that. What shall I do with my legacy when I have got it?'

'Put it out at interest,' Henry suggested. 'Get so much a year for it, you know.'

'How much shall I get?' the nurse asked.

'If you put your hundred pounds into the Funds, you will get between three and four pounds a year.'

The nurse shook her head. 'Three or four pounds a year? That won't do! I want more than that. Look here, Master Henry. I don't care about this bit of money—I never did like the man who has left it to me, though he *was* your brother. If I lost it all to-morrow, I shouldn't break my heart; I'm well enough off, as it is, for the rest of my days. They say you're a speculator. Put me in for a good thing, there's a dear! Neck-or-nothing—and *that* for the Funds!' She snapped her fingers to express her contempt for security of investment at three per cent.

Henry produced the prospectus of the Venetian Hotel Company. 'You're a funny old woman,' he said. 'There, you dashing speculator—there is neck-or-nothing for you! You must keep it a secret from Miss Agnes, mind. I'm not at all sure that she would approve of my helping you to this investment.'

The nurse took out her spectacles. 'Six per cent. guaranteed,' she read;

'and the Directors have every reason to believe that ten per cent., or more, will be ultimately realised to the shareholders by the hotel.' 'Put me into that, Master Henry! And, wherever you go, for Heaven's sake recommend the hotel to your friends!'

So the nurse, following Henry's mercenary example, had *her* pecuniary interest, too, in the house in which Lord Montbarry had died.

Three days passed before Henry was able to visit Agnes again. In that time, the little cloud between them had entirely passed away. Agnes received him with even more than her customary kindness. She was in better spirits than usual. Her letter to Mrs. Stephen Westwick had been answered by return of post; and her proposal had been joyfully accepted, with one modification. She was to visit the Westwicks for a month—and, if she really liked teaching the children, she was then to be governess, aunt, and cousin, all in one—and was only to go away in an event which her friends in Ireland persisted in contemplating, the event of her marriage.

'You see I was right,' she said to Henry.

He was still incredulous. 'Are you really going?' he asked.

'I am going next week.'

'When shall I see you again?'

'You know you are always welcome at your brother's house. You can see me when you like.' She held out her hand. 'Pardon me for leaving you—I am beginning to pack up already.'

Henry tried to kiss her at parting. She drew back directly.

'Why not? I am your cousin,' he said.

'I don't like it,' she answered.

Henry looked at her, and submitted. Her refusal to grant him his privilege as a cousin was a good sign—it was indirectly an act of encouragement to him in the character of her lover.

On the first day in the new week, Agnes left London on her way to Ireland. As the event proved, this was not destined to be the end of her journey. The way to Ireland was only the first stage on a roundabout road—the road that led to the palace at Venice.

# THE THIRD PART

## CHAPTER XIII

In the spring of the year 1861, Agnes was established at the country-seat of her two friends—now promoted (on the death of the first lord, without offspring) to be the new Lord and Lady Montbarry. The old nurse was not separated from her mistress. A place, suited to her time of life, had been found for her in the pleasant Irish household. She was perfectly happy in her new sphere; and she spent her first half-year's dividend from the Venice Hotel Company, with characteristic prodigality, in presents for the children.

Early in the year, also, the Directors of the life insurance offices submitted to circumstances, and paid the ten thousand pounds. Immediately afterwards, the widow of the first Lord Montbarry (otherwise, the dowager Lady Montbarry) left England, with Baron Rivar, for the United States. The Baron's object was announced, in the scientific columns of the newspapers, to be investigation into the present state of experimental chemistry in the great American republic. His sister informed inquiring friends that she accompanied him, in the hope of finding consolation in change of scene after the bereavement that had fallen on her. Hearing this news from Henry Westwick (then paying a visit at his brother's house), Agnes was conscious of a certain sense of relief. 'With the Atlantic between us,' she said, 'surely I have done with that terrible woman now!'

Barely a week passed after those words had been spoken, before an event happened which reminded Agnes of 'the terrible woman' once more.

On that day, Henry's engagements had obliged him to return to London. He had ventured, on the morning of his departure, to press his suit once more on Agnes; and the children, as he had anticipated, proved to be innocent obstacles in the way of his success. On the other hand, he had privately secured a firm ally in his sister-in-law. 'Have a little patience,' the new Lady Montbarry had said, 'and leave me to turn the influence of the children in the right direction. If they can persuade her to listen to you—they shall!'

The two ladies had accompanied Henry, and some other guests who went away at the same time, to the railway station, and had just driven back to the house, when the servant announced that 'a person of the name of Rolland was waiting to see her ladyship.'

'Is it a woman?'

'Yes, my lady.'

Young Lady Montbarry turned to Agnes.

'This is the very person,' she said, 'whom your lawyer thought likely to help him, when he was trying to trace the lost courier.'

'You don't mean the English maid who was with Lady Montbarry at Venice?'

'My dear! don't speak of Montbarry's horrid widow by the name which is *my* name now. Stephen and I have arranged to call her by her foreign title, before she was married. I am "Lady Montbarry," and she is "the Countess." In that way there will be no confusion.—Yes, Mrs. Rolland was in my service before she became the Countess's maid. She was a perfectly trustworthy person, with one defect that obliged me to send her away—a sullen temper which led to perpetual complaints of her in the servants' hall. Would you like to see her?'

Agnes accepted the proposal, in the faint hope of getting some information for the courier's wife. The complete defeat of every attempt to trace the lost man had been accepted as final by Mrs. Ferrari. She had deliberately arrayed herself in widow's mourning; and was earning her livelihood in an employment which the unwearied kindness of Agnes had procured for her in London. The last chance of penetrating the mystery of Ferrari's disappearance seemed to rest now on what Ferrari's former fellow-servant might be able to tell. With highly-wrought expectations, Agnes followed her friend into the room in which Mrs. Rolland was waiting.

A tall bony woman, in the autumn of life, with sunken eyes and iron-grey hair, rose stiffly from her chair, and saluted the ladies with stern submission as they opened the door. A person of unblemished character, evidently—but not without visible drawbacks. Big bushy eyebrows, an awfully deep and solemn voice, a harsh unbending manner, a complete absence in her figure of the undulating lines characteristic of the sex, presented Virtue in this excellent person under its least alluring aspect. Strangers, on a first introduction to her, were accustomed to wonder why she was not a man.

'Are you pretty well, Mrs. Rolland?'

'I am as well as I can expect to be, my lady, at my time of life.'

'Is there anything I can do for you?'

'Your ladyship can do me a great favour, if you will please speak to my character while I was in your service. I am offered a place, to wait on an invalid lady who has lately come to live in this neighbourhood.'

'Ah, yes—I have heard of her. A Mrs. Carbury, with a very pretty niece I am told. But, Mrs. Rolland, you left my service some time ago. Mrs. Carbury will surely expect you to refer to the last mistress by whom you were employed.'

A flash of virtuous indignation irradiated Mrs. Rolland's sunken eyes. She coughed before she answered, as if her 'last mistress' stuck in her throat.

'I have explained to Mrs. Carbury, my lady, that the person I last served—I really cannot give her her title in your ladyship's presence!—has left England for America. Mrs. Carbury knows that I quitted the person of my own free will, and knows why, and approves of my conduct so far. A word from your ladyship will be amply sufficient to get me the situation.'

'Very well, Mrs. Rolland, I have no objection to be your reference, under the circumstances. Mrs. Carbury will find me at home to-morrow until two o'clock.'

'Mrs. Carbury is not well enough to leave the house, my lady. Her niece, Miss Haldane, will call and make the inquiries, if your ladyship has no objection.'

'I have not the least objection. The pretty niece carries her own welcome with her. Wait a minute, Mrs. Rolland. This lady is Miss Lockwood— my husband's cousin, and my friend. She is anxious to speak to you about the courier who was in the late Lord Montbarry's service at Venice.'

Mrs. Rolland's bushy eyebrows frowned in stern disapproval of the new topic of conversation. 'I regret to hear it, my lady,' was all she said.

'Perhaps you have not been informed of what happened after you left Venice?' Agnes ventured to add. 'Ferrari left the palace secretly; and he has never been heard of since.'

Mrs. Rolland mysteriously closed her eyes—as if to exclude some vision of the lost courier which was of a nature to disturb a respectable woman. 'Nothing that Mr. Ferrari could do would surprise me,' she replied in her deepest bass tones.

'You speak rather harshly of him,' said Agnes.

Mrs. Rolland suddenly opened her eyes again. 'I speak harshly of nobody without reason,' she said. 'Mr. Ferrari behaved to me, Miss Lockwood, as no man living has ever behaved—before or since.'

'What did he do?'

Mrs. Rolland answered, with a stony stare of horror:—

'He took liberties with me.'

Young Lady Montbarry suddenly turned aside, and put her handkerchief over her mouth in convulsions of suppressed laughter.

Mrs. Rolland went on, with a grim enjoyment of the bewilderment which her reply had produced in Agnes: 'And when I insisted on an apology, Miss, he had the audacity to say that the life at the palace was dull, and he didn't know how else to amuse himself!'

'I am afraid I have hardly made myself understood,' said Agnes. 'I am not speaking to you out of any interest in Ferrari. Are you aware that he is married?'

'I pity his wife,' said Mrs. Rolland.

'She is naturally in great grief about him,' Agnes proceeded.

'She ought to thank God she is rid of him,' Mrs. Rolland interposed.

Agnes still persisted. 'I have known Mrs. Ferrari from her childhood, and I am sincerely anxious to help her in this matter. Did you notice anything, while you were at Venice, that would account for her husband's extraordinary disappearance? On what sort of terms, for instance, did he live with his master and mistress?'

'On terms of familiarity with his mistress,' said Mrs. Rolland, 'which were simply sickening to a respectable English servant. She used to encourage him to talk to her about all his affairs—how he got on with his wife, and how pressed he was for money, and such like—just as if they were equals. Contemptible—that's what I call it.'

'And his master?' Agnes continued. 'How did Ferrari get on with Lord Montbarry?'

'My lord used to live shut up with his studies and his sorrows,' Mrs. Rolland answered, with a hard solemnity expressive of respect for his lordship's memory. Mr. Ferrari got his money when it was due; and he cared for nothing else. "If I could afford it, I would leave the place too; but I can't afford it." Those were the last words he said to me, on the morning when I left the palace. I made no reply. After what had happened (on that other occasion) I was naturally not on speaking terms with Mr. Ferrari.'

'Can you really tell me nothing which will throw any light on this matter?'

'Nothing,' said Mrs. Rolland, with an undisguised relish of the disappointment that she was inflicting.

'There was another member of the family at Venice,' Agnes resumed, determined to sift the question to the bottom while she had the chance. 'There was Baron Rivar.'

Mrs. Rolland lifted her large hands, covered with rusty black gloves, in mute protest against the introduction of Baron Rivar as a subject of inquiry. 'Are you aware, Miss,' she began, 'that I left my place in consequence of what I observed ——?'

Agnes stopped her there. 'I only wanted to ask,' she explained, 'if anything was said or done by Baron Rivar which might account for Ferrari's strange conduct.'

'Nothing that I know of,' said Mrs. Rolland. 'The Baron and Mr. Ferrari (if I may use such an expression) were "birds of a feather," so far as I could see—I mean, one was as unprincipled as the other. I am a just woman; and I will give you an example. Only the day before I left, I heard the Baron say (through the open door of his room while I was passing along the corridor), "Ferrari, I want a thousand pounds. What would you do for a thousand pounds?" And I heard Mr. Ferrari answer, "Anything, sir, as long as I was not found out." And then they both burst out laughing. I heard no more than that. Judge for yourself, Miss.'

Agnes reflected for a moment. A thousand pounds was the sum that had been sent to Mrs. Ferrari in the anonymous letter. Was that enclosure in any way connected, as a result, with the conversation between the Baron and Ferrari? It was useless to press any more inquiries on Mrs. Rolland. She could give no further information which was of the slightest importance to the object in view. There was no alternative but to grant her dismissal. One more effort had been made to find a trace of the lost man, and once again the effort had failed.

They were a family party at the dinner-table that day. The only guest left in the house was a nephew of the new Lord Montbarry—the eldest son of his sister, Lady Barrville. Lady Montbarry could not resist telling the story of the first (and last) attack made on the virtue of Mrs. Rolland, with a comically-exact imitation of Mrs. Rolland's deep and dismal voice. Being asked by her husband what was the object which had brought that formidable person to the house, she naturally mentioned the expected visit of Miss Haldane. Arthur Barville, unusually silent and pre-occupied so far, suddenly struck into the conversation with a burst of enthusiasm. 'Miss Haldane is the most charming girl in all Ireland!' he said. 'I caught sight of her yesterday, over the wall of her garden, as I was riding by. What time is she coming to-morrow? Before two? I'll look into the drawing-room by accident—I am dying to be introduced to her!'

Agnes was amused by his enthusiasm. 'Are you in love with Miss Haldane already?' she asked.

Arthur answered gravely, 'It's no joking matter. I have been all day at the garden wall, waiting to see her again! It depends on Miss Haldane to make me the happiest or the wretchedest man living.'

'You foolish boy! How can you talk such nonsense?'

He was talking nonsense undoubtedly. But, if Agnes had only known it, he was doing something more than that. He was innocently leading her another stage nearer on the way to Venice.

## CHAPTER XIV

As the summer months advanced, the transformation of the Venetian palace into the modern hotel proceeded rapidly towards completion.

The outside of the building, with its fine Palladian front looking on the canal, was wisely left unaltered. Inside, as a matter of necessity, the rooms were almost rebuilt—so far at least as the size and the arrangement of them were concerned. The vast saloons were partitioned off into 'apartments' containing three or four rooms each. The broad corridors in the upper regions afforded spare space enough for rows of little bedchambers, devoted to servants and to travellers with limited means. Nothing was spared but the solid floors and the finely-carved ceilings. These last, in excellent preservation as to workmanship, merely required cleaning, and regilding here and there, to add greatly to the beauty and importance of the best rooms in the hotel. The only exception to the complete re-organization of the interior was at one extremity of the edifice, on the first and second floors. Here there happened, in each case, to be rooms of such comparatively moderate size, and so attractively decorated, that the architect suggested leaving them as they were. It was afterwards discovered that these were no other than the apartments formerly occupied by Lord Montbarry (on the first floor), and by Baron Rivar (on the second). The room in which Montbarry had died was still fitted up as a bedroom, and was now distinguished as Number Fourteen. The room above it, in which the Baron had slept, took its place on the hotel-register as Number Thirty-Eight. With the ornaments on the walls and ceilings cleaned and brightened up, and with the heavy old-fashioned beds, chairs, and tables replaced by bright, pretty, and luxurious modern furniture, these two promised to be at once the most attractive and the most comfortable bedchambers in the hotel. As for the once-desolate and disused ground floor of the building, it was now transformed, by means of splendid dining-rooms, reception-rooms, billiard-rooms, and smoking-rooms, into a palace by itself. Even the dungeon-like vaults beneath, now lighted and ventilated on the most approved modern plan, had been turned as if by magic into kitchens, servants' offices, ice-rooms, and wine cellars, worthy of the splendour of the grandest hotel in Italy, in the now bygone period of seventeen years since.

Passing from the lapse of the summer months at Venice, to the lapse of the summer months in Ireland, it is next to be recorded that Mrs. Rolland obtained the situation of attendant on the invalid Mrs. Carbury; and that the fair Miss Haldane, like a female Caesar, came, saw, and conquered, on her first day's visit to the new Lord Montbarry's house.

The ladies were as loud in her praises as Arthur Barville himself. Lord Montbarry declared that she was the only perfectly pretty woman he had ever seen, who was really unconscious of her own attractions. The old nurse said she looked as if she had just stepped out of a picture, and wanted nothing but a gilt frame round her to make her complete. Miss Haldane, on her side, returned from her first visit to the Montbarrys charmed with her new acquaintances. Later on the same day, Arthur called with an offering of fruit and flowers for Mrs. Carbury, and with instructions to ask if she was well enough to receive Lord and Lady Montbarry and Miss Lockwood on the morrow. In a week's time, the two households were on the friendliest terms. Mrs. Carbury, confined to the sofa by a spinal malady, had been hitherto dependent on her niece for one of the few pleasures she could enjoy, the pleasure of having the best new novels read to her as they came out. Discovering this, Arthur volunteered to relieve Miss Haldane, at intervals, in the office of reader. He was clever at mechanical contrivances of all sorts, and he introduced improvements in

Mrs. Carbury's couch, and in the means of conveying her from the bed-chamber to the drawing-room, which alleviated the poor lady's sufferings and brightened her gloomy life. With these claims on the gratitude of the aunt, aided by the personal advantages which he unquestionably possessed, Arthur advanced rapidly in the favour of the charming niece. She was, it is needless to say, perfectly well aware that he was in love with her, while he was himself modestly reticent on the subject—so far as words went. But she was not equally quick in penetrating the nature of her own feelings towards Arthur. Watching the two young people with keen powers of observation, necessarily concentrated on them by the complete seclusion of her life, the invalid lady discovered signs of roused sensibility in Miss Haldane, when Arthur was present, which had never yet shown themselves in her social relations with other admirers eager to pay their addresses to her. Having drawn her own conclusions in private, Mrs. Carbury took the first favourable opportunity (in Arthur's interests) of putting them to the test.

'I don't know what I shall do,' she said one day, 'when Arthur goes away.'

Miss Haldane looked up quickly from her work. 'Surely he is not going to leave us!' she exclaimed.

'My dear! he has already stayed at his uncle's house a month longer than he intended. His father and mother naturally expect to see him at home again.'

Miss Haldane met this difficulty with a suggestion, which could only have proceeded from a judgment already disturbed by the ravages of the tender passion. 'Why can't his father and mother go and see him at Lord Montbarry's?' she asked. 'Sir Theodore's place is only thirty miles away, and Lady Barville is Lord Montbarry's sister. They needn't stand on cere-mony.'

'They may have other engagements,' Mrs. Carbury remarked.

'My dear aunt, we don't know that! Suppose you ask Arthur?'

'Suppose *you* ask him?'

Miss Haldane bent her head again over her work. Suddenly as it was done, her aunt had seen her face—and her face betrayed her.

When Arthur came the next day, Mrs. Carbury said a word to him in private, while her niece was in the garden. The last new novel lay neglected on the table. Arthur followed Miss Haldane into the garden. The next day he wrote home, enclosing in his letter a photograph of Miss Haldane. Before the end of the week, Sir Theodore and Lady Barville arrived at Lord Montbarry's, and formed their own judgment of the fidelity of the portrait. They had themselves married early in life—and, strange to say, they did not object on principle to the early marriages of other people. The question of age being thus disposed of, the course of true love had no other obstacles to encounter. Miss Haldane was an only child, and was possessed of an ample fortune. Arthur's career at the university had been creditable, but certainly not brilliant enough to present his withdrawal in the light of a disaster. As Sir Theodore's eldest son, his position was already made for him. He was two-and-twenty years of age; and the young lady was eighteen. There was really no producible reason for keeping the lovers waiting, and no excuse for deferring the wedding-day beyond the first week in September. In the interval, while the bride and bridegroom would be necessarily absent on the inevitable tour abroad, a sister of Mrs. Carbury volunteered to stay with her during the temporary separation from her niece. On the conclusion of the honeymoon, the young couple were to return to Ireland, and were to establish themselves in Mrs. Carbury's spacious and comfortable house.

These arrangements were decided upon early in the month of August. About the same date, the last alterations in the old palace at Venice were completed. The rooms were dried by steam; the cellars were stocked; the manager collected round him his army of skilled servants; and the new hotel was advertised all over Europe to open in October.

## CHAPTER XV

### (MISS AGNES LOCKWOOD TO MRS. FERRARI)

'I promised to give you some account, dear Emily, of the marriage of Mr. Arthur Barville and Miss Haldane. It took place ten days since. But I have had so many things to look after in the absence of the master and mistress of this house, that I am only able to write to you to-day.

'The invitations to the wedding were limited to members of the families on either side, in consideration of the ill health of Miss Haldane's aunt. On the side of the Montbarry family, there were present, besides Lord and Lady Montbarry, Sir Theodore and Lady Barville; Mrs. Norbury (whom you may remember as his lordship's second sister); and Mr. Francis Westwick, and Mr. Henry Westwick. The three children and I attended the ceremony as bridesmaids. We were joined by two young ladies, cousins of the bride and very agreeable girls. Our dresses were white, trimmed with green in honour of Ireland; and we each had a handsome gold bracelet given to us as a present from the bridegroom. If you add to the persons whom I have already mentioned, the elder members of Mrs. Carbury's family, and the old servants in both houses—privileged to drink the healths of the married pair at the lower end of the room—you will have the list of the company at the wedding-breakfast complete.

'The weather was perfect, and the ceremony (with music) was beautifully performed. As for the bride, no words can describe how lovely she looked, or how well she went through it all. We were very merry at the breakfast, and the speeches went off on the whole quite well enough. The last speech, before the party broke up, was made by Mr. Henry Westwick, and was the best of all. He offered a happy suggestion, at the end, which has produced a very unexpected change in my life here.

'As well as I remember, he concluded in these words:—"On one point, we are all agreed—we are sorry that the parting hour is near, and we should be glad to meet again. Why should we not meet again? This is the autumn time of the year; we are most of us leaving home for the holidays. What do you say (if you have no engagements that will prevent it) to joining our young married friends before the close of their tour, and renewing the social success of this delightful breakfast by another festival in honour of the honeymoon? The bride and bridegroom are going to Germany and the Tyrol, on their way to Italy. I propose that we allow them a month to themselves, and that we arrange to meet them afterwards in the North of Italy—say at Venice."

'This proposal was received with great applause, which was changed into shouts of laughter by no less a person than my dear old nurse. The moment Mr. Westwick pronounced the word "Venice," she started up among the servants at the lower end of the room, and called out at the top of her voice, "Go to our hotel, ladies and gentlemen! We get six per cent. on our money already; and if you will only crowd the place and call for the best of everything, it will be ten per cent in our pockets in no time. Ask Master Henry!"

'Appealed to in this irresistible manner, Mr. Westwick had no choice but to explain that he was concerned as a shareholder in a new Hotel Company at Venice, and that he had invested a small sum of money for the nurse (not very considerately, as I think) in the speculation. Hearing this, the company, by way of humouring the joke, drank a new toast:— Success to the nurse's hotel, and a speedy rise in the dividend!

'When the conversation returned in due time to the more serious question of the proposed meeting at Venice, difficulties began to present themselves, caused of course by invitations for the autumn which many of the guests had already accepted. Only two members of Mrs. Carbury's family were at liberty to keep the proposed appointment. On our side we were more at leisure to do as we pleased. Mr. Henry Westwick decided to go to Venice in advance of the rest, to test the accommodation of the new hotel on the opening day. Mrs. Norbury and Mr. Francis Westwick volunteered to follow him; and, after some persuasion, Lord and Lady Montbarry consented to a species of compromise. His lordship could not conveniently spare time enough for the journey to Venice, but he and Lady Montbarry arranged to accompany Mrs. Norbury and Mr. Francis Westwick as far on their way to Italy as Paris. Five days since, they took their departure to meet their travelling companions in London; leaving me here in charge of the three dear children. They begged hard, of course, to be taken with papa and mamma. But it was thought better not to interrupt the progress of their education, and not to expose them (especially the two younger girls) to the fatigues of travelling.

'I have had a charming letter from the bride, this morning, dated Cologne. You cannot think how artlessly and prettily she assures me of her happiness. Some people, as they say in Ireland, are born to good luck—and I think Arthur Barville is one of them.

'When you next write, I hope to hear that you are in better health and spirits, and that you continue to like your employment. Believe me, sincerely your friend,—A. L.'

Agnes had just closed and directed her letter, when the eldest of her three pupils entered the room with the startling announcement that Lord Montbarry's travelling-servant had arrived from Paris! Alarmed by the idea that some misfortune had happened, she ran out to meet the man in the hall. Her face told him how seriously he had frightened her, before she could speak. 'There's nothing wrong, Miss,' he hastened to say. 'My lord and my lady are enjoying themselves at Paris. They only want you and the young ladies to be with them.' Saying these amazing words, he handed to Agnes a letter from Lady Montbarry.

'Dearest Agnes,' (she read), 'I am so charmed with the delightful change in my life—it is six years, remember, since I last travelled on the Continent—that I have exerted all my fascinations to persuade Lord Montbarry to go on to Venice. And, what is more to the purpose, I have actually succeeded! He has just gone to his room to write the necessary letters of excuse in time for the post to England. May you have as good a husband, my dear, when your time comes! In the mean while, the one thing wanting now to make my happiness complete, is to have you and the darling children with us. Montbarry is just as miserable without them as I am—though he doesn't confess it so freely. You will have no difficulties to trouble you. Louis will deliver these hurried lines, and will take care of you on the journey to Paris. Kiss the children for me a thousand times—and never mind their education for the present! Pack up instantly, my dear, and I will be fonder of you than ever. Your affectionate friend, Adela Montbarry.'

Agnes folded up the letter; and, feeling the need of composing herself, took refuge for a few minutes in her own room.

Her first natural sensations of surprise and excitement at the prospect of going to Venice were succeeded by impressions of a less agreeable kind. With the recovery of her customary composure came the unwelcome remembrance of the parting words spoken to her by Montbarry's widow:— 'We shall meet again—here in England, or there in Venice where my husband died—and meet for the last time.'

It was an odd coincidence, to say the least of it, that the march of events should be unexpectedly taking Agnes to Venice, after those words had been spoken! Was the woman of the mysterious warnings and the wild black eyes still thousands of miles away in America? Or was the march of events taking *her* unexpectedly, too, on the journey to Venice? Agnes started out of her chair, ashamed of even the momentary concession to superstition which was implied by the mere presence of such questions as these in her mind.

She rang the bell, and sent for her little pupils, and announced their approaching departure to the household. The noisy delight of the children, the inspiriting effort of packing up in a hurry, roused all her energies. She dismissed her own absurd misgivings from consideration, with the contempt that they deserved. She worked as only women *can* work, when their hearts are in what they do. The travellers reached Dublin that day, in time for the boat to England. Two days later, they were with Lord and Lady Montbarry at Paris.

# THE FOURTH PART

## CHAPTER XVI

It was only the twentieth of September, when Agnes and the children reached Paris. Mrs. Norbury and her brother Francis had then already started on their journey to Italy—at least three weeks before the date at which the new hotel was to open for the reception of travellers.

The person answerable for this premature departure was Francis Westwick.

Like his younger brother Henry, he had increased his pecuniary resources by his own enterprise and ingenuity; with this difference, that his speculations were connected with the Arts. He had made money, in the first instance, by a weekly newspaper; and he had then invested his profits in a London theatre. This latter enterprise, admirably conducted, had been rewarded by the public with steady and liberal encouragement. Pondering over a new form of theatrical attraction for the coming winter season, Francis had determined to revive the languid public taste for the ballet by means of an entertainment of his own invention, combining dramatic interest with dancing. He was now, accordingly, in search of the best dancer (possessed of the indispensable personal attractions) who was to be found in the theatres of the Continent. Hearing from his foreign correspondents of two women who had made successful first appearances, one at Milan and one at Florence, he had arranged to visit those cities, and to judge of the merits of the dancers for himself, before he joined the bride and bridegroom. His widowed sister, having friends at Florence whom she was anxious to see, readily accompanied him. The Montbarrys remained at Paris, until it was time to present themselves at the family meeting in Venice. Henry found them still in the Franch capital, when he arrived from London on his way to the opening of the new hotel.

Against Lady Montbarry's advice, he took the opportunity of renewing his addresses to Agnes. He could hardly have chosen a more unpropitious time for pleading his cause with her. The gaieties of Paris (quite incomprehensibly to herself as well as to everyone about her) had a depressing effect on her spirits. She had no illness to complain of; she shared willingly in the ever-varying succession of amusements offered to strangers by the ingenuity of the liveliest people in the world—but nothing roused her: she remained persistently dull and weary through it all. In this frame of mind and body, she was in no humour to receive Henry's ill-timed addresses with favour, or even with patience: she plainly and positively refused to listen to him. 'Why do you remind me of what I have suffered?' she asked petulantly. 'Don't you see that it has left its mark on me for life?'

'I thought I knew something of women by this time,' Henry said, appealing privately to Lady Montbarry for consolation. 'But Agnes completely puzzles me. It is a year since Montbarry's death; and she remains as devoted to his memory as if he had died faithful to her—she still feels the loss of him, as none of *us* feel it!'

'She is the truest woman that ever breathed the breath of life,' Lady Montbarry answered. 'Remember that, and you will understand her. Can such a woman as Agnes give her love or refuse it, according to circumstances? Because the man was unworthy of her, was he less the man of her choice? The truest and best friend to him (little as he deserved it) in his lifetime, she naturally remains the truest and best friend to his memory now. If you really love her, wait; and trust to your two best friends—to time and to me. There is my advice; let your own experience decide whether it is not the best advice that I can offer. Resume your journey to Venice to-morrow; and when you take leave of Agnes, speak to her as cordially as if nothing had happened.'

Henry wisely followed this advice. Thoroughly understanding him, Agnes made the leave-taking friendly and pleasant on her side. When he stopped at the door for a last look at her, she hurriedly turned her head so that her face was hidden from him. Was that a good sign? Lady Montbarry, accompanying Henry down the stairs, said, 'Yes, decidedly! Write when you get to Venice. We shall wait here to receive letters from Arthur and his wife, and we shall time our departure for Italy accordingly.'

A week passed, and no letter came from Henry. Some days later, a telegram was received from him. It was despatched from Milan, instead of from Venice; and it brought this strange message:—'I have left the hotel. Will return on the arrival of Arthur and his wife. Address, meanwhile, Albergo Reale, Milan.'

Preferring Venice before all other cities of Europe, and having arranged to remain there until the family meeting took place, what unexpected event had led Henry to alter his plans? and why did he state the bare fact, without adding a word of explanation? Let the narrative follow him—and find the answer to those questions at Venice.

# CHAPTER XVII

The Palace Hotel, appealing for encouragement mainly to English and American travellers, celebrated the opening of its doors, as a matter of course, by the giving of a grand banquet, and the delivery of a long succession of speeches.

Delayed on his journey, Henry Westwick only reached Venice in time to join the guests over their coffee and cigars. Observing the splendour of the reception rooms, and taking note especially of the artful mixture of comfort and luxury in the bedchambers, he began to share the old nurse's view of the future, and to contemplate seriously the coming dividend of ten per cent. The hotel was beginning well, at all events. So much interest in the enterprise had been aroused, at home and abroad, by profuse advertising, that the whole accommodation of the building had been secured by travellers of all nations for the opening night. Henry only obtained one of the small rooms on the upper floor, by a lucky accident—the absence of the gentleman who had written to engage it. He was quite satisfied, and was on his way to bed, when another accident altered his prospects for the night, and moved him into another and a better room.

Ascending on his way to the higher regions as far as the first floor of the hotel, Henry's attention was attracted by an angry voice protesting, in a strong New England accent, against one of the greatest hardships that can be inflicted on a citizen of the United States—the hardship of sending him to bed without gas in his room.

The Americans are not only the most hospitable people to be found on the face of the earth—they are (under certain conditions) the most patient and good-tempered people as well. But they are human; and the limit of American endurance is found in the obsolete institution of a bedroom candle. The American traveller, in the present case, declined to believe that his bedroom was in a complete finished state without a gas-burner. The manager pointed to the fine antique decorations (renewed and regilt) on the walls and the ceiling, and explained that the emanations of burning gas-light would certainly spoil them in the course of a few months. To this the traveller replied that it was possible, but that he did not understand decorations. A bedroom with gas in it was what he was used to, was what he wanted, and was what he was determined to have. The compliant manager volunteered to ask some other gentleman, housed on the inferior upper storey (which was lit throughout with gas), to change rooms. Hearing this, and being quite willing to exchange a small bedchamber for a large one, Henry volunteered to be the other gentleman. The excellent American shook hands with him on the spot. 'You are a cultured person, sir,' he said; 'and *you* will no doubt understand the decorations.'

Henry looked at the number of the room on the door as he opened it. The number was Fourteen.

Tired and sleepy, he naturally anticipated a good night's rest. In the thoroughly healthy state of his nervous system, he slept as well in a bed abroad as in a bed at home. Without the slightest assignable reason, however, his just expectations were disappointed. The luxurious bed, the well-ventilated room, the delicious tranquillity of Venice by night, all were in favour of his sleeping well. He never slept at all. An indescribable sense of depression and discomfort kept him waking through darkness and daylight alike. He went down to the coffee-room as soon as the hotel was astir, and ordered some breakfast. Another unaccountable change in himself appeared with the appearance of the meal. He was absolutely without appetite. An excellent omelette, and cutlets cooked to perfection, he sent away untasted—he, whose appetite never failed him, whose digestion was still equal to any demands on it!

The day was bright and fine. He sent for a gondola, and was rowed to the Lido.

Out on the airy Lagoon, he felt like a new man. He had not left the hotel ten minutes before he was fast asleep in the gondola. Waking, on reaching the landing-place, he crossed the Lido, and enjoyed a morning's swim in the Adriatic. There was only a poor restaurant on the island, in those days; but his appetite was now ready for anything; he ate whatever was offered to him, like a famished man. He could hardly believe, when he reflected on it, that he had sent away untasted his excellent breakfast at the hotel.

Returning to Venice, he spent the rest of the day in the picture-galleries and the churches. Towards six o'clock his gondola took him back, with another fine appetite, to meet some travelling acquaintances with whom he had engaged to dine at the table d'hôte.

The dinner was deservedly rewarded with the highest approval by every guest in the hotel but one. To Henry's astonishment, the appetite with which he had entered the house mysteriously and completely left him when he sat down to table. He could drink some wine, but he could literally eat nothing. 'What in the world is the matter with you?' his travelling acquaintances asked. He could honestly answer, 'I know no more than you do.'

When night came, he gave his comfortable and beautiful bedroom another trial. The result of the second experiment was a repetition of the result of the first. Again he felt the all-pervading sense of depression and discomfort. Again he passed a sleepless night. And once more, when he tried to eat his breakfast, his appetite completely failed him!

This personal experience of the new hotel was too extraordinary to be passed over in silence. Henry mentioned it to his friends in the public room, in the hearing of the manager. The manager, naturally zealous in defence of the hotel, was a little hurt at the implied reflection cast on Number Fourteen. He invited the travellers present to judge for themselves whether Mr. Westwick's bedroom was to blame for Mr. Westwick's sleepless nights; and he especially appealed to a grey-headed gentleman, a guest at the breakfast-table of an English traveller, to take the lead in the investigation. 'This is Doctor Bruno, our first physician in Venice,' he explained. 'I appeal to him to say if there are any unhealthy influences in Mr. Westwick's room.'

Introduced to Number Fourteen, the doctor looked round him with a certain appearance of interest which was noticed by everyone present. 'The last time I was in this room,' he said, 'was on a melancholy occasion. It was before the palace was changed into an hotel. I was in professional attendance on an English nobleman who died here.' One of the persons present inquired the name of the nobleman. Doctor Bruno answered (without the slightest suspicion that he was speaking before a brother of the dead man), 'Lord Montbarry.'

Henry quietly left the room, without saying a word to anybody.

He was not, in any sense of the term, a superstitious man. But he felt, nevertheless, an insurmountable reluctance to remaining in the hotel. He decided on leaving Venice. To ask for another room would be, as he could plainly see, an offence in the eyes of the manager. To remove to another hotel, would be to openly abandon an establishment in the success of which he had a pecuniary interest. Leaving a note for Arthur Barville, on his arrival in Venice, in which he merely mentioned that he had gone to look at the Italian lakes, and that a line addressed to his hotel at Milan would bring him back again, he took the afternoon train to Padua—and dined with his usual appetite, and slept as well as ever that night.

The next day, a gentleman and his wife (perfect strangers to the Montbarry family), returning to England by way of Venice, arrived at the hotel and occupied Number Fourteen.

Still mindful of the slur that had been cast on one of his best bedchambers, the manager took occasion to ask the travellers the next morning how they liked their room. They left him to judge for himself how well they were satisfied, by remaining a day longer in Venice than they had originally planned to do, solely for the purpose of enjoying the excellent accommodation offered to them by the new hotel. 'We have met with nothing like it in Italy,' they said; 'you may rely on our recommending you to all our friends.'

On the day when Number Fourteen was again vacant, an English lady travelling alone with her maid arrived at the hotel, saw the room, and at once engaged it.

The lady was Mrs. Norbury. She had left Francis Westwick at Milan, occupied in negotiating for the appearance at his theatre of the new dancer at the Scala. Not having heard to the contrary, Mrs. Norbury supposed that Arthur Barville and his wife had already arrived at Venice. She was more interested in meeting the young married couple than in awaiting the result of the hard bargaining which delayed the engagement of the new dancer; and she volunteered to make her brother's apologies, if his theatrical business caused him to be late in keeping his appointment at the honeymoon festival.

Mrs. Norbury's experience of Number Fourteen differed entirely from her brother Henry's experience of the room.

Falling asleep as readily as usual, her repose was disturbed by a succession of frightful dreams; the central figure in every one of them being the figure of her dead brother, the first Lord Montbarry. She saw him starving in a loathsome prison; she saw him pursued by assassins, and dying under their knives; she saw him drowning in immeasurable depths of dark water; she saw him in a bed on fire, burning to death in the flames; she saw him tempted by a shadowy creature to drink, and dying of the poisonous draught. The reiterated horror of these dreams had such an effect on her that she rose with the dawn of day, afraid to trust herself again in bed. In the old times, she had been noted in the family as the one member of it who lived on affectionate terms with Montbarry. His other sister and his brothers were constantly quarrelling with him. Even his mother owned that her eldest son was of all her children the child whom she least liked. Sensible and resolute woman as she was, Mrs. Norbury shuddered with terror as she sat at the window of her room, watching the sunrise, and thinking of her dreams.

She made the first excuse that occurred to her, when her maid came in at the usual hour, and noticed how ill she looked. The woman was of so superstitious a temperament that it would have been in the last degree indiscreet to trust her with the truth. Mrs. Norbury merely remarked that she had not found the bed quite to her liking, on account of the large size of it. She was accustomed at home, as her maid knew, to sleep in a small bed. Informed of this objection later in the day, the manager regretted that he could only offer to the lady the choice of one other bedchamber, numbered Thirty-eight, and situated immediately over the bedchamber which she desired to leave. Mrs. Norbury accepted the proposed change of quarters. She was now about to pass her second night in the room occupied in the old days of the palace by Baron Rivar.

Once more, she fell asleep as usual. And, once more, the frightful dreams of the first night terrified her, following each other in the same succession. This time her nerves, already shaken, were not equal to the renewed torture of terror inflicted on them. She threw on her dressing-gown, and rushed out of her room in the middle of the night. The porter, alarmed by the banging of the door, met her hurrying headlong down the stairs, in search of the first human being she could find to keep her company. Considerably surprised at this last new manifestation of the famous 'English eccentricity,' the man looked at the hotel register, and led the lady upstairs again to the room occupied by her maid. The maid was not asleep, and, more wonderful still, was not even undressed. She received her mistress quietly. When they were alone, and when Mrs. Norbury had, as a matter of necessity, taken her attendant into her confidence, the woman made a very strange reply.

'I have been asking about the hotel, at the servants' supper to-night,' she said. 'The valet of one of the gentlemen staying here has heard that the late Lord Montbarry was the last person who lived in the palace, before it was made into an hotel. The room he died in, ma'am, was the room you slept in last night. Your room tonight is the room just above it. I said nothing for fear of frightening you. For my own part, I have passed the night as you see, keeping my light on, and reading my Bible. In my opinion, no member of your family can hope to be happy or comfortable in this house.'

'What do you mean?'

'Please to let me explain myself, ma'am. When Mr. Henry Westwick was here (I have this from the valet, too) he occupied the room his brother died in (without knowing it), like you. For two nights he never closed his eyes. Without any reason for it (the valet heard him tell the gentlemen in the coffee-room) he could *not* sleep; he felt so low and so wretched in himself. And what is more, when daytime came, he couldn't even eat while he was under this roof. You may laugh at me, ma'am—but even a servant may draw her own conclusions. It's my conclusion that something happened to my lord, which we none of us know about, when he died in this house. His ghost walks in torment until he can tell it—and the living persons related to him are the persons who feel he is near them. Those persons may yet see him in the time to come. Don't, pray don't stay any longer in this dreadful place! I wouldn't stay another night here myself— no, not for anything that could be offered me!'

Mrs. Norbury at once set her servant's mind at ease on this last point.

'I don't think about it as you do,' she said gravely. 'But I should like to speak to my brother of what has happened. We will go back to Milan.'

Some hours necessarily elapsed before they could leave the hotel, by the first train in the forenoon.

In that interval, Mrs. Norbury's maid found an opportunity of confidentially informing the valet of what had passed between her mistress and herself. The valet had other friends to whom he related the circumstances in his turn. In due course of time, the narrative, passing from mouth to mouth, reached the ears of the manager. He instantly saw that the credit of the hotel was in danger, unless something was done to retrieve the character of the room numbered Fourteen. English travellers, well acquainted with the peerage of their native country, informed him that Henry Westwick and Mrs. Norbury were by no means the only members of the Montbarry family. Curiosity might bring more of them to the hotel, after hearing what had happened. The manager's ingenuity easily hit on the obvious means of misleading them, in this case. The numbers of all the rooms were enamelled in blue, on white china plates, screwed to the doors. He ordered a new plate to be prepared, bearing the number, '13 A'; and he kept the room empty, after its tenant for the time being had gone away, until the plate was ready. He then re-numbered the room; placing the removed Number Fourteen on the door of his own room (on the second floor), which, not being to let, had not previously been numbered at all. By this device, Number Fourteen disappeared at once and for ever from the books of the hotel, as the number of a bedroom to let.

Having warned the servants to beware of gossiping with travellers, on the subject of the changed numbers, under penalty of being dismissed, the manager composed his mind with the reflection that he had done his duty to his employers. 'Now,' he thought to himself, with an excusable sense of triumph, 'let the whole family come here if they like! The hotel is a match for them.'

## CHAPTER XVIII

Before the end of the week, the manager found himself in relations with 'the family' once more. A telegram from Milan announced that Mr. Francis Westwick would arrive in Venice on the next day; and would be obliged if Number Fourteen, on the first floor, could be reserved for him, in the event of its being vacant at the time.

The manager paused to consider, before he issued his directions.

The re-numbered room had been last let to a French gentleman. It would be occupied on the day of Mr. Francis Westwick's arrival, but it would be empty again on the day after. Would it be well to reserve the room for the special occupation of Mr. Francis? and when he had passed the night unsuspiciously and comfortably in 'No. 13 A,' to ask him in the presence of witnesses how he liked his bedchamber? In this case, if the reputation of the room happened to be called in question again, the answer would vindicate it, on the evidence of a member of the very family which had first given Number Fourteen a bad name. After a little reflection, the manager decided on trying the experiment, and directed that '13 A' should be reserved accordingly.

On the next day, Francis Westwick arrived in excellent spirits.

He had signed agreements with the most popular dancer in Italy; he had transferred the charge of Mrs. Norbury to his brother Henry, who had joined him in Milan; and he was now at full liberty to amuse himself by testing in every possible way the extraordinary influence exercised over his relatives by the new hotel. When his brother and sister first told him what their experience had been, he instantly declared that he would go to Venice in the interest of his theatre. The circumstances related to him contained invaluable hints for a ghost-drama. The title occurred to him in the railway: 'The Haunted Hotel.' Post that in red letters six feet high, on a black ground, all over London—and trust the excitable public to crowd into the theatre!

Received with the politest attention by the manager, Francis met with a disappointment on entering the hotel. 'Some mistake, sir. No such room on the first floor as Number Fourteen. The room bearing that number is on the second floor, and has been occupied by me, from the day when the hotel opened. Perhaps you meant number 13 A, on the first floor? It will be at your service to-morrow—a charming room. In the mean time, we will do the best we can for you, to-night.'

A man who is the successful manager of a theatre is probably the last man in the civilized universe who is capable of being impressed with favourable opinions of his fellow-creatures. Francis privately set the manager down as a humbug, and the story about the numbering of the rooms as a lie.

On the day of his arrival, he dined by himself in the restaurant, before the hour of the table d'hôte, for the express purpose of questioning the waiter, without being overheard by anybody. The answer led him to the conclusion that '13 A' occupied the situation in the hotel which had been described by his brother and sister as the situation of '14.' He asked next for the Visitors' List; and found that the French gentleman who then occupied '13 A,' was the proprietor of a theatre in Paris, personally well known to him. Was the gentleman then in the hotel? He had gone out, but would certainly return for the table d'hôte. When the public dinner was over, Francis entered the room, and was welcomed by his Parisian colleague, literally, with open arms. 'Come and have a cigar in my room,' said the friendly Frenchman. 'I want to hear whether you have really engaged that woman at Milan or not.' In this easy way, Francis found his opportunity of comparing the interior of the room with the description which he had heard of it at Milan.

Arriving at the door, the Frenchman bethought himself of his travelling companion. 'My scene-painter is here with me,' he said, 'on the look-out for materials. An excellent fellow, who will take it as a kindness if we ask him to join us. I'll tell the porter to send him up when he comes in.' He handed the key of his room to Francis. 'I will be back in a minute. It's at the end of the corridor—13 A.'

Francis entered the room alone. There were the decorations on the walls and the ceiling, exactly as they had been described to him! He had just time to perceive this at a glance, before his attention was diverted to himself and his own sensations, by a grotesquely disagreeable occurrence which took him completely by surprise.

He became conscious of a mysteriously offensive odour in the room, entirely new in his experience of revolting smells. It was composed (if such a thing could be) of two mingling exhalations, which were separately-discoverable exhalations nevertheless. This strange blending of odours consisted of something faintly and unpleasantly aromatic, mixed with another underlying smell, so unutterably sickening that he threw open the window, and put his head out into the fresh air, unable to endure the horribly infected atmosphere for a moment longer.

The French proprietor joined his English friend, with his cigar already lit. He started back in dismay at a sight terrible to his countrymen in general—the sight of an open window. 'You English people are perfectly mad on the subject of fresh air!' he exclaimed. 'We shall catch our deaths of cold.'

Francis turned, and looked at him in astonishment. 'Are you really not aware of the smell there is in the room?' he asked.

'Smell!' repeated his brother-manager. 'I smell my own good cigar. Try one yourself. And for Heaven's sake shut the window!'

Francis declined the cigar by a sign. 'Forgive me,' he said. 'I will leave you to close the window. I feel faint and giddy—I had better go out.' He put his handkerchief over his nose and mouth, and crossed the room to the door.

The Frenchman followed the movements of Francis, in such a state of bewilderment that he actually forgot to seize the opportunity of shutting out the fresh air. 'Is it so nasty as that?' he asked, with a broad stare of amazement.

'Horrible!' Francis muttered behind his handkerchief. 'I never smelt anything like it in my life!'

There was a knock at the door. The scene-painter appeared. His employer instantly asked him if he smelt anything.

'I smell your cigar. Delicious! Give me one directly!'

'Wait a minute. Besides my cigar, do you smell anything else—vile, abominable, overpowering, indescribable, never-never-never-smelt before?'

The scene-painter appeared to be puzzled by the vehement energy of the language addressed to him. 'The room is as fresh and sweet as a room can be,' he answered. As he spoke, he looked back with astonishment at Francis Westwick, standing outside in the corridor, and eyeing the interior of the bedchamber with an expression of undisguised disgust.

The Parisian director approached his English colleague, and looked at him with grave and anxious scrutiny.

'You see, my friend, here are two of us, with as good noses as yours, who smell nothing. If you want evidence from more noses, look there!' He pointed to two little English girls, at play in the corridor. 'The door of my room is wide open—and you know how fast a smell can travel. Now listen, while I appeal to these innocent noses, in the language of their own dismal island. My little loves, do you sniff a nasty smell here—ha?' The children burst out laughing, and answered emphatically, 'No.' 'My good Westwick,' the Frenchman resumed, in his own language, 'the conclusion is surely plain? There is something wrong, very wrong, with your own nose. I recommend you to see a medical man.'

Having given that advice, he returned to his room, and shut out the horrid fresh air with a loud exclamation of relief. Francis left the hotel, by the lanes that led to the Square of St. Mark. The night-breeze soon revived him. He was able to light a cigar, and to think quietly over what had happened.

## CHAPTER XIX

Avoiding the crowd under the colonnades, Francis walked slowly up and down the noble open space of the square, bathed in the light of the rising moon.

Without being aware of it himself, he was a thorough materialist. The strange effect produced on him by the room—following on the other strange effects produced on the other relatives of his dead brother—exercised no perplexing influence over the mind of this sensible man. 'Perhaps,' he reflected, 'my temperament is more imaginative than I supposed it to be—and this is a trick played on me by my own fancy? Or, perhaps, my friend is right; something is physically amiss with me? I don't feel ill, certainly. But that is no safe criterion sometimes. I am not going to sleep in that abominable room to-night—I can well wait till to-morrow to decide whether I shall speak to a doctor or not. In the mean time, the hotel doesn't seem likely to supply me with the subject of a piece. A terrible smell from an invisible ghost is a perfectly new idea. But it has one drawback. If I realise it on the stage, I shall drive the audience out of the theatre.'

As his strong common sense arrived at this facetious conclusion, he became aware of a lady, dressed entirely in black, who was observing him with marked attention. 'Am I right in supposing you to be Mr. Francis Westwick?' the lady asked, at the moment when he looked at her.

'That is my name, madam. May I inquire to whom I have the honour of speaking?'

'We have only met once,' she answered a little evasively, 'when your late brother introduced me to the members of his family. I wonder if you have quite forgotten my big black eyes and my hideous complexion?' She lifted her veil as she spoke, and turned so that the moonlight rested on her face.

Francis recognised at a glance the woman of all others whom he most cordially disliked—the widow of his dead brother, the first Lord Montbarry. He frowned as he looked at her. His experience on the stage, gathered at innumerable rehearsals with actresses who had sorely tried his temper, had accustomed him to speak roughly to women who were distasteful to him. 'I remember you,' he said. 'I thought you were in America!'

She took no notice of his ungracious tone and manner; she simply stopped him when he lifted his hat, and turned to leave her.

'Let me walk with you for a few minutes,' she quietly replied. 'I have something to say to you.'

He showed her his cigar. 'I am smoking,' he said.

'I don't mind smoking.'

After that, there was nothing to be done (short of downright brutality) but to yield. He did it with the worst possible grace. 'Well?' he resumed. 'What do you want of me?'

'You shall hear directly, Mr. Westwick. Let me first tell you what my position is. I am alone in the world. To the loss of my husband has now been added another bereavement, the loss of my companion in America, my brother—Baron Rivar.'

The reputation of the Baron, and the doubt which scandal had thrown on his assumed relationship to the Countess, were well known to Francis. 'Shot in a gambling-saloon?' he asked brutally.

'The question is a perfectly natural one on your part,' she said, with the impenetrably ironical manner which she could assume on certain occasions. 'As a native of horse-racing England, you belong to a nation of gamblers. My brother died no extraordinary death, Mr. Westwick. He sank, with many other unfortunate people, under a fever prevalent in a Western city which we happened to visit. The calamity of his loss made the United States unendurable to me. I left by the first steamer that sailed from New York—a French vessel which brought me to Havre. I continued my lonely journey to the South of France. And then I went on to Venice.'

'What does all this matter to me?' Francis thought to himself. She paused, evidently expecting him to say something. 'So you have come to Venice?' he said carelessly. 'Why?'

'Because I couldn't help it,' she answered.

Francis looked at her with cynical curiosity. 'That sounds odd,' he remarked. 'Why couldn't you help it?'

'Women are accustomed to act on impulse,' she explained. 'Suppose we say that an impulse has directed my journey? And yet, this is the last place in the world that I wish to find myself in. Associations that I detest are connected with it in my mind. If I had a will of my own, I would never see it again. I hate Venice. As you see, however, I am here. When did you meet with such an unreasonable woman before? Never, I am sure!' She stopped, eyed him for a moment, and suddenly altered her tone. 'When is Miss Agnes Lockwood expected to be in Venice?' she asked.

It was not easy to throw Francis off his balance, but that extraordinary question did it. 'How the devil did you know that Miss Lockwood was coming to Venice?' he exclaimed.

She laughed—a bitter mocking laugh. 'Say, I guessed it!'

Something in her tone, or perhaps something in the audacious defiance of her eyes as they rested on him, roused the quick temper that was in Francis Warwick. 'Lady Montbarry ——!' he began.

'Stop there!' she interposed. 'Your brother Stephen's wife calls herself Lady Montbarry now. I share my title with no woman. Call me by my name before I committed the fatal mistake of marrying your brother. Address me, if you please, as Countess Narona.'

'Countess Narona,' Francis resumed, 'if your object in claiming my acquaintance is to mystify me, you have come to the wrong man. Speak plainly, or permit me to wish you good evening.'

'If your object is to keep Miss Lockwood's arrival in Venice a secret,' she retorted, 'speak plainly, Mr. Westwick, on *your* side, and say so.'

Her intention was evidently to irritate him; and she succeeded. 'Nonsense!' he broke out petulantly. 'My brother's travelling arrangements are secrets to nobody. He brings Miss Lockwood here, with Lady Montbarry and the children. As you seem so well informed, perhaps you know why she is coming to Venice?'

The Countess had suddenly become grave and thoughtful. She made no reply. The two strangely associated companions, having reached one extremity of the square, were now standing before the church of St. Mark. The moonlight was bright enough to show the architecture of the grand cathedral in its wonderful variety of detail. Even the pigeons of St. Mark were visible, in dark closely packed rows, roosting in the archways of the great entrance doors.

'I never saw the old church look so beautiful by moonlight,' the Countess said quietly; speaking, not to Francis, but to herself. 'Good-bye, St. Mark's by moonlight! I shall not see you again.'

She turned away from the church, and saw Francis listening to her with wondering looks. 'No,' she resumed, placidly picking up the lost thread of the conversation, 'I don't know why Miss Lockwood is coming here, I only know that we are to meet in Venice.'

'By previous appointment?'

'By Destiny,' she answered, with her head on her breast, and her eyes on the ground. Francis burst out laughing. 'Or, if you like it better,' she instantly resumed, 'by what fools call Chance.' Francis answered easily, out of the depths of his strong common sense. 'Chance seems to be taking a queer way of bringing the meeting about,' he said. 'We have all arranged to meet at the Palace Hotel. How is it that your name is not on the Visitors' List? Destiny ought to have brought you to the Palace Hotel too.'

She abruptly pulled down her veil. 'Destiny may do that yet!' she said. 'The Palace Hotel?' she repeated, speaking once more to herself. 'The old hell, transformed into the new purgatory. The place itself! Jesu Maria! the place itself!' She paused and laid her hand on her companion's arm. 'Perhaps Miss Lockwood is not going there with the rest of you?' she burst out with sudden eagerness. 'Are you positively sure she will be at the hotel?'

'Positively! Haven't I told you that Miss Lockwood travels with Lord and Lady Montbarry? and don't you know that she is a member of the family? You will have to move, Countess, to our hotel.'

She was perfectly impenetrable to the bantering tone in which he spoke. 'Yes,' she said faintly, 'I shall have to move to your hotel.' Her hand was still on his arm—he could feel her shivering from head to foot while she spoke. Heartily as he disliked and distrusted her, the common instinct of humanity obliged him to ask if she felt cold.

'Yes,' she said. 'Cold and faint.'

'Cold and faint, Countess, on such a night as this?'

'The night has nothing to do with it, Mr. Westwick. How do you suppose the criminal feels on the scaffold, while the hangman is putting the rope around his neck? Cold and faint, too, I should think. Excuse my grim fancy. You see, Destiny has got the rope round *my* neck—and *I* feel it.'

She looked about her. They were at that moment close to the famous café known as 'Florian's.' 'Take me in there,' she said; 'I must have something to revive me. You had better not hesitate. You are interested in reviving me. I have not said what I wanted to say to you yet. It's business, and it's connected with your theatre.'

Wondering inwardly what she could possibly want with his theatre, Francis reluctantly yielded to the necessities of the situation, and took her into the café. He found a quiet corner in which they could take their places without attracting notice. 'What will you have?' he inquired resignedly. She gave her own orders to the waiter, without troubling him to speak for her.

'Maraschino. And a pot of tea.'

The waiter stared; Francis stared. The tea was a novelty (in connection with maraschino) to both of them. Careless whether she surprised them or not, she instructed the waiter, when her directions had been complied with, to pour a large wine-glass-full of the liqueur into a tumbler, and to fill it up from the teapot. 'I can't do it for myself,' she remarked, 'my hand trembles so.' She drank the strange mixture eagerly, hot as it was. 'Maraschino punch—will you taste some of it?' she said. 'I inherit the discovery of this drink. When your English Queen Caroline was on the Continent, my mother was attached to her Court. That much injured Royal Person invented, in her happier hours, maraschino punch. Fondly attached to her gracious mistress, my mother shared her tastes. And I, in my turn, learnt from my mother. Now, Mr. Westwick, suppose I tell you what my business is. You are manager of a theatre. Do you want a new play?'

'I always want a new play—provided it's a good one.'

'And you pay, if it's a good one?'

'I pay liberally—in my own interests.'

'If *I* write the play, will you read it?'

Francis hesitated. 'What has put writing a play into your head?' he asked.

'Mere accident,' she answered. 'I had once occasion to tell my late brother of a visit which I paid to Miss Lockwood, when I was last in England. He took no interest at what happened at the interview, but something struck him in my way of relating it. He said, "You describe what passed between you and the lady with the point and contrast of good stage dialogue. You have the dramatic instinct—try if you can write a play. You might make money." *That* put it into my head.'

Those last words seemed to startle Francis. 'Surely you don't want money!' he exclaimed.

'I always want money. My tastes are expensive. I have nothing but my poor little four hundred a year—and the wreck that is left of the other money: about two hundred pounds in circular notes—no more.'

Francis knew that she was referring to the ten thousand pounds paid by the insurance offices. 'All those thousands gone already!' he exclaimed.

She blew a little puff of air over her fingers. 'Gone like that!' she answered coolly.

'Baron Rivar?'

She looked at him with a flash of anger in her hard black eyes.

'My affairs are my own secret, Mr. Westwick. I have made you a proposal—and you have not answered me yet. Don't say No, without thinking first. Remember what a life mine has been. I have seen more of the world than most people, playwrights included. I have had strange adventures; I have heard remarkable stories; I have observed; I have remembered. Are there no materials, here in my head, for writing a play—if the opportunity is granted to me?' She waited a moment, and suddenly repeated her strange question about Agnes.

'When is Miss Lockwood expected to be in Venice?'

'What has that to do with your new play, Countess?'

The Countess appeared to feel some difficulty in giving that question its fit reply. She mixed another tumbler full of maraschino punch, and drank one good half of it before she spoke again.

'It has everything to do with my new play,' was all she said. 'Answer me.' Francis answered her.

'Miss Lockwood may be here in a week. Or, for all I know to the contrary, sooner than that.'

'Very well. If I am a living woman and a free woman in a week's time—or if I am in possession of my senses in a week's time (don't interrupt me; I know what I am talking about)—I shall have a sketch or outline of my play ready, as a specimen of what I can do. Once again, will you read it?'

'I will certainly read it. But, Countess, I don't understand ——'

She held up her hand for silence, and finished the second tumbler of maraschino punch.

'I am a living enigma—and you want to know the right reading of me,' she said. 'Here is the reading, as your English phrase goes, in a nutshell. There is a foolish idea in the minds of many persons that the natives of the warm climates are imaginative people. There never was a greater mistake. You will find no such unimaginative people anywhere as you find in Italy, Spain, Greece, and the other Southern countries. To anything fanciful, to anything spiritual, their minds are deaf and blind by nature. Now and then, in the course of centuries, a great genius springs up among them; and he is the exception which proves the rule. Now see! I, though I am no genius—I am, in my little way (as I suppose), an exception too. To my sorrow, I have some of that imagination which is so common among the English and the Germans—so rare among the Italians, the Spaniards, and the rest of them! And what is the result? I think it has become a disease in me. I am filled with presentiments which make this wicked life of mine one long terror to me. It doesn't matter, just now, what they are. Enough that they absolutely govern me—they drive me over land and sea at their own horrible will; they are in me, and torturing me, at this moment! Why don't I resist them? Ha! but I do resist them. I am trying (with the help of the good punch) to resist them now. At intervals I cultivate the difficult virtue of common sense. Sometimes, sound sense makes a hopeful woman of me. At one time, I had the hope that what seemed reality to me was only mad delusion, after all—I even asked the question of an English doctor! At other times, other sensible doubts of myself beset me. Never mind dwelling on them now—it always ends in the old terrors and super-stitions taking possession of me again. In a week's time, I shall know whether Destiny does indeed decide my future for me, or whether I decide it for myself. In the last case, my resolution is to absorb this self-tormenting fancy of mine in the occupation that I have told you of already. Do you understand me a little better now? And, our business being settled, dear Mr. Westwick, shall we get out of this hot room into the nice cool air again?'

They rose to leave the café. Francis privately concluded that the maraschino punch offered the only discoverable explanation of what the Countess had said to him.

## CHAPTER XX

'Shall I see you again?' she asked, as she held out her hand to take leave. 'It is quite understood between us, I suppose, about the play?'

Francis recalled his extraordinary experience of that evening in the re-numbered room. 'My stay in Venice is uncertain,' he replied. 'If you have anything more to say about this dramatic venture of yours, it may be as well to say it now. Have you decided on a subject already? I know the public taste in England better than you do—I might save you some waste of time and trouble, if you have not chosen your subject wisely.'

'I don't care what subject I write about, so long as I write,' she an-swered carelessly. 'If *you* have got a subject in your head, give it to me. I answer for the characters and the dialogue.'

'You answer for the characters and the dialogue,' Francis repeated. 'That's a bold way of speaking for a beginner! I wonder if I should shake your sublime confidence in yourself, if I suggested the most ticklish sub-ject to handle which is known to the stage? What do you say, Countess, to entering the lists with Shakespeare, and trying a drama with a ghost in it? A true story, mind! founded on events in this very city in which you and I are interested.'

She caught him by the arm, and drew him away from the crowded colonnade into the solitary middle space of the square. 'Now tell me!' she said eagerly. 'Here, where nobody is near us. How am I interested in it? How? how?'

Still holding his arm, she shook him in her impatience to hear the coming disclosure. For a moment he hesitated. Thus far, amused by her ignorant belief in herself, he had merely spoken in jest. Now, for the first time, impressed by her irresistible earnestness, he began to consider what he was about from a more serious point of view. With her knowledge of all that had passed in the old palace, before its transformation into an hotel, it was surely possible that she might suggest some explanation of what had happened to his brother, and sister, and himself. Or, failing to do this, she might accidentally reveal some event in her own experience which, acting as a hint to a competent dramatist, might prove to be the making of a play. The prosperity of his theatre was his one serious object in life. 'I may be on the trace of another "Corsican Brothers," ' he thought. 'A new piece of that sort would be ten thousand pounds in my pocket, at least.'

With these motives (worthy of the single-hearted devotion to dramatic business which made Francis a successful manager) he related, without further hesitation, what his own experience had been, and what the experience of his relatives had been, in the haunted hotel. He even described the outbreak of superstitious terror which had escaped Mrs. Norbury's ignorant maid. 'Sad stuff, if you look at it reasonably,' he remarked. 'But there is something dramatic in the notion of the ghostly influence making itself felt by the relations in succession, as they one after another enter the fatal room—until the one chosen relative comes who will see the Unearthly Creature, and know the terrible truth. Material for a play, Countess—first-rate material for a play!'

There he paused. She neither moved nor spoke. He stooped and looked closer at her.

What impression had he produced? It was an impression which his utmost ingenuity had failed to anticipate. She stood by his side—just as she had stood before Agnes when her question about Ferrari was plainly answered at last—like a woman turned to stone. Her eyes were vacant and rigid; all the life in her face had faded out of it. Francis took her by the hand. Her hand was as cold as the pavement that they were standing on. He asked her if she was ill.

Not a muscle in her moved. He might as well have spoken to the dead.

'Surely,' he said, 'you are not foolish enough to take what I have been telling you seriously?'

Her lips moved slowly. As it seemed, she was making an effort to speak to him.

'Louder,' he said. 'I can't hear you.'

She struggled to recover possession of herself. A faint light began to soften the dull cold stare of her eyes. In a moment more she spoke so that he could hear her.

'I never thought of the other world,' she murmured, in low dull tones, like a woman talking in her sleep.

Her mind had gone back to the day of her last memorable interview with Agnes; she was slowly recalling the confession that had escaped her, the warning words which she had spoken at that past time. Necessarily incapable of understanding this, Francis looked at her in perplexity. She went on in the same dull vacant tone, steadily following out her own train of thought, with her heedless eyes on his face, and her wandering mind far away from him.

'I said some trifling event would bring us together the next time. I was wrong. No trifling event will bring us together. I said I might be the person who told her what had become of Ferrari, if she forced me to it. Shall I feel some other influence than hers? Will *he* force me to it? When *she* sees him, shall *I* see him too?'

Her head sank a little; her heavy eyelids dropped slowly; she heaved a long low weary sigh. Francis put her arm in his, and made an attempt to rouse her.

'Come, Countess, you are weary and over-wrought. We have had enough talking to-night. Let me see you safe back to your hotel. Is it far from here?'

She started when he moved, and obliged her to move with him, as if he had suddenly awakened her out of a deep sleep.

'Not far,' she said faintly. 'The old hotel on the quay. My mind's in a strange state; I have forgotten the name.'

'Danieli's?'

'Yes!'

He led her on slowly. She accompanied him in silence as far as the end of the Piazzetta. There, when the full view of the moonlit Lagoon revealed itself, she stopped him as he turned towards the Riva degli Schiavoni. 'I have something to ask you. I want to wait and think.'

She recovered her lost idea, after a long pause.

'Are you going to sleep in the room to-night?' she asked.

He told her that another traveller was in possession of the room that night. 'But the manager has reserved it for me to-morrow,' he added, 'if I wish to have it.'

'No,' she said. 'You must give it up.'

'To whom?'

'To me!'

He started. 'After what I have told you, do you really wish to sleep in that room to-morrow night?'

'I *must* sleep in it.'

'Are you not afraid?'

'I am horribly afraid.'

'So I should have thought, after what I have observed in you to-night. Why should you take the room? you are not obliged to occupy it, unless you like.'

'I was not obliged to go to Venice, when I left America,' she answered. 'And yet I came here. I must take the room, and keep the room, until ——' She broke off at those words. 'Never mind the rest,' she said. 'It doesn't interest you.'

It was useless to dispute with her. Francis changed the subject. 'We can do nothing to-night,' he said. 'I will call on you to-morrow morning, and hear what you think of it then.'

They moved on again to the hotel. As they approached the door, Francis asked if she was staying in Venice under her own name.

She shook her head. 'As your brother's widow, I am known here. As Countess Narona, I am known here. I want to be unknown, this time, to strangers in Venice; I am travelling under a common English name.' She hesitated, and stood still. 'What has come to me?' she muttered to herself. 'Some things I remember; and some I forget. I forgot Danieli's—and now I forget my English name.' She drew him hurriedly into the hall of the hotel, on the wall of which hung a list of visitors' names. Running her finger slowly down the list, she pointed to the English name that she had assumed:—'Mrs. James.'

'Remember that when you call to-morrow,' she said. 'My head is heavy. Good night.'

Francis went back to his own hotel, wondering what the events of the next day would bring forth. A new turn in his affairs had taken place in his absence. As he crossed the hall, he was requested by one of the servants to walk into the private office. The manager was waiting there with a gravely pre-occupied manner, as if he had something serious to say. He regretted to hear that Mr. Francis Westwick had, like other members of the family, discovered serious sources of discomfort in the new hotel. He had been informed in strict confidence of Mr. Westwick's extraordinary objection to the atmosphere of the bedroom upstairs. Without presuming to discuss the matter, he must beg to be excused from reserving the room for Mr. Westwick after what had happened.

Francis answered sharply, a little ruffled by the tone in which the manager had spoken to him. 'I might, very possibly, have declined to sleep in the room, if you *had* reserved it,' he said. 'Do you wish me to leave the hotel?'

The manager saw the error that he had committed, and hastened to repair it. 'Certainly not, sir! We will do our best to make you comfortable while you stay with us. I beg your pardon, if I have said anything to offend you. The reputation of an establishment like this is a matter of very serious importance. May I hope that you will do us the great favour to say nothing about what has happened upstairs? The two French gentlemen have kindly promised to keep it a secret.'

This apology left Francis no polite alternative but to grant the manager's request. 'There is an end to the Countess's wild scheme,' he thought to himself, as he retired for the night. 'So much the better for the Countess!'

He rose late the next morning. Inquiring for his Parisian friends, he was informed that both the French gentlemen had left for Milan. As he crossed the hall, on his way to the restaurant, he noticed the head porter chalking the numbers of the rooms on some articles of luggage which were waiting to go upstairs. One trunk attracted his attention by the extraordinary number of old travelling labels left on it. The porter was marking it at the moment—and the number was, '13 A.' Francis instantly looked at the card fastened on the lid. It bore the common English name, 'Mrs. James'! He at once inquired about the lady. She had arrived early that morning, and she was then in the Reading Room. Looking into the room, he discovered a lady in it alone. Advancing a little nearer, he found himself face to face with the Countess.

She was seated in a dark corner, with her head down and her arms crossed over her bosom. 'Yes,' she said, in a tone of weary impatience, before Francis could speak to her. 'I thought it best not to wait for you—I determined to get here before anybody else could take the room.'

'Have you taken it for long?' Francis asked.

'You told me Miss Lockwood would be here in a week's time. I have taken it for a week.'

'What has Miss Lockwood to do with it?'

'She has everything to do with it—she must sleep in the room. I shall give the room up to her when she comes here.'

Francis began to understand the superstitious purpose that she had in view. 'Are you (an educated woman) really of the same opinion as my sister's maid!' he exclaimed. 'Assuming your absurd superstition to be a serious thing, you are taking the wrong means to prove it true. If I and my brother and sister have seen nothing, how should Agnes Lockwood discover what was not revealed to *us*? She is only distantly related to the Montbarrys—she is only our cousin.'

'She was nearer to the heart of the Montbarry who is dead than any of you,' the Countess answered sternly. 'To the last day of his life, my miserable husband repented his desertion of her. She will see what none of you have seen—she shall have the room.'

Francis listened, utterly at a loss to account for the motives that animated her. 'I don't see what interest *you* have in trying this extraordinary experiment,' he said.

'It is my interest *not* to try it! It is my interest to fly from Venice, and never set eyes on Agnes Lockwood or any of your family again!'

'What prevents you from doing that?'

She started to her feet and looked at him wildly. 'I know no more what prevents me than you do!' she burst out. 'Some will that is stronger than mine drives me on to my destruction, in spite of my own self!' She suddenly sat down again, and waved her hand for him to go. 'Leave me,' she said. 'Leave me to my thoughts.'

Francis left her, firmly persuaded by this time that she was out of her senses. For the rest of the day, he saw nothing of her. The night, so far as he knew, passed quietly. The next morning he breakfasted early, determining to wait in the restaurant for the appearance of the Countess. She came in and ordered her breakfast quietly, looking dull and worn and self-absorbed, as she had looked when he last saw her. He hastened to her table, and asked if anything had happened in the night.

'Nothing,' she answered.

'You have rested as well as usual?'

'Quite as well as usual. Have you had any letters this morning? Have you heard when she is coming?'

'I have had no letters. Are you really going to stay here? Has your experience of last night not altered the opinion which you expressed to me yesterday?'

'Not in the least.'

The momentary gleam of animation which had crossed her face when she questioned him about Agnes, died out of it again when he answered her. She looked, she spoke, she eat her breakfast, with a vacant resignation, like a woman who had done with hopes, done with interests, done with everything but the mechanical movements and instincts of life.

Francis went out, on the customary travellers' pilgrimage to the shrines of Titian and Tintoret. After some hours of absence, he found a letter waiting for him when he got back to the hotel. It was written by his brother Henry, and it recommended him to return to Milan immediately. The proprietor of a French theatre, recently arrived from Venice, was trying to induce the famous dancer whom Francis had engaged to break faith with him and accept a higher salary.

Having made this startling announcement, Henry proceeded to inform his brother that Lord and Lady Montbarry, with Agnes and the children, would arrive in Venice in three days more. 'They know nothing of our adventures at the hotel,' Henry wrote; 'and they have telegraphed to the manager for the accommodation that they want. There would be something absurdly superstitious in our giving them a warning which would frighten the ladies and children out of the best hotel in Venice. We shall be a strong party this time—too strong a party for ghosts! I shall meet the travellers on their arrival, of course, and try my luck again at what you call the Haunted Hotel. Arthur Barville and his wife have already got as far on their way as Trent; and two of the lady's relations have arranged to accompany them on the journey to Venice.'

Naturally indignant at the conduct of his Parisian colleague, Francis made his preparations for returning to Milan by the train of that day.

On his way out, he asked the manager if his brother's telegram had been received. The telegram had arrived, and, to the surprise of Francis, the rooms were already reserved. 'I thought you would refuse to let any more of the family into the house,' he said satirically. The manager answered (with the due dash of respect) in the same tone. 'Number 13 A is safe, sir, in the occupation of a stranger. I am the servant of the Company; and I dare not turn money out of the hotel.'

Hearing this, Francis said good-bye—and said nothing more. He was ashamed to acknowledge it to himself, but he felt an irresistible curiosity to know what would happen when Agnes arrived at the hotel. Besides, 'Mrs. James' had reposed a confidence in him. He got into his gondola, respecting the confidence of 'Mrs. James.'

Towards evening on the third day, Lord Montbarry and his travelling companions arrived, punctual to their appointment.

'Mrs. James,' sitting at the window of her room watching for them, saw the new Lord land from the gondola first. He handed his wife to the steps. The three children were next committed to his care. Last of all, Agnes appeared in the little black doorway of the gondola cabin, and, taking Lord Montbarry's hand, passed in her turn to the steps. She wore no veil. As she ascended to the door of the hotel, the Countess (eyeing her through an opera-glass) noticed that she paused to look at the outside of the building, and that her face was very pale.

# CHAPTER XXI

Lord and Lady Montbarry were received by the housekeeper; the manager being absent for a day or two on business connected with the affairs of the hotel.

The rooms reserved for the travellers on the first floor were three in number; consisting of two bedrooms opening into each other, and communicating on the left with a drawing-room. Complete so far, the arrangements proved to be less satisfactory in reference to the third bedroom required for Agnes and for the eldest daughter of Lord Montbarry, who usually slept with her on their travels. The bed-chamber on the right of the drawing-room was already occupied by an English widow lady. Other bed-chambers at the other end of the corridor were also let in every case. There was accordingly no alternative but to place at the disposal of Agnes a comfortable room on the second floor. Lady Montbarry vainly complained of this separation of one of the members of her travelling party from the rest. The housekeeper politely hinted that it was impossible for her to ask other travellers to give up their rooms. She could only express her regret, and assure Miss Lockwood that her bed-chamber on the second floor was one of the best rooms in that part of the hotel.

On the retirement of the housekeeper, Lady Montbarry noticed that Agnes had seated herself apart, feeling apparently no interest in the question of the bedrooms. Was she ill? No; she felt a little unnerved by the railway journey, and that was all. Hearing this, Lord Montbarry proposed that she should go out with him, and try the experiment of half an hour's walk in the cool evening air. Agnes gladly accepted the suggestion. They directed their steps towards the square of St. Mark, so as to enjoy the breeze blowing over the lagoon. It was the first visit of Agnes to Venice. The fascination of the wonderful city of the waters exerted its full influence over her sensitive nature. The proposed half-hour of the walk had passed away, and was fast expanding to half an hour more, before Lord Montbarry could persuade his companion to remember that dinner was waiting for them. As they returned, passing under the colonnade, neither of them noticed a lady in deep mourning, loitering in the open space of the square. She started as she recognised Agnes walking with the new Lord Montbarry—hesitated for a moment—and then followed them, at a discreet distance, back to the hotel.

Lady Montbarry received Agnes in high spirits—with news of an event which had happened in her absence.

She had not left the hotel more than ten minutes, before a little note in pencil was brought to Lady Montbarry by the housekeeper. The writer proved to be no less a person than the widow lady who occupied the room on the other side of the drawing-room, which her ladyship had vainly hoped to secure for Agnes. Writing under the name of Mrs. James, the polite widow explained that she had heard from the housekeeper of the disappointment experienced by Lady Montbarry in the matter of the rooms. Mrs. James was quite alone; and as long as her bed-chamber was airy and comfortable, it mattered nothing to her whether she slept on the first or the second floor of the house. She had accordingly much pleasure in proposing to change rooms with Miss Lockwood. Her luggage had already been removed, and Miss Lockwood had only to take possession of the room (Number 13 A), which was now entirely at her disposal.

'I immediately proposed to see Mrs. James,' Lady Montbarry continued, 'and to thank her personally for her extreme kindness. But I was informed that she had gone out, without leaving word at what hour she might be expected to return. I have written a little note of thanks, saying that we hope to have the pleasure of personally expressing our sense of Mrs. James's courtesy to-morrow. In the mean time, Agnes, I have ordered your boxes to be removed downstairs. Go!—and judge for yourself, my dear, if that good lady has not given up to you the prettiest room in the house!'

With those words, Lady Montbarry left Miss Lockwood to make a hasty toilet for dinner.

The new room at once produced a favourable impression on Agnes. The large window, opening into a balcony, commanded an admirable view of the canal. The decorations on the walls and ceiling were skilfully copied from the exquisitely graceful designs of Raphael in the Vatican. The massive wardrobe possessed compartments of unusual size, in which double the number of dresses that Agnes possessed might have been conveniently hung at full length. In the inner corner of the room, near the head of the bedstead, there was a recess which had been turned into a little dressing-room, and which opened by a second door on the inferior stair-case of the hotel, commonly used by the servants. Noticing these aspects of the room at a glance, Agnes made the necessary change in her dress, as quickly as possible. On her way back to the drawing-room she was addressed by a chambermaid in the corridor who asked for her key. 'I will put your room tidy for the night, Miss,' the woman said, 'and I will then bring the key back to you in the drawing-room.'

While the chambermaid was at her work, a solitary lady, loitering about the corridor of the second storey, was watching her over the bannisters. After a while, the maid appeared, with her pail in her hand, leaving the room by way of the dressing-room and the back stairs. As she passed out of sight, the lady on the second floor (no other, it is needless to add, than the Countess herself) ran swiftly down the stairs, entered the bed-chamber by the principal door, and hid herself in the empty side compartment of the wardrobe. The chambermaid returned, completed her work, locked the door of the dressing-room on the inner side, locked the principal entrance-door on leaving the room, and returned the key to Agnes in the drawing-room.

The travellers were just sitting down to their late dinner, when one of the children noticed that Agnes was not wearing her watch. Had she left it in her bed-chamber in the hurry of changing her dress? She rose from the table at once in search of her watch; Lady Montbarry advising her, as she went out, to see to the security of her bed-chamber, in the event of there being thieves in the house. Agnes found her watch, forgotten on the toilet table, as she had anticipated. Before leaving the room again she acted on Lady Montbarry's advice, and tried the key in the lock of the dressing-room door. It was properly secured. She left the bed-chamber, locking the main door behind her.

Immediately on her departure, the Countess, oppressed by the confined air in the wardrobe, ventured on stepping out of her hiding place into the empty room.

Entering the dressing-room, she listened at the door, until the silence outside informed her that the corridor was empty. Upon this, she un-locked the door, and, passing out, closed it again softly; leaving it to all appearance (when viewed on the inner side) as carefully secured as Agnes had seen it when she tried the key in the lock with her own hand.

While the Montbarrys were still at dinner, Henry Westwick joined them, arriving from Milan.

When he entered the room, and again when he advanced to shake hands with her, Agnes was conscious of a latent feeling which secretly recipro-cated Henry's unconcealed pleasure on meeting her again. For a moment only, she returned his look; and in that moment her own observation told her that she had silently encouraged him to hope. She saw it in the sudden glow of happiness which overspread his face; and she confusedly took refuge in the usual conventional inquiries relating to the relatives whom he had left at Milan.

Taking his place at the table, Henry gave a most amusing account of the position of his brother Francis between the mercenary opera-dancer on one side, and the unscrupulous manager of the French theatre on the other. Matters had proceeded to such extremities, that the law had been called on to interfere, and had decided the dispute in favour of Francis. On winning the victory the English manager had at once left Milan, recalled to London by the affairs of his theatre. He was accompanied on the journey back, as he had been accompanied on the journey out, by his sister. Resolved, after passing two nights of terror in the Venetian hotel, never to enter it again, Mrs. Norbury asked to be excused from appearing at the family festival, on the ground of ill-health. At her age, travelling fatigued her, and she was glad to take advantage of her brother's escort to return to England.

While the talk at the dinner-table flowed easily onward, the evening-time advanced to night—and it became necessary to think of sending the children to bed.

As Agnes rose to leave the room, accompanied by the eldest girl, she observed with surprise that Henry's manner suddenly changed. He looked serious and pre-occupied; and when his niece wished him good night, he abruptly said to her, 'Marian, I want to know what part of the hotel you sleep in?' Marian, puzzled by the question, answered that she was going to sleep, as usual, with 'Aunt Agnes.' Not satisfied with that reply, Henry next inquired whether the bedroom was near the rooms occupied by the other members of the travelling party. Answering for the child, and wondering what Henry's object could possibly be, Agnes mentioned the polite sacrifice made to her convenience by Mrs. James. 'Thanks to that lady's kindness,' she said, 'Marian and I are only on the other side of the drawing-room.' Henry made no remark; he looked incomprehensibly discontented as he opened the door for Agnes and her companion to pass out. After wishing them good night, he waited in the corridor until he saw them enter the fatal corner-room—and then he called abruptly to his brother, 'Come out, Stephen, and let us smoke!'

As soon as the two brothers were at liberty to speak together privately, Henry explained the motive which had led to his strange inquiries about the bedrooms. Francis had informed him of the meeting with the Countess at Venice, and of all that had followed it; and Henry now carefully repeated the narrative to his brother in all its details. 'I am not satisfied,' he added, 'about that woman's purpose in giving up her room. Without alarming the ladies by telling them what I have just told you, can you not warn Agnes to be careful in securing her door?'

Lord Montbarry replied, that the warning had been already given by his wife, and that Agnes might be trusted to take good care of herself and her little bed-fellow. For the rest, he looked upon the story of the Countess and her superstitions as a piece of theatrical exaggeration, amusing enough in itself, but unworthy of a moment's serious attention.

While the gentlemen were absent from the hotel, the room which had been already associated with so many startling circumstances, became the scene of another strange event in which Lady Montbarry's eldest child was concerned.

Little Marian had been got ready for bed as usual, and had (so far) taken hardly any notice of the new room. As she knelt down to say her prayers, she happened to look up at that part of the ceiling above her which was just over the head of the bed. The next instant she alarmed Agnes, by starting to her feet with a cry of terror, and pointing to a small brown spot on one of the white panelled spaces of the carved ceiling. 'It's a spot of blood!' the child exclaimed. 'Take me away! I won't sleep here!'

Seeing plainly that it would be useless to reason with her while she was in the room, Agnes hurriedly wrapped Marian in a dressing-gown, and carried her back to her mother in the drawing-room. Here, the ladies did their best to soothe and reassure the trembling girl. The effort proved to be useless; the impression that had been produced on the young and sensitive mind was not to be removed by persuasion. Marian could give no explanation of the panic of terror that had seized her. She was quite unable to say why the spot on the ceiling looked like the colour of a spot of blood. She only knew that she should die of terror if she saw it again. Under these circumstances, but one alternative was left. It was arranged that the child should pass the night in the room occupied by her two younger sisters and the nurse.

In half an hour more, Marian was peacefully asleep with her arm around her sister's neck. Lady Montbarry went back with Agnes to her room to see the spot on the ceiling which had so strangely frightened the child. It was so small as to be only just perceptible, and it had in all probability been caused by the carelessness of a workman, or by a dripping from water accidentally spilt on the floor of the room above.

'I really cannot understand why Marian should place such a shocking interpretation on such a trifling thing,' Lady Montbarry remarked.

'I suspect the nurse is in some way answerable for what has happened,' Agnes suggested. 'She may quite possibly have been telling Marian some tragic nursery story which has left its mischievous impression behind it. Persons in her position are sadly ignorant of the danger of exciting a child's imagination. You had better caution the nurse to-morrow.'

Lady Montbarry looked round the room with admiration. 'Is it not prettily decorated?' she said. 'I suppose, Agnes, you don't mind sleeping here by yourself?'

Agnes laughed. 'I feel so tired,' she replied, 'that I was thinking of bidding you good-night, instead of going back to the drawing-room.'

Lady Montbarry turned towards the door. 'I see your jewel-case on the table,' she resumed. 'Don't forget to lock the other door there, in the dressing-room.'

'I have already seen to it, and tried the key myself,' said Agnes. 'Can I be of any use to you before I go to bed?'

'No, my dear, thank you; I feel sleepy enough to follow your example. Good night, Agnes—and pleasant dreams on your first night in Venice.'

# CHAPTER XXII

Having closed and secured the door on Lady Montbarry's departure, Agnes put on her dressing-gown, and, turning to her open boxes, began the business of unpacking. In the hurry of making her toilet for dinner, she had taken the first dress that lay uppermost in the trunk, and had thrown her travelling costume on the bed. She now opened the doors of the wardrobe for the first time, and began to hang her dresses on the hooks in the large compartment on one side.

After a few minutes only of this occupation, she grew weary of it, and decided on leaving the trunks as they were, until the next morning. The oppressive south wind, which had blown throughout the day, still prevailed at night. The atmosphere of the room felt close; Agnes threw a shawl over her head and shoulders, and, opening the window, stepped into the balcony to look at the view.

The night was heavy and overcast: nothing could be distinctly seen. The canal beneath the window looked like a black gulf; the opposite houses were barely visible as a row of shadows, dimly relieved against the starless and moonless sky. At long intervals, the warning cry of a belated gondolier was just audible, as he turned the corner of a distant canal, and called to invisible boats which might be approaching him in the darkness. Now and then, the nearer dip of an oar in the water told of the viewless passage of other gondolas bringing guests back to the hotel. Excepting these rare sounds, the mysterious night-silence of Venice was literally the silence of the grave.

Leaning on the parapet of the balcony, Agnes looked vacantly into the black void beneath. Her thoughts reverted to the miserable man who had broken his pledged faith to her, and who had died in that house. Some change seemed to have come over her since her arrival in Venice; some new influence appeared to be at work. For the first time in her experience of herself, compassion and regret were not the only emotions aroused in her by the remembrance of the dead Montbarry. A keen sense of the wrong that she had suffered, never yet felt by that gentle and forgiving nature, was felt by it now. She found herself thinking of the bygone days of her humiliation almost as harshly as Henry Westwick had thought of them— she who had rebuked him the last time he had spoken slightingly of his brother in her presence! A sudden fear and doubt of herself, startled her physically as well as morally. She turned from the shadowy abyss of the dark water as if the mystery and the gloom of it had been answerable for the emotions which had taken her by surprise. Abruptly closing the window, she threw aside her shawl, and lit the candles on the mantelpiece, impelled by a sudden craving for light in the solitude of her room.

The cheering brightness round her, contrasting with the black gloom outside, restored her spirits. She felt herself enjoying the light like a child!

Would it be well (she asked herself) to get ready for bed? No! The sense of drowsy fatigue that she had felt half an hour since was gone. She returned to the dull employment of unpacking her boxes. After a few minutes only, the occupation became irksome to her once more. She sat down by the table, and took up a guide-book. 'Suppose I inform myself,' she thought, 'on the subject of Venice?'

Her attention wandered from the book, before she had turned the first page of it.

The image of Henry Westwick was the presiding image in her memory now. Recalling the minutest incidents and details of the evening, she could think of nothing which presented him under other than a favourable and interesting aspect. She smiled to herself softly, her colour rose by fine gradations, as she felt the full luxury of dwelling on the perfect truth and modesty of his devotion to her. Was the depression of spirits from which she had suffered so persistently on her travels attributable, by any chance, to their long separation from each other—embittered perhaps by her own vain regret when she remembered her harsh reception of him in Paris? Suddenly conscious of this bold question, and of the self-abandonment which it implied, she returned mechanically to her book, distrusting the unrestrained liberty of her own thoughts. What lurking temptations to forbidden tenderness find their hiding-places in a woman's dressing-gown, when she is alone in her room at night! With her heart in the tomb of the dead Montbarry, could Agnes even think of another man, and think of love? How shameful! how unworthy of her! For the second time, she tried to interest herself in the guide-book—and once more she tried in vain. Throwing the book aside, she turned desperately to the one resource that was left, to her luggage—resolved to fatigue herself without mercy, until she was weary enough and sleepy enough to find a safe refuge in bed.

For some little time, she persisted in the monotonous occupation of transferring her clothes from her trunk to the wardrobe. The large clock in the hall, striking mid-night, reminded her that it was getting late. She sat down for a moment in an arm-chair by the bedside, to rest.

The silence in the house now caught her attention, and held it—held it disagreeably. Was everybody in bed and asleep but herself? Surely it was time for her to follow the general example? With a certain irritable nervous haste, she rose again and undressed herself. 'I have lost two hours of rest,' she thought, frowning at the reflection of herself in the glass, as she arranged her hair for the night. 'I shall be good for nothing to-morrow!'

She lit the night-light, and extinguished the candles—with one exception, which she removed to a little table, placed on the side of the bed opposite to the side occupied by the arm-chair. Having put her travelling-box of matches and the guide-book near the candle, in case she might be sleepless and might want to read, she blew out the light, and laid her head on the pillow.

The curtains of the bed were looped back to let the air pass freely over her. Lying on her left side, with her face turned away from the table, she could see the arm-chair by the dim night-light. It had a chintz covering—representing large bunches of roses scattered over a pale green ground. She tried to weary herself into drowsiness by counting over and over again the bunches of roses that were visible from her point of view. Twice her attention was distracted from the counting, by sounds outside—by the clock chiming the half-hour past twelve; and then again, by the fall of a pair of boots on the upper floor, thrown out to be cleaned, with that barbarous disregard of the comfort of others which is observable in humanity when it inhabits an hotel. In the silence that followed these passing disturbances, Agnes went on counting the roses on the arm-chair, more and more slowly. Before long, she confused herself in the figures—tried to begin counting again—thought she would wait a little first—felt her eyelids drooping, and her head reclining lower and lower on the pillow—sighed faintly—and sank into sleep.

How long that first sleep lasted, she never knew. She could only remember, in the after-time, that she woke instantly.

Every faculty and perception in her passed the boundary line between insensibility and consciousness, so to speak, at a leap. Without knowing why, she sat up suddenly in the bed, listening for she knew not what. Her head was in a whirl; her heart beat furiously, without any assignable cause. But one trivial event had happened during the interval while she had been asleep. The night-light had gone out; and the room, as a matter of course, was in total darkness.

She felt for the match-box, and paused after finding it. A vague sense of confusion was still in her mind. She was in no hurry to light the match. The pause in the darkness was, for the moment, agreeable to her.

In the quieter flow of her thoughts during this interval, she could ask herself the natural question:—What cause had awakened her so suddenly, and had so strangely shaken her nerves? Had it been the influence of a dream? She had not dreamed at all—or, to speak more correctly, she had no waking remembrance of having dreamed. The mystery was beyond her fathoming: the darkness began to oppress her. She struck the match on the box, and lit her candle.

As the welcome light diffused itself over the room, she turned from the table and looked towards the other side of the bed.

In the moment when she turned, the chill of a sudden terror gripped her round the heart, as with the clasp of an icy hand.

She was not alone in her room!

There—in the chair at the bedside—there, suddenly revealed under the flow of light from the candle, was the figure of a woman, reclining. Her head lay back over the chair. Her face, turned up to the ceiling, had the eyes closed, as if she was wrapped in a deep sleep.

The shock of the discovery held Agnes speechless and helpless. Her first conscious action, when she was in some degree mistress of herself again, was to lean over the bed, and to look closer at the woman who had so incomprehensibly stolen into her room in the dead of night. One glance was enough: she started back with a cry of amazement. The person in the chair was no other than the widow of the dead Montbarry—the woman who had warned her that they were to meet again, and that the place might be Venice!

Her courage returned to her, stung into action by the natural sense of indignation which the presence of the Countess provoked.

'Wake up!' she called out. 'How dare you come here? How did you get in? Leave the room—or I will call for help!'

She raised her voice at the last words. It produced no effect. Leaning farther over the bed, she boldly took the Countess by the shoulder and shook her. Not even this effort succeeded in rousing the sleeping woman. She still lay back in the chair, possessed by a torpor like the torpor of death—insensible to sound, insensible to touch. Was she really sleeping? Or had she fainted?

Agnes looked closer at her. She had not fainted. Her breathing was audible, rising and falling in deep heavy gasps. At intervals she ground her teeth savagely. Beads of perspiration stood thickly on her forehead. Her clenched hands rose and fell slowly from time to time on her lap. Was she in the agony of a dream? or was she spiritually conscious of something hidden in the room?

The doubt involved in that last question was unendurable. Agnes determined to rouse the servants who kept watch in the hotel at night.

The bell-handle was fixed to the wall, on the side of the bed by which the table stood.

She raised herself from the crouching position which she had assumed in looking close at the Countess; and, turning towards the other side of the bed, stretched out her hand to the bell. At the same instant, she stopped and looked upward. Her hand fell helplessly at her side. She shuddered, and sank back on the pillow.

What had she seen?

She had seen another intruder in her room.

Midway between her face and the ceiling, there hovered a human head—severed at the neck, like a head struck from the body by the guillotine.

Nothing visible, nothing audible, had given her any intelligible warning of its appearance. Silently and suddenly, the head had taken its place above her. No supernatural change had passed over the room, or was perceptible in it now. The dumbly-tortured figure in the chair; the broad window opposite the foot of the bed, with the black night beyond it; the candle burning on the table—these, and all other objects in the room, remained unaltered. One object more, unutterably horrid, had been added to the rest. That was the only change—no more, no less.

By the yellow candlelight she saw the head distinctly, hovering in mid-air above her. She looked at it steadfastly, spell-bound by the terror that held her.

*She was not alone in her room.*

The flesh of the face was gone. The shrivelled skin was darkened in hue, like the skin of an Egyptian mummy—except at the neck. There it was of a lighter colour; there it showed spots and splashes of the hue of that brown spot on the ceiling, which the child's fanciful terror had distorted into the likeness of a spot of blood. Thin remains of a discoloured moustache and whiskers, hanging over the upper lip, and over the hollows where the cheeks had once been, made the head just recognisable as the head of a man. Over all the features death and time had done their obliterating work. The eyelids were closed. The hair on the skull, discoloured like the hair on the face, had been burnt away in places. The bluish lips, parted in a fixed grin, showed the double row of teeth. By slow degrees, the hovering head (perfectly still when she first saw it) began to descend towards Agnes as she lay beneath. By slow degrees, that strange doubly-blended odour, which the Commissioners had discovered in the vaults of the old palace—which had sickened Francis Westwick in the bed-chamber of the new hotel—spread its fetid exhalations over the room. Downward and downward the hideous apparition made its slow progress, until it stopped close over Agnes—stopped, and turned slowly, so that the face of it confronted the upturned face of the woman in the chair.

There was a pause. Then, a supernatural movement disturbed the rigid repose of the dead face.

The closed eyelids opened slowly. The eyes revealed themselves, bright with the glassy film of death—and fixed their dreadful look on the woman in the chair.

Agnes saw that look; saw the eyelids of the living woman open slowly like the eyelids of the dead; saw her rise, as if in obedience to some silent command—and saw no more.

Her next conscious impression was of the sunlight pouring in at the window; of the friendly presence of Lady Montbarry at the bedside; and of the children's wondering faces peeping in at the door.

## CHAPTER XXIII

' . . . You have some influence over Agnes. Try what you can do, Henry, to make her take a sensible view of the matter. There is really nothing to make a fuss about. My wife's maid knocked at her door early in the morning, with the customary cup of tea. Getting no answer, she went round to the dressing-room—found the door on that side unlocked—and discovered Agnes on the bed in a fainting fit. With my wife's help, they brought her to herself again; and she told the extraordinary story which I have just repeated to you. You must have seen for yourself that she has been over-fatigued, poor thing, by our long railway journeys: her nerves are out of order—and she is just the person to be easily terrified by a dream. She obstinately refuses, however, to accept this rational view. Don't suppose that I have been severe with her! All that a man can do to humour her I have done. I have written to the Countess (in her assumed name) offering to restore the room to her. She writes back, positively declining to return to it. I have accordingly arranged (so as not to have the thing known in the hotel) to occupy the room for one or two nights, and to leave Agnes to recover her spirits under my wife's care. Is there anything more that I can do? Whatever questions Agnes has asked of me I have answered to the best of my ability; she knows all that you told me about Francis and the Countess last night. But try as I may I can't quiet her mind. I have given up the attempt in despair, and left her in the drawing-room. Go, like a good fellow, and try what you can do to compose her.'

In those words, Lord Montbarry stated the case to his brother from the rational point of view. Henry made no remark, he went straight to the drawing-room.

He found Agnes walking rapidly backwards and forwards, flushed and excited. 'If you come here to say what your brother has been saying to me,' she broke out, before he could speak, 'spare yourself the trouble. I don't want common sense—I want a true friend who will believe in me.'

'I am that friend, Agnes,' Henry answered quietly, 'and you know it.'

'You really believe that I am not deluded by a dream?'

'I know that you are not deluded—in one particular, at least.'

'In what particular?'

'In what you have said of the Countess. It is perfectly true —'

Agnes stopped him there. 'Why do I only hear this morning that the Countess and Mrs. James are one and the same person?' she asked distrustfully. 'Why was I not told of it last night?'

'You forget that you had accepted the exchange of rooms before I reached Venice,' Henry replied. 'I felt strongly tempted to tell you, even then—but your sleeping arrangements for the night were all made; I should only have inconvenienced and alarmed you. I waited till the morning, after hearing from my brother that you had yourself seen to your security from any intrusion. How that intrusion was accomplished it is impossible to say. I can only declare that the Countess's presence by your bedside last night was no dream of yours. On her own authority I can testify that it was a reality.'

'On her own authority?' Agnes repeated eagerly. 'Have you seen her this morning?'

'I have seen her not ten minutes since.'

'What was she doing?'

'She was busily engaged in writing. I could not even get her to look at me until I thought of mentioning your name.'

'She remembered me, of course?'

'She remembered you with some difficulty. Finding that she wouldn't answer me on any other terms, I questioned her as if I had come direct from you. Then she spoke. She not only admitted that she had the same superstitious motive for placing you in that room which she had acknowledged to Francis—she even owned that she had been by your bedside, watching through the night, "to see what you saw," as she expressed it. Hearing this, I tried to persuade her to tell me how she got into the room. Unluckily, her manuscript on the table caught her eye; she returned to her writing. "The Baron wants money," she said; "I must get on with my play." What she saw or dreamed while she was in your room last night, it is at present impossible to discover. But judging by my brother's account of her, as well as by what I remember of her myself, some recent influence has been at work which has produced a marked change in this wretched woman for the worse. Her mind (since last night, perhaps) is partially deranged. One proof of it is that she spoke to me of the Baron as if he were still a living man. When Francis saw her, she declared that the Baron was dead, which is the truth. The United States Consul at Milan showed us the announcement of the death in an American newspaper. So far as I can see, such sense as she still possesses seems to be entirely absorbed in one absurd idea—the idea of writing a play for Francis to bring out at his theatre. He admits that he encouraged her to hope she might get money in this way. I think he did wrong. Don't you agree with me?'

Without heeding the question, Agnes rose abruptly from her chair.

'Do me one more kindness, Henry,' she said. 'Take me to the Countess at once.'

Henry hesitated. 'Are you composed enough to see her, after the shock that you have suffered?' he asked.

She trembled, the flush on her face died away, and left it deadly pale. But she held to her resolution. 'You have heard of what I saw last night?' she said faintly.

'Don't speak of it!' Henry interposed. 'Don't uselessly agitate yourself.'

'I must speak! My mind is full of horrid questions about it. I know I can't identify it—and yet I ask myself over and over again, in whose likeness did it appear? Was it in the likeness of Ferrari? or was it ——?' she stopped, shuddering. 'The Countess knows, I must see the Countess!' she resumed vehemently. 'Whether my courage fails me or not, I must make the attempt. Take me to her before I have time to feel afraid of it!'

Henry looked at her anxiously. 'If you are really sure of your own resolution,' he said, 'I agree with you—the sooner you see her the better. You remember how strangely she talked of your influence over her, when she forced her way into your room in London?'

'I remember it perfectly. Why do you ask?'

'For this reason. In the present state of her mind, I doubt if she will be much longer capable of realizing her wild idea of you as the avenging angel who is to bring her to a reckoning for her evil deeds. It may be well to try what your influence can do while she is still capable of feeling it.'

He waited to hear what Agnes would say. She took his arm and led him in silence to the door.

They ascended to the second floor, and, after knocking, entered the Countess's room.

She was still busily engaged in writing. When she looked up from the paper, and saw Agnes, a vacant expression of doubt was the only expression in her wild black eyes. After a few moments, the lost remembrances and associations appeared to return slowly to her mind. The pen dropped from her hand. Haggard and trembling, she looked closer at Agnes, and recognised her at last. 'Has the time come already?' she said in low awe-struck tones. 'Give me a little longer respite, I haven't done my writing yet!'

She dropped on her knees, and held out her clasped hands entreatingly. Agnes was far from having recovered, after the shock that she had suffered in the night: her nerves were far from being equal to the strain that was now laid on them. She was so startled by the change in the Countess, that she was at a loss what to say or to do next. Henry was obliged to speak to her. 'Put your questions while you have the chance,' he said, lowering his voice. 'See! the vacant look is coming over her face again.'

Agnes tried to rally her courage. 'You were in my room last night —' she began. Before she could add a word more, the Countess lifted her hands, and wrung them above her head with a low moan of horror. Agnes shrank back, and turned as if to leave the room. Henry stopped her, and whispered to her to try again. She obeyed him after an effort. 'I slept last night in the room that you gave up to me,' she resumed. 'I saw —'

The Countess suddenly rose to her feet. 'No more of that,' she cried. 'Oh, Jesu Maria! do you think I want to be told what you saw? Do you think I don't know what it means for you and for me? Decide for yourself, Miss. Examine your own mind. Are you well assured that the day of reckoning has come at last? Are you ready to follow me back, through the crimes of the past, to the secrets of the dead?'

She returned again to the writing-table, without waiting to be answered. Her eyes flashed; she looked like her old self once more as she spoke. It was only for a moment. The old ardour and impetuosity were nearly worn out. Her head sank; she sighed heavily as she unlocked a desk which stood on the table. Opening a drawer in the desk, she took out a leaf of vellum, covered with faded writing. Some ragged ends of silken thread were still attached to the leaf, as if it had been torn out of a book.

'Can you read Italian?' she asked, handing the leaf to Agnes.

Agnes answered silently by an inclination of her head.

'The leaf,' the Countess proceeded, 'once belonged to a book in the old library of the palace, while this building was still a palace. By whom it was torn out you have no need to know. For what purpose it was torn out you may discover for yourself, if you will. Read it first—at the fifth line from the top of the page.'

Agnes felt the serious necessity of composing herself. 'Give me a chair,' she said to Henry; 'and I will do my best.' He placed himself behind her chair so that he could look over her shoulder and help her to understand the writing on the leaf. Rendered into English, it ran as follows:—

I have now completed my literary survey of the first floor of the palace. At the desire of my noble and gracious patron, the lord of this glorious edifice, I next ascend to the second floor, and continue my catalogue or description of the pictures, decorations, and other treasures of art therein contained. Let me begin with the corner room at the western extremity of the palace, called the Room of the Caryatides, from the statues which support the mantel-piece. This work is of comparatively recent execution: it dates from the eighteenth century only, and reveals the corrupt taste of the period in every part of it. Still, there is a certain interest which attaches to the mantel-piece: it conceals a cleverly constructed hiding-place, between the floor of the room and the ceiling of the room beneath, which was made during the last evil days of the Inquisition in Venice, and which is reported to have saved an ancestor of my gracious lord pursued by that terrible tribunal. The machinery of this curious place of concealment has been kept in good order by the present lord, as a species of curiosity. He condescended to show me the method of working it. Approaching the two Caryatides, rest your hand on the forehead (midway between the eyebrows) of the figure which is on your left as you stand opposite to the fireplace, then press the head inwards as if you were pushing it against the wall behind. By doing this, you set in motion the hidden machinery in the wall which turns the hearthstone on a pivot, and discloses the hollow place below. There is room enough in it for a man to lie easily at full length. The method of closing the cavity again is equally simple. Place both your hands on the temples of the figures; pull as if you were pulling it towards you—and the hearthstone will revolve into its proper position again.

'You need read no farther,' said the Countess. 'Be careful to remember what you have read.'

She put back the page of vellum in her writing-desk, locked it, and led the way to the door.

'Come!' she said; 'and see what the mocking Frenchman called "The beginning of the end." '

Agnes was barely able to rise from her chair; she trembled from head to foot. Henry gave her his arm to support her. 'Fear nothing,' he whispered; 'I shall be with you.'

The Countess proceeded along the westward corridor, and stopped at the door numbered Thirty-eight. This was the room which had been inhabited by Baron Rivar in the old days of the palace: it was situated immediately over the bedchamber in which Agnes had passed the night. For the last two days the room had been empty. The absence of luggage in it, when they opened the door, showed that it had not yet been let.

'You see?' said the Countess, pointing to the carved figure at the fireplace; 'and you know what to do. Have I deserved that you should temper justice with mercy?' she went on in lower tones. 'Give me a few hours more to myself. The Baron wants money—I must get on with my play.'

She smiled vacantly, and imitated the action of writing with her right hand as she pronounced the last words. The effort of concentrating her weakened mind on other and less familiar topics than the constant want of money in the Baron's lifetime, and the vague prospect of gain from the still unfinished play, had evidently exhausted her poor reserves of strength. When her request had been granted, she addressed no expressions of gratitude to Agnes; she only said, 'Feel no fear, miss, of my attempting to escape you. Where you are, there I must be till the end comes.'

Her eyes wandered round the room with a last weary and stupefied look. She returned to her writing with slow and feeble steps, like the steps of an old woman.

## CHAPTER XXIV

Henry and Agnes were left alone in the Room of the Caryatides.

The person who had written the description of the palace—probably a poor author or artist—had correctly pointed out the defects of the mantel-piece. Bad taste, exhibiting itself on the most costly and splendid scale, was visible in every part of the work. It was nevertheless greatly admired by ignorant travellers of all classes; partly on account of its imposing size, and partly on account of the number of variously-coloured marbles which the sculptor had contrived to introduce into his design. Photographs of the mantel-piece were exhibited in the public rooms, and found a ready sale among English and American visitors to the hotel.

Henry led Agnes to the figure on the left, as they stood facing the empty fire-place. 'Shall I try the experiment,' he asked, 'or will you?' She abruptly drew her arm away from him, and turned back to the door. 'I can't even look at it,' she said. 'That merciless marble face frightens me!'

Henry put his hand on the forehead of the figure. 'What is there to alarm you, my dear, in this conventionally classical face?' he asked jesting-ly. Before he could press the head inwards, Agnes hurriedly opened the door. 'Wait till I am out of the room!' she cried. 'The bare idea of what you may find there horrifies me!' She looked back into the room as she crossed the threshold. 'I won't leave you altogether,' she said, 'I will wait outside.'

She closed the door. Left by himself, Henry lifted his hand once more to the marble forehead of the figure.

For the second time, he was checked on the point of setting the machinery of the hiding-place in motion. On this occasion, the interruption came from an outbreak of friendly voices in the corridor. A woman's voice exclaimed, 'Dearest Agnes, how glad I am to see you again!' A man's voice followed, offering to introduce some friend to 'Miss Lockwood.' A third voice (which Henry recognised as the voice of the manager of the hotel) became audible next, directing the housekeeper to show the ladies and gentlemen the vacant apartments at the other end of the corridor. 'If more accommodation is wanted,' the manager went on, 'I have a charming room to let here.' He opened the door as he spoke, and found himself face to face with Henry Westwick.

'This is indeed an agreeable surprise, sir!' said the manager cheerfully. 'You are admiring our famous chimney-piece, I see. May I ask, Mr. West-wick, how you find yourself in the hotel, this time? Have the supernatural influences affected your appetite again?'

'The supernatural influences have spared me, this time,' Henry answered. 'Perhaps you may yet find that they have affected some other member of the family.' He spoke gravely, resenting the familiar tone in which the manager had referred to his previous visit to the hotel. 'Have you just returned?' he asked, by way of changing the topic.

'Just this minute, sir. I had the honour of travelling in the same train with friends of yours who have arrived at the hotel—Mr. and Mrs. Arthur Barville, and their travelling companions. Miss Lockwood is with them, looking at the rooms. They will be here before long, if they find it convenient to have an extra room at their disposal.'

This announcement decided Henry on exploring the hiding-place, before the interruption occurred. It had crossed his mind, when Agnes left him, that he ought perhaps to have a witness, in the not very probable event of some alarming discovery taking place. The too-familiar manager, suspecting nothing, was there at his disposal. He turned again to the Caryan figure, maliciously resolving to make the manager his witness.

'I am delighted to hear that our friends have arrived at last,' he said. 'Before I shake hands with them, let me ask you a question about this queer work of art here. I see photographs of it downstairs. Are they for sale?'

'Certainly, Mr. Westwick!'

'Do you think the chimney-piece is as solid as it looks?' Henry proceeded. 'When you came in, I was just wondering whether this figure here had not accidentally got loosened from the wall behind it.' He laid his hand on the marble forehead, for the third time. 'To my eye, it looks a little out of the perpendicular. I almost fancied I could jog the head just now, when I touched it.' He pressed the head inwards as he said those words.

A sound of jarring iron was instantly audible behind the wall. The solid hearthstone in front of the fire-place turned slowly at the feet of the two men, and disclosed a dark cavity below. At the same moment, the strange and sickening combination of odours, hitherto associated with the vaults of the old palace and with the bed-chamber beneath, now floated up from the open recess, and filled the room.

The manager started back. 'Good God, Mr. Westwick!' he exclaimed, 'what does this mean?'

Remembering, not only what his brother Francis had felt in the room beneath, but what the experience of Agnes had been on the previous night, Henry was determined to be on his guard. 'I am as much surprised as you are,' was his only reply.

'Wait for me one moment, sir,' said the manager. 'I must stop the ladies and gentlemen outside from coming in.'

He hurried away—not forgetting to close the door after him. Henry opened the window, and waited there breathing the purer air. Vague apprehensions of the next discovery to come, filled his mind for the first time. He was doubly resolved, now, not to stir a step in the investigation without a witness.

The manager returned with a wax taper in his hand, which he lighted as soon as he entered the room.

'We need fear no interruption now,' he said. 'Be so kind, Mr. Westwick, as to hold the light. It is my business to find out what this extraordinary discovery means.'

Henry held the taper. Looking into the cavity, by the dim and flickering light, they both detected a dark object at the bottom of it. 'I think I can reach the thing,' the manager remarked, 'if I lie down, and put my hand into the hole.'

He knelt on the floor—and hesitated. 'Might I ask you, sir, to give me my gloves?' he said. 'They are in my hat, on the chair behind you.'

Henry gave him the gloves. 'I don't know what I may be going to take hold of,' the manager explained, smiling rather uneasily as he put on his right glove.

He stretched himself at full length on the floor, and passed his right arm into the cavity. 'I can't say exactly what I have got hold of,' he said. 'But I have got it.'

Half raising himself, he drew his hand out.

The next instant, he started to his feet with a shriek of terror. A human head dropped from his nerveless grasp on the floor, and rolled to Henry's feet. It was the hideous head that Agnes had seen hovering above her, in the vision of the night!

The two men looked at each other, both struck speechless by the same emotion of horror. The manager was the first to control himself. 'See to the door, for God's sake!' he said. 'Some of the people outside may have heard me.'

Henry moved mechanically to the door.

Even when he had his hand on the key, ready to turn it in the lock in case of necessity, he still looked back at the appalling object on the floor. There was no possibility of identifying those decayed and distorted features with any living creature whom he had seen—and, yet, he was conscious of feeling a vague and awful doubt which shook him to the soul. The questions which had tortured the mind of Agnes, were now *his* questions too. *He* asked himself, 'In whose likeness might I have recognised it before the decay set in? The likeness of Ferrari? or the likeness of——?' He paused trembling, as Agnes had paused trembling before him. Agnes! The name, of all women's names the dearest to him, was a terror to him now! What was he to say to her? What might be the consequence if he trusted her with the terrible truth?

No footsteps approached the door; no voices were audible outside. The travellers were still occupied in the rooms at the eastern end of the corridor.

In the brief interval that had passed, the manager had sufficiently recovered himself to be able to think once more of the first and foremost interests of his life—the interests of the hotel. He approached Henry anxiously.

'If this frightful discovery becomes known,' he said, 'the closing of the hotel and the ruin of the Company will be the inevitable results. I feel sure that I can trust your discretion, sir, so far?'

'You can certainly trust me,' Henry answered. 'But surely discretion has its limits,' he added, 'after such a discovery as we have made?'

The manager understood that the duty which they owed to the community, as honest and law-abiding men, was the duty to which Henry now referred. 'I will at once find the means,' he said, 'of conveying the remains privately out of the house, and I will myself place them in the care of the police authorities. Will you leave the room with me? or do you not object to keep watch here, and help me when I return?'

While he was speaking, the voices of the travellers made themselves heard again at the end of the corridor. Henry instantly consented to wait in the room. He shrank from facing the inevitable meeting with Agnes if he showed himself in the corridor at that moment.

The manager hastened his departure, in the hope of escaping notice. He was discovered by his guests before he could reach the head of the stairs. Henry heard the voices plainly as he turned the key. While the terrible drama of discovery was in progress on one side of the door, trivial questions about the amusements of Venice, and facetious discussions on the relative merits of French and Italian cookery, were proceeding on the other. Little by little, the sound of the talking grew fainter. The visitors, having arranged their plans of amusement for the day, were on their way out of the hotel. In a minute or two, there was silence once more.

Henry turned to the window, thinking to relieve his mind by looking at the bright view over the canal. He soon grew wearied of the familiar scene. The morbid fascination which seems to be exercised by all horrible sights, drew him back again to the ghastly object on the floor.

Dream or reality, how had Agnes survived the sight of it? As the question passed through his mind, he noticed for the first time something lying on the floor near the head. Looking closer, he perceived a thin little plate of gold, with three false teeth attached to it, which had apparently dropped out (loosened by the shock) when the manager let the head fall on the floor.

The importance of this discovery, and the necessity of not too readily communicating it to others, instantly struck Henry. Here surely was a chance—if any chance remained—of identifying the shocking relic of humanity which lay before him, the dumb witness of a crime! Acting on this idea, he took possession of the teeth, purposing to use them as a last means of inquiry when other attempts at investigation had been tried and had failed.

He went back again to the window: the solitude of the room began to weigh on his spirits. As he looked out again at the view, there was a soft knock at the door. He hastened to open it—and checked himself in the act. A doubt occurred to him. Was it the manager who had knocked? He called out, 'Who is there?'

The voice of Agnes answered him. 'Have you anything to tell me, Henry?'

He was hardly able to reply. 'Not just now,' he said, confusedly. 'Forgive me if I don't open the door. I will speak to you a little later.'

The sweet voice made itself heard again, pleading with him piteously. 'Don't leave me alone, Henry! I can't go back to the happy people downstairs.'

How could he resist that appeal? He heard her sigh—he heard the rustling of her dress as she moved away in despair. The very thing that he had shrunk from doing but a few minutes since was the thing that he did now! He joined Agnes in the corridor. She turned as she heard him, and pointed, trembling, in the direction of the closed room. 'Is it so terrible as that?' she asked faintly.

He put his arm round her to support her. A thought came to him as he looked at her, waiting in doubt and fear for his reply. 'You shall know what I have discovered,' he said, 'if you will first put on your hat and cloak, and come out with me.'

She was naturally surprised. 'Can you tell me your object in going out?' she asked.

He owned what his object was unreservedly. 'I want, before all things,' he said, 'to satisfy your mind and mine, on the subject of Montbarry's death. I am going to take you to the doctor who attended him in his illness, and to the consul who followed him to the grave.'

Her eyes rested on Henry gratefully. 'Oh, how well you understand me!' she said. The manager joined them at the same moment, on his way up the stairs. Henry gave him the key of the room, and then called to the servants in the hall to have a gondola ready at the steps. 'Are you leaving the hotel?' the manager asked. 'In search of evidence,' Henry whispered, pointing to the key. 'If the authorities want me, I shall be back in an hour.'

# CHAPTER XXV

The day had advanced to evening. Lord Montbarry and the bridal party had gone to the Opera. Agnes alone, pleading the excuse of fatigue, remained at the hotel. Having kept up appearances by accompanying his friends to the theatre, Henry Westwick slipped away after the first act, and joined Agnes in the drawing-room.

'Have you thought of what I said to you earlier in the day?' he asked, taking a chair at her side. 'Do you agree with me that the one dreadful doubt which oppressed us both is at least set at rest?'

Agnes shook her head sadly. 'I wish I could agree with you, Henry—I wish I could honestly say that my mind is at ease.'

The answer would have discouraged most men. Henry's patience (where Agnes was concerned) was equal to any demands on it.

'If you will only look back at the events of the day,' he said, 'you must surely admit that we have not been completely baffled. Remember how Dr. Bruno disposed of our doubts:—"After thirty years of medical practice, do you think I am likely to mistake the symptoms of death by bronchitis?" If ever there was an unanswerable question, there it is! Was the consul's testimony doubtful in any part of it? He called at the palace to offer his services, after hearing of Lord Montbarry's death; he arrived at the time when the coffin was in the house; he himself saw the corpse placed in it, and the lid screwed down. The evidence of the priest is equally beyond dispute. He remained in the room with the coffin, reciting the prayers for the dead, until the funeral left the palace. Bear all these statements in mind, Agnes; and how can you deny that the question of Montbarry's death and burial is a question set at rest? We have really but one doubt left: we have still to ask ourselves whether the remains which I discovered are the remains of the lost courier, or not. There is the case, as I understand it. Have I stated it fairly?'

Agnes could not deny that he had stated it fairly.

'Then what prevents you from experiencing the same sense of relief that I feel?' Henry asked.

'What I saw last night prevents me,' Agnes answered. 'When we spoke of this subject, after our inquiries were over, you reproached me with taking what you called the superstitious view. I don't quite admit that—but I do acknowledge that I should find the superstitious view intelligible if I heard it expressed by some other person. Remembering what your brother and I once were to each other in the bygone time, I can understand the apparition making itself visible to *me*, to claim the mercy of Christian burial, and the vengeance due to a crime. I can even perceive some faint possibility of truth in the explanation which you described as the mesmeric theory—that what I saw might be the result of magnetic influence communicated to me, as I lay between the remains of the murdered husband above me and the guilty wife suffering the tortures of remorse at my bedside. But what I do *not* understand is, that I should have passed through that dreadful ordeal; having no previous knowledge of the murdered man in his lifetime, or only knowing him (if you suppose that I saw the apparition of Ferrari) through the interest which I took in his wife. I can't dispute your reasoning, Henry. But I feel in my heart of hearts that you are deceived. Nothing will shake my belief that we are still as far from having discovered the dreadful truth as ever.'

Henry made no further attempt to dispute with her. She had impressed him with a certain reluctant respect for her own opinion, in spite of himself.

'Have you thought of any better way of arriving at the truth?' he asked. 'Who is to help us? No doubt there is the Countess, who has the clue to the mystery in her own hands. But, in the present state of her mind, is her testimony to be trusted—even if she were willing to speak? Judging by my own experience, I should say decidedly not.'

'You don't mean that you have seen her again?' Agnes eagerly interposed.

'Yes. I disturbed her once more over her endless writing; and I insisted on her speaking out plainly.'

'Then you told her what you found when you opened the hiding-place?'

'Of course I did!' Henry replied. 'I said that I held her responsible for the discovery, though I had not mentioned her connection with it to the authorities as yet. She went on with her writing as if I had spoken in an unknown tongue! I was equally obstinate, on my side. I told her plainly that the head had been placed under the care of the police, and that the manager and I had signed our declarations and given our evidence. She paid not the slightest heed to me. By way of tempting her to speak, I added that the whole investigation was to be kept a secret, and that she might depend on my discretion. For the moment I thought I had succeeded. She looked up from her writing with a passing flash of curiosity, and said, "What are they going to do with it?"—meaning, I suppose, the head. I answered that it was to be privately buried, after photographs of it had first been taken. I even went the length of communicating the opinion of the surgeon consulted, that some chemical means of arresting decomposition had been used and had only partially succeeded—and I asked her point-blank if the surgeon was right? The trap was not a bad one—but it completely failed. She said in the coolest manner, "Now you are here, I should like to consult you about my play; I am at a loss for some new incidents." Mind! there was nothing satirical in this. She was really eager to read her wonderful work to me—evidently supposing that I took a special interest in such things, because my brother is the manager of a theatre! I left her, making the first excuse that occurred to me. So far as I am concerned, I can do nothing with her. But it is possible that *your* influence may succeed with her again, as it has succeeded already. Will you make the attempt, to satisfy your own mind? She is still upstairs; and I am quite ready to accompany you.'

Agnes shuddered at the bare suggestion of another interview with the Countess.

'I can't! I daren't!' she exclaimed. 'After what has happened in that horrible room, she is more repellent to me than ever. Don't ask me to do it, Henry! Feel my hand—you have turned me as cold as death only with talking of it!'

She was not exaggerating the terror that possessed her. Henry hastened to change the subject.

'Let us talk of something more interesting,' he said. 'I have a question to ask you about yourself. Am I right in believing that the sooner you get away from Venice the happier you will be?'

'Right?' she repeated excitedly. 'You are more than right! No words can say how I long to be away from this horrible place. But you know how I am situated—you heard what Lord Montbarry said at dinner-time?'

'Suppose he has altered his plans, since dinner-time?' Henry suggested.

Agnes looked surprised. 'I thought he had received letters from England which obliged him to leave Venice to-morrow,' she said.

'Quite true,' Henry admitted. 'He had arranged to start for England to-morrow, and to leave you and Lady Montbarry and the children to enjoy your holiday in Venice, under my care. Circumstances have occurred, however, which have forced him to alter his plans. He must take you all back with him to-morrow because I am not able to assume the charge of you. I am obliged to give up my holiday in Italy, and return to England too.'

Agnes looked at him in some little perplexity: she was not quite sure whether she understood him or not.

'Are you really obliged to go back?' she asked.

Henry smiled as he answered her. 'Keep the secret,' he said, 'or Montbarry will never forgive me!'

She read the rest in his face. 'Oh!' she exclaimed, blushing brightly, 'you have not given up your pleasant holiday in Italy on my account?'

'I shall go back with you to England, Agnes. That will be holiday enough for *me*.'

She took his hand in an irrepressible outburst of gratitude. 'How good you are to me!' she murmured tenderly. 'What should I have done in the troubles that have come to me, without your sympathy? I can't tell you, Henry, how I feel your kindness.'

She tried impulsively to lift his hand to her lips. He gently stopped her. 'Agnes,' he said, 'are you beginning to understand how truly I love you?'

That simple question found its own way to her heart. She owned the whole truth, without saying a word. She looked at him—and then looked away again.

He drew her nearer to him. 'My own darling!' he whispered—and kissed her. Softly and tremulously, the sweet lips lingered, and touched his lips in return. Then her head drooped. She put her arms round his neck, and hid her face on his bosom. They spoke no more.

The charmed silence had lasted but a little while, when it was mercilessly broken by a knock at the door.

Agnes started to her feet. She placed herself at the piano; the instrument being opposite to the door, it was impossible, when she seated herself on the music-stool, for any person entering the room to see her face. Henry called out irritably, 'Come in.'

The door was not opened. The person on the other side of it asked a strange question.

'Is Mr. Henry Westwick alone?'

Agnes instantly recognised the voice of the Countess. She hurried to a second door, which communicated with one of the bedrooms. 'Don't let her come near me!' she whispered nervously. 'Good night, Henry! good night!'

If Henry could, by an effort of will, have transported the Countess to the uttermost ends of the earth, he would have made the effort without remorse. As it was, he only repeated, more irritably than ever, 'Come in!'

She entered the room slowly with her everlasting manuscript in her hand. Her step was unsteady; a dark flush appeared on her face, in place of its customary pallor; her eyes were bloodshot and widely dilated. In approaching Henry, she showed a strange incapability of calculating her distances—she struck against the table near which he happened to be sitting. When she spoke, her articulation was confused, and her pronunciation of some of the longer words was hardly intelligible. Most men would have suspected her of being under the influence of some intoxicating liquor. Henry took a truer view—he said, as he placed a chair for her, 'Countess, I am afraid you have been working too hard: you look as if you wanted rest.'

She put her hand to her head. 'My invention has gone,' she said. 'I can't write my fourth act. It's all a blank—all a blank!'

Henry advised her to wait till the next day. 'Go to bed,' he suggested; 'and try to sleep.'

She waved her hand impatiently. 'I must finish the play,' she answered. 'I only want a hint from you. You must know something about plays. Your brother has got a theatre. You must often have heard him talk about fourth and fifth acts—you must have seen rehearsals, and all the rest of it.' She abruptly thrust the manuscript into Henry's hand. 'I can't read it to you,' she said; 'I feel giddy when I look at my own writing. Just run your eye over it, there's a good fellow—and give me a hint.'

Henry glanced at the manuscript. He happened to look at the list of the persons of the drama. As he read the list he started and turned abruptly to the Countess, intending to ask her for some explanation. The words were suspended on his lips. It was but too plainly useless to speak to her. Her head lay back on the rail of the chair. She seemed to be half asleep already. The flush on her face had deepened: she looked like a woman who was in danger of having a fit.

He rang the bell, and directed the man who answered it to send one of the chambermaids upstairs. His voice seemed to partially rouse the Countess; she opened her eyes in a slow drowsy way. 'Have you read it?' she asked.

It was necessary as a mere act of humanity to humour her. 'I will read it willingly,' said Henry, 'if you will go upstairs to bed. You shall hear what I think of it to-morrow morning. Our heads will be clearer, we shall be better able to make the fourth act in the morning.'

The chambermaid came in while he was speaking. 'I am afraid the lady is ill,' Henry whispered. 'Take her up to her room.' The woman looked at the Countess and whispered back, 'Shall we send for a doctor, sir?'

Henry advised taking her upstairs first, and then asking the manager's opinion. There was great difficulty in persuading her to rise, and accept the support of the chambermaid's arm. It was only by reiterated promises to read the play that night, and to make the fourth act in the morning, that Henry prevailed on the Countess to return to her room.

Left to himself, he began to feel a certain languid curiosity in relation to the manuscript. He looked over the pages, reading a line here and a line there. Suddenly he changed colour as he read—and looked up from the manuscript like a man bewildered. 'Good God! what does this mean?' he said to himself.

His eyes turned nervously to the door by which Agnes had left him. She might return to the drawing-room, she might want to see what the Countess had written. He looked back again at the passage which had startled him—considered with himself for a moment—and, snatching up the unfinished play, suddenly and softly left the room.

## CHAPTER XXVI

Entering his own room on the upper floor, Henry placed the manuscript on his table, open at the first leaf. His nerves were unquestionably shaken; his hand trembled as he turned the pages, he started at chance noises on the staircase of the hotel.

The scenario, or outline, of the Countess's play began with no formal prefatory phrases. She presented herself and her work with the easy familiarity of an old friend.

'Allow me, dear Mr. Francis Westwick, to introduce to you the persons in my proposed Play. Behold them, arranged symmetrically in a line.

'My Lord. The Baron. The Courier. The Doctor. The Countess.

'I don't trouble myself, you see, to invest fictitious family names. My characters are sufficiently distinguished by their social titles, and by the striking contrast which they present one with another.

'The First Act opens ——

'No! Before I open the First Act, I must announce, in justice to myself, that this Play is entirely the work of my own invention. I scorn to borrow from actual events; and, what is more extraordinary still, I have not stolen one of my ideas from the Modern French drama. As the manager of an English theatre, you will naturally refuse to believe this. It doesn't matter. Nothing matters—except the opening of my first act.

'We are at Homburg, in the famous Salon d'Or, at the height of the season. The Countess (exquisitely dressed) is seated at the green table. Strangers of all nations are standing behind the players, venturing their money or only looking on. My Lord is among the strangers. He is struck by the Countess's personal appearance, in which beauties and defects are fantastically mingled in the most attractive manner. He watches the Countess's game, and places his money where he sees her deposit her own little stake. She looks round at him, and says, "Don't trust to my colour; I have been unlucky the whole evening. Place your stake on the other colour, and you may have a chance of winning." My Lord (a true Englishman) blushes, bows, and obeys. The Countess proves to be a prophet. She loses again. My Lord wins twice the sum that he has risked.

'The Countess rises from the table. She has no more money, and she offers my Lord her chair.

'Instead of taking it, he politely places his winnings in her hand, and begs her to accept the loan as a favour to himself. The Countess stakes again, and loses again. My Lord smiles superbly, and presses a second loan on her. From that moment her luck turns. She wins, and wins largely. Her brother, the Baron, trying his fortune in another room, hears of what is going on, and joins my Lord and the Countess.

'Pay attention, if you please, to the Baron. He is delineated as a remarkable and interesting character.

'This noble person has begun life with a single-minded devotion to the science of experimental chemistry, very surprising in a young and handsome man with a brilliant future before him. A profound knowledge of the occult sciences has persuaded the Baron that it is possible to solve the famous problem called the "Philosopher's Stone." His own pecuniary resources have long since been exhausted by his costly experiments. His sister has next supplied him with the small fortune at her disposal: reserving only the family jewels, placed in the charge of her banker and friend at Frankfort. The Countess's fortune also being swallowed up, the Baron has in a fatal moment sought for new supplies at the gaming table. He proves, at starting on his perilous career, to be a favourite of fortune; wins largely, and, alas! profanes his noble enthusiasm for science by yielding his soul to the all-debasing passion of the gamester.

'At the period of the Play, the Baron's good fortune has deserted him. He sees his way to a crowning experiment in the fatal search after the secret of transmuting the baser elements into gold. But how is he to pay the preliminary expenses? Destiny, like a mocking echo, answers, How?

'Will his sister's winnings (with my Lord's money) prove large enough to help him? Eager for this result, he gives the Countess his advice how to play. From that disastrous moment the infection of his own adverse fortune spreads to his sister. She loses again, and again—loses to the last farthing.

'The amiable and wealthy Lord offers a third loan; but the scrupulous Countess positively refuses to take it. On leaving the table, she presents her brother to my Lord. The gentlemen fall into pleasant talk. My Lord asks leave to pay his respects to the Countess, the next morning, at her hotel. The Baron hospitably invites him to breakfast. My Lord accepts, with a last admiring glance at the Countess which does not escape her brother's observation, and takes his leave for the night.

'Alone with his sister, the Baron speaks out plainly. "Our affairs," he says, "are in a desperate condition, and must find a desperate remedy. Wait for me here, while I make inquiries about my Lord. You have evidently produced a strong impression on him. If we can turn that impression into money, no matter at what sacrifice, the thing must be done."

'The Countess now occupies the stage alone, and indulges in a soliloquy which develops her character.

'It is at once a dangerous and attractive character. Immense capacities for good are implanted in her nature, side by side with equally remarkable capacities for evil. It rests with circumstances to develop either the one or the other. Being a person who produces a sensation wherever she goes, this noble lady is naturally made the subject of all sorts of scandalous reports. To one of these reports (which falsely and abominably points to the Baron as her lover instead of her brother) she now refers with just indignation. She has just expressed her desire to leave Homburg, as the place in which the vile calumny first took its rise, when the Baron returns, overhears her last words, and says to her, "Yes, leave Homburg by all means; provided you leave it in the character of my Lord's betrothed wife!"

'The Countess is startled and shocked. She protests that she does not reciprocate my Lord's admiration for her. She even goes the length of refusing to see him again. The Baron answers, "I must positively have command of money. Take your choice, between marrying my Lord's income, in the interest of my grand discovery—or leave me to sell myself and my title to the first rich woman of low degree who is ready to buy me."

'The Countess listens in surprise and dismay. Is it possible that the Baron is in earnest? He is horribly in earnest. "The woman who will buy me," he says, "is in the next room to us at this moment. She is the wealthy widow of a Jewish usurer. She has the money I want to reach the solution of the great problem. I have only to be that woman's husband, and to make myself master of untold millions of gold. Take five minutes to consider what I have said to you, and tell me on my return which of us is to marry for the money I want, you or I."

'As he turns away, the Countess stops him.

'All the noblest sentiments in her nature are exalted to the highest pitch. "Where is the true woman," she exclaims, "who wants time to consummate the sacrifice of herself, when the man to whom she is devoted demands it? She does not want five minutes—she does not want five seconds—she holds out her hand to him, and she says, Sacrifice me on the altar of your glory! Take as stepping-stones on the way to your triumph, my love, my liberty, and my life!"

'On this grand situation the curtain falls. Judging by my first act, Mr. Westwick, tell me truly, and don't be afraid of turning my head:—Am I not capable of writing a good play?'

Henry paused between the First and Second Acts; reflecting, not on the merits of the play, but on the strange resemblance which the incidents so far presented to the incidents that had attended the disastrous marriage of the first Lord Montbarry.

Was it possible that the Countess, in the present condition of her mind, supposed herself to be exercising her invention when she was only exercising her memory?

The question involved considerations too serious to be made the subject of a hasty decision. Reserving his opinion, Henry turned the page, and devoted himself to the reading of the next act. The manuscript proceeded as follows:—

'The Second Act opens at Venice. An interval of four months has elapsed since the date of the scene at the gambling table. The action now takes place in the reception-room of one of the Venetian palaces.

'The Baron is discovered, alone, on the stage. He reverts to the events which have happened since the close of the First Act. The Countess has sacrificed herself; the mercenary marriage has taken place—but not without obstacles, caused by difference of opinion on the question of marriage settlements.

'Private inquiries, instituted in England, have informed the Baron that my Lord's income is derived chiefly from what is called entailed property. In case of accidents, he is surely bound to do something for his bride? Let him, for example, insure his life, for a sum proposed by the Baron, and let him so settle the money that his widow shall have it, if he dies first.

'My Lord hesitates. The Baron wastes no time in useless discussion. "Let us by all means" (he says) "consider the marriage as broken off." My Lord shifts his ground, and pleads for a smaller sum than the sum proposed. The Baron briefly replies, "I never bargain." My lord is in love; the natural result follows—he gives way.

'So far, the Baron has no cause to complain. But my Lord's turn comes, when the marriage has been celebrated, and when the honeymoon is over. The Baron has joined the married pair at a palace which they have hired in

Venice. He is still bent on solving the problem of the "Philosopher's Stone." His laboratory is set up in the vaults beneath the palace—so that smells from chemical experiments may not incommode the Countess, in the higher regions of the house. The one obstacle in the way of his grand discovery is, as usual, the want of money. His position at the present time has become truly critical. He owes debts of honour to gentlemen in his own rank of life, which must positively be paid; and he proposes, in his own friendly manner, to borrow the money of my Lord. My Lord positively refuses, in the rudest terms. The Baron applies to his sister to exercise her conjugal influence. She can only answer that her noble husband (being no longer distractedly in love with her) now appears in his true character, as one of the meanest men living. The sacrifice of the marriage has been made, and has already proved useless.

'Such is the state of affairs at the opening of the Second Act.

'The entrance of the Countess suddenly disturbs the Baron's reflections. She is in a state bordering on frenzy. Incoherent expressions of rage burst from her lips: it is some time before she can sufficiently control herself to speak plainly. She has been doubly insulted—first, by a menial person in her employment; secondly, by her husband. Her maid, an Englishwoman, has declared that she will serve the Countess no longer. She will give up her wages, and return at once to England. Being asked her reason for this strange proceeding, she insolently hints that the Countess's service is no service for an honest woman, since the Baron has entered the house. The Countess does, what any lady in her position would do; she indignantly dismisses the wretch on the spot.

'My Lord, hearing his wife's voice raised in anger, leaves the study in which he is accustomed to shut himself up over his books, and asks what this disturbance means. The Countess informs him of the outrageous language and conduct of her maid. My Lord not only declares his entire approval of the woman's conduct, but expresses his own abominable doubts of his wife's fidelity in language of such horrible brutality that no lady could pollute her lips by repeating it. "If I had been a man," the Countess says, "and if I had had a weapon in my hand, I would have struck him dead at my feet!"

'The Baron, listening silently so far, now speaks. "Permit me to finish the sentence for you," he says. "You would have struck your husband dead at your feet; and by that rash act, you would have deprived yourself of the insurance money settled on the widow—the very money which is wanted to relieve your brother from the unendurable pecuniary position which he now occupies!"

'The Countess gravely reminds the Baron that this is no joking matter. After what my Lord has said to her, she has little doubt that he will communicate his infamous suspicions to his lawyers in England. If nothing is done to prevent it, she may be divorced and disgraced, and thrown on the world, with no resource but the sale of her jewels to keep her from starving.

'At this moment, the Courier who has been engaged to travel with my Lord from England crosses the stage with a letter to take to the post. The Countess stops him, and asks to look at the address on the letter. She takes it from him for a moment, and shows it to her brother. The handwriting is my Lord's; and the letter is directed to his lawyers in London.

'The Courier proceeds to the post-office. The Baron and the Countess look at each other in silence. No words are needed. They thoroughly understand the position in which they are placed; they clearly see the terrible remedy for it. What is the plain alternative before them? Disgrace and ruin—or, my Lord's death and the insurance money!

'The Baron walks backwards and forwards in great agitation, talking to himself. The Countess hears fragments of what he is saying. He speaks of my Lord's constitution, probably weakened in India—of a cold which my Lord has caught two or three days since—of the remarkable manner in which such slight things as colds sometimes end in serious illness and death.

'He observes that the Countess is listening to him, and asks if she has anything to propose. She is a woman who, with many defects, has the great merit of speaking out. "Is there no such thing as a serious illness," she asks, "corked up in one of those bottles of yours in the vaults downstairs?"

'The Baron answers by gravely shaking his head. What is he afraid of?—a possible examination of the body after death? No: he can set any post-mortem examination at defiance. It is the process of administering the poison that he dreads. A man so distinguished as my Lord cannot be taken seriously ill without medical attendance. Where there is a Doctor, there is always danger of discovery. Then, again, there is the Courier, faithful to my Lord as long as my Lord pays him. Even if the Doctor sees nothing suspicious, the Courier may discover something. The poison, to do its work with the necessary secrecy, must be repeatedly administered in graduated doses. One trifling miscalculation or mistake may rouse suspicion. The insurance offices may hear of it, and may refuse to pay the money. As things are, the Baron will not risk it, and will not allow his sister to risk it in his place.

'My Lord himself is the next character who appears. He has repeatedly rung for the Courier, and the bell has not been answered. "What does this insolence mean?"

'The Countess (speaking with quiet dignity—for why should her infamous husband have the satisfaction of knowing how deeply he has wounded her?) reminds my Lord that the Courier has gone to the post. My Lord asks suspiciously if she has looked at the letter. The Countess informs him coldly that she has no curiosity about his letters. Referring to the cold from which he is suffering, she inquires if he thinks of consulting a medical man. My Lord answers roughly that he is quite old enough to be capable of doctoring himself.

'As he makes this reply, the Courier appears, returning from the post.

My Lord gives him orders to go out again and buy some lemons. He proposes to try hot lemonade as a means of inducing perspiration in bed. In that way he has formerly cured colds, and in that way he will cure the cold from which he is suffering now.

'The Courier obeys in silence. Judging by appearances, he goes very reluctantly on this second errand.

'My Lord turns to the Baron (who has thus far taken no part in the conversation) and asks him, in a sneering tone, how much longer he proposes to prolong his stay in Venice. The Baron answers quietly, "Let us speak plainly to one another, my Lord. If you wish me to leave your house, you have only to say the word, and I go." My Lord turns to his wife, and asks if she can support the calamity of her brother's absence—laying a grossly insulting emphasis on the word "brother." The Countess preserves her impenetrable composure; nothing in her betrays the deadly hatred with which she regards the titled ruffian who has insulted her. "You are master in this house, my Lord," is all she says. "Do as you please."

'My Lord looks at his wife; looks at the Baron—and suddenly alters his tone. Does he perceive in the composure of the Countess and her brother something lurking under the surface that threatens him? This is at least certain, he makes a clumsy apology for the language that he has used. (Abject wretch!)

'My Lord's excuses are interrupted by the return of the Courier with the lemons and hot water.

'The Countess observes for the first time that the man looks ill. His hands tremble as he places the tray on the table. My Lord orders his Courier to follow him, and make the lemonade in the bedroom. The Countess remarks that the Courier seems hardly capable of obeying his orders. Hearing this, the man admits that he is ill. He, too, is suffering from a cold; he has been kept waiting in a draught at the shop where he bought the lemons; he feels alternately hot and cold, and he begs permission to lie down for a little while on his bed.

'Feeling her humanity appealed to, the Countess volunteers to make the lemonade herself. My Lord takes the Courier by the arm, leads him aside, and whispers these words to him: "Watch her, and see that she puts nothing into the lemonade; then bring it to me with your own hands; and, then, go to bed, if you like."

'Without a word more to his wife, or to the Baron, my Lord leaves the room.

'The Countess makes the lemonade, and the Courier takes it to his master.

'Returning, on the way to his own room, he is so weak, and feels, he says, so giddy, that he is obliged to support himself by the backs of the chairs as he passes them. The Baron, always considerate to persons of low degree, offers his arm. "I am afraid, my poor fellow," he says, "that you are really ill." The Courier makes this extraordinary answer: "It's all over with me, Sir: I have caught my death."

'The Countess is naturally startled. "You are not an old man," she says, trying to rouse the Courier's spirits. "At your age, catching cold doesn't surely mean catching your death?" The Courier fixes his eyes despairingly on the Countess.

"My lungs are weak, my Lady," he says; "I have already had two attacks of bronchitis. The second time, a great physician joined my own doctor in attendance on me. He considered my recovery almost in the light of a miracle. Take care of yourself," he said. "If you have a third attack of bronchitis, as certainly as two and two make four, you will be a dead man. I feel the same inward shivering, my Lady, that I felt on those two former occasions—and I tell you again, I have caught my death in Venice."

'Speaking some comforting words, the Baron leads him to his room. The Countess is left alone on the stage.

'She seats herself, and looks towards the door by which the Courier has been led out. "Ah! my poor fellow," she says, "if you could only change constitutions with my Lord, what a happy result would follow for the Baron and for me! If *you* could only get cured of a trumpery cold with a little hot lemonade, and if *he* could only catch his death in your place ——!"

'She suddenly pauses—considers for a while—and springs to her feet, with a cry of triumphant surprise: the wonderful, the unparalleled idea has crossed her mind like a flash of lightning. Make the two men change names and places—and the deed is done! Where are the obstacles? Remove my Lord (by fair means or foul) from his room; and keep him secretly prisoner in the palace, to live or die as future necessity may determine. Place the Courier in the vacant bed, and call in the doctor to see him—ill, in my Lord's character, and (if he dies) dying under my Lord's name!'

The manuscript dropped from Henry's hands. A sickening sense of horror overpowered him. The question which had occurred to his mind at the close of the First Act of the Play assumed a new and terrible interest now. As far as the scene of the Countess's soliloquy, the incidents of the Second Act had reflected the events of his late brother's life as faithfully as the incidents of the First Act. Was the monstrous plot, revealed in the lines which he had just read, the offspring of the Countess's morbid imagination? or had she, in this case also, deluded herself with the idea that she was inventing when she was really writing under the influence of her own guilty remembrances of the past? If the latter interpretation were the true one, he had just read the narrative of the contemplated murder of his brother, planned in cold blood by a woman who was at that moment inhabiting the same house with him. While, to make the fatality complete, Agnes herself had innocently provided the conspirators with the one man who was fitted to be the passive agent of their crime.

Even the bare doubt that it might be so was more than he could endure. He left his room; resolved to force the truth out of the Countess, or to denounce her before the authorities as a murderess at large.

Arrived at her door, he was met by a person just leaving the room. The person was the manager. He was hardly recognisable; he looked and spoke like a man in a state of desperation.

'Oh, go in, if you like!' he said to Henry. 'Mark this, sir! I am not a superstitious man; but I do begin to believe that crimes carry their own curse with them. This hotel is under a curse. What happens in the morning? We discover a crime committed in the old days of the palace. The night comes, and brings another dreadful event with it—a death; a sudden and shocking death, in the house. Go in, and see for yourself! I shall resign my situation, Mr. Westwick: I can't contend with the fatalities that pursue me here!'

Henry entered the room.

The Countess was stretched on her bed. The doctor on one side, and the chambermaid on the other, were standing looking at her. From time to time, she drew a heavy stertorous breath, like a person oppressed in sleeping. 'Is she likely to die?' Henry asked.

'She is dead,' the doctor answered. 'Dead of the rupture of a blood-vessel on the brain. Those sounds that you hear are purely mechanical—they may go on for hours.'

Henry looked at the chambermaid. She had little to tell. The Countess had refused to go to bed, and had placed herself at her desk to proceed with her writing. Finding it useless to remonstrate with her, the maid had left the room to speak to the manager. In the shortest possible time, the doctor was summoned to the hotel, and found the Countess dead on the floor. There was this to tell—and no more.

Looking at the writing-table as he went out, Henry saw the sheet of paper on which the Countess had traced her last lines of writing. The characters were almost illegible. Henry could just distinguish the words, 'First Act,' and 'Persons of the Drama.' The lost wretch had been thinking of her Play to the last, and had begun it all over again!

## CHAPTER XXVII

Henry returned to his room.

His first impulse was to throw aside the manuscript, and never to look at it again. The one chance of relieving his mind from the dreadful uncertainty that oppressed it, by obtaining positive evidence of the truth, was a chance annihilated by the Countess's death. What good purpose could be served, what relief could he anticipate, if he read more?

He walked up and down the room. After an interval, his thoughts took a new direction; the question of the manuscript presented itself under another point of view. Thus far, his reading had only informed him that the conspiracy had been planned. How did he know that the plan had been put in execution?

The manuscript lay just before him on the floor. He hesitated; then picked it up; and, returning to the table, read on as follows, from the point at which he had left off.

'While the Countess is still absorbed in the bold yet simple combination of circumstances which she has discovered, the Baron returns. He takes a serious view of the case of the Courier; it may be necessary, he thinks, to send for medical advice. No servant is left in the palace, now the English maid has taken her departure. The Baron himself must fetch the doctor, if the doctor is really needed.

' "Let us have medical help, by all means," his sister replies. "But wait and hear something that I have to say to you first." She then electrifies the Baron by communicating her idea to him. What danger of discovery have they to dread? My Lord's life in Venice has been a life of absolute seclusion: nobody but his banker knows him, even by personal appearance. He has presented his letter of credit as a perfect stranger; and he and his banker have never seen each other since that first visit. He has given no parties, and gone to no parties. On the few occasions when he has hired a gondola or taken a walk, he has always been alone. Thanks to the atrocious suspicion which makes him ashamed of being seen with his wife, he has led the very life which makes the proposed enterprise easy of accomplishment.

'The cautious Baron listens—but gives no positive opinion, as yet. "See what you can do with the Courier," he says; "and I will decide when I hear the result. One valuable hint I may give you before you go. Your man is easily tempted by money—if you only offer him enough. The other day, I asked him, in jest, what he would do for a thousand pounds. He answered, 'Anything.' Bear that in mind; and offer your highest bid without bargaining."

'The scene changes to the Courier's room, and shows the poor wretch with a photographic portrait of his wife in his hand, crying. The Countess enters.

'She wisely begins by sympathising with her contemplated accomplice. He is duly grateful; he confides his sorrows to his gracious mistress. Now that he believes himself to be on his death-bed, he feels remorse for his neglectful treatment of his wife. He could resign himself to die; but despair overpowers him when he remembers that he has saved no money, and that he will leave his widow, without resources, to the mercy of the world.

'On this hint, the Countess speaks. "Suppose you were asked to do a perfectly easy thing," she says; "and suppose you were rewarded for doing it by a present of a thousand pounds, as a legacy for your widow?"

'The Courier raises himself on his pillow, and looks at the Countess with an expression of incredulous surprise. She can hardly be cruel enough (he thinks) to joke with a man in his miserable plight. Will she say plainly what this perfectly easy thing is, the doing of which will meet with such a magnificent reward?

'The Countess answers that question by confiding her project to the Courier, without the slightest reserve.

'Some minutes of silence follow when she has done. The Courier is not weak enough yet to speak without stopping to think first. Still keeping his eyes on the Countess, he makes a quaintly insolent remark on what he has just heard. "I have not hitherto been a religious man; but I feel myself on the way to it. Since your ladyship has spoken to me, I believe in the Devil." It is the Countess's interest to see the humorous side of this confession of faith. She takes no offence. She only says, "I will give you half an hour by yourself, to think over my proposal. You are in danger of death. Decide, in your wife's interests, whether you will die worth nothing, or die worth a thousand pounds."

'Left alone, the Courier seriously considers his position—and decides. He rises with difficulty; writes a few lines on a leaf taken from his pocketbook; and, with slow and faltering steps, leaves the room.

'The Countess, returning at the expiration of the half-hour's interval, finds the room empty. While she is wondering, the Courier opens the door. What has he been doing out of his bed? He answers, "I have been protecting my own life, my lady, on the bare chance that I may recover from the bronchitis for the third time. If you or the Baron attempts to hurry me out of this world, or to deprive me of my thousand pounds reward, I shall tell the doctor where he will find a few lines of writing, which describe your ladyship's plot. I may not have strength enough, in the case supposed, to betray you by making a complete confession with my own lips; but I can employ my last breath to speak the half-dozen words which will tell the doctor where he is to look. Those words, it is needless to add, will be addressed to your Ladyship, if I find your engagements towards me faithfully kept."

'With this audacious preface, he proceeds to state the conditions on which he will play his part in the conspiracy, and die (if he does die) worth a thousand pounds.

'Either the Countess or the Baron are to taste the food and drink brought to his bedside, in his presence, and even the medicines which the doctor may prescribe for him. As for the promised sum of money, it is to be produced in one bank-note, folded in a sheet of paper, on which a line is to be written, dictated by the Courier. The two enclosures are then to be sealed up in an envelope, addressed to his wife, and stamped ready for the post. This done, the letter is to be placed under his pillow; the Baron or the Countess being at liberty to satisfy themselves, day by day, at their own time, that the letter remains in its place, with the seal unbroken, as long as the doctor has any hope of his patient's recovery. The last stipulation follows. The Courier has a conscience; and with a view to keeping it easy, insists that he shall be left in ignorance of that part of the plot which relates to the sequestration of my Lord. Not that he cares particularly what becomes of his miserly master—but he does dislike taking other people's responsibilities on his own shoulders.

'These conditions being agreed to, the Countess calls in the Baron, who has been waiting events in the next room.

'He is informed that the Courier has yielded to temptation; but he is still too cautious to make any compromising remarks. Keeping his back turned on the bed, he shows a bottle to the Countess. It is labelled "Chloroform." She understands that my Lord is to be removed from his room in a convenient state of insensibility. In what part of the palace is he to be hidden? As they open the door to go out, the Countess whispers that question to the Baron. The Baron whispers back, "In the vaults!" The curtain falls.'

# CHAPTER XXVIII

So the Second Act ended.

Turning to the Third Act, Henry looked wearily at the pages as he let them slip through his fingers. Both in mind and body, he began to feel the need of repose.

In one important respect, the later portion of the manuscript differed from the pages which he had just been reading. Signs of an overwrought brain showed themselves, here and there, as the outline of the play approached its end. The handwriting grew worse and worse. Some of the longer sentences were left unfinished. In the exchange of dialogue, questions and answers were not always attributed respectively to the right speaker. At certain intervals the writer's failing intelligence seemed to recover itself for a while; only to relapse again, and to lose the thread of the narrative more hopelessly than ever.

After reading one or two of the more coherent passages Henry recoiled from the ever-darkening horror of the story. He closed the manuscript, heartsick and exhausted, and threw himself on his bed to rest. The door opened almost at the same moment. Lord Montbarry entered the room.

'We have just returned from the Opera,' he said; 'and we have heard the news of that miserable woman's death. They say you spoke to her in her last moments; and I want to hear how it happened.'

'You shall hear how it happened,' Henry answered; 'and more than that. You are now the head of the family, Stephen; and I feel bound, in the position which oppresses me, to leave you to decide what ought to be done.'

With those introductory words, he told his brother how the Countess's play had come into his hands. 'Read the first few pages,' he said. 'I am anxious to know whether the same impression is produced on both of us.'

Before Lord Montbarry had got half-way through the First Act, he stopped, and looked at his brother. 'What does she mean by boasting of this as her own invention?' he asked. 'Was she too crazy to remember that these things really happened?'

This was enough for Henry: the same impression had been produced on both of them. 'You will do as you please,' he said. 'But if you will be guided by me, spare yourself the reading of those pages to come, which describe our brother's terrible expiation of his heartless marriage.'

'Have *you* read it all, Henry?'

'Not all. I shrank from reading some of the latter part of it. Neither you nor I saw much of our elder brother after we left school; and, for my part, I felt, and never scrupled to express my feeling, that he behaved infamously to Agnes. But when I read that unconscious confession of the murderous conspiracy to which he fell a victim, I remembered, with something like remorse, that the same mother bore us. I have felt for him to-night, what I am ashamed to think I never felt for him before.'

Lord Montbarry took his brother's hand.

'You are a good fellow, Henry,' he said; 'but are you quite sure that you have not been needlessly distressing yourself? Because some of this crazy creature's writing accidentally tells what we know to be the truth, does it follow that all the rest is to be relied on to the end?'

'There is no possible doubt of it,' Henry replied.

'No possible doubt?' his brother repeated. 'I shall go on with my reading, Henry—and see what justification there may be for that confident conclusion of yours.'

He read on steadily, until he had reached the end of the Second Act. Then he looked up.

'Do you really believe that the mutilated remains which you discovered this morning are the remains of our brother?' he asked. 'And do you believe it on such evidence as this?'

Henry answered silently by a sign in the affirmative.

Lord Montbarry checked himself—evidently on the point of entering an indignant protest.

'You acknowledge that you have not read the later scenes of the piece,' he said. 'Don't be childish, Henry! If you persist in pinning your faith on such stuff as this, the least you can do is to make yourself thoroughly acquainted with it. Will you read the Third Act? No? Then I shall read it to you.'

He turned to the Third Act, and ran over those fragmentary passages which were clearly enough written and expressed to be intelligible to the mind of a stranger.

'Here is a scene in the vaults of the palace,' he began. 'The victim of the conspiracy is sleeping on his miserable bed; and the Baron and the Countess are considering the position in which they stand. The Countess (as well as I can make it out) has raised the money that is wanted by borrowing on the security of her jewels at Frankfort; and the Courier upstairs is still declared by the Doctor to have a chance of recovery. What are the conspirators to do, if the man does recover? The cautious Baron suggests setting the prisoner free. If he ventures to appeal to the law, it is easy to declare that he is subject to insane delusion, and to call his own wife as witness. On the other hand, if the Courier dies, how is the sequestrated and unknown nobleman to be put out of the way? Passively, by letting him starve in his prison? No: the Baron is a man of refined tastes; he dislikes needless cruelty. The active policy remains—say, assassination by the knife of a hired bravo? The Baron objects to trusting an accomplice; also to spending money on anyone but himself. Shall they drop their prisoner into the canal? The Baron declines to trust water; water will show him on the surface. Shall they set his bed on fire? An excellent idea; but the smoke might be seen. No: the circumstances being now entirely altered, poisoning him presents the easiest way out of it. He has simply become a superfluous person. The cheapest poison will do.—Is it possible, Henry, that you believe this consultation really took place?'

Henry made no reply. The succession of the questions that had just been read to him, exactly followed the succession of the dreams that had terrified Mrs. Norbury, on the two nights which she had passed in the hotel. It was useless to point out this coincidence to his brother. He only said, 'Go on.'

Lord Montbarry turned the pages until he came to the next intelligible passage.

'Here,' he proceeded, 'is a double scene on the stage—so far as I can understand the sketch of it. The Doctor is upstairs, innocently writing his certificate of my Lord's decease, by the dead Courier's bedside. Down in the vaults, the Baron stands by the corpse of the poisoned lord, preparing the strong chemical acids which are to reduce it to a heap of ashes—Surely, it is not worth while to trouble ourselves with deciphering such melodramatic horrors as these? Let us get on! let us get on!'

He turned the leaves again; attempting vainly to discover the meaning of the confused scenes that followed. On the last page but one, he found the last intelligible sentences.

'The Third Act seems to be divided,' he said, 'into two Parts or Tableaux. I think I can read the writing at the beginning of the Second Part. The Baron and the Countess open the scene. The Baron's hands are mysteriously concealed by gloves. He has reduced the body to ashes by his own system of cremation, with the exception of the head — —'

Henry interrupted his brother there. 'Don't read any more!' he exclaimed.

'Let us do the Countess justice,' Lord Montbarry persisted. 'There are not half a dozen lines more that I can make out! The accidental breaking of his jar of acid has burnt the Baron's hands severely. He is still unable to proceed to the destruction of the head—and the Countess is woman enough (with all her wickedness) to shrink from attempting to take his place—when the first news is received of the coming arrival of the commission of inquiry despatched by the insurance offices. The Baron feels no alarm. Inquire as the commission may, it is the natural death of the Courier (in my Lord's character) that they are blindly investigating. The head not being destroyed, the obvious alternative is to hide it—and the Baron is equal to the occasion. His studies in the old library have informed him of a safe place of concealment in the palace. The Countess may recoil from handling the acids and watching the process of cremation; but she can surely sprinkle a little disinfecting powder ——'

'No more!' Henry reiterated. 'No more!'

'There is no more that can be read, my dear fellow. The last page looks like sheer delirium. She may well have told you that her invention had failed her!'

'Face the truth honestly, Stephen, and say her memory.'

Lord Montbarry rose from the table at which he had been sitting, and looked at his brother with pitying eyes.

'Your nerves are out of order, Henry,' he said. 'And no wonder, after that frightful discovery under the hearth-stone. We won't dispute about it; we will wait a day or two until you are quite yourself again. In the meantime, let us understand each other on one point at least. You leave the question of what is to be done with these pages of writing to me, as the head of the family?'

'I do.'

Lord Montbarry quietly took up the manuscript, and threw it into the fire. 'Let this rubbish be of some use,' he said, holding the pages down with the poker. 'The room is getting chilly—the Countess's play will set some of these charred logs flaming again.' He waited a little at the fireplace, and returned to his brother. 'Now, Henry, I have a last word to say, and then I have done. I am ready to admit that you have stumbled, by an unlucky chance, on the proof of a crime committed in the old days of the palace, nobody knows how long ago. With that one concession, I dispute everything else. Rather than agree in the opinion you have formed, I won't believe anything that has happened. The supernatural influences that some of us felt when we first slept in this hotel—your loss of appetite, our sister's dreadful dreams, the smell that overpowered Francis, and the head that appeared to Agnes—I declare them all to be sheer delusions! I believe in nothing, nothing, nothing!' He opened the door to go out, and looked back into the room. 'Yes,' he resumed, 'there is one thing I believe in. My wife has committed a breach of confidence—I believe Agnes will marry you. Good night, Henry. We leave Venice the first thing to-morrow morning.'

So Lord Montbarry disposed of the mystery of The Haunted Hotel.

## POSTSCRIPT

A last chance of deciding the difference of opinion between the two brothers remained in Henry's possession. He had his own idea of the use to which he might put the false teeth as a means of inquiry when he and his fellow-travellers returned to England.

The only surviving depositary of the domestic history of the family in past years, was Agnes Lockwood's old nurse. Henry took his first opportunity of trying to revive her personal recollections of the deceased Lord Montbarry. But the nurse had never forgiven the great man of the family for his desertion of Agnes; she flatly refused to consult her memory. 'Even the bare sight of my lord, when I last saw him in London,' said the old woman, 'made my finger-nails itch to set their mark on his face. I was sent on an errand by Miss Agnes; and I met him coming out of his dentist's door—and, thank God, that's the last I ever saw of him!'

Thanks to the nurse's quick temper and quaint way of expressing herself, the object of Henry's inquiries was gained already! He ventured on asking if she had noticed the situation of the house. She had noticed, and still remembered the situation—did Master Henry suppose she had lost the use of her senses, because she happened to be nigh on eighty years old? The same day, he took the false teeth to the dentist, and set all further doubt (if doubt had still been possible) at rest for ever. The teeth had been made for the first Lord Montbarry.

Henry never revealed the existence of this last link in the chain of discovery to any living creature, his brother Stephen included. He carried his terrible secret with him to the grave.

There was one other event in the memorable past on which he preserved the same compassionate silence. Little Mrs. Ferrari never knew that her husband had been—not, as she supposed, the Countess's victim—but the Countess's accomplice. She still believed that the late Lord Montbarry had sent her the thousand-pound note, and still recoiled from making use of a present which she persisted in declaring had 'the stain of her husband's blood on it.' Agnes, with the widow's entire approval, took the money to the Children's Hospital; and spent it in adding to the number of the beds.

In the spring of the new year, the marriage took place. At the special request of Agnes, the members of the family were the only persons present at the ceremony. There was no wedding breakfast—and the honeymoon was spent in the retirement of a cottage on the banks of the Thames.

During the last few days of the residence of the newly married couple by the riverside, Lady Montbarry's children were invited to enjoy a day's play in the garden. The eldest girl overheard (and reported to her mother) a little conjugal dialogue which touched on the topic of The Haunted Hotel.

'Henry, I want you to give me a kiss.'

'There it is, my dear.'

'Now I am your wife, may I speak to you about something?'

'What is it?'

'Something that happened the day before we left Venice. You saw the

'*Let this rubbish be of some use.*'

Countess, during the last hours of her life. Won't you tell me whether she made any confession to you?'

'No conscious confession, Agnes—and therefore no confession that I need distress you by repeating.'

'Did she say nothing about what she saw or heard, on that dreadful night in my room?'

'Nothing. We only know that her mind never recovered the terror of it.'

Agnes was not quite satisfied. The subject troubled her. Even her own brief intercourse with her miserable rival of other days suggested questions that perplexed her. She remembered the Countess's prediction. 'You have to bring me to the day of discovery, and to the punishment that is my doom.' Had the prediction simply failed, like other mortal prophecies?—or had it been fulfilled on the terrible night when she had seen the apparition, and when she had innocently tempted the Countess to watch her in her room?

Let it, however, be recorded, among the other virtues of Mrs. Henry Westwick, that she never again attempted to persuade her husband into betraying his secrets. Other men's wives, hearing of this extraordinary conduct (and being trained in the modern school of morals and manners), naturally regarded her with compassionate contempt. They spoke of Agnes, from that time forth, as 'rather an old-fashioned person.'

Is that all?

That is all.

Is there no explanation of the mystery of The Haunted Hotel?

Ask yourself if there is any explanation of the mystery of your own life and death.—Farewell.

# THE
# HAUNTED
# HOUSE
# AT
# LATCHFORD

by *Mrs. J. H. Riddell*

# CHAPTER I

## MR. H. STAFFORD TREVOR, BARRISTER-AT-LAW, INTRODUCED BY HIMSELF

No one who has met me in society will be in the least degree astonished when he, or haply she, hears I have at length decided to appear before the British, American, Foreign, and Colonial public, as a writer of tales.

I am one of those people concerning whom partial friends remark: "He can do anything he likes."

Considering the number of people about whom the same observation is made, it is painful to reflect how few must like to do anything.

It is late in life, no doubt, for me to take to a new profession, but having been most courteously asked to contribute to the literature of my country, I feel it impossible to refuse.

Besides, at the present time, literature is the fashion, and I have always tried to be in the fashion. I am perpetually meeting young men, and (more especially) young women, who are the precocious parents of books more or less absurd, inane, objectionable, recondite, who have new views about morals, religion, Moses, and Catherine of Russia, and am expected to derive pleasure from their acquaintance.

For the future when people meet me, they can go home and mention that amongst the company at Mr. So and So's, was Mr. Stafford Trevor, the author.

At how cheap a rate can we confer pleasure! It gives quite a zest to the idea of writing this story to reflect the amount of gratification friends and enemies (supposing I have any of the latter) will extract from the narrative and the author.

As I have already remarked, the fact of my turning author will surprise no one. Often after I have repeated some of my best stories for the benefit of a single listener, he has inquired:

"Why, Mr. Trevor, do you not reproduce all these good things in a book?"

Had I been quite frank, I should have informed him I refrained from doing so because, in fact, the good things were not mine to reproduce; but as he would have disbelieved my statement, I never thought it worth while to enlighten him on the subject.

Now, however, it so happens I have a little story all my own to relate, I consent to appearing in print.

Besides other people, places, and things, the story concerns a place called Fairy Water, and a lady of whom I was and am very fond, a cousin of mine by marriage—that is to say, she married my cousin Geoffrey Trevor, and he left her a widow, whereon hangs a tale—that I am about to tell.

Naturally, however, before I say much about Mr. Geoffrey Trevor, I wish to state, and the reader wishes to hear, some facts relating to myself.

The world nowadays is extremely curious concerning genius. Whether this curiosity arises from any abstract interest in genius, or a belief that genius is to be caught like small-pox, fever, whooping-cough, or the measles, it would be presumptuous in me to decide.

Certain, however, it is, that the smallest details of the domestic life, habits, manners, modes of thought of eminent people are listened to with a rapt attention wonderful to contemplate; and many of my own later successes in life I can trace to the fact of being able to tell enthusiastic ladies that Mr. A——'s novel, which drew tears from so many eyes, was absolutely a photograph from life—his own; that in spite of the Bohemianism of her plots, Mrs. B—— is a devoted wife and affectionate mother; that Mr. C——, whose style is neat and epigrammatic, suggestive of a quiet study, can write anywhere, under any circumstances.

"Give him a waiting room at the Paddington Station full of people, an express train; the wilds of Connemara, or the snowy peaks of Switzerland; it is immaterial; his sentences will be as finished, his sentences as complete," I say, in my best manner.

Concerning Mr. D——, I am only able to state, with a reserve which elicits the remark that I am such a dear satirical creature, whenever he brings out a new book he flies to the Continent for fear of seeing a bad review, which is, indeed, a simple impossibility, unless a new race of reviewers should spring up ignorant of the traditions of the elders.

Mrs. E——, I tell my neighbour in strict confidence, draws her ideas of life from going disguised as a sister of mercy through St. Giles' in the morning, and finishing the day, not disguised, at a supper-house near the theatres. As for Miss F——, I state, when she girds up her loins to write a book, she clothes herself in white, drinks *eau sucrée*, and refuses to eat her meals like an ordinary mortal.

Thus I go through the alphabet, and each hearer in succession tries, I believe, the white dress, and the *eau sucrée,* and the sister of mercy business, in hopes that by such eccentricities she too may be able to make some fabulous sum per volume, per page, per line.

And why, then, if the limited public I meet at dinners, at lawn-parties, at kettledrums, at crowded evenings, delight to listen to such weak details of the minor doings of great people; why, I ask, should the general public not care to hear of the great doings of a small man like myself?

If there is one thing about me which ought to win praise, it is this—I am non-assuming.

I never put down a man nor condescend to a woman; I am not clever, or sarcastic, or energetic, or anything except useful.

There you have me in a nutshell. If I have been anything in my life I have been useful. If I have not been useful I have been nothing.

Permit me to explain. I have not been a drudge, not useful in the cart-horse and maid-of-all-work sense, but useful as flowers, as music, as perfume, as colour, as sunshine, as painting, as trees in the distance, as water in the foreground.

I have been ornamentally useful; I have filled up corners in the world's economy which must, otherwise, have remained hideously bare of bud and blossom, and the world has evidenced extreme gratitude for my trouble.

When I am gone to swell the ranks of that "great majority," of which a daily paper, more funny than any comic periodical, speaks in terms of intimate familiarity, the world will perhaps forget me—indeed, I think it extremely probable the world may then have something else to do than remember me; but whilst I am still "in the lobby," to quote our comic friend once more, few of my acquaintances forget the fact of my existence; and to those I have not lately had the pleasure of meeting, the advertisement of this Annual will be an agreeable reminder that H. Stafford Trevor is up to the present hour in the minority.

Naturally, those persons whom I have not already the happiness of knowing will wish me to divide my personal explanation into two heads—viz. Who am I? Whence am I?

Truth compels me at this juncture to confess I have heard those two questions propounded ere now from the pulpit, but the reader may rest tranquil; I have no intention of analysing my own position, as an individual: I am about considering it in common with that society for which I live, and move, and have my being.

At the head of this chapter you have my profession. I am H. Stafford Trevor, barrister-at-law.

As a barrister-at-law I have done very little. Law is one of those things in which I might have achieved success had I liked, but then I did not like.

Once I overheard a man ask: "What does Trevor do?" to which his friend replied: "He dines out."

The creature who said this *is* a barrister-at-law, and his friends have decided he can do nothing; nevertheless, I am bound to confess he summed up the case neatly.

I do dine out. If I have a profession it is dining out; if upon any settled system I do anything, it is accepting invitations. That is how I am useful. Perhaps, reader, you are inclined to sneer at this; but before you sneer, pause, and let me ask—

"Do you ever dine out?"

"No," you answer, for two reasons. I may say one, expressed, "You would not if you could"; the second, and more cogent, non-expressed, "You could not if you would."

Now I can: that is one of the things I have liked to do; and it is an accomplished fact, more dinners have been graced by my presence than you could well count; but as the lesser is included in the greater, there are many things included in the art of dining out.

First, you wish to know how I managed to get invited to so many houses, that my face is as well known to butlers, footmen, and—yes—why should I hesitate?—hired waiters, as that of Mr. D'Israeli is to the readers of *Punch*.

Ah, friend, Rome was not built in a day, and many a year of my life has gone in making myself free of London society.

There is a fate in these things. By all rules, known and unknown, I ought to have been a doctor jingling guineas, or a barrister making his way to the Woolsack, or a professor discovering all sorts of unpleasant natural facts, or solving an equal number of useless scientific problems; but genius knows no law. As Turner was born a painter, Beethoven a composer, Grisi a singer, and Palmer a poisoner, so I was born a diner out.

It is not given to everyone to find out his especial talent in early youth, and there was a period of my life when I not merely studied law, but frequented evening parties.

As we see the needle oscillating violently when its equilibrium is disturbed, so I went from reading to dancing, and dancing to reading, with a distracted mind.

I felt unhappy, restless, dissatisfied; I had not found my vocation. Even when I was first inducted into its mysteries, I failed—such is the occasional modesty of genius—to perceive that success lay that way. I had doubts, qualms, throes. I questioned my own fitness for the career—I overrated the gifts possessed by others—I underrated my own; but that is all gone and passed.

Many men can write, paint, sing, talk, conduct business affairs, shine as orators, rise to eminence at the bar, lead armies to victory or death, command vessels, grow fat oxen and fatter sheep, but there are few, indeed, who can dine out. I can; that inane barrister was right: I dine out. I have dined out since I was twenty-five years of age. I shall go on dining out till Death knocks loudly, and tells me to make haste and come with him; or till I grow old and feeble, and one I wot of brings me gruel and other like abominations, which, however, her gentle voice and my growing infirmities may then make bearable.

But bah! why should I look forward? Has she not but just left me saying I grow younger with the years? Is not her kiss—it seems so strange for a woman's lips to touch my face, that I feel as if she must have left a mark, still visible on my cheek. It is all about her and somebody else this story has to be told; so I must hasten onward; and to hasten on, as is the way of those who are—well—who are not so young as they were at twenty-five, I must go back.

My father was a wonderfully clever man! He was one of those people whom the world thinks so much of, and his family consider as only a degree better than an idiot. Amongst his fellow-professors he was an authority; at home his second wife treated him like a child. There was not a secret in the heavens above, the earth below, and the waters under the earth, with which he did not believe himself to be *au courant*; but he never knew where his spectacles were—no, not when they were elevated on his forehead; he did not detect the fraud when I took him a branch of gorse, decked with laurustine blossoms, and introduced it to his notice as a new and curious wild flower I had discovered on Hampstead Heath; he could not imagine why his flute—on which it was his mild pleasure to accompany the pianoforte and harp performances of two limp old maids of our acquaintance—on one occasion refused to give forth any sound save a gurgling groan, till my stepmother found the end of it was plugged up with a cork; in short, a theoretical man who, never having had any business to marry at all, found himself at forty a widower with one son, and then married for the second time a woman utterly dowerless, who bore him various children, who have no connection whatsoever with this narrative.

There are various ways in which a parent may be useful to one. In my capacity the professor has been infinitely useful to me, and has made by his memory many a dinner-party more agreeable than he ever made the social board at home.

His first wife, my mother, had a modest fortune. Happily it was secured to her children. She had no children, only a child, a son; and at twenty-one I found myself a man easy as regarded money matters, and possessed of a father totally indifferent as to what I did or left undone, so long as I did not trouble him with my affairs, or contradict him when any of his pet theories chanced to be on the carpet.

I was a model son. He spent his last breath in blessing me.

"You have never contradicted me, Hercules," he whispered, pressing my hand. Dear, simple old man. If he only would come back and sit with me in the twilight I would not contradict him, supposing he pleased to tell me fire was not hot or ice cold.

Negative qualities are often accounted great virtues. In the later years of my father's lifetime, silence and consent seemed grateful where many words usually broke the stillness, and acquiescence was a thing almost unknown.

"I ought never to have married," he said to me once, piteously.

The result of his first mistake in that line, I profited by his experience. I have never married.

The feminine reader has already decided this point. Had I married I could not have dined out.

But you wish to know how I gained the power of dining out. I tell you it was my speciality; once the opportunity occurred for me to distinguish myself, my genius, not my other self, achieved success.

"What a nice, modest young man Mr. Stafford Trevor is," said my hostess. She has told me all this since.

That is a long time ago. I have been nice, modest, self-possessed, well-bred, handsome, clever, sarcastic, good-natured in the interim; now I am useful. The world, my world, could little spare a better man. Old friends welcome me for the sake of Auld Lang Syne, to speak in the hideous idiom of a people whose accent I detest, and whose ways are abhorrent to me—one degree less abhorrent only than their primitive ballads, always suggestive of the screech of a bagpipe. Young couples welcome me for the sake of the dead and gone; people whose position is assured, because, like dear Lady Mary, who plays a little part in this story, it is quite safe to whisper secret scandals, and the latest and most wicked *bon mot* in my ear; and the *nouveau riche*, because, poor wretches, they believe I must be somebody.

They see me apparently on equal terms with those who dine off silver and gold, and call all the upper ten thousand friends, and some of them relations, and they rush to conclusions.

If I cared much for their heavy repasts, or their insufferable time-serving, I should fear for my future; but both are growing wearisome.

Give me rather impertinent, ugly, vulgar Lady Mary, who calling me, as is her pleasant habit, by my christian-name, will say:

"I always knew you meant to have it out of us, Stafford, but it is of no use. Till *we* can produce an author—not an outsider—not one like you, introduced by accident and tolerated on sufferance—the English public will not understand the demerits of the nobility. And that will be never. *We* never have produced a novelist, and, mark my words, Stafford, *we never will.*"

In which opinion that I shall certainly hear announced I quite agree with her ladyship.

Though, upon the whole, I am disposed to doubt whether the lower ten millions have so much the advantage as Lady Mary sometimes seems to imply.

The capacity for producing fools is not, I fear, confined to any class. That, I am convinced, can scarcely, seeing what one sees, be considered a monopoly. Would to heaven it were!

## CHAPTER II

### I ASSIST AT A WEDDING

It is curious how the traditions of one's youth influence the actions of our later years.

When I was an extremely small child I heard some person remark that strawberries preserved the whiteness of the teeth. Sedulously each season since I attained my majority I have eaten strawberries. When people left London earlier than they do now, I partook of them in the gardens of my

father's cousin, Admiral Trevor; subsequently, when his son succeeded to
the small property which gives a title to this story, I went down each
summer, and eat strawberries as I might join in some religious rite; and
now that Parliament unhappily sits later and later, and that pleasant dinner-parties obtain to the very end of the season, far past Midsummer-day,
the fruit—small, sweet, fresh, utterly unlike anything one can buy at Cov-
ent Garden—comes to me in dainty baskets, embowered in cool green
leaves, from Fairy Water.

"And where is Fairy Water?" you ask.

Dear reader, every person has his secret, and the *locale* of Fairy Water is
mine. About this time in each year I begin to dream of it, but I am not
bound to tell my dreams to all the world.

I will describe it to you as I saw it first in the reign of Admiral Trevor, a
quaint building seen from the avenue: a long, low cottage, overgrown with
wistaria and ivy, with climbing roses, and Virginian creepers, and jasmine,
and honeysuckle, all tangled together.

"A poor place, though picturesque," you say.

Wait a little—wait till having entered the large, though low, square hall,
and passed through the drawing-room and conservatory, you emerge on
the western front, where all delicious plants climb along the verandah;
where myrtles shed their blossoms on grass which slopes down to the
loveliest sheet of water ever contrived by human skill; where the ash and
the willow droop over lawns smooth and soft as velvet; where great trees
shade the winding walks; and within and without peace reigns—such peace
as is to be found in very few homes on the face of this quarrelsome earth.

That is where I used to eat my strawberries, that is the place whence
they are sent to me now. There was a time when even at Fairy Water they
lost their relish, and I will tell you why. It happened in this wise: one day,
in an abrupt note, my second cousin, Captain Trevor, son of the admiral
formerly alluded to and deceased, informed me he was about to get married.

To most men this announcement would have been disagreeable. If he
died unmarried, Fairy Water must come to me; and to the generality of
persons, no doubt, Fairy Water would have seemed a desirable inheritance,
but to me certainly not. What should I have done with the place? It would
have cost money to keep up; the expense must have proved a source of
eternal worry to me. I know within a trifle what I shall have to pay my
landlady, at the end of each month, for breakfast, washing, and lodging;
but how should I ever know, without employing a professional accountant, or going through the Bankruptcy Court, whether a place in the
country, with lawns, flower-gardens—stables, and horses in them—pigstyes,
and pigs in them—poultry-houses, and fowls in them—a sheet of water, and
swans on it—to say nothing of Aylesbury ducks, were producing a profit or
loss?

I want no secluded dwelling before I repair to one quiet enough in all
conscience, where the landlord and the collectors may knock till they

break their knuckles, without injuring the peace of my repose. Let others have what suits them; for me a first floor in a vague western district is sufficient. I should say a second, but from my youth climbing many stairs has been distasteful to me.

Further, to revert to the Fairy Water question, I fear I should prove but a poor host if heaven ever gave me the means to enact the part. Some persons can dine out, and others can give dinners; but, as a rule, I do not think the best giver of dinners is the best diner out; a different set of qualities is required in each. An admirable host is often a poor guest; an admirable guest often proves a wretched, incompetent host.

Unless, indeed, in Bohemian society, where the two qualities, like others equally incongruous, are sometimes, though not always, united. But, then, of what use is it referring to that vague, beautiful land, which is as a fairy country to one not free of it by nature or inheritance?

For myself I have visited the place, and am bound to confess I found it exceedingly beautiful, spite of the spectacle of duns, debts, and writs; but I do not know how the inhabitants manage to sustain life. Dining out may seem a mere matter of chance, but I could not dine out if I once proclaimed myself so total a creature of circumstances as the dear delightful inhabitants of the London city of Prague.

Some try to reduce Bohemianism to a science, but they fail, and they will fail. To be liked, Bohemianism must be pure and simple. The Bohemian must have no *arrière pensée* when he hobnobs with my lord; and his wife, if her husband is to prove successful, had better leave the mutual and to-be-provided-for olive branches hanging to the parent tree if the nobility and others are to be favourably impressed.

I have dined so often at houses in which everything has been solid from the furniture to the plate, that, when I find myself at the table of a man who has to get everything he sets before his guests on credit, and whose chance of ever being able to pay for the repast is extremely remote, an odd sense of wonder is perpetually cropping up in my mind as I watch that man and his friends making merry over a banquet which has for an unbidden guest the skeleton—Debt.

I cannot understand the nature of a host able to eat, drink, make jests, laugh at the jests of others to-day, when all the time he must feel tolerably certain of being arrested at some not very remote to-morrow; and yet I am bound to say that never, even when gold and silver dishes have lent an unpleasant flavour to food, can I remember such dinners as I have seen served on stone-china, with wit for *sauce piquante.*

Only in that vague region the meats are secondary to the wine, and the few morning headaches which I ever experienced have always followed excursions into Bohemia.

Perhaps, as one of the race suggested, these may be induced by too much laughter; such exercise being strange to me and unwonted. This remark contained a sneer, no doubt, for at the houses where I dine out ebullitions of merriment would be considered bad form.

As Eastern grandees do not dance for themselves, so people in the upper walks of society in England do not laugh for themselves. It may be all very well for persons who have to earn their livings by laughter and jesting, as it may be well for an acrobat to stand on his head; but the possessor of ten thousand a year and upwards should maintain a gravity of manner and stateliness of deportment commensurate to the dignity fate has conferred upon him, and as a rule he does this.

To add that occasionally he overdoes it is but to say that he is human.

But I am wandering away from Fairy Water. Let me return to the swans of that enchanted lake—to the Aylesbury ducks, which turn up such plump breasts on the hospitable board, and, with a rare generosity, fatten themselves in readiness for that season of the year when green peas are most tender and succulent.

Much as I loved the place I never longed to possess it. I was in the position of the Frenchman, who, having lost his wife, was asked if he intended to marry a lady he had been in the constant habit of visiting.

"*Ma foi!*" he said, "where should I then spend my evenings?"

And, in faith, had Fairy Water come down, where should I have spent my holidays?

As a guest I delighted in Fairy Water; as a host I should have grown to loathe the place.

It was well I thought so—for I had always expected to step into Captain Trevor's shoes.

He was that rare phenomenon, a sea-monster—an ugly, ill-tempered, cross-grained brute, who bawled at the servants as if a perpetual hurricane were blowing through the house; and who was as much disliked by all his inferiors in station, as his father, the admiral, had been beloved by those below him in rank.

Further, he was fifteen years older than myself, and had lived fast and drank hard so long as gout, the only thing which ever obtained a mastery over him, would permit.

It would not have astonished me any morning to hear he was dead; but to hear he was about to be married certainly proved a surprise.

He had always been civil to me. So far as he was capable of the feeling, I think he had a liking for Staff—so he persisted in abbreviating my name; and therefore, though his news appeared astounding, his request that I would be the best man on the occasion seemed nothing extraordinary.

I consented; ordered a new suit of clothes, bought a wedding present—the expense of which I secretly grudged; and on the day before that fixed for the wedding went down to Winchelsea, near which cheerful town the lady, as he gave me to understand, resided.

There is a funny little inn at Winchelsea, the windows of which over-look the principal, and I think only, square of the town, which happens to be the churchyard likewise, and here Geoffrey and I took up our quarters for the night.

Naturally I wished to know something about the bride elect, and asked her name.

"Mary Ashwell," he answered. "Her people, however, call her Polly, and I daresay I shall do the same."

I thought this over for a moment. There was a friskiness about the *sobriquet* which gave me an idea of an elderly young lady with a red nose, a flat chest, a long neck, light eyes, and ringlets.

"She has a pot of money, no doubt?" I suggested.

"Not a shilling. Her father was once comfortably off, I believe, but he is as poor now as a church mouse."

"Oh, then she has a father ——"

"And a mother," he condescended to add.

"Is she young?" I inquired, finding he did not seem inclined to volunteer further information.

"Well, you couldn't call her old," he said, wincing, as it seemed to me.

"Is she pretty?"

"I daresay you would not think her so—I do," was his reply; and this time I distinctly saw a dull red colour appear through the brown of his weather-beaten face, of which sign of emotion he seemed to be conscious, for he put his hand to his forehead so as to hide the flush.

I confess I was puzzled. Evidently he was ashamed of his choice; and yet what could have induced him to make it?

He was no longer young, it is true—indeed, he was growing elderly; but "surely," I thought, "he might have found somebody willing to marry him more suitable than a plain old maid, possessed of kitten-like proclivities and not possessed of sixpence."

I was not one half so much surprised to hear of the proposed marriage as I was at his evident dislike to speak of the bride. Of all the men I ever met, Geoffrey was the last I should have supposed likely to be taken in by a woman; but that he had been taken in was impossible to doubt, and I was confirmed in this impression when, in answer to some leading question, he said:

"You will see her to-morrow, and can then judge for yourself what she is like. I am tired now, so do not torment me with questions, Staff."

No pleasant dreams of Fairy Water visited my pillow that night. I had visions of a mistress not unlike a cruet bottle as to shape, and with mind and temper an even mixture of cayenne and vinegar.

"Stafford Trevor," I said, addressing myself as I stood next morning brushing my hair, "you will have to look out a new place at which to spend your holidays. No more cakes and ale at Fairy Water; black looks and scant courtesy are all you need expect when the new mistress comes to her own"; and having arrived at this conclusion, I walked into the sitting-room, feeling like a man who knows the worst and is prepared for it.

Geoffrey himself was nervous and uneasy, I could see that. He ate little breakfast, a sure sign with him of uneasiness of mind or sickness of body; and when he pushed away his cup he rose and paced the room, his hands buried deep in his pockets.

It was quite a relief when at last he said we ought to be going.

I looked at my watch, and saw it was twenty-five minutes past eleven, Greenwich time.

"They have a long way to drive, I suppose?" I remarked.

"Two miles," he answered.

"Madame's get-up requires both leisure and thought," was my mental comment as we took our hats and walked from the inn door to the church porch.

I should not care to pass the fifteen minutes which followed over again.

The clergyman was waiting, the clerk in readiness, the sextoness all impatience, Geoffrey working himself up into such a state of mind that although it was not a warm morning, and a pleasant breeze stirred the ivy, the perspiration stood on his forehead, and he grew white and red by turns.

"What time were they to be here?" I asked.

"Half-past eleven; her own hour," he answered.

We waited a little longer; then I looked at my watch again.

"Quarter to twelve," I said. "If they do not come soon ——"

He put his hand—a great strong hand it was too—over my mouth with such force he actually drove me back against the wall.

"Don't say that," he entreated, and his tone was so agitated I should scarcely have recognised his voice. "Ah! here they are!" he cried out next minute, as the hired carriages turned into the square.

The first contained the bride, closely veiled, and her father and mother; the other two elderly spinsters, one of whom officiated as bridesmaid.

I could not catch even a glimpse of the bride's face as she passed up the aisle, holding down her head, and keeping her veil drawn in folds, as if she wished to remain hidden.

There was a mystery, and I could not penetrate it. She was not old; the walk was that of a young person, and the hand from which her bridesmaid drew the glove belonged most certainly to no lady of a doubtful age. Her answers were almost inaudible, and she trembled so violently when it came to the ring ceremony that Geoffrey could scarcely slip it on her finger.

"She is not old," I decided, watching her as she knelt; "I am afraid she must be very ugly."

It was all over; they were man and wife. Still keeping her veil folded over her face, she went with Geoffrey into the vestry, we following.

About this time it occurred to me we had somehow made a mistake, and that instead of witnessing a marriage we had been assisting at a funeral.

As a rule I know how to say the right thing in the right place, but I did not then feel in the right place, and consequently I could not say the right thing.

The churchyard, with a couple of gravediggers hard at work, would have seemed to me a much more fitting locality at that moment than the vestry, with its limp curate, elderly bridesmaid, silent bride, and sulky though triumphant bridegroom.

Still without lifting her veil, the bride, who had to ask, and did ask in an almost inaudible whisper what name she must sign, wrote "Mary Ashwell," in a shaky, tremulous hand.

When she finished, her father, who had not conducted himself through the ceremony with the same resolute fortitude as his wife, said, with tears in his weak eyes and a suspicious twitching about his mouth:

"Polly darling, kiss me: kiss your poor old father." Then before she could prevent it he threw back her veil and held her to his heart.

Shall I ever forget the sight of that face?—ever forget the eyes, heavy and swollen with weeping; the cheeks white as death, worn and grief-stained; the expression of utter misery, such as I had never seen in the countenance of a living being before—never anywhere save on the canvas of some old master?

But it was not the heavy eyes, or the white face, or the look of anguish it bore, which caused me to forget where I was; I forgot all sense of propriety, all idea of fitness and decorum—in a word, I forgot myself, and exclaimed out loud—just as if I had been alone and not in a church:

"Good God! why, she is a child!"

In a moment, as though I had uttered some form of incantation, a change took place amongst the company.

With a look at me, which, to say the least of it, was not pleasant, Geoffrey drew his wife's hand in his arm, and marched out of the vestry with her, leaving us all to follow or not, as we liked.

The curate turned his eyes up to the ceiling, as if he expected it to fall in and crush one at least of the party. Out of his prayers I believe he had never heard such an expression before; the two ladies, spinsters, were gazing fixedly on the floor; Mrs. Ashwell was transfixing me with looks like daggers; Mr. Ashwell was in the aisle, sobbing into a white handkerchief.

As for me, I was so stunned that I failed even to apologise for my misdemeanour. I knew of course all these people were standing round and about, but I could see nothing, think of nothing, except my elderly cousin and his child-wife.

Old enough to be her father!—why, he might have been her grandfather!

To this hour I do not know how we got out of the church, and in what form of words I took leave of the curate. I have no distinct memory of anything after I saw the bride's face, till I found myself sitting on the box beside the coachman, driving along a country road, and feeling like one who, having beheld a vision, is gradually and painfully struggling back to consciousness and recollection.

# CHAPTER III

## MY COUSIN'S WILL

After all, I had not to find another place in which to spend my holidays, for Geoffrey condoned the offence of which I had been guilty, and, together with his wife, welcomed me to Fairy Water cordially as ever.

But Fairy Water was not now what it had once been. I could not endure the place, yet I was perpetually going there. I always felt thankful to leave it, and yet when I was away, a pleading face, a pair of soft brown eyes, a meek beseeching voice, seemed always dragging first my thoughts and then myself thither.

She was such a mere child, and he such an uncultivated savage, frantically in love with, and equally frantically jealous of her. It was the old story, not an uncommon one, in which the characters are a ruined father, a rich and generous suitor, a worldly mother, a loving, yielding child, willing to sacrifice her young life on the altar of duty.

She had never cared for anyone; that was the solitary consolation I could find in the transaction. She had never seen a man to care for, I fancy, so utterly secluded and nun-like had been her previous experience. She was innocent as an infant; pure as one of the angels; sweet-natured, docile, truthful, loyal; and I believe, after a time, when a child was born, and she had something all her own to pet and care for, and concentrate all her affections upon, the match—unequal and unsuitable, horribly unsuitable as it was—might not have proved altogether miserable, had anyone been clever enough to lay the devil of jealousy with which Geoffrey was possessed.

He could not bear her to have a look or a thought excepting for himself. His affection for his children was weak in comparison to the vehement and unreasoning attachment he bore his wife. She had loved her father with a clinging devotion beautiful to behold, and so he separated them—would not bid the old man to Fairy Water, or suffer her to visit her former home. When Mr. Ashwell died, he was jealous of her very grief. When she had a new baby, he grudged the caresses she lavished upon it.

Poor Polly! poor little girl! poor child-wife! poor baby-mother! How often has my heart ached for you with a sympathy I feared to show!

But you knew I felt it, my dear! You could tell I was your true friend, and would have stood by you through good and evil, had any advocacy of mine been likely to serve your cause.

Often and often I felt it hard to stand by silent and see the spirit, and the hope, and the joy crushed out of your young life by slow degrees—to see you growing old almost before you had done growing tall; but what could I do?

He was your husband, you his wife; and you have told me since my very silence gave you strength to bear the inevitable—taught you how hopeless it was to struggle against that which was irrevocable.

I shall never forget one day in the earlier part of her married life, when Mrs. Geoffrey Trevor came to me as I was sauntering along a path through the strawberry-beds.

She was a pretty, dainty creature, I thought, as I watched her tripping along; dress a little uplifted above her small feet; head held erect, as if filled and balanced with a new idea.

"Mr. Stafford," she began—she was shy, at first, of calling me by my christian-name; and no wonder, for I must have been baptised some five-and-twenty years before she was thought of, and had been knocking about the world, and learning its wickedness, long ere she crossed life's threshold —"Mr. Stafford, I want to ask you something so much. You have known my husband longer, of course, than I have. Tell me what I can do to make him trust me more."

She said it all in a breath, like a child who has learned a lesson—conning it over and over till she knows it off by heart.

What a child she was! what an unsuspecting, guileless creature! Thank God, I never, not even for a moment, held a thought in my soul about her I might not have held for a daughter of my own; and, in his blind and stupid way, I believe Geoffrey knew this.

Certainly, however, this appeal—for which I was wholly unprepared—staggered me. It took me, indeed, so much by surprise, that I stared at her till she coloured to her temples. After a moment, her eyes drooped, her cheeks paled, and she stood before me abashed and silent, as though she had done something wrong.

Then I spoke.

"I do not know that you can do anything, Mrs. Trevor," I answered, "unless you discover some way to make him less fond of you."

Then the blood flew up again into her face, and she lifted her eyes to mine.

"Do you think he is very fond of me?" she asked, touching unconsciously the strawberry-leaves with her foot, as she moved it restlessly to and fro.

"Yes," I said. "His love for you is *the* love of his life."

She did not say another word. She walked back—not briskly, as she came, but slowly and thoughtfully.

A daughter of whom any man might have been proud—a sweet, tender girl, already developing a woman's soul.

She never tried to make him less fond. With all her strength, I believe, she tried to please him more, and do her duty better.

I watched her efforts. I saw how futile they were. The more tender, gentle, and patient she strove to be—the more lovable he learned her nature really was—so in precise proportion did his jealousy wax greater. He knew, as well as I knew, that while the sun rose and set she never could love him. What he had hoped or expected when he married her, Heaven alone knows; but it is possible—since men in love are unreasoning animals— he trusted eventually to win from her something besides obedience and sweetness; and, as time passed by, and found her unchanged, save that she grew more still, more tranquil, more submissive, I think his heart must occasionally have stopped beating at the thought that someone might yet win her affection when he was dead and forgotten.

After a couple of children had been born, he asked me if I would object to my name being inserted as one of the executors of his will?

"Mr. Henderson will act with you," he added.

Mr. Henderson was a very respectable solicitor; and, having no objection to being associated with him, I said so.

"I hope, however," I went on, "you have done all that is right by your wife."

"What do you mean?" he asked.

"I mean that I hope you have made ample provision for her."

"I have left everything to her," he replied, and I must say I felt surprise, though I did not evince any; "everything except Fairy Water, which, as you know, I cannot will; unless she should marry again."

"And in that case?" I suggested.

"She has nothing. I suppose you do not expect me to leave my money for the benefit of another man?"

"Well, no," I replied; "I do not think I should be so philanthropic myself; although I might, for the sake of memory, just as a mere matter of sentiment, leave a woman some trifle a year, settled on herself, of course strictly."

"I will not do that," he answered, and the subject dropped.

Time went on; they had been married eight years. Mrs. Trevor called me Stafford and I called her Mary. Somehow, Polly had dropped out of our recollections as it assuredly had out of her face, and there were five children at Fairy Water and one in the churchyard, all boys, all except the very last comer, to whom I stood godfather—to whom, for her mother's sake, I presented the handsomest conventional mug, knife, fork, and spoon I could possibly afford, and which was called—a graceful piece of thoughtfulness on the part of Mrs. Trevor—Isobel, after my own dear mother.

How this young wife went through those eight years is to me a puzzle even now. How she preserved her amiability, how she kept her temper from souring, how she retained her timid, trembling, and yet certain faith in all things holy, could have been only by reason of God's great mercy to his weakest and most helpless children.

But there was a slow, gradual change in her which made my heart ache to behold. She was as staid as a matron of forty. The sweet laughter of a happy wife and mother never echoed through the rooms at Fairy Water. She was grave even with her children. Young as she was, she had lost the ability to play with them. Geoffrey had gained his desire, and wedded a young wife whom he loved, pretty, faithful, true, and yet he found no happiness in the years, whilst she—I have told how she was affected by their passage, and can only guess the anguish of soul each day they contained had brought with its dawn.

But a change was very near at hand. One night Geoffrey, always a bad, reckless whip, managed to upset his dogcart, and in doing so contrived, besides breaking his leg, to inflict serious internal injuries on himself.

That was the beginning of the end. The leg knitted, the injuries were patched up, but he could never hope to be the same man again. He grew thin and worn, and month after month wasted away visibly.

At times also he suffered cruelly; whatever was the matter with him, and the doctors could only vaguely diagnose his disease, there were hours when it seemed to fasten upon him tooth and nail, almost gnawing the life out of that once robust, loud-voiced, strong-limbed boor.

Under this discipline he grew, wonderful to relate, gentle.

In health one of the most discontented, restless, impatient mortals that ever existed, in sickness and in pain he became a different being.

"Spite of his sufferings," said his wife, tears in her eyes at the thought of them, "we have never been so happy. Oh, Stafford, if he had only been like this always."

Two years after the accident a letter from Fairy Water told me the end had come. It was the dead of the winter time, and I do not like travelling in winter, or going into residence with a corpse, but I started for the old place at once. The little woman, with her five young children, all alone in the world but for me, would have need of my presence.

I can see her now as she crossed the hall to meet and thank me for coming. Her face was very pale, and thin, and sad, but peaceful.

"He had no pain at the last," she told me, as we passed into the library together; and then, holding her hand, I sat silent for a minute, thinking—as we all must at some period or another—of the last change, of the awful mystery.

All it was possible to do for her at this juncture I did; and when the short days drew to a close, and we talked quietly by the firelight, she always led the conversation to her late husband—she liked to speak of him, I perceived—liked to tell me how, by almost imperceptible degrees, he had been softened and altered.

"At last," she said, on the evening before the funeral, and her voice dropped and trembled a little as she spoke, "at last he told me how much he regretted that we had not been so happy as we might have been. He said, poor dear, it was all his fault; he said he had distrusted me once, and made his own life miserable in consequence; and then he would, spite of my entreaties, go on to talk about his will. It would 'show how I trust you,' those were his words, 'what full confidence I place in Stafford and you.' "

At that point she broke down. I had not mixed with my species for a considerable number of years without having had many such utterances confided to me. For a week after his death a man is generally well spoken of, and I ought to have remembered this, and been on my guard as to consequences accordingly; but I was off guard, and, I confess, Mrs. Trevor's grief for the departed, and her account of Geoffrey's supposed repentance, touched me exceedingly.

As a rule, I wait to form my opinion of the regret of the survivors and the real character of the deceased until the day after the funeral; but in this case, as has been stated, I was weak and premature, and went to bed with a newly-developed liking and pity for the poor gentleman who lay stiff and stark in unpleasant proximity to my own bedchamber.

"I wonder what his will is?" I marvelled, as I put out my candle; and then a dreadful idea, a most shocking and horrible notion struck me.

"If he has expressed a wish for me to marry his widow, what shall I do?"

What should I do, indeed? I could not sleep for hours, so fearful did I feel that in some mood of maudlin repentance, when his mind was weakened with illness, he might have committed such a desire to paper; and when at last I sank off into slumber it was only to dream I was standing once again in Winchelsea Church, this time as an unwilling bridegroom, with Geoffrey Trevor in his shroud officiating as clergyman, and one of the elderly spinsters vowing as fast and hard as she knew how she would cling to me till death did us part.

I awoke in a cold perspiration, and though day had not yet broken, got up, dressed myself, went out for a walk, and on my return finished my nap, rolled up in a rug on a sofa in the dining-room.

Funerals, like weddings, take place at too early an hour. Though it was an immense relief to me to think Geoffrey was out of his own house, I confess, as we drove back to Fairy Water, I wished his departure had been arranged for at a later period of the day.

I wondered what I could find to do until it was time to retire to rest. I marvelled how long Mrs. Trevor would wish me to remain in the house of mourning; I speculated on the number of invitations which must be by this time lying on my table in town, and through all there was a curious under-current of thought as to what my own end would be like, where I should die, what I should die of, where I should be buried, and who would follow me to the grave.

"Mr. Stafford"—it was Mr. Henderson who thus broke into my reverie— "do you know whether your cousin left any other will than that made some years since?"

"He told Mrs. Trevor," I answered, "he had made a will which would show how fully he trusted her."

"Has she got that will?"

"No; at least I should think not."

"Has she looked for it?"

"Decidedly not, I should say."

"Have you?"

"No; if I ever thought about the matter, I concluded you had the will in your possession."

"I have not," he replied; "and, what is more, I never drew out any but the one which, against my most earnest advice, he executed. I often urged upon him to reconsider the matter, but he always either turned the subject or refused to do so."

"Then you think my cousin did not make a second will?" I suggested.

"I am afraid he did not."

"Is that you hold so very bad?" I inquired.

"I think it so," he replied.

"What is to be done?" I asked.

"His papers had better be examined, to ascertain if he has left a later will before that I hold is produced."

"There can be no objection to such a course," I said; "will you examine them?"

"I am in the hands of yourself. and Mrs. Trevor," he answered, and we drove on in silence.

It was lucky for us that the widow had not the faintest idea the usual course of procedure ordered a will to be read as soon as possible after the man who made it had been got safely into the churchyard.

Though twenty-six, she remained to that hour as ignorant of worldly affairs as she was when she had to ask what name she should sign in the register at Winchelsea, and she accepted in simple good faith my suggestion that she should give the keys of her late husband's desks, drawers, boxes, and so forth to Mr. Henderson, on whom the duty of looking over his papers now devolved.

"I fancy he wanted something out of that old oak cabinet, which stood near his bedside," she said, as she handed me the keys. "He pointed and nodded to it several times just before—before he died, and tried to speak, but he was not able. Perhaps Mr. Henderson may find out what it was."

"We must look there for the will," I said, as the lawyer and I ascended the staircase together.

He bowed gravely. He had formed his opinion, which the result of our search justified. Geoffrey had made no second will. There was no such document to be found.

All the letters and papers in the oak cabinet related to matters stale as the deluge, with the exception, indeed, of some few notes from Geoffrey's young wife, and a lock of her hair tied with a thread of silver twist. We found also a knot of ribbon and a few flowers pressed in tissue paper. When we showed these to Mrs. Trevor she burst into tears.

"He wanted them buried with him," said Mr. Henderson to me, *sotto voce.* "The desire is not uncommon. I assure you, Mr. Stafford, elderly men are often more romantic than young ones."

"No doubt you speak truly," I replied; "nevertheless I wish, sentiment notwithstanding, he had forgotten those relics, and executed his will."

"He did not wish to make another," said the lawyer; "rely upon that."

The worst of lawyers is, they are always telling one something one is forced to believe, whether one likes to do so or not.

I was forced to believe, and, indeed, my long experience of his amiable nature made that belief unpleasantly easy, that my cousin Geoffrey had made no second will, and that the document which Mr. Henderson described as containing some curious and stringent clauses was the only keepsake he had left us.

"I will bring it over in a day or two," said Mr. Henderson, "and read it quietly to you and Mrs. Trevor."

"Bring it to-morrow," I suggested, "and let us have done with the matter. If medicine has to be swallowed, the sooner it is taken the better."

"True," he commented; but there was a twinkle in his eye and a smile on his lip as he took his leave, which seemed to say, "I understand you, Mr. H. Stafford Trevor. You find Fairy Water dull; you are longing for the fleshpots of Egypt—for the cucumbers of course—leeks are not esteemed luxurious now as they were some four thousand years back—which even in December grace the tables of those rich enough to pay for them."

There was a certain amount of truth in this unspoken sentence. I had eaten too long out of the fleshpots to care very much for anything they contain, but still I was tired of Fairy Water. The country in summer, as a change from town, is delightful; the country in winter is something not delightful, beginning with a d—— also.

That night I slept with a quiet heart. I saw a prospect of returning to my beloved London. I had no fear of having to regard any last wishes chronicled by the late owner of Fairy Water.

Dreamily I wondered what Mr. Henderson meant by a bad will; but being too much tired to try to work out the problem, closed my eyes, and left it for him to solve next day.

When I awoke in the night I felt glad to remember I was not the owner of Fairy Water, but that an extremely delicate child, sleeping in a distant wing, would some day be master in it.

Unless, indeed, he died; in which case the other youngsters were ready to step into and wait for the vacant shoes.

I never liked Fairy Water so little as on the night following the noon when we helped to lay Geoffrey Trevor under a great slab of granite, there to lie quiet till the Judgment-day.

Men of my temperament generally strive to eschew assisting at these unpleasant ceremonies, but I have always tried to do my duty, however disagreeable it may be; and really, excepting a christening, I know no ceremony so utterly distasteful to me as a funeral.

I have never shirked accompanying any dear brother who had a claim upon me, either of relationship or friendship, to the only home where men can do no more harm to anybody. Nevertheless it is one thing to perform a duty, and another to like performing it. There are persons who take a positive pleasure in the black business, who do not object to strolling through cemeteries and examining in ancient churchyards old tombs and inscriptions as false as those graven in our own day. To me, however, the whole thing is objectionable, and the idea of Goeffrey sleeping out in a damp piece of consecrated ground, with rank grass waving around his last bed, made me shiver.

Still, as the ceremony had to be gone through, I was glad it was over; and when I rose the next morning I felt sufficiently reconciled to my loss and composed in my mind, to consider how Mr. Geoffrey Trevor's death would in the future affect my previous relations with Fairy Water. Of course in my capacity as executor I should have to visit the place occasionally, but my knowledge of the world told me it would not do, even for a man old enough to be the widow's father, to continue free of the house now its master was dead.

True, he had told me she would lose her fortune if she married again. Nevertheless, the children were certain to be well provided for, and in the case of one, at all events, there would be a minority of between eighteen and nineteen years.

For myself, of course any remarks which might be made in a place so utterly remote from the centre of civilisation as Fairy Water, were of no consequence; but it behoved me to be very careful as to what might be said about Mary; and I decided, as I had decided nearly ten years previously, that I must find some other house in which to spend my holidays, recruit my health, and eat my strawberries.

I had never seen Fairy Water look so utterly dreary as it did during that forenoon when I stood watching the rain dripping into the lake, and making the already sodden ground more sodden.

The sky looked as if it had never done anything but rain since the second day of the world, and as if it never meant to do anything except rain till the last day. The leafless forest trees waved their long bare arms slowly to and fro, as though they were burdened with the weight of some speechless agony. The swans looked dirty and draggled, the ducks had collected together under the shelter of a clump of evergreens, and were suggestive of utter misery. Mrs. Trevor was making belief to execute some impossible piece of needlework; the children, as is the pleasing habit of children on wet days, were flattening their unformed noses against the window-panes; while their father, out in the weather, could not tell whether the rain were raining, or the sun shining.

After luncheon Mr. Henderson arrived. Out of consideration for my London habits, Geoffrey had always dined later on the occasion of my visits to Fairy Water.

Ordinarily, I believe, the family partook of that meal with the children at one o'clock.

In honour of the solicitor's visit, a fire had been lighted in the drawing-room, and thither we three repaired, leaving the heir, his two brothers, and his sister to amuse themselves as they could.

Mrs. Trevor seated herself on a sofa drawn up beside the fire; Mr. Henderson took a chair at a little distance from her, and unfolding the will, laid it solemnly on a table close to his hand.

I stood leaning against the mantelpiece; a long course of after-dinner drawing-room experience having rendered standing a more natural attitude to me than sitting.

"Shall I commence reading, Mrs. Trevor?" inquired Mr. Henderson.

"If you please," she said softly, and after the lawyer had cleared his throat he began.

It was a long document, copiously interlarded with legal phrases, which were plainly so much Greek to my unsophisticated cousin. There was first a long preamble, setting forth the particulars of the will under which Captain Trevor held Fairy Water, but which left him no power in the devising of it. Then were enumerated the different sources whence his income was derived; then a statement that in the year of grace 18— he married, at Winchelsea Church, Mary, only surviving child of Justin Ashwell, Esq., and Rebecca his wife.

"A will made as much by client as by lawyer," was my mental comment, while Mr. Henderson turned over folio after folio. "Ah! now we are coming to the gist of the matter."

His eldest son, Geoffrey Bertrand, being heir to Fairy Water and whatever moneys might accrue from that property during his minority, it was Captain Trevor's will that the moneys derived from such and such sources, or invested in such and such securities, should be equally divided between such other children as might be born to him, always excluding Geoffrey Bertrand or the son who, in the event of the death of Geoffrey Bertrand, might succeed to the estate called Fairy Water. Subject, however, to an annuity of three hundred pounds per annum to his wife Mary, after the youngest child attained the age of twenty-one, and to a yearly allowance to the said Mary of one hundred pounds per annum for each child of herself and the said Geoffrey Trevor, whom she might undertake to maintain and educate in a manner satisfactory to the before-named executors, viz., Hercules Stafford Trevor, of London, Barrister-at-Law, and Reuben Henderson, Attorney.

In the event of no child, except that son who might at any time be heir to Fairy Water, surviving, one-half the annuity mentioned was to be paid at once to the said Mary, and it was his will that she should continue to reside at Fairy Water, and that the furniture, not including, however, plate and pictures, was to be at her order and disposal.

At this juncture Mr. Henderson paused.

"Come," I thought, "considering the testator was Geoffrey, the will is not so bad a one."

"Providing always," continued the lawyer, and then I found that the sting of the document lay in its tail.

Mrs. Trevor was to be entitled to the sums of money of which mention has been made only in the event of her remaining unmarried. If she married, not merely was she to lose her annuity, and the hundreds per annum to which she was entitled during the minority of her children, but also her children. They were to be placed at such schools as the executors might decide, and all intercourse with their mother was to cease. Further, in the event of her second marriage, she must leave Fairy Water.

There were other clauses, but I forget them; other legacies, but unimportant, including fifty guineas to Mr. Henderson and myself. As I listened to that comprehensive sentence, which must prove, as I knew, a sentence to Mrs. Trevor of perpetual widowhood, I glanced at her for one moment stealthily, and saw the Parthian dart flung at her almost, as it seemed, from eternity, had done its work.

If she grasped no other part of her husband's will, she did that portion which, while contemplating the possibility of her meeting in the future with someone she might wish to marry, virtually placed an insuperable barrier in the way of her becoming his wife.

She did not utter a word, however. When, having finished the reading of the will, Mr. Henderson asked if she understood its purport, she said:

"I think so," in that grave, repressed tone which of late years had become habitual to her, but which I had heard less frequently than formerly since my last arrival at Fairy Water.

"If there is anything you do not quite understand, I can explain it to you hereafter."

"Thank you," she said. Then after an instant's pause, "I suppose you do not require me any longer."

Mr. Henderson at these words rose and bowed. As I opened the door for her to pass out she never once looked at me. She kept her head resolutely bent down, as I remembered seeing it drooped on that bright spring morning at Winchelsea.

Was that day present with her at the moment as it was with me, I wondered, as I watched her slowly move across the hall and enter a little room which she preferred to any other in the house.

"Mrs. Trevor takes it badly, I am afraid," said Mr. Henderson, when I returned to my position near the fire. "Ah! it is a cruel will."

"What a pity we cannot put it between the bars," I remarked, looking longingly at the blazing coals.

Mr. Henderson seized the document as if he imagined I really had some thoughts of disposing of it summarily.

"Geoffrey always was a brute," I went on, seeming not to notice his gesture, "and he appears to have been true to his character to the last."

"Mrs. Trevor takes it worse than I expected she would do," said my companion. "I should not have thought she was the sort of woman to entertain the idea of marrying again, not, at all events, in the first week of her widowhood."

"She never did entertain an idea of the kind," I answered resolutely.

"No doubt; how could she? Her husband never allowed her to exchange half-a-dozen words with any man, except myself."

There was something about this I did not like.

"I beg your pardon, Mr. Henderson," I said, with a little stiffness of manner, "I have exchanged many half-dozen words with her."

"Of course! of course! I meant also excepting you."

Although I had, and have, a perfect horror of any woman imagining she has formed an attachment for me, I felt my anger rise at the tone in which Mr. Henderson put the very idea of my being anybody in such affairs aside.

I looked at the man, and a suspicion struck me that perhaps, had Geoffrey's will been different, Mr. Henderson might have aspired to marrying the widow. He was younger than I, and much better-looking. To Mrs. Trevor, his want of that *je ne sais quoi*, which produces a freemasonry amongst persons accustomed to mix in good society, would not be apparent.

Well, thank Heaven, there was no necessity to vex myself about the chance of such a *mésalliance* now. Some man there might be on earth willing to give up her money for the sake of calling her wife, but she would never give up her children.

I expressed this idea very openly to Mr. Henderson, who said, no doubt I was right. At the same time he once more hinted his surprise at the way in which Mrs. Trevor received the intelligence.

"Depend upon it," I said, "she is not vexed because she cannot marry again. There is some other cause at the bottom of her grief."

"Well, it has been a miserable business first and last," he remarked, as he drew on his gloves, and buttoned up his coat, and drank off a couple of glasses of Madeira preparatory to facing the weather. "I have seen so much unhappiness resulting from unsuitable marriages, Mr. Trevor, that, sooner than one of my girls should wed a man like your late lamented cousin, I would put her in a convent or her coffin."

"You mean a hypothetical girl, I suppose," was my reply. "You have not any of your own."

"Haven't I!" was his answer. "I have a round dozen of children, one sort and another, some of them as tall as Mrs. Trevor."

"Why, I had no idea you were a married man!" I exclaimed.

He looked at me for a minute, and then broke into a ringing laugh, which he instantly suppressed.

"I beg ten thousand pardons. I forgot, I quite forgot. If Mrs. Trevor unfortunately heard me, assure her I meant no disrespect," and he was so earnest in this matter that he kept me at least a minute hatless in a damp country air, begging me to believe he would not have done it for the world—he intended no offence.

When at last I got rid of Mr. Henderson, I went to the door of the room I had seen Mrs. Trevor enter, and asked if I might come in.

"Yes," she answered, and she took her hands away from her face, and greeted me with the same gentle smile which had been growing more gentle ever since I first knew her.

"I do not think I deserved this," she began. "I do not wish to speak ill of the dead, but I think this was a cruel insult to put upon me."

I ventured to suggest that probably her husband had looked upon it in the light of a precaution.

"As if I was likely to marry again—as if—but there, I will not speak of that —— Captain Trevor used to tell me women were not fit to be trusted with anything. I am certain there is one thing with which men cannot be trusted."

"And that is ——?"

"A woman's happiness."

Neither of us spoke for a few minutes; then she broke the silence.

"I shall be sorry to-morrow for what I have said to you to-day; but I was hurt—I was shocked. When my boys grow up and see their father's will, they cannot fail to wonder what manner of woman their mother was in her youth that it was necessary to have such restrictions in case she failed in her trust to them. And beyond all that," she went on, "it was a revulsion. We had seemed so much closer together—he had been so much kinder to me—I seemed to have won his confidence so completely—he appeared so thankful for and pleased with the little things I was able to do to lighten his pain—he had told me so certainly and truly, as I thought— not with a sneer as he might once have done—I should find in his will how thoroughly he trusted me, that I feel I cannot bear the reality of that cruel, cruel paper I heard read to-day. I feel I cannot understand at all what he meant."

It was not my place to tell her I believed the late Captain Trevor had, for purposes of his own, improvised the fiction she repeated to me on the evening before his funeral; so I said no doubt he considered he had showed his trust in her by leaving his children almost completely to her care.

"For, of course, Henderson and I will not consider it necessary to interfere with them," I finished.

"But what did he mean by showing the confidence he placed in you?" she inquired.

"It shows that one man places confidence in another when he asks him to become his executor," I replied.

"You are trying to make the best of this to me," she said, "and I shall be grateful to you hereafter for not making the worst, but I know what you think of it all in your heart. Now, we will never talk of it again."

We had, however, to talk of it again in years to come; but that was not her fault, poor girl, or mine by reason of any intention I had to bring more trouble upon her.

# CHAPTER IV

## I STRIKE A BARGAIN

For the second time I found I had made a mistake about those strawberries. The little world—heavens! what a diminutive world it was round
and about Fairy Water—accepted with a unanimity rare in even smaller
communities three facts—one, that Captain Trevor, having treated his wife
infamously while living, had treated her still worse when dead; another,
that she, being different from most people, would not feel the restrictions
placed upon her as a woman of a different type might; the third, that it
was a great comfort she had one male relation—myself to wit—who, in her
difficult position, could visit and advise her.

The little world previously referred to took me into its confidence
concerning these and many other subjects, and I accepted its opinions.

As for Mary, the idea that her husband's death should make any difference in my visits to Fairy Water clearly never occurred to her.

She called me Stafford, and the boys Uncle Stafford, and the little girl
Godpa Stafford; and if I had suggested taking up my home with them all, I
am confident she would have seen no impropriety in the arrangement.

Altogether, the visits I paid at Fairy Water after Geoffrey's death were
not unhappy ones. They would have been happier, but that the eldest lad
was developing symptoms which no one, not even the local doctor, understood, and which certainly no one could like.

"The boy will be lame for life, if we do not try some different treatment," I said to his mother, as we paced the lawn one day side by side. "I
wonder what course we ought to pursue? I think we must have some
first-rate doctor to see him."

"Do anything you consider best so long as my darling is cured," she
said. "I never look at him without a feeling of self-reproach. My own sinful
fretting after I was first married was the cause of this. I know that perfectly well."

And Mrs. Trevor spoke so decidedly on the matter that I doubt if the
whole College of Physicians could have brought her to a different opinion.

Not being one of that body I never tried. Beyond all things, she was
now a mother. Her whole soul, thoughts, interest, hopes were bound up in
her children, and if she liked to accuse herself of having induced delicacy
in the constitution of her first-born, why should I deprive her of the
pleasure?

"Mary," said I, and I stopped in my walk suddenly, "I have a notion. I
know a man. He is a very dear friend of mine—one of the few dear friends

I have in the world. He is also a clever surgeon—wonderfully clever. Should you object to my asking him down to spend a fortnight here? He is ill himself, poor fellow, and wants a change to some quiet place like this, and he would tell us what to do about Geoff ——"

Before I knew where I was she had led me in an ecstasy of excitement into the library, put pen, ink, and paper before me, and commanded that I should write to my friend.

"Make haste," she said. "You will have just time to catch the post," and she rang the bell. "Tell Robert," she added, while I scribbled my note, "to come here directly. I want him to take a letter to the office at once. Valentine Waldrum, Esq.," she proceeded, taking up my note and reading the address. "What a weak pair of names, Stafford. I am afraid he is not clever. I am indeed."

"He is one of the cleverest men I know," I said, with a little pleasant severity of manner, at which she put her finger to her lip and drew back a step or two, and said, "Hush-sh-sh!" to an imaginary audience.

Even at nine-and-twenty, or thereabouts, I could see now and then in such ways and actions as these a spectre of the Polly Ashwell, at whose death and burial I had assisted thirteen years before.

"I suppose he is very old as he is so clever?" she said after the note was despatched.

"He is not at all old," I answered, at which intelligence she made a *moue* of disappointment.

One of the oddest traits about her was a fancy for elderly gentlemen. Considering what her life had been with one of them, I could not understand this, till in a moment of confidence she told me she felt *gauche* with young ones, never having associated with them.

"Is his wife nice?" she asked.

"He has no wife," I replied. "He never will have one."

"Why not?"

"His father died mad, and in consequence he considers it his duty to remain single."

"Does his mother live with him?"

"No, she is dead too. She did not long survive her husband."

"How sad. Did you know her?"

"Yes, very well indeed. I knew her when she was no taller than your little Isobel; but I knew her best when she was ten years older than you are now."

"'ere you attached to her?" she asked, with that directness which is as often a proof of want of knowledge of the world as of intimate acquaintance with all its ways.

"If I ever loved a woman it was Val Waldrum's mother," I answered; "but make no mistake, Mary; that she married another man has caused no great disturbance in my life. When I began to love her I was at an age when sentiment is paramount. She was to me just what a favourite heroine might have appeared. She was my ideal love, and for the sake of that romance in the first instance, and because afterwards I found her to be a woman, sweet, true, devoted, I liked her son first for his mother's sake, and then for his own. I hope you will be very amiable to him, my dear, for he is much to be pitied."

She took both my hands in hers and kissed first the right and then the left.

"Do you suppose I should not be amiable to any friend of yours?" she answered. "Am I a monster of ingratitude, that I should forget the kindness you have unceasingly showed to me?"

She had her ways and her words, which never permitted me to forget, no, not for a moment, what she might have been under happier auspices, what she might have developed had not Geoffrey decided to celebrate the obsequies of everything which was young, cheerful, light-hearted, about her on her bridal morning. We did two things that noon in Winchelsea, I decided. We buried the original Polly, and we dragged a resuscitated Mary to the altar, and married her to a man old enough to be her grandfather.

"My dear," I said, "you are not a monster of ingratitude, neither am I. Nevertheless, if you could find something else to kiss than my hands, I should feel obliged."

"You wretch," she said, and boxed my ears, or rather made belief to do so.

I tried to understand, but utterly failed to do so, why on that day, and for several days afterwards, Mrs. Trevor treated me like a person who had just sustained some great loss, or experienced some serious misfortune. Had my first love ascertained her real sentiments towards me in the same hour in which I made my confession, instead of—well it does not particularly matter how many years before—it would have been impossible for Mary to evince a keener sympathy with my disappointment than she showed by a hundred little attentions, by a certain tone of her voice, by a pitying expression in her face.

I could have laughed at her intense simplicity, but that between me and laughter there stood, at the moment, the spectre of that which seems only beautiful to us when we can grasp it no more—youth.

I had been young and I was old, and yet a few words, spoken almost at random, raised a fair illusion from the grave of the past.

Around me were the flowers, and the waters, and the beauty of the long ago; above my head shone a sun, the glory of which had faded many and many a year before; in my ears sounded the voices of the dead and gone; and there is something about phantoms such as these which chills the merriment even of a man of the world.

Nevertheless, the form which Mary's sympathy took was not disagreeable to me in my last capacity.

Intuition teaches the sex many things wonderful to consider. Intuition taught her that after forty, and sometimes before, men find in creature comforts a marvellous solace for disappointed affections, and therefore when we sat down to dinner I found my tastes had been consulted even more scrupulously than was the case in general; and when dessert appeared, the wine she pressed me so much to try turned out to be taken from a bin that had been held so sacred in Geoffrey's time, that I never recollect but once his asking any person to share a bottle of the vintage.

That was on the day of his father's death. I happened to be in the house at the time, and perhaps in honour of his new authority he produced some of this wonderful wine, saying it would do us both good.

Afterwards thinking that what might be enough for one would not be for two, he treated himself on high festivals to a bottle in private. Those high festivals must have occurred frequently, judging from the small quantity left.

"I am so glad I thought of it," said Mrs. Trevor, when I remonstrated with her on the extravagance of decanting such wine for me. "I cannot imagine what is the use of having things unless they are used." Which article of faith she had learned, no doubt, from her father, who went on using everything he had till there was nothing left.

When I told her Valentine Waldrum was one of the few dear friends I had left in the world, I spoke the truth. One of the benefits attached to my profession is that it acts as an almost complete deterrent to personal dislikes; on the other hand, it places bars in the way of forming strong attachments. Dear friends being frequently a little *exigeant*, diners-out can scarcely run the risk of offending non-*exigeant* friends by making too many of them. I could not at all events, and the few I did make I took care to keep, by letting none of my useful acquaintances know, if I could help it, of their existence. Each rule has, however, its exception, and Waldrum proved that to mine. From the time he first came to London, I tried to get him into society, but, unfortunately, I could not make him like society; then I tried to get society to recognise his professional merits.

Always graceful, society expressed itself certain Waldrum's abilities were of the highest order, but at this point it stopped. When it wanted an arm cut off, or any other remunerative operation performed, it sent for some well-known man, even if he were half blind, half deaf, half doting, instead of my *protégé*.

Do you think I quarrelled with society for this? On the contrary, I only set my wits to work to overcome its prejudices.

The only man whom I asked as a favour to put business in the way of my young friend was an old doctor who had grown gray in feeling pulses, in pocketing guineas, and doing as little for his money as even a fashionable physician was able to manage.

I took Valentine to call upon him, and the young fellow's good sense, cleverness, and modesty impressed the ancient humbug favourably.

As we rose to take our leave, the latter asked Valentine where he lived? to which he replied he was trying to work up a small practice in Islington.

"Where is Islington?" said the doctor, as though he had never heard of that suburb before.

When I explained its topography to him, and enlarged upon the fact that at one time London physicians sent their consumptive patients to die in its salubrious air, as they send them nowadays for the same purpose to Torquay, Madeira, and other such favourite resorts, he said he had no doubt it must be a charming neighbourhood, and that my anecdotes were most interesting. Further, he observed, if I happened to be passing in the course of a day or two, he should like to see me.

When I called he rushed to the point at once. "A fine young fellow," he remarked, "something in him, should not wonder if he makes his mark; but, my dear sir, get him away from his present quarters. How could I recommend a man who lives in a place of which no one who is anybody ever heard? He ought to rent a house in a good street, furnish it well, set up a carriage and pair, or at least a well-appointed brougham. If he follow my advice he may earn a handsome income ere long; if he do not, he may make up his mind to remain in 'Merrie Islington' an unknown surgeon to the end of his days."

"You are right, very probably," I replied.

"Right, to be sure I am right! and you, who have been mixing in society for a quarter of a century at least, know I am. It is all very well for those who do not want to live by their fellows to talk about worth, and talent, and genius, and industry, and other nice qualities of a similar description, but we who must get money out of the upper ten thousand, or else starve, comprehend that the aristocracy must be humoured. And quite correct, too," he added; "if I paid a man a guinea every time he looked at my tongue, I should expect him to find out my especial weakness, and respect it."

That same evening I went to Islington, and found my young friend domiciled in a house which presented a front of a window and a hall-door, adorned with a brass plate, to one street, while round the corner was another door, smaller than the first, adorned by a second and more diminutive plate, on which was engraved, "Surgery."

One does not grow less sensitive to the value of external appearances as one gets older, and I confess it shocked me very greatly to find Mrs. Waldrum's son making his professional *début* in such a locality.

I found him reading the last handbook of surgery, and writing his own opinions on certain passages as he went on.

"Still on the mill, Val," I remarked.

"Yes," he said, laughing; "there are some people on whom sentence of 'hard labour for life' is passed the moment they enter the world, and I am one of them."

"Well, we must see that you get something in return for your labour," I answered; and then I repeated all the words of wisdom which had fallen from the lips of my friend, the ancient humbug, and watched the effect they produced upon Mr. Waldrum.

He took the matter in a different spirit to that I expected. I thought he would pooh-pooh the experience of his elders—break out into invectives against the rottenness of a state of society which looked to what a man seemed, instead of first asking what he was. I imagined it quite possible he would tell me he preferred the poor to the rich, that he asked for no other emolument out of his profession than the power of alleviating pain, of benefiting the sufferings of his fellow-creatures, with much more to the same effect, uttered in the vehement language with which inexperienced persons clothe their crude notions until time has taught them both the fallacy of their ideas, and the folly of expressing them.

Mr. Waldrum, however, disappointed my expectations in the most agreeable manner. He waited quite patiently till I had finished, seemingly listening to and weighing every word; then he looked round his sitting-room with a most suggestive glance—a glance which took in the six second-hand chairs, covered with horsehair; the sofa, upholstered in a like cheerful and comfortable manner; the pembroke table, its deal top concealed by a tablecloth of washing damask, the washing capabilities of which had, however, apparently never yet been put to the test; curtains, ditto, ditto; carpet, neither bright nor new; ornaments on the chimney-piece to match.

When he had completed the survey, he knocked the ashes out of his pipe, and commenced refilling it, with a smile.

"It is good advice," he said, "but, like all good advice, impossible to follow. I had trouble enough to gather sufficient money together to buy this excellent practice and superior house of furniture; how, therefore, shall I ever be able to move to the West End, and decorate my rooms as West End rooms should be decorated, and purchase a brougham and horse, and feed the latter, to say nothing of a man in livery to open the door, and another in livery also, to drive me to the dwellings of problematical patients who may require my services, or who may not—very possibly the latter."

For the time being I ignored the conclusion of his sentence, and inquired:

"Why, when you were short of money, did you not come to me?"

"Well, for one reason—because I am a queer fellow, and have a fancy to be independent."

"Independence is an excellent virtue, in moderation," I replied.

"I wonder if you mean, now, by that remark, to imply what I heard a lady say the other day, that people who begin with being extremely independent, usually end by making eminently ungrateful beggars."

"A sweeping assertion," was my answer; "but still no virtue ought to be pushed to extremities."

"You did not ask me what my second reason was," he remarked.

"I shall be most happy to hear it, nevertheless," I said, politely.

"Well, the fact is, if I ever thought about the matter, I thought you had no money to speak of. I knew you had a lot of friends, and influence likely to prove useful, say to a young lady whose relatives wanted her brought out and put in the way of making a good marriage, but I never supposed you had a hundred pounds lying at your bankers in your life."

"I do not suppose I ever had," I replied, humouring him.

"And that is the reason," he went on, "that I have liked to know you. I felt you could not imagine I had any ulterior object in visiting you. It was very good of you to get me invited to grand parties, and affairs of that kind, and I am glad to understand, thanks to you, what is going on inside one of the big houses in a fashionable quarter, when I see the windows lighted up, and the carpet laid across the pavement, and carriages driving up, and footmen lounging about; but society and I are not suited for each other, and therefore you cannot now think, when I say I like to know and talk to you, it is for anything than for your own sake, and the sake of one who understood you better than I think you do yourself."

Really an extremely difficult sentence to answer, and as I dislike difficulties, I did not attempt to answer it.

He had refilled and lighted his pipe by this time, and began smoking vigorously. I walked to the window and made some observation about the quietness of the street.

"Yes, it is quiet enough," he agreed, "if that be an advantage; still even on that score I think I might have secured a more desirable residence at a lower figure."

We were on ground now where I felt I could meet him.

"Val," I observed, "I have a fancy that when you bought this excellent practice and superior house of furniture, you were deceived by someone."

"I was sold," he said, doggedly; whereupon I read him a small lecture. Slang might suit fast young ladies and vulgar young men, I informed my listener, but for anyone who wished to succeed in life it was inadmissible. I suggested that a perusal of Addison might improve his style; that a study of Dr. Johnson would teach him the capabilities of the English language; that Swift would show him the way to apply the axe of satire to everyday doings; and how do you suppose he met this. Really, I grieve to record his answer!

"Damn them all!" he said, "I have read and re-read till I wish no man had ever written, in which case I must have gone out and spent my strength in manual labour instead of vegetating in this cursed hole!"

As a narrator I am bound to be accurate as to conversation; as an individual I must apologise for the vehement language of my friend.

It is as useless to argue with a man who is miserable as one who is angry. Val Waldrum, I saw, was miserable. He had, or he imagined he had, which comes to very much the same thing, capabilities in him for rising to eminence, were a chance given; but no chance seemed likely to present itself.

He had hoped from a small beginning to make a great ending, but there are some professions in which small beginnings mean a struggle from first to last, with no end worth speaking about, let a man fight as long and as bravely as he will.

He had spent his small capital in buying a practice which was evidently perfectly valueless, and though he had ample leisure for thought and study, both seemed destined to produce but poor worldly fruits, unless by a miracle he could be translated to some different sphere.

I am not a person who, as a rule, jumps to conclusions very rapidly, and I felt almost startled at the swiftness with which I formed the foregoing opinion.

"I suppose," I began, "that if by any means it was practicable to follow the advice of our experienced friend, you would not object to do so?"

"Object!" he repeated, with a forced laugh, then went on, "I should not object—that is to say, if the thing could be done without borrowing money or running into debt. I think a man must be a fool who walks into ——" the reader will excuse my merely indicating the place which this vehement young surgeon mentioned, "with his eyes open. Many a poor devil has, I daresay, done so in ignorance; but I! have I not seen the evils of debt all my life? Am I not, though through no fault of my own, eating its bitter fruits now? And for all these reasons, if anyone assured me I could earn five thousand a year by adopting such and such a course, I would not go into debt to secure it. At the same time I feel—do not think me vain—so certain that I have it in me to make a name, that if I had enough money to stand the racket for twelve months I would risk losing it in order to give myself a chance; but as I have not the money I must e'en content myself in this charming house, in this delightful locality, and try to work up a practice. I might sell the practice now, I daresay, if I could make up my mind to take in some unhappy wretch as I was taken in myself."

"Is not the old place yours still?" I asked. "I do not, of course, mean the Grange, but the other property, where ——"

He stopped me, wincing as if I had touched some unhealed wound.

"Yes; I get fifty pounds a year from the land. Of course, it is let far below its value; but we were glad to let it on any terms."

"Do you mean that the house is included in the fifty pounds?" I inquired.

"No one would take the house," he replied. "We had the greatest difficulty to get anyone to live in it, even as caretaker. The woman who does so has the reputation of being a witch."

"Oh!" I said, and we sat silent for a minute. Then I asked:

"Suppose the house and grounds and farm were let at a fair rental, how much ought the whole thing to produce?"

"A hundred a year at the least," he answered; "but then it would cost a lot of money to put the house and grounds in order. I wish I could afford to paint and repair it a little, for there is some talk of a railway cutting a corner off the garden, and I might then ask for handsome compensation."

"If a purchaser could be found, should you mind selling the place?"

"Not if I got anything like a price for it."

"What should you call a fair price?"

"If a man offered me fifteen hundred pounds he might have it to-night. But, there, what is the use of talking? No one would have it at any price. I did try to raise some money on it, and what do you think was the highest amount offered on mortgage?"

"Five hundred, perhaps," I suggested.

"Two," he replied, "and I can't wonder at it. The land is impoverished, the fences broken down, the gates gone, the barns going to wreck and ruin. If I only could forget," he went on passionately, "if the horror were ever likely to leave my mind, I should take the land into my own hands, and see if I could not make the property of some value once again. But I cannot—I cannot; the very thought of the place makes me feel not quite right myself. I shall not be able to sleep to-night after talking about it."

This was a view of the question on which I felt no desire to enlarge. Not from anyone had I ever been able to hear a succinct account of the circumstances which preceded the death of Mr. Waldrum, senior. For years before the Waldrums moved from the Grange to Crow Hall the latter place had the reputation of being haunted, and all I could elicit from Valentine on the subject of his father's mania was that he began to "see things" and to talk strangely.

"There was a garden at the back of the house," the young man told me, "and one day as he was sauntering along the side walk he suddenly stopped, and declared he saw a woman looking out of the window of a room where no living woman was. To all appearance, up to that time he was as sensible as you are," continued his son; "but after that he got worse and worse to the end."

There was something more in the affair than I had ever heard, I felt satisfied; but curiosity is not my besetting sin, and I consequently accepted his version as complete, without cross-questioning him about the matter.

The most singular thing to me in the whole business seemed that Mrs. Waldrum could not be induced to speak on the subject at all. If the place were ever mentioned in her presence, she was at once seized with a nervous shuddering that she appeared powerless to control. Valentine accounted for this by stating it was she who had been instrumental in inducing his father to take up his residence at Crow Hall, and that she reproached herself for having done so.

"As if the disease would not have developed itself sooner or later wherever he had been," said the young man, taking a strictly medical view of the case.

Of course I could form no opinion about it; I could only believe that, from some cause or other, Mr. Waldrum had died raving mad, and that the subject was too painful a one for son or mother to discuss.

Crow Hall was the place of which I had been talking—to return to Islington and business.

"Val," said I, "suppose I could sell that delightful residence for you—might I reckon on a commission?"

"That you might," he replied. "I tell you what, if, amongst your friends, you know any eccentric gentleman who wants a haunted house, and is willing to give fifteen hundred pounds for it and the land attached—and to anybody with money the place is honestly worth every penny I have named—you shall have two hundred out of it."

"Is it a bargain?" I asked, holding out my hand.

"Yes," he replied, wringing it in a manner which caused me to remonstrate, and—well—to exclaim, "only, the man, whoever he may prove, must be told there is a story attached to the place."

"Of course," I agreed. "And now, you had better give me a letter to the witch, instructing her to allow me or any friend to view the premises. I must see the house before I can talk about it, you know."

"If you do not mind sleeping there for one night," he said, hesitating, "you could do so. I have always told her to keep a room ready for me, though I have never been able to summon up sufficient courage to cross its threshold since the day we left."

"I will see about that," I answered, as I took the letter; "and now continue to work up this practice till you hear from me Crow Hall is—sold."

## CHAPTER V

### THE LEGEND OF CROW HALL

The intelligent reader, no doubt, clearly understands that I meant to buy Crow Hall myself. I calculated the cost mentally whilst I sat in the apartment, already—to quote the house-agency lists—"fully described on page 160."

I am one of those people who may be described as eminently non-speculative. To me promoters post their circulars in vain; for me the prospectuses of new companies have no charm; banks place their dividends before my eyes without dazzling those organs in the least; whilst in mines I have no faith at all.

Naturally, then, you will wish to know in what I have faith? A question easily answered. I believe in ground-rents; I respect the Three per Cents.; and, to a certain extent, I have a liking for land. Not to enlarge, however, on opinions which have little or nothing to do with the progress of this story, I did a little sum in mental arithmetic whilst Valentine Waldrum was talking. Given that fifteen hundred pounds in the Three per Cents. returned me forty-five pounds a year, I certainly could not lose much money supposing Crow Hall only produced forty.

But I intended, if I purchased the place, to make it produce a great deal more.

There are some persons who can make money, and there are others who can take care of it; but the two qualities are rarely combined. My speciality is taking care of money—getting full value for it in some shape or other. It is not easy to delude me into making a bad bargain, and I was certainly not likely to permit Crow Hall to depreciate in the market if I became its possessor.

Before, however, I moved further in the matter, I meant to see the place, so I wrote a letter to the woman in charge, informing her I was a friend of Mr. Waldrum's, who had kindly sanctioned my making use of his house for a few days; and that I should feel obliged by her having a bed in readiness for me by such a date.

When that date came, I started for Essex, in which county Crow Hall was situated.

From Valentine I had received minute directions as to its whereabouts.

I was to go a certain distance by rail, and then a stage by coach; and after that I might post six miles by road, or walk through lanes and across fields (of which he drew me an accurate plan), which lessened the distance by one-third, to Crow Hall.

I have always been a tolerable pedestrian. In one's own interest, as well as that of one's friends, it is desirable to follow such rules as conduce to the maintenance of health; and therefore, even when dining out most constantly, the heights of Hampstead, the lanes round Willesden, the banks of the Thames, the windings of the Brent, have found me a frequent visitor.

In the country I always walk, and therefore, of course, I elected to go by the lanes and fields to Crow Hall.

It was late in the afternoon of an autumn day when I found myself standing at the entrance-pillars—gate there was none—of that ancient house; and I am bound to state that the eye of man never beheld a picture of more utter desolation than it presented.

A long, straight avenue, overgrown with weeds, led to a sort of semicircle enclosed with hedges of ivy, privet, and thorn, outside of which the drive bore away to the right, and terminated apparently in the farmyard.

To the left of the avenue lay a lawn, on which the grass had seeded and was now rotting; beyond this a belt of trees, chiefly pine; and beyond that the lake of the dismal swamp, which had furnished Crow Hall with no less than two tragedies.

Not a place, certainly, to tempt a capitalist possessed of an imaginative mind; but then no one was ever less imaginative than myself.

I merely beheld so much ground which had for years been kept in extremely bad order; a rather good approach; and an old-fashioned two-storey red brick house, with a high pitched roof, and dormer windows projecting from it.

"There are capabilities about the place, certainly," I decided, as I looked at Valentine's inheritance with critical eyes; "but the first thing to do will be to alter its character. I shall cut down those fir-trees; drain the lake; fill it up; lay the whole front down in grass; and plant clumps of evergreens here and there to break the monotony—hollies and yews with their red berries for the winter; laurestinas for the spring; Portuguese laurels for the summer; gorse for the autumn; and variegated laurels, the evergreen oak, and *arbor vitae* for all the year."

Man proposes! I fully determined to perfect all the plans above enumerated, and many others beside. It pleases me now to remember I did not carry out one of them.

When I reached the enclosure previously mentioned I paused again, and decided to grub up the hedges surrounding it. What to do with the front—at that time ornamented by a garden wilder than any wilderness, which had been laid out originally in the Dutch style, and still presented some traces of the prim, curiously-shaped flower-beds, and rank box-edgings—I had not time to decide; for before I had quite compassed the design of this curious parterre, the front door grated on its hinges, and a woman (who was certainly old enough and ugly enough to answer to Mr. Waldrum's description) inquired if I was Mr. Trevor.

For some unexplained reason, she called me "Mr. Treevor." It is a peculiarity of the lower classes in England that they either cannot or will not pronounce a surname properly.

Being, of course, entirely ignorant of the cause of my visit, and having her own reasons for wishing to propitiate her employer, the old creature had done, and did do, her best to make me comfortable.

She made me tea; she toasted bread for my benefit; she fried ham and poached eggs; and, I doubt not, did ample justice to the reversionary interest in the repast which fell to her share.

It had been a lowering afternoon, and the clouds now seemed drawing up for a wet evening and night; so I decided to defer my tour round the premises till the next day, and, drawing up a chair to the fire blazing on the hearth, drew out a book, and began to read.

Towards eight o'clock, the woman—who was, I afterwards discovered, in the habit of going to bed at most proper and most unwitch-like hours—namely, seven in summer and six in winter—tapped at the door to know if I should like to see my room.

"It is well aired, sir," she took care to assure me. "I always keep it aired in case Mr. Valentine, poor dear, should come back; and the sheets have had a good sight of the fire; and the bed was before it all day yesterday. I hope you will sleep sound, that I do, sir. You are sure there is nothing more I can bring you? Then I'll wish you 'Good-night,' sir." And she actually went out and shut the door, as if she never expected to see me open it and walk downstairs after her.

Great is the influence of earnest conviction. So satisfied was the woman that I meant to go to bed, that I actually did so; and lay watching the blazing fire, and the flickering shadows it threw on the wall, till the first died out, and the latter, missing their playfellow, fled away into the darkness.

At the same time in London I should probably have been saying, "Sherry," in answer to some liveried murderer of the English language who had just asked, " 'Ock or sherry, sir?" and yet at Crow Hall, only forty miles off, I was, notwithstanding the fact that I had partaken of no soup, no fish, no entrées, no joints, no pudding, no game, no gruyère, no fruit, and, most particularly, no wine—lying contentedly in bed, with the sheet drawn up under my chin, thinking what a very singular thing life is, and what very wonderful, though somewhat monotonous, patterns the kaleidoscope of existence presents for our inspection.

It is needless to say I did not fall asleep for hours. The fire had died out, and the shadows were all hidden away for the night ere slumber condescended to visit my pillow; and when at length I did close my eyes, and forgetting reality, wandered away into the silent dreamland, I found wakefulness perpetually calling me back to discuss with it some utterly unimportant event.

And now I am about to state a singular fact.

*I never awoke that night, or any other night I spent in the house, with a feeling of being alone.*

I have no theory on the subject. I am quite unable to form any just opinion about it. I can only repeat that, sleeping—heavily sleeping, as I always seemed to be—when something dragged me back to consciousness, I always had the sensation of someone moving away from the side of my bed.

So strong did this conviction become at last, that, rising, I struck a light, examined the bolt of the door, looked in the cupboards, and in every conceivable place where any person or thing could be hidden.

"Pshaw!" I thought; "it is the tea and the strange room."

Shall we say it was the tea and the strange room? Yes—very well—then be it so. I have no wish to argue the point. I only desire to get on with my story, and back into daylight once more.

Next morning, the old woman hoped I rested well, with a look in her face which seemed to express she expected me to say, "No."

"Admirably," I told her; which reply she received with a look of mingled disbelief and disappointment.

After breakfast—at which meal more tea, more toast, more ham, and more eggs made their appearance—I went out to view my future property, and found the account Valentine had given of its dilapidated condition by no means exaggerated.

His tenant, an individual of eccentric habits, I found loading manure into a cart, whilst his man stood by the horse's head.

When I had ingratiated myself with him by the offer of a trifle *pour boire*, which he was not above taking, he informed me, evidently imagining I was a spy sent down by Valentine, that the land was so poor he thought he couldn't hold it much longer; in fact, he had only paid rent so far out of regard to Mr. Waldrum.

"The garden," he added, "is running wild like; the seeds blow into the land, and fill it choke up with weeds." If Mr. Waldrum would throw the gardens in, he wouldn't mind trying it a bit longer, he wouldn't. Did I think I should see Mr. Waldrum soon? Yes; then perhaps I wouldn't mind telling him, with Mr. Dogset's dooty, that if the garden was throwed in, he would keep them clear of weeds for the fruit.

I replied that I should be most happy to deliver his message.

"And you can tell him how shocking poor the land is."

"Yes; that I certainly can."

"And you won't forget about the garden and the weeds?"

"No; I will tell him all. But don't you think, Mr. Dogset," I added, "you could make some use of the house as well?"

"No, sir; that I couldn't," replied Mr. Dogset; and he pulled down his shirt-sleeves, and slipped on his coat, and pulled an old straw hat low over his eyes, and gave one defiant glance ere saying "Mornin'," and turning on his heel.

Clearly, there was some very unpleasant story mixed up with Crow Hall; about *that* part of the business Mr. Dogset was genuine.

When I re-entered the house, I penetrated to Mrs. Paul's domain. Paul was the name of the witch, which struck me with a sense of unfitness.

She had selected for her own living apartment a front kitchen, the most comfortable room I had yet beheld in Crow Hall. It looked out on a little grass-plot, which Mrs. Paul informed me she kept clipped with a pair of garden-shears. Beyond this was a privet hedge, which likewise presented a good appearance; and in the broad window-seats the old lady had a goodly collection of geraniums, fuchsias, and musk. Apparently, also, she was not unskilled in the use of the whitewash brush, since the ceiling looked clean and newly done up; and the jambs of the fireplace had received a coat at some not remote period.

In a cage hung near one of the windows a bullfinch was singing away to its heart's content, whilst on the hearth a black cat with white paws and a very white shirt-front sat gravely watching the operations of his mistress, who was engaged in singeing a fowl I had seen sacrificed an hour before, and off which I dined two hours later.

A man in town selects what he shall eat; a man in the country has to be thankful for anything he can get.

"May I come in, Mrs. Paul?" I asked.

"And welcome, sir; but you must excuse the place being a bit through other."

I replied, and truly, that I thought the place looked very clean and nice indeed. I could not have said as much for its occupant, but then happily she had not considered it necessary to apologise for her own dilapidated appearance.

"Do you not find it dull here, living all by yourself?" I inquired.

"No, sir; I did at first, but I have got used to it. A lone woman must content herself to be a bit dull at times, or else put up with all sorts of people. I have always tried to keep myself to myself, and folks hate a body that strives to do that. No; it is not particular lonesome here, unless indeed in the long winter nights and days, when the snow is on the ground. I do feel a bit bad then, sir; but, law! I think how much better it is than the work'us, and I thank God I was not afraid to come here when Mrs. Waldrum gave me the chance."

"As a rule people were afraid, I suppose?"

"You may say that, sir. Before Mrs. Waldrum left, she could not get a servant for love or money to stay a night in the house. I did not know how she was situated, or I would have come to her sooner; for many a half-a-crown, and many a quarter of tea, and many a pound of sugar she has brought down with her own hands when I lived on the other side Latchford Common; and it would have been a wonderful ghost could have frightened me away from her when she was in need of help. At last I happened to hear, and walked over.

" 'Is there anything Betty can do?' I asked, and then she broke out crying.

" 'Would you be afraid to stay in the house and take care of it after all that has happened?' she sobbed. 'I can find nobody to take care of it, and if I cannot get away soon I shall go mad myself.'

"Then I helped her pack up, and she sent for a fly and drove off, and I said to her:

" 'Make your mind easy, missus; I will take care of everything till you come back.'

"But she never did come back. They took away a little of the furniture, and they sold the rest, except what you see is left; and Mr. Valentine, he seems to hate the place worse than his mother did, and what will be the end of it, God knows. I only hope I shan't have to shift out from the place till I am carried out feet foremost."

"The house has been haunted for a long time," I suggested.

"So it is always said, sir," she replied.

Meanwhile, I should observe, the fowl, in a limp and dejected attitude, was lying between us on the table. I was ensconced on the dresser, and Mrs. Paul, at my earnest entreaty, was seated on a rush-bottomed chair.

"Do you think it is haunted?" I asked.

"I know nothing about the matter, sir. I have lived in the new part ever since I came here."

"This is the new part?"

"Yes, sir"; and she rose as if about to recommence her work.

"Mrs. Paul," I began, "to be perfectly frank, it is a matter of importance to me to know exactly what story is connected with this house. I do not want to take up your time without paying for it, but if you can spare me half-an-hour I shall be much obliged."

I held out five shillings to her as I spoke, at which she looked wistfully.

"I do not think, sir," she said, "Mr. Valentine would like the thing talked about."

"But, my good friend," I remonstrated, "everyone has talked about it. Every person speaks of the house as a haunted house, and, even by your showing, shuns it like a pestilence."

"Besides," she went on, ignoring my last remark, "I know nothing but what I have been told, just hearsay—a parcel of idle stories. I might have been frightened enough if I had believed one-half the neighbours say."

"If you do not believe what they say, why need you object to repeat those idle stories?"

"I did not say, sir, I exactly disbelieved. I know nothing about ghosts, and such like, and I want to know nothing. I have never seen worse than myself in the house since I came to it, nor heard anything except the whistling of the wind, or the creaking of a broken branch, or the hoot of an owl."

"But what happened in the first instance to give the place such a bad name?" I persisted. "When, for instance, was the man found dead, in that dismal-looking piece of water in the front?"

"I would rather say nothing about it, sir." And Mrs. Paul took up the fowl and a sharp knife, and looked as if she were going to disembowel the animal before my very eyes.

"As you please," I said, taking up my hat: "I suppose there is someone in the parish can tell me all I want to know."

"Oh, sir, if you must know it, I may as well speak as another." This remark had reference clearly to the crown-piece, and I recognised the fact by placing it on the table. "But I think you had better not ask me to say more as long as you are sleeping in the house."

For a moment there came over me a strange creeping feeling of chilliness. It was as if, on a warm summer's day, an icy hand had been passed suddenly, though slowly, down my spine. Never before had I quite understood to what an extent the force of imagination is capable of carrying one.

I did not hesitate, however, for one-half the time it has required to write the foregoing sentence. Before I ever entered the house I had formed a theory concerning its care-taker, and I felt quite satisfied that, notwithstanding her assumed reticence and apparent reluctance to speak about the phantom residents in Crow Hall, she desired to encourage the belief in their existence.

Of course it was to her interest that the place should remain unlet; and although she spoke as though she had, out of gratitude, conferred upon Mrs. Waldrum the obligation of taking up her abode in extremely comfortable quarters, still I could not be blind to the fact that having no rent to pay, having the run of the neglected gardens, having the use of an orchard where her fowls could almost pick up their own living, having likewise as much wood for the gathering and chopping as she could well burn, not to mention a gift at Christmas and Easter from Mr. Waldrum, was altogether a good thing for Mrs. Paul.

"Thank you," I said, in answer to her last remark, "but I should prefer to hear the story now. I am not at all afraid of its disturbing my rest."

The witch sighed—in justice I ought here perhaps to state that on one shelf of the dresser I had ere this time espied a Bible, a tattered hymn-book, and a few tracts—shook her head mournfully, turned up her eyes with an expression which seemed to mean:

"A wilful man must have his way, no matter how bad that way may be for him"; and said:

"I have never seen anything myself, sir, you must remember."

"My dear soul," I observed, "you have told me that several times already; and as I have no reason to suppose you are telling me a falsehood, there is not any necessity for you to repeat it again. Somebody, I suppose, must have seen something?"

"Well, yes, sir; the housekeeper who lived here with old Mr. Bragshaw told me herself that one day when he had gone to Chelmsford, and she was quite alone in the house, she was scrubbing the stairs, when all at once she heard a rustling above her, and looking up she saw a lady coming down. She was so astonished she stood on one side to let her pass, and it was not till the figure vanished—'seeming to melt into air'—those were her very words, that she knew it must be 'the foreigner.' "

"What foreigner?" I asked.

"The story goes, sir, and is, I believe, quite true, that a couple of hundred years ago this was an old manor-house, where in the time of the troubles, Catholic gentry used to be hidden till they could get safe off to France and other faraway places; and they do say that when old Madam Waldrum lived here, this was like a dower dwelling for the widows of the family—priests and soldiers, and all sorts of people were concealed, one and two at once, and no one knew the secret of where they put them, except madam and her old butler.

"At her death she left him a good bit of money, and her son leased him the house and farm, and he turned the house into an inn, and called it 'The Black Crow,' and made a mint of gold; not out of tavern keeping, people said, but by smuggling.

"To this day it is thought there are passages underground that lead away to other houses accessible to the sea and the river, though the secret of them died with the man who was found drowned.

"Well, the old butler died, but his son and his grandson and his great-grandson held the place after him, and kept it still on as an inn. The road ran right up to and past it then, instead of turning off as it does now; and instead of a lawn there was a great strip of common land, and there were larger trees and thicker; almost a wood, indeed, growing round the water.

"Each landlord made money in the place, but all were not careful of it alike, and at last there came one who wasted his substance as fast as he made it by consorting with a lot of wild young men, by betting at races, laying guineas by the handful down at cockfights, and such like.

"About this time old Squire Waldrum, the old squire, lay a dying, and as he could leave the property just how he liked, and as the younger son had got an inkling of his eldest brother having a wife and child abroad, what does he do but post off to bring her to England, so as to get his father to leave the estate to him instead of to the son who had married a woman who was two things the old squire couldn't abear—a foreigner and a Papist.

"By some means he did induce her to come to England with him; the child, as I have heard is the fashion in those parts, was out at nurse away from his mother, and she came alone. They had such a frightful passage she was forced to leave her maid sick at the port where they landed, and it was such a night of wind and rain when they got so far as this on their road, that he was fain to seek shelter for the night for himself and the lady at 'The Black Crow.'

"They had supper together, and the landlord himself waited on them. His wife was dead, but he had a niece who looked after the house, and she often spoke afterwards of the wonderful beauty and value of the rings and other jewels the lady wore.

"They were all set with precious stones—diamonds, I think someone told me. 'She had more, too, with her,' she said to her brother-in-law. The niece heard her speak the words.

" 'My dear Filipe'—she had a queer foreign tongue, I am given to understand—'had usage of being often out of moneys. Since he last left me I have received much value from an aunt who had great jewels. He need have want no more.'

"At which Mr. Francis laughed; perhaps because he was glad to think if his brother did lose The Grange, he would not be a beggar; perhaps for another reason; no one can know anything about it for certain till the judgment-day."

Here Mrs. Paul stopped short, as if she never meant to go on again.

"Waiving the day of judgment for the present, will you kindly proceed with your narrative?" I suggested.

Mrs. Paul looked at me. Though she bore the reputation of being a witch, I ascertained subsequently her proclivities were methodistical, and that she refrained from public worship, not merely because of her scanty wardrobe, but also because there was no church in the neighbourhood of the doctrines which she affected.

Whatever her thoughts about me may have been, and I feel satisfied they were not complimentary, she resumed her story.

"Next morning, when they went to call the lady, she was nowhere to be found, neither was the landlord. Mr. Francis behaved like a madman; he sent out people to scour the country, he went to the magistrates, he rode home to The Grange, and tried to make the squire understand his eldest son was married, and that to a foreigner and a Papist; but the old man was nearly gone and wandering, and only said, 'Good boy, good boy,' before he died.

"Three days after, the landlord's body was found floating on the piece of water. The men who rowed out to bring it to land struck the boat on a sunken root, and had some work to save themselves, but the body was after a time recovered.

"Of the lady from that hour to this nothing has been heard. She was Mr. Val's great-grandmother, and since her disappearance nothing has prospered with the family.

"Mr. Francis was arrested, but as nothing could be proved against him, he was set at liberty, and went to foreign parts, where he died, protesting to the last, as I have heard tell, that in Mrs. Philip Waldrum's disappearance he had neither act nor part.

"Mr. Philip shut himself up at The Grange, and led the life of a hermit till his death, when the child of the foreign lady—Louis, I think he was called—succeeded to the property.

"He lived much in London and abroad, married a lady of fashion with no money and little sense, and left The Grange in debt, as I have heard tell, to its very gates, to Val's father.

"While those things were going on at The Grange, someone took 'The Black Crow' and turned it back again to a private dwelling-house. But it often lay empty; people said it was haunted; people could not rest in the old rooms. It was not that they saw anything, or that they heard anything; but they felt as if *somebody was there.*

"I daresay you know what I mean, sir; I would not need to turn my head or hear a footfall, but still I should know if anybody came into this kitchen."

"I can quite understand that," I agreed, remembering my experience of the previous night.

"To people with plenty to do and think about," proceeded Mrs. Paul, sententiously, "that did not signify much, so long as they kept well; but after a while no one kept well in the place. Some laid it to the water, and some to the drainage, and some to the air, and some to the lake; but none spoke up, though everybody suspected, the place lost its tenants that were able to pay rent, because they found somebody who paid no rent at all had been in possession before they were thought of.

"The man that lived the longest here was a foreigner. He could scarcely speak any English when he came to the place, and he could speak little more when he went away, but he drank a great deal of sour stuff they make in his country, stronger than brandy it is said, smelling of herbs. He gave me a drop of it once, and I felt strange for a week after. He came over on account of something he had done against his own king, Mrs. Waldrum told me, but the people round about would have it he was some friend to the lady Mr. Philip had married, and the place was looked on worse than ever after that; my notion is, when he had taken some of his stuff he would not have seen a dozen ghosts if they had been walking backwards and forwards through the room."

"And when he left, or died?" I suggested.

"The place stood empty again, till the trouble came at The Grange, and then nothing would content Mrs. Waldrum but to come here and see if they could not live off the farm. Ah! she was a good lady, she was, and clever, but she made a mistake about that. She had a high spirit of her own, and laughed at the idea of ghosts and such like.

" 'They rise out of the pond,' she said, 'and we will drain it.'

"They tried, but they could not drain it. More was the pity."

Suddenly Mrs. Paul discontinued the "Chronicles of Crow Hall."

"You must excuse my tongue, sir," she said; "it has run the last hour away, and the fowl for your dinner is not trussed yet."

"So I see," I answered, and walked discreetly out of the kitchen.

It was no use disguising the fact, I relished the bird. He had no adjuncts to speak of. There was no bread sauce, no tongue, no ham, no anything to recommend him to a man who was in the habit of dining well; further, he laboured under the disadvantage of having been seen in almost all steps of preparation, and yet I liked him.

There was not much on his bones, as he had been earning a precarious living in the orchard, but what I found was sweet.

How much the man who stated "Hunger is good sauce," would have contributed to the happiness of his fellow-creatures had he only given some receipt, stating how hunger was to be compassed short of travelling forty miles into the wilderness to find it.

# CHAPTER VI

## MAD! MY MASTERS

Dinner over, I went out into the garden, and sat ruminating in a ridiculous arbour, which someone had built evidently for the accommodation of spiders, daddy-long-legs, moths, snails with shells on their backs, and other such creatures.

I could not lie on the grass, because it was a couple of feet high, going to seed, and full of various insects and reptiles even worse than those enumerated above; the dingy, old-fashioned, only quarter-furnished room which had been appropriated to my living use, was not an inviting or exhilarating apartment, and, as has been said, I went out to the arbour, lit a cigar, and began to think.

The roof had disappeared, and, as I thought and smoked, I looked up into the bright green foliage of a chestnut-tree.

I was trying to solve two problems: one which concerned the present, and one which did not; the first, why such an impression of horror should have been left upon the mind of Mrs. Waldrum and her son regarding the manner of Mr. Waldrum's death; the other, what had really become of that lady. It seemed impossible to acquit Mr. Francis Waldrum of some guilty knowledge in the matter.

As to the landlord's disappearance, and the subsequent recovery of his body, I felt satisfied he had fallen accidentally in the water, more especially as I could in no way connect the fact of his death with that of the flight or abduction of the foreign lady.

Continuing the family history down to the time of Valentine's father, I failed to discover why the manner of his death should so powerfully have affected both Mrs. Waldrum and her son.

There seemed nothing very wonderful in the affair after all. A man, with mind no doubt already weakened by long and wearying pecuniary anxieties, came to reside in a house haunted by a ghost related by the closest ties to himself and his family. The loneliness of the life, the change even from excitement to mere vegetation, began in due course to tell. He got low-spirited, and, wandering about the place, began to recall the memories connected with it.

From that point, the distance to dreaming dreams and seeing visions could not be considered remote.

He had fallen into a weak nervous state, and instead of removing from the scene of his delusions, those around tried to argue and reason him out of them, by which treatment the fancy remained impressed more indelibly on him.

All this I went over in my own mind, looking at the matter from various points of view, and dovetailing in the story told me by Mrs. Paul with the few facts furnished by Valentine.

"There is something more in the affair than I know," I decided; "and Mrs. Paul is not the person to tell it to me, neither is Valentine. To whom then should I apply?"

No answer presenting itself, I resolved to take a walk and think out this question.

Latchford was the nearest village; thither I bent my steps. Half an hour brought me to a small, old-fashioned church shaded by fir and elm trees. A great cypress grew half way between the church gate and the porch. Under the shade of that cypress, under the green billow of grass, all alone with the daisies and the dead, the birds, and God, Harold Waldrum lay dreamless, an unexplained mystery buried with him.

Who should expose it to me, I wondered, as I stood beside his grave; not the clergyman, no—his province was naturally with the wise and the responsible, not with the mad and the irresponsible. If not the clergyman, who then could repeat to me anything but vague gossip? Who? why, the doctor of course. How was it I had not thought of that before? I asked the first labourer I met where "The Doctor" lived, and was directed to a house overlooking the village-green, and standing back from the road—a house with a well-established garden surrounding, and creepers, which had evidently been growing for years, not a few almost covering it.

"Come," thought I, "this looks well"; and I rang the bell, and was answered by a neat maid-servant, who showed me into a sitting-room, where I was soon joined by an extremely limp-looking young man, tall, long-necked, light-haired, blue-eyed, large-mouthed, who evidently thought Heaven had sent him a patient from The Grange.

He looked unaffectedly disappointed when he heard the nature of my business, but bore the disappointment with greater courage than might have been supposed, and set himself to work to give me such assistance as he could, in a manner which, though it has certainly not added to his riches, has probably caused him to partake of more champagne than may, I fear, have been good for a person of habitually abstinent instincts.

"No; he was very sorry—very sorry indeed, but he could tell me nothing about Mr. Waldrum's last illness. Of course he had heard rumours—vague rumours, but they were not to be depended on. He bought the practice a year previously from Doctor Wickham. It was that gentleman who attended Mr. Waldrum."

"Could he give me Doctor Wickham's address?"

"Yes, certainly, with the greatest pleasure: 1, Waterloo Terrace, New North Road, London. He did not himself exactly know where the New North Road was, but most probably it might be on the way to—or beyond Highgate, but perhaps I knew London better than he."

This I thought extremely likely, but contented myself by saying I did know London tolerably well, and had little doubt but I should be able to find Waterloo Terrace.

Subsequently, under the impression evidently that he had not been able to do as much for me as could be desired, he took his hat, and volunteered to accompany me part of the way back.

When we reached the church he offered to procure the keys, as he thought it contained some monuments and brasses which might interest me. I saw both, and they had not the slightest interest in my eyes.

Once we were out of the churchyard he said he would walk a little way farther, and in fact he did walk so far that he accompanied me to the place where a gate should have been at the entrance to Crow Hall, and indeed left me no resource but to ask him if he would walk in and take a cup of tea.

He partook of several, and he smoked various cigars and several pipes; indeed, he only persuaded himself to leave me when Mrs. Paul, who, I could see, was indignant and uneasy at the turn affairs were taking, brought in my candle, and setting it down with a bang, inquired:

"Will you be pleased, sir, to want anything more?"

"Nothing, Mrs. Paul," I replied, in my most gracious manner; and when the woman disappeared I availed myself of the opportunity to inform him I had unfortunately forgotten wine, and such like commodities could not be purchased in the village, but upon the occasion of my next visit to that part of the world I hoped he would do me the pleasure of partaking of a friendly tumbler.

To do the young man justice, I believe it was no thought of either vinous or spirituous liquors which had induced him to prolong his stay, but he took the hint nevertheless, and made many apologies for having remained so late.

It was at this time about half-past eight o'clock.

I do not think I should have cared to invite that young man to pass an evening with me in town, but country life certainly produces a wonderful effect upon one, mentally as well as physically.

Like the simple fowl innocent of town artifices—deprived of all the advantages of skilful cookery and those adjuncts so necessary to his fellow, who makes his appearance in the busy haunts of men—I found the unsophisticated manners and habits of my new acquaintance pleasing rather than otherwise.

Musing about the sort of life he must lead in these remote wilds, I lighted my candle, and following the admirable example set by Mrs. Paul, at a much earlier hour of the evening, proceeded upstairs to bed.

As I did so, with nothing less in my mind, I can declare, at the moment than the ghost, I could have sworn that something brushed past me, and I was sensible of a sudden and chilling change of temperature.

"There is some trick in it," I mentally exclaimed. After bolting my door, I examined, as on the previous night, every corner and cupboard in my room. "No doubt in an old house like this there are secret panels and passages known only to the initiated. Mrs. Paul looks as if she might have defrauded the Queen a little herself in days gone by."

Thus I tried to reassure myself, but in vain. In whichever direction I turned it seemed to me there was someone behind me; some one or thing who moved as I moved, who with impalpable presence followed my steps.

Not that I heard a sound. Whatever the thing might be, it did not even breathe. I knew that, because I held my own breath over and over again in order to make certain.

"I am getting nervous," I thought; and putting out the light, I placed the candlestick and matches ready to hand, got into bed, drew the clothes over me, laid my head on the pillow, and my invisible friend having also apparently retired for the night, fell asleep.

I slept sound until morning—sounder than I ever did in my lodgings, with the familiar and delightful London noises to lull me into peace and oblivion; and when I awoke, as I did with a start, the sun was shining in the east window, having a mind, as it seemed, to make the most of that day.

There was a noise close beside me too. Yes; a noise had awakened me. Turning to the point whence it seemed to proceed, I was surprised, and I may add mortified, to find the disturbance was caused by a mouse, which, seated on the top of the candle, was partaking of an extremely hearty meal.

When he found I was looking at him, he paused for a moment, and returned my stare with interest, his long tail hanging within reach of my hand.

After this greeting he seemed to think the exigencies of politeness satisfied, for he set to work again at the candle.

I made a feint of catching him, and he scuttled off to his hole.

When I woke again I found he had returned during the interval, and eaten one side of the tallow candle off, leaving the wick bare.

"I wonder what may be his opinion on the subject of ghosts," I thought, as I sprang out of bed, and flinging open the window, looked forth over the country bathed in the morning glory of glittering dew and molten gold.

Perhaps it might have been more to the purpose had I marvelled what my own opinion was on the same matter; but I shrank from a strict mental examination at the time.

I would defer analysing my feelings and the conclusions I deduced from them until I returned to London.

All I could bring myself to confess was that I believed there was something the matter with Crow Hall; whether that something was the air, the water, the trees, the drainage, or the story connected with the place, I could not, like others who had preceded me, decide; on one point, however, I experienced no doubts or misgivings—Crow Hall agreed with Mrs. Paul. Let the climate of the place or its invisible inhabitants militate against the health of other people, the house and her company suited that worthy lady.

Clearly I was beginning to suspect Mrs. Paul of a complicity with spirits, not exactly indicated by the term "witch." On the other hand, there was this in her favour; unless she were really a witch it was impossible she could have been in existence in the time of Philip Waldrum, neither could she have had any hand in getting up the appearances, or non-appearances, which alarmed successive tenants. Neither did it appear she ever was employed about the house in any capacity during the time when Valentine's father resided at Crow Hall. So far she seemed guiltless in the matter.

But the idea occurred to me, that perhaps she might be a descendant of some of those daring smugglers to whom the runs under and surrounding "The Black Crow" had been familiar.

Supposing the grounds were honeycombed with underground passages, and that Mrs. Paul possessed a knowledge of secret doors and hiding-places in the house, unsuspected by any other living person, it became very clear that unless with her permission, no one would stand a very good chance of living either comfortably or peaceably in Crow Hall.

"I must propitiate her," I thought; and I did this without meaning to do so, when I stated my intention of returning to London that afternoon.

Her eyes glistened, and one especially ugly tooth, which was eminently distasteful to me, showed more distinctly than ever whilst she listened.

"I hope to return next week," I went on; hearing which Mrs. Paul evidently thought her exultation had been premature, for her face clouded over, and the tooth retired behind her lips, disappearing totally from view.

Back in London, dirty, delightful, home-like London.

"Dearer art thou to me," I said, apostrophising the streets, lanes, and houses of the metropolis, "with thy fogs, rain, dust, than the finest country to which man could take me."

"Better," I thought, unconsciously parodying the Laureate, but similar ideas do occur to extremely different orders of mind; "better an hour in London than a year in Essex." Spite of an aptitude for eating lean fowls and ham and eggs, and existing without wine, all acquired at Crow Hall, I should have become nervous had I remained there, I should indeed.

The very sight of the London pavements, the smell of the smoke, the well-remembered blacks settling on my handkerchief—all these things acted upon me like tonics, and I was myself once more. I pooh-poohed the ghosts; I decided Crow Hall might be rendered habitable, and money made of it. I felt certain Mrs. Paul had been only trying to frighten me; and, after all, what was there in her story? Nothing.

I went to my club and dined, and felt better satisfied still. Yes, I could help Val, and still not hurt myself; full of which idea I wrote to him as follows:

"DEAR VAL,—I think I know a man who will buy your place. I have been to see it; kindly let me know, at your convenience, if you will take sixteen hundred and fifty.

"Yours faithfully,
"STAFFORD TREVOR."

To which he sent this reply by the very next post. I was still in bed when it arrived:

"DEAR MR. TREVOR,—Yes; I will thankfully take sixteen hundred and fifty pounds, and our agreement can remain as it was, plus commission on the extra one hundred and fifty.

"Indeed, I know not how to express my obligations.

"Yours truly,
"V. WALDRUM."

"I am in for it, then," I considered; "it is said that the woman who deliberates is lost. Surely the converse holds good with men. I have not deliberated, and I am bound in honour, at all events, to buy the place. I will, however, hear Doctor Wickham's report this evening, though that can make little difference now one way or another."

At a remote period of my life I had been in the habit of thinking the New North Road one of the dreariest thoroughfares in London; but that was in far-distant days, when my knowledge of modern Babylon was by no means so extensive as is the case at present.

Several localities present themselves at this moment as even less inviting than the road which at St. John's Church, Hoxton, debouches into a singularly nondescript and undesirable neighbourhood.

Men cannot always choose where they shall reside, more especially men without a large private income and with a large personal family. Can a person ever feel sufficiently thankful for not having a large personal family, if he be not possessed of a large private income?

I, at all events, felt thankful for the fact when I was ushered into Doctor Wickham's consulting-room.

A creature extremely diminutive in stature and painfully lean in person, clad in tight trousers and a jacket covered with buttons, supposed to represent his rank as a page, answered the door, and informed me that the Doctor would be with me in a minute, ere he shut me into an ailment-inspiring apartment commanding a view over a back garden—the ordinary back garden, in fact, of middle-class London.

Next instant the Doctor himself appeared—a small man, with sandy hair, keen gray eyes, and resolute mouth, who would, I am positive, have made a name in the world, had he not possessed that fatal soft spot in his character which prompted him to marry a wife prematurely.

"I am grieved to disturb you at your dinner-hour," I said.

Having heard the clatter of cups and saucers, as well as smelt the odour of grilled meat, I knew he must have been assisting at the purely feminine, moral, and domestic institution called a meat tea; but as people always like it to be supposed they dine late, I thought it as well to yield to the popular prejudice.

"A medical man ——" he began.

"Is always ready to lend his time to a patient, I am aware," I added; "but I am not a patient. I have no malady, and yet I want to consult you on a matter which is important to me—the health of a dear friend deceased."

"Really, sir," said Doctor Wickham.

"I think my name will tell you I am not a person likely to intrude unnecessarily upon the time or patience of a busy man like yourself," I replied. "I am the son of Professor Trevor, with whose works you are, doubtless, well acquainted, and I am most anxious to learn a few particulars from you about the illness of Mr. Harold Waldrum, of Crow Hall."

"I make it a rule never to speak of the cases I attend," he said, stiffening up in a moment.

"A most admirable rule," I agreed. "Would that all medical men adhered to it. But, supposing Mr. Valentine Waldrum requested you to be confidential, should you then object to open your mind to me fully about the matter?"

"I apprehend, sir," he answered, "that Mr. Valentine Waldrum, being a professional man himself, could afford you all the information you desire."

"Possibly, but the subject is a painful one to him."

"No doubt, and I can well believe he would wish as little said about it in the future as may be."

Here was a dilemma. I could not offer this man a five-pound note to bribe him to speak, acceptable as I felt certain such a sum would prove. I could not force him to open his mouth, and so I rose to take my leave without further parley, merely remarking:

"You perhaps imagine you are doing Mr. Waldrum a service in this matter, but I can assure you the contrary is the case. It is my intention to purchase Crow Hall, but I am quite determined not to do so till I know all the particulars of the late owner's illness and death."

"Purchase Crow Hall!" repeated the little doctor.

"Yes; is there anything very wonderful about that?" I inquired.

"I should not like to purchase it," he remarked.

"Why not?" I asked. "Surely the fancies and utterances of a madman ought not to be allowed to prejudice one against so cheap and desirable a property."

"Perhaps not; but after my experiences at Crow Hall, I would rather you bought it than I," he persisted.

"Come," I remarked, "you have said as much against the place as you well can; you may as well tell me the story straightforwardly. I know all about the reputed ghost. I have slept in the house; I shall sleep there again next week."

"Don't," he said. "Take my advice. Buy Crow Hall if you like; pull it down, or let it stand empty, but do not sleep in it—do not."

"May I ask why?" I said. "You cannot surely expect any .sane man to allow his money to remain unproductive, merely because at some remote period a foreign lady disappeared from a strange house, no one knew why or how."

He motioned me to sit down again, and he took a chair himself, looking with a perplexed expression at the depressing garden, with its two straight bordered walks and its strip of grass, terminating in a dreary-looking summer-house not much larger than a dog-kennel, where, doubtless, he smoked his pipe, and ruminated on ways and means after the youngsters were safely packed away in the sheets.

"Mr. Waldrum is, of course, aware that you mean to buy Crow Hall?" he said, after a pause.

"He fancies I want it for a friend of mine," I replied; "in fact, there is a note referring to the subject," and I handed Val's epistle to the Doctor.

He read it over, folded the paper, and returned the note to me.

"You had heard, of course, there were stories afloat concerning the place?" he suggested.

"Yes, and Mr. Waldrum said he wished no one to purchase it who was ignorant of them."

"Precisely so, and then ——"

"Then I went to the fountain-head and heard all about Philip Waldrum's wife, and the landlord of 'The Black Crow,' and the tenants who could not rest at night, or keep their health in the house."

"Anything else?"

"Nothing except what I had previously heard from Valentine Waldrum —namely, that his father died raving mad; that his disease first indicated itself by seeing visions and faces, and all that kind of thing. I never questioned either him or his mother much about the matter, as they always seemed to avoid it."

"May I inquire your object in wishing to purchase Crow Hall?"

"Yes; I wish to do the son of my old friend, Mrs. Waldrum, a good turn, if it be possible, without losing much by the transaction."

Once again he sat silent for a moment, looking out over his small domain, without, I am satisfied, seeing any single thing it contained; then he said:

"Sometimes, Mr. Trevor, I think there may be as much harm done by silence as by speech, and I am satisfied Mr. Waldrum would not wish you or anyone to buy that doomed house ignorant of what has happened in it. I attended Mr. Waldrum at The Grange in the latter days of his residence there; and, naturally, when he removed to Crow Hall, I used frequently to call there non-professionally, and oftener still to meet him and exchange a few words when I was walking about the parish or visiting patients who lived on the other side of Latchford Common. Before he had been in the place very long I was struck by a change in his appearance. It came on gradually, and I did not notice it till one day when he happened to be walking before me on the road; and something in his gait, in the droop of his head, in the slouch of his shoulders, struck me with that sort of uneasiness which a medical man's instinct feels at any physical alteration for which there is not, so far as he is aware, any actual cause.

" 'You walk as if you were tired,' I said to him. It was a bracing, frosty day—a day on which a healthy man had no business to feel tired. 'Are not you well?'

" 'Yes, I am well,' he answered; 'but there is something the matter with me. I have always latterly felt weary. I sleep soundly, not to say heavily, and yet I wake in the morning more tired than when I lie down at night; and my head is heavy—it does not ache, you know, but there is a weight across my forehead. I have curious dreams too; and when I wake, as I often do suddenly, I have a feeling as if someone were standing beside my pillow. It is all nonsense of course,' he finished.

" 'There is something amiss with your liver,' I observed.

" 'Very likely,' he agreed; 'you had better put it to rights for me.'

"We were close by my house at that moment, so I asked him in, and inquired more particularly as to his symptoms, but I could not find out what was the matter with him.

"His forehead was not hot, his tongue was in good order; he did not complain of cold feet, or ache or pain anywhere; his lungs were sound, I knew. I could not discover anything wrong with his liver.

"The only things about him I did not like were his appearance and his pulse. There was an indescribable grey look on his face, and there was a nervous flutter in his pulse that made me ask him:

" 'Have you anything on your mind?'

" 'I have had much on my mind for many a day past,' he said evasively.

" 'But anything extra—anything unconnected with worldly matters—with money?'

" 'I do not quite understand what you mean.'

" 'I mean, have you any fresh trouble; has anything occurred latterly to annoy you?'

" 'No,' he said, 'except that I do not like this feeling in my head.'

"I told him that feeling was a consequence, not a cause, and tried hard to get him to confide to me what he had on his mind. All in vain; he either had nothing at that time to tell, or he was determined not to tell it, so I sent him some medicine, and thought no more about the matter till one day when his son, who was at home at the time, came rushing up to my house to entreat me to go to his father immediately.

" 'He has gone suddenly mad, I think,' he said; 'persists he saw a woman's face at the window, and declares it is Philip Waldrum's wife come back.'

" 'He must be delirious,' I said.

" 'He is no more delirious than you are,' said his son, almost rudely; 'he is mad, and I have been afraid matters were tending to this for some time past.'

"When we reached Crow Hall, Mrs. Waldrum was sitting in the drawing-room crying, the servants were talking together in whispers, and Mr. Waldrum was standing in that bit of neglected garden lying under the oldest part of the house, staring up at a small window in one of the gables. He greeted me without the slightest evidence of insanity.

" 'Seeing is believing, Doctor,' he said, laying his hand on my shoulder. 'Now, you follow my eyes; you will not have long to wait; she has come to that window half-a-dozen times within the last half-hour.'

"I stood beside him for a few minutes, and then observed:

" 'Now, Mr. Waldrum, I cannot see anything, and what is more, I do not believe you can see anything either, and you must not try to frighten your household by talking such nonsense—you must not, really.'

" 'Well, perhaps I had better not talk of it,' he answered; 'but, Doctor, one word,' and he lowered his voice, 'it is true for all that. She has been haunting me for a long time, and I know who she is at last—Philip Waldrum's lost wife; you remember her portrait at The Grange. Well, I saw her at that window, looking as if she had stepped out of the frame.'

"Of course it was no use arguing with a man in such a state of mind, so I merely advised Mrs. Waldrum and his son to try the effect of change of air.

"It is easy for a doctor to tell the friends of a patient to take him away, but it is not always so simple a matter for the friends to follow his advice.

"It was difficult for Mrs. Waldrum to adopt my suggestion, I knew; but somehow she managed to get her husband to Hastings.

"They stayed away for three months; at the end of that time they returned, he being, as she, poor soul, imagined, cured. One look was enough for me. I knew the man had come home to die; and I suppose I must have shown something of my dismay, for he said, when his wife left the room:

" 'Doctor, what I saw before I left here was a warning to me. I hope I have taken it to heart.'

"By the same night's post I wrote to his son, and, after a very short delay, he came and stayed to the end.

"It would have been almost impossible to trace how he sank. Week by week he grew weaker; until one morning a message arrived, asking me to step up to Crow Hall. Mr. Waldrum wanted to see me particularly. He was still in bed, and looked worn and exhausted.

" 'No, I am not so well to-day,' he said, in answer to my inquiry; 'I am tired, tired, tired; but that is no matter. Doctor, I wanted to tell you a curious dream I had last night. I do not speak of any of these things to my wife or Valentine now. They do not like it, and they cannot understand; but I felt I must repeat it to someone. First, I dreamt I was awake; that it was a bright moonlight night; that I could see patches of light on the walls, the floor, the curtains. The door was open between this room and the next, and I could hear by Esther's light breathing that she was asleep, poor dear. I was lying looking at the moon, and thinking about the past and the future—about the world to which I am travelling so fast, Doctor, and wondering how my wife and boy will get on in this—when feeling that nameless something I have mentioned before, I turned my head, and saw Philip Waldrum's wife standing in the middle of a patch of moonlight that streamed against the wall. She was dressed all in black, her head was uncovered, round her neck she wore the traditional necklace, and on her hands she had the rings we have heard of so often. They gleamed in the moon's beams like stars. She beckoned me to follow her, and I could not choose but do so. She seemed to pass into the wall, and I did the same. Lighted by her diamonds we went down a narrow winding passage, the stairs rotted away with age, and the walls dirty and covered with mould, and wet with damp. She turned now and then to see if I was following, and at last we found ourselves in a square room that smelt like a charnel-house, and was close and suffocating as the grave. In a passage leading out of it something lay in a heap. She pointed to it; and, looking more closely, I saw these were bones on which jewels sparkled as on the hands and neck of my companion. As I stood, the face of Philip's wife changed—her cheeks dropped in, her eyes grew lustreless, her mouth fell, the skin tightened over her forehead. While I looked her countenance altered to that of a grinning death's-head; then the whole body collapsed, and I was alone with a heap of bones. How I got back I do not know. I have forgotten that part of the dream; but when I awoke it was broad day, and I felt weary enough to have been walking half the night.'

"It certainly did not occur to me then that he was describing this vision as a dream, merely because he was afraid to define it even to himself as anything else; so, instead of trying to lead him from the subject, as Mrs. Waldrum and his son always tried to do, I let him talk on, and hark back to the subject as often as he liked.

"While he was, for the third or fourth time, describing to me the very spot in the wall which had seemed to open, and was pointing it out with his hand, I said:

" 'What have you got on your sleeve, Mr. Waldrum?'

" 'On my sleeve?' he repeated.

" 'Yes; it is one mass of dirt,' I answered; and turning the folds round, I showed him the marks, as if it had been rubbed against some black, moist substance.

"He looked at it, and then at me. Next instant he fell back on his pillow in a dead faint.

"I thought we never should get him out of it. He lay like one dead, till I began to despair of his recovery; but he did recover.

"Of course, the one idea suggested to me by his story, and the black marks on his sleeve, was that he walked in his sleep; and after telling Valentine he had better be in the room at night instead of his mother, and keep the door locked, I went away, feeling all that could be done had been.

"But he grew more and more restless; as his physical strength decreased his mental irritability increased, and he was unable to control his speech, or to keep silence concerning the visions he saw, and the terrible sight which had been revealed to him.

"Ill though he was, I urged his being removed from Crow Hall. I offered the use of my own house, if none other were available; but he would not hear of it. If the subject were broached, he burst into a paroxysm of either grief or rage—sometimes weeping like a child—again, inveighing against the cruelty of those about him.

"They wanted to take away his last hope; wealth, wealth untold lay hidden away about the house, and he would find it for them. He should never enjoy it himself—that, of course, was a vain hope, a past expectation —but he might leave it for his wife and his son; he would have it if we could only be persuaded to let him alone.

"What were we to do? I put it to you, sir; what were we to do?"

"Humour him," I suggested.

"We did humour him. Mrs. Waldrum watched him by day, his son by night. The doors were kept locked; the keys removed. I saw him every day. I knew the end was a mere question of weeks; when about four o'clock one morning I was awakened by a tremendous knocking at the door.

" 'What is the matter?' I asked.

" 'It's Mr. Waldrum, sir, drownded in the pond!'

"I don't know how I got my clothes on. I don't know how I got to Crow Hall. He lay on his bed like one departed, but he was not dead. He spoke to me quite rationally once. I had cleared the room, and we were alone together.

" 'You remember what I told you about Philip's wife?' he said.

"I nodded.

" 'She has come often since, but particularly last night. We went down as before, but this time I could not get back. I went groping, groping on till I came to water. Then it caught me, and I shouted for help. It came. You know the rest.'

"After that he lapsed into delirium. He talked of hidden treasures; of a dark, beautiful woman; of bodies buried in subterranean chambers; of passages known to none but himself. And then he died. I was with him when he passed away.

"He stretched out his hands to the phantom which had cursed his later life, and said:

" 'Forgive me! I had not strength ——'

"That was all."

"And the moral you deduce from this," I said, "is that Crow Hall is an 'uncanny' sort of place?"

"It is a weird place," he answered. "Laugh if you like; it drove me from the neighbourhood."

"I have no inclination to laugh," I replied. "Nevertheless, I intend to buy."

"Do not blame me, then, sir, for anything that may ensue," he remarked.

"I am not one of the Waldrums," I replied; "and if I were, I do not think Mrs. Philip could induce me to take nocturnal rambles with her."

He looked at me, and shook his head gravely.

"I have a good digestion," I observed.

"There can be no doubt of that, or you would never buy Crow Hall," he replied.

After all we parted good friends. That is how, when the grand moment arrives, I should like to part with the world; but I think such a desirable exit improbable.

# CHAPTER VII

## MR. WALDRUM UNDERSTANDS

Crow Hall was mine, and with the purchase-money Valentine Waldrum furnished, not a house, but a waiting and consulting-room—to say nothing of a suite of private apartments—in a mansion once inhabited by nobility, but which had, in due course of time, come into the possession of a retired butler; who, with his wife, an ex-lady's maid, were very glad indeed to make mutually satisfactory arrangements with so desirable a tenant.

If I may say so without the charge of vainglory being preferred against me, Valentine would never of himself have found any residence or person likely to meet his requirements; consequently, the credit of house, furniture, servants, and moderate charges, may fairly be given to me.

Yet it was not without a struggle I agreed to abandon my first scheme, and permit him to settle down into bachelor chambers.

I wanted him to marry. I wished him to look for a wife before a state of celibacy became chronic. I told him surgeons and doctors ought to be husbands and fathers; and that, if he wished to succeed in his profession, he ought to make it his business to find a lady—if an heiress, so much the better—but in any case a lady, amiable, educated, intelligent; who could order his household, sit at the head of his table, and help him to push his way in society as only a clever woman can.

In answer to these remarks, for some time he only fenced or laughed; but at last he said plainly he never intended to marry.

"If I ever felt myself attracted by a girl, and likely to fall in love with her," he said, "I should flee away as swiftly as though I knew she were one of the Lorlei. The Waldrums have been a queer lot for many a long day, and I will not perpetuate the evil. Every man, I suppose, has a natural longing to hold his son on his knee—to think his name will be perpetuated through his children; but how should I look my son in the face without a shudder, remembering the legacy I must bequeath him? What delight should I feel thinking of one sprung from my loins ending his days a gibbering idiot, or a raving maniac in an asylum? No; marriage is not for me. I have taken my profession to wife instead of a woman; and, no matter what my own latter years may have in store, I know I shall leave behind me brain-children that may yet do the world good service."

"Pooh!" I said. "Your father was no more mad than I am. He got into a low state of health; saw visions and dreamt dreams; walked in his sleep, and talked nonsense about hidden wealth and a woman who wrought much trouble in the Waldrum family—as foreigners, male and female, are apt to do in regular, well-conducted British households. That is the sensible, matter-of-fact way of looking at the business."

At this juncture, Mr. Valentine Waldrum rose from his chair, and, taking my arm in his, held me as if I were in a vice.

"My good fellow," I observed; "if you are strong, be merciful!" But he never heeded my remonstrance.

"Once for all," he said, "let this matter end between us. As a medical man, I might be inclined to adopt your view of the question, if what you have stated were all; but it is not all. There is mad blood in the Waldrums, I tell you. *I saw that woman too!* I never thought to speak of this to living being again; but I saw her. It was before the funeral, and I had gone into the room where he lay to look at him once more. At the foot of the coffin stood a lady. She was dressed all in black, and she was wringing her hands like one in some terrible agony. For a moment I stood still, looking at her. Then she turned her face towards me, and I recognised her as the original of the picture at The Grange—a woman with black hair, and great sorrowful black eyes. She wore the fatal necklace of precious stones, and had diamonds sparkling on her hands. I must have lost consciousness for the time. When I came to myself, I was alone with the dead!"

"And the next time?" I inquired.

"Was the night before we left Crow Hall. I had sat up late, smoking, and, as I went up the staircase to bed, I distinctly felt the skirt of a woman's dress brush against me. Nothing was visible then; but when I reached the landing, I saw, in the moonlight which streamed through the window, a dark figure standing with her back to me. As before, she slowly turned her head, and I beheld Philip Waldrum's wife again, with her fatal beauty, with her decking of gems.

"She beckoned me to follow her. I felt something I could not define drawing me into the room where my father died; but with a last effort I called back my reason and fled. I do not mind confessing to you that I spent the whole of the night in prayer; I entreated God to deliver me from the haunting of that terrible presence, and to enable me to keep to my solemn resolution of living single all my days, rather than that child of mine should inherit so fearful a doom."

I sat for a moment silent, ashamed to confess in that ghostly house I too had felt the something he described sweep past me, and yet I dared not altogether refrain from expressing my belief.

"Val," I said at last, "do you know I think there really is a ghost at Crow Hall, or else someone who considers it worth while to personate the foreign lady. It could be easily done, you know."

"No!" he interrupted; "do you suppose I did not exhaust every possible and impossible conjecture before deciding the place was accursed, and we all mad together? By-the-bye, what is your friend going to do with it?"

He did not know till long afterwards I was the actual purchaser.

"He will put it in order, and charge the new railway company a fancy price for spoiling the seclusion of so charming a property."

"He does not intend to live there, then?"

"No; he buys as a mere speculation. He buys for a rise; if it proves a fall, he must put up with the loss and can afford to do so. By-the-way, I am going to Crow Hall next month. Can I deliver any message to the lady with the diamonds?"

"She will never appear to any but one of our doomed race," he answered gloomily.

"I fancy she is a lady of an extremely erratic and capricious turn of mind," was my reply; "and it would, therefore, be extremely difficult to say what she might or might not do."

Mr. Valentine Waldrum turned away offended: a pet ghost is like a cherished ailment—no man parts with either readily.

So far, however, he proved right. I never saw the lady with the diamonds. Philip Waldrum's dead wife did not care evidently to exhibit her charms to strangers; nevertheless, I could not sleep comfortably in the house. I always had that sense of a second presence after my door was locked, and I apparently alone, which, I may as well state at once, tried my courage as nothing before or since ever tried it.

Still, I was not going to be beaten. I had bought the place and meant to make money out of it. To make money it was absolutely necessary the popular belief in the idea of previous tenants should be shaken, and so I shook it. Once Mrs. Paul understood I was the owner of Crow Hall, all trouble in that quarter ceased. She waited upon me "hand and foot," to use her own vague phrase. When I suggested that I should like a room with a western aspect, a front apartment was scrubbed and prepared for my reception; and in it man nor woman, smuggler nor ghost, disturbed my repose.

Further, I at once gave Mr. Dogset notice, that on and after a certain date I should require him to relinquish his tenancy of the Crow Hall acres, which so astonished him, that he offered me a pound an acre more rental, which I accepted, and bound him to keep the fences in a state of proper repair.

For my own part, I had the out and inside of the house painted, the drive gravelled, the grass mown, the gates replaced, the gardens dug over and put in order. Mrs. Paul's fowls had to confine their scientific researches to their yard and the adjacent paddock, and it came to be rumoured throughout the parish that the Crow Hall ghost was laid.

I did not contradict the rumours, though I knew it was not true. When the railway surveyors came to inspect the property, they found a country-house in good repair, the grounds in order and well kept, the farm let at an increased rental, and better cropped and stocked than had been the case for years.

They were impressed, and offered me a very fair price for the slip of land they wanted.

At once, as an idle man who did not want to be troubled, I accepted their offer. After the purchase-money was paid I felt secure. I was not afraid of the future; I knew I should see my outlay back again, and doubled possibly. In which event I meant Valentine should share in my prosperity.

As has been already stated, I am eminently non-speculative. Perhaps it is for this reason that when I do speculate fortune favours me.

For example: no worse whist-player ever existed; and yet, when I consent to make a fourth, such cards are dealt to me that success is absolutely certain.

Again: suppose I see, as I sometimes do, a mine or a company in which I feel disposed to buy a few shares, those shares are sure to go up, and then I sell. I do not hold my poor purchase, no matter how promising things look, in the expectation of gaining two hundred per cent. No; I wait for a certain rise, and then find a customer.

Of course I sometimes see the shares of a company, in which I have no further interest, touch a fabulous price, but that does not fret me in the least. More frequently I see the grand programme collapse, and the final scene of the drama played out in the Vice-Chancellor's Court or else patronised in person by the Chief Judge in Bankruptcy, to say nothing of a host of clamorous creditors.

As I have before remarked, I believe in nothing as a really secure investment except the Three per Cents. and a first mortgage on land.

Nevertheless, occasionally I coquette with the Money Market to the extent of a few hundreds. To please fair patronesses I buy a lottery-ticket now and then; and for the sake of times long past, I take a little trouble about such a place as Crow Hall, for instance.

To pick up, however, once more the thread of my story.

In a fashionable quarter, in well-furnished rooms, with an unexceptional gentleman in black to show gentlemen and ladies into the apartment, which may well, I think, to borrow a City phrase, be called a sweating-room, by reason of the feverish agony there undergone, Mr. Valentine Waldrum did fairly well. He did not succeed as my friend the medical humbug prophesied; perhaps because he lacked some of the elements of success—perhaps because my friend never sent him but three patients—one a governess, one an artist, and one an eccentric country squire, who screwed him down to perform an operation any old practitioner would have charged fifty guineas for, at, to quote the advertising agents, a nominal price of five.

Nevertheless he succeeded pretty well. He was paying his way and gaining a name, and seemed sufficiently happy. All his leisure moments he devoted to some abstruse studies connected with those parts of the human internal economy which are connected with the spleen, or the lights, or the liver, or the kidneys. I beg to assure the reader I have no feeling of favouritism as regards the internal mechanism of man, and it is quite immaterial to me to which organ Mr. Waldrum directed his attention. A copy of his book containing the author's autograph is on my bookshelves, but I never read it, and I can conscientiously say I never shall.

All this, however, has nothing to do with the fact that he did make some part of the human body his study; that he discovered something in it, or deduced something from it never previously deduced or discovered; that he wrote a book on the subject which was well reviewed in *The Lancet*, and which gave him a certain standing in the opinion of his professional brethren.

It is quite one thing, however, to stand well with brother-surgeons, and another to hit the fancy of the general public. Perhaps surgeons are like other men of the world, and like those in their own line best who have not the faculty of climbing very fast or very high. Anyhow, if Valentine Waldrum won favour, he did not make guineas so rapidly as I had hoped would prove the case. Further, by the time his book was finished, the reviews had appeared, and his brethren had begun to remark: "Waldrum is a clever fellow; he has something in him. He will make his mark yet ——" Waldrum fell ill.

He had tried his sight by staring at unpleasant objects through the microscope. He had been examining and torturing all sorts of animals. He had been reading books, old and new, on the subject nearest his heart. He had been attending people who did not pay him, in the interests of science; and he had been sitting up at night, when he could have done his work just as well in the middle of the day.

All this and more I remarked to him, but he only smiled in answer, as though the production of a book never likely to be read out of his own profession, and by very few of the members composing it, were a more than sufficient off-set against impaired sight, low spirits, and a generally depressed state of health.

This was the position—pecuniary, sanitary, and moral—of Mr. Valentine Waldrum when I left town to pay my usual visit to Fairy Water, and this was how it came to pass I suggested the expediency of inviting him to stay there.

I and one of the boys, a riotous young imp, between whom and the pony there seemed a sort of *rapport* which carried us up hill, and down dale, and along the level, as fast as the creature could tear, went over to the station to meet our visitor, who mightily astonished Master Ralph by taking the reins from him.

"I have no doubt you are a capital whip," he remarked, "but for all that I cannot submit to be driven by a lad of your size."

"All right," said Master Ralph; "that is, if you can drive."

"You want your ears boxed, young gentleman," I observed.

"If I did want them boxed, I don't know who is to do it," retorted Ralph, whom I had heard on one occasion call me an old fogie.

"Very likely I shall," said Valentine, with a genial smile.

The boy looked him over, and then bursting into a hoarse laugh, exclaimed:

"Come, you ain't a muff, that is one comfort."

"What would your mamma say if she heard you use such expressions, Ralph?" I inquired.

"Oh! she'd cry; but we never let her hear. She's a woman, and she does not understand, so we don't vex mother—none of us."

"See you never do, my lad," said Mr. Waldrum. "Time may bring you many good gifts, but it will never bring you a second mother."

Ralph did not make any direct reply to this, but I saw the young rascal turn up his eyes and clasp his hands, and heard him mutter to himself:

"My! ain't it better than copy!"

Mrs. Trevor came to the door to meet us. She had seen so little of the world, she was such a child still in many respects, that she thought so distinguished a guest as Valentine ought to be received with all the honours.

She was a staid, quiet little matron; and as I watched her shyly holding out her hand to the new arrival, I felt irresistibly reminded of some plant grown in a cellar, of some creature kept long in confinement, of some bird in its earliest flight, utterly ignorant of the ways and manners of those of its fellows who have been accustomed to liberty from their youth upwards.

Of course she was not, even in her early youth, the sort of woman Valentine was likely to admire. I had not seen him in society without understanding precisely the lady fair to whom he would have inclined had he permitted himself to incline to anybody.

Juno-like beauties were his favourites. To them he directed his eyes, his attention, his discourse. Given a woman with well-developed and better-exposed shoulders, full face, decided features, large eyes, red-lipped mouth, filled with regular white teeth, and a fluent tongue, and round and about that shrine my *protégé* wandered.

Making, however, every due allowance for this proclivity, I felt disappointed at the expression which came over his face when he first saw my cousin.

I could not tell what it implied, whether contempt or derision, or simple astonishment.

At any rate, if I ever felt inclined to pick a quarrel with him it was then; but immediately I reproached myself for the feeling.

"He knows nothing of her past life," I considered. "He is judging her as he might a woman of society, and thinks her small, plain, *gauche*. He has no idea of her worth, nor suspicion of what she has suffered, poor darling"; and when she kissed me, as was her innocent mode of receiving her late husband's cousin, I returned the salute, which was not my innocent mode, as a rule, and glanced at Valentine after I had done so.

He was looking at me, I found, with a very queer twinkle in his eyes, and the desire to pick a quarrel grew almost irresistible.

After the first ten minutes, however, things went on smoothly. Once he saw the sick lad he was in his element. Having met with a human being more than ordinarily ill, whose case nevertheless was not beyond hope, his spirits rose at once. He forgot his own ailments; he forgot that so far he had won less money than fame; he forgot everything save his skill, and devoted it and himself to the heir of Fairy Water.

During the first part of his stay I was his constant companion. We walked, drove, smoked, sat together. Mrs. Trevor and the lads kept themselves to themselves with a pertinacity for which I am only able to account on the ground that they were all, mother and boys, afraid of the newcomer. Miss Isobel had her own views on the subject, however, and haunted my friend with a pertinacity which seemed to be troublesome; but he would not let me send her away.

"There are not many who care for me," he said with a pathetic break in his voice. "If this little one likes to say she will marry me, where is the harm to either of us?"

Where indeed! And yet there was something in the tiny maiden's repeated assertion: "I love you; I will marry you when I am a woman," which seemed to me to be a discord in the calm harmony of that almost monastic home.

I had assisted at the sacrifice of the mother, who might never now hope to love or marry; and yet here was the child, all unconscious of what marrying and giving in marriage had proved to one of the *dramatis personae* present that morning in Winchelsea church, inventing her own little domestic story, and assigning to herself and this man, whom I could remember running about in short frocks and red shoes before Mrs. Trevor was thought of, the parts of hero and heroine.

After a time there came a change, however, in our order of proceeding. As Valentine recovered his health and spirits, I found myself more alone with Mrs. Trevor and the invalid, whilst Mr. Waldrum and the boys took long rambles over the hills; or hired a boat, and rowed up and down the river; or went fishing or playing cricket.

In a few days after he began to make companions of them, the lads worshipped him, as lads do worship muscular men, whether Christians or sinners. They were never happy except in his presence; they followed him about like dogs; and wearied not in reciting his feats of strength, his acts of valour, and his performances with bat, rod, and oar, for the edification of their mother, Geoffrey, and myself.

Gradually I observed Mrs. Trevor seemed to weary of their ecstasies; the smile with which she listened to their narratives grew forced; and whilst they chatted on she would often look away, as if thinking of something foreign to their conversation.

I could not imagine what was the reason for this. It was natural enough I should feel tired to death both of Valentine and the lads, but with her the case was different. Hitherto, she had been in the habit of evincing the keenest sympathy with their few sports; and when they brought, to my intense disgust, a bottle filled with sticklebacks into the drawing-room, she actually attempted to count the victims.

Now, all this interest had died out. Like me, she seemed to loathe the name of trout, whilst cricket became as great a word of dread to her as to me.

Knowledge came one evening as we sat by the window, looking down on the water which gave its name to the place. The sun was shining through the trees, and threw long patches of shifting and glimmering light upon the lake, making it look a fitting haunt for the most fanciful fairy that ever danced on greensward, or hid herself in the cup of the floating lily. Under a great walnut-tree Valentine sat on a bench, the sick boy lying on a couch near him, and the others grouped around, making the summer stillness hideous with peals of laughter.

People talk of the music of children's voices, but anything less resembling music than those shouts of merriment I never heard, save, perhaps, the braying of a German band when every instrument is out of tune.

I had been discoursing about the beauty of the landscape, and was pointing out to Mrs. Trevor the perpetual changes that flitted over the face of the water as the sunlight fell now here, now there upon it.

"I do not think I ever saw Fairy Water look so worthy of its name," I remarked at last, as a stately swan came slowly sailing across a patch of light, which made it seem as though he were floating through a sea of molten gold.

"Yes," she answered, and there was something in her tone which caused me to turn from my contemplation of the external prospect.

She was not looking at the lake, or the flickering sunbeams, or the heavy foliage of the solemn trees; her eyes were fastened on the group gathered on the lawn, and they were full of unbidden, perhaps unconscious, tears.

"Why, Mary," I exclaimed, "what is the matter?"

She covered her face with her hands, and wept softly.

"I am very foolish—very wicked, perhaps; but I can't help it. My children are all I have, and till he came I was first in their hearts. Now they leave me for a total stranger."

"Don't be a baby, Mary," I expostulated; "your boys love you just as much as ever; but it is natural that a man like Mr. Waldrum, who in many ways," I added, loftily, "seems little more than a lad himself, should attract their fancy. It is far better they should openly show their attachment for a person in their own rank of life, than be sneaking secretly after grooms, rat-catchers, and poachers."

"I never felt afraid of my boys doing anything of that kind," she replied, with spirit.

"Nevertheless," was my answer, "it is precisely what your boys have been doing. When you are present they conduct themselves like saints; but when your back is turned, there are no greater young Turks on earth. I do not say this in any disparagement of the lads. They are fine, spirited children, and though they would not, I believe, vex you for any consideration, still they cannot help their young blood, and light hearts, and muscles asking to be used, and minds wanting to be occupied. You cannot go fishing, shooting, boating, and cricketing with them; and fond as they are of their mother, they delight in the company of any man able to share in their sports. Because I never had any taste for such things, I have heard that young rascal Ralph call me a 'duffer,' and other equally opprobrious names. Why, he tried to get the best of Mr. Waldrum the first evening we met him at the station; but Valentine threatened to box his ears, and the boy was delighted."

She sat thinking for a minute over all I had said, and then she remarked:

"So it comes to this—I shall not be able to bring up my boys myself."

There was a pathetic quiver about her mouth, a beseeching look in her eyes which tempted me to shirk telling her the truth, but I put aside the temptation. My own views had been enlarged since I saw the influence a man could acquire over the young termagants, and I was not going to run the risk of breaking her heart in the future for the sake of uttering pleasant things in the present.

"My dear," I said, and I took her hand in mine as I spoke, "I am afraid we ought not to blind ourselves any longer. No woman can, after a certain age, bring up boys properly. She can train them to be hypocrites, selfish tyrants, milksops, absorbed students, shy recluses; but she cannot educate them to be men. The mother's influence exercised in her own especial province is almighty for good; but another influence is needed, and you must send your boys away that they may be fitted for the battle of life, that when they grow into men you may be proud instead of ashamed of them. The girl is all your own of course ——"

"Ah!" she interrupted, "Isobel is more a boy even than Ralph. She has not an instinct or taste of a girl about her."

At this I laughed outright.

"Mary," I said, "when you were Isobel's age, what were your instincts and tastes?"

"I do not remember," she answered. "Mamma never let me have any, I think."

"In my opinion you must have greatly resembled your little girl," I observed. "But now you must promise me to be brave. You will try not to be jealous of poor Val's influence over your children; you will, like a wise little woman, remember you cannot alter human nature or ——"

At this juncture she suddenly withdrew her hand, which, quite unconsciously, I had retained.

"Here they come," she said, and the colour rose in her face as if she had been doing something eminently wrong; "I—I will just go upstairs and bathe my eyes."

And she left the room as Valentine, with that curious expression in his face I had noticed the first evening of his arrival, came up to the open French window, and asked me if I would come out for a stroll and a cigar.

"These lads have quite exhausted me," he explained. "Let us have a walk for half an hour."

"I will go with you," shouted Ralph.

"That you shall not," declared Mr. Waldrum, with commendable decision; "I have had quite enough of you for one evening"; which statement was a great relief to me—Ralph's company being about the last thing I should ever have thought of desiring.

For a time we paced along in silence, then said Valentine, knocking the ash off his cigar:

"I suppose Mr. Trevor has not been long dead?"

"Captain Trevor has been dead for many years," I replied.

"Mrs. Trevor still wears very deep mourning," he remarked.

"I suppose she will do so till the end," I replied.

"The end of what?" he asked.

"Her life," I said shortly, and then ensued another silence.

"It was the old story, I presume," he began after a pause; "a love-match, an early death."

"There was no love on her side," I answered; "and Captain Trevor lived to a sufficient age. It is a tale I have never cared to repeat, but as there is no secret in Mrs. Trevor's life, I will tell you all I know about it if you like."

"She puzzles me," he replied; and then I understood his curiosity was piqued.

It did not take me long to finish the narrative. How bald and naked it seemed when reduced to words, and yet what did the whole thing mean? Simply the loss of the best part of a woman's life—the annihilation of youth, hope, love.

He comprehended it all now, even to the will which rendered it impossible for her to make a better or a worse of the future than the past had proved. I told him everything, even to my own remorse at the part I had acted in Winchelsea church.

"We won't talk about this thing again," he said. "I misjudged you very much; I thought you had a *tendresse* for *la belle cousine*, but refrained from speaking, deterred by the idea of losing your liberty and gaining the boys."

"My dear fellow," I observed, "I love and honour Mrs. Trevor, but I never was a marrying man; and if I had been, I am a quarter of a century at least older than she."

"True," he said, "I had forgotten that"; and we walked back to Fairy Water in silence.

## CHAPTER VIII

### VALENTINE'S FIRST CHANCE

Shortly after that evening Mr. Valentine Waldrum began to tire of the country; he grew weary, I could see, of the still, tranquil, stagnant life, of the remorselessly monotonous meals, of the utter lack of congenial society, of the riotous fondness of the children, of the gentle amiability of his hostess, of the uninviting existence, of which nothing disturbed the routine save the advent of a fresh calf, or the hatching of a successful brood of chickens.

His spirits, at first so much improved, fell to zero; his appetite followed suit, his manners grew restrained, and his face gradually assumed an expression of penitential weariness. Altogether I did not feel in the least degree surprised when he announced to me one morning, after breakfast, that he had received letters which compelled him to return to town.

"I shall not forget Geoffrey, though, Mrs. Trevor," he said to her before his departure; "I will run down as often as I possibly can to see him."

She knew too little of the world—she was so utterly ignorant of the ways and doings of that London near "which she had once lived," to understand fully the extent of the kindness already done by Valentine to her boy, but she was of so grateful and humble a nature that intuition stood her in almost as good stead as experience.

With a pretty colour in her cheeks and tears in her eyes, with a sweet simplicity that made me feel very proud of my cousin, and that I am sure touched Mr. Waldrum sensibly, she thanked him for all he had already done.

"You have laid me under a debt of gratitude I can never repay," she said.

"And Mr. Trevor has laid me under a debt of gratitude I can never repay," answered Valentine, frankly. "He has done far, far more for me than I could ever hope to do for him or his."

"Has he, really? I am so glad," she exclaimed eagerly.

"It was nothing, Mary. He is given to exaggeration," I remarked, with becoming modesty.

"It is no exaggeration," said Valentine, with a look which reminded me of his mother. Ah! welladay, that story was indeed an old one.

"Mrs. Trevor, everything I have I owe to your cousin. If I ever achieve any fame or success worth speaking of, I can never forget he gave me the first shove from shore; he found me at Islington, depressed, disgusted, eating my heart out, and he put courage into me at once. I had a poor little place down in Essex, which no one would buy, upon which no one would lend money. He found a friend to purchase it, and on the strength of that purchase I set up as a West End surgeon, tried the experiments in which I was interested, wrote a book, and am a known man, making a fair income. That is *all* your cousin did for me," with a satirical expression on the "all"; "and as of course it was not worth remembering, I forgot it immediately."

"Do not pay any attention to what he says, Mary," I entreated; "he was a bad boy from the beginning."

"He has been very good to me and mine," she answered, holding out her hand, which he took reluctantly, as it seemed to me, and released immediately.

"I will cure the boy if it be in human power to do so," he said confidently, and thus we parted.

About that time my attention was much engaged concerning a variety of business letters that were perpetually arriving on the subject of Crow Hall, nevertheless it certainly struck me as curious that Mary found nothing to say concerning her late guest.

If I introduced him as a topic of conversation, she listened and tried to seem interested, but she never voluntarily alluded to his existence.

Of course I understood the reason for her silence—she was jealous of his influence over her children.

Well, it was natural; she had only them, and, thanks to my cousin, she had lived out her young life, whilst they might have many another interest beside her; and had, moreover, their lives all before them.

I could not argue the matter with her; nevertheless, I felt hurt. When one introduces a friend to a woman, one expects her to evince some interest in him; more especially when he has tried to serve her and hers.

My cousin Mary was gracious in manner to Mr. Waldrum, but I misdoubted me that she was ungrateful at heart; and he, I think, felt this, for when he did come down to Fairy Water for his promised visits to Geoffrey, he made his stay as short as possible, and, always alleging professional engagements, returned to London with as much speed as might be.

Meanwhile the words I had spoken to Mrs. Trevor about the boys bore fruit. She herself suggested a thing I should never have dared to do—that Ralph should be removed from the mild sway of the neighbouring vicar, and the unrestrained liberty of Fairy Water, to a good school, the selection of which she left to me.

"I cannot part with them all at once," she said, with a forced smile; "but I want to do my duty by them now I understand clearly which way duty lies."

"You are a dear, good little woman," I exclaimed, delighted to find that, even on the subject of her children, she possessed some small share of that common sense so unusual amongst mothers.

At which outbreak she laughed, and asked if I were certain I really thought so, which question I answered in the affirmative with some slight mental reservation.

I had found her good in all relations of life, except it might be in her non-appreciation of my friend; and, after all, was she to be blamed for failing to understand his character?

It rarely happens that a man's friends take kindly to each other. Why should Mr. Waldrum and Mrs. Trevor prove exceptions to this rule?

Besides the strawberry season, there were other festive occasions and high saint days and holidays which I had been in the habit of spending at Fairy Water for more years than there is any necessity to specify.

Christmas Day, of course; Shrove Tuesday, and Ash Wednesday, generally; Mid Lent Sunday occasionally; and Good Friday and Easter time, I may say, without exception. Sometimes I ran down about Whitsuntide for a day or two, and since boyhood I had assisted at the sacrifice of the traditional goose, the appearance of which, smoking hot on the domestic board, is supposed to insure good fortune for twelve months to come. I am not certain that these anniversaries were seasons of any real festivity to me, but the habit of observing them had been growing for years; and as Doctor Johnson felt a sense of uneasiness if he passed one of the familiar posts in Fleet Street without touching it, so I should have experienced a sensation of mental discomfort had the days above enumerated come round and found me absent from my accustomed place.

It was the 28th September in the same year when I had first introduced Mr. Waldrum to Fairy Water—how well I remember the day by reason of what followed after—when Valentine, coming to my lodging, found me dawdling over the remains of a late breakfast.

"I have called," he said, "to know if I can take any message or parcel to Mrs. Trevor. I am going to Fairy Water to-morrow."

"I am going there this evening," I answered. "Come with me, and stay over Sunday."

He demurred to this proposition, but finally agreed that we should travel together, if I would let him return the following afternoon.

"You seem to be as loath to leave London as I am, Val," I remarked.

"Yes," he said; "I think it is the only place for a solitary man."

"You mean, I suppose, that it is the only place where a man need never feel solitary," I observed.

"You have expressed my meaning better than I did," he answered, and then fell into a brown study.

"What is the matter?" I asked, at last; "what is preying on your mind now?"

"Only the loss of a patient," was his reply. "I wonder how old I shall be before people will believe I have sufficient experience to attend the upper ten?"

"Your patient then has left you, not departed this life?" I commented; for at first I really imagined a casualty had occurred.

"Oh! he is not dead," said Valentine. "You know the man I mean—Keith, who has just become Sir Henry Keith, and succeeded to his uncle's estates. He could afford now to pay one a decent fee, and I suppose that is the reason why he has thought fit to send for Cock."

"Never mind, your turn will come some day," I said consolingly.

"Yes, when I am too old to care whether it does or not."

"A man is never too old to be indifferent to success," I replied. "Besides, Keith is not a patient worth fretting after. He used to be a poor snob, and now he is a rich one; that is all. When you begin to attend the Royal Family he will remember he used to consult you, and send a polite note to that effect at once. But you may take my word for it," I proceeded; "you will do no good for yourself unless you go into general society."

"I have no inclination to enter into general society," he answered; and then I understood the old wound was still open, that the previous year had failed to obliterate the memory of that tragedy enacted at Crow Hall.

When we reached Fairy Water, we found the local doctor sitting beside the sick boy.

It was he who had written to tell Mr. Waldrum their patient seemed retrograding, and to judge from the expression of his face, Geoffrey might have been *in articulo mortis*.

Mrs. Trevor looked as though she had been crying night and day for a fortnight previously, and in this cheerful mental atmosphere the lad's own spirits had fallen to zero.

At a glance almost, Valentine took in the position of affairs.

"You must not distress yourself, Mrs. Trevor," he said; "Geoffrey does not seem so well as I should like to find him, certainly, but there is nothing the matter that cannot be put right very easily."

And then he and Dr. Sloane went into another room and had a long chat together, whilst I took the first convenient opportunity of telling Mary what a baby she was, and relieving my own feelings by scolding her.

Next to Isobel, Geoffrey of all the children was my favourite. His health had prevented his indulging in the riotous pastimes which were the delight of Master Ralph, and his constant and enforced companionship with his mother had imparted to him somewhat of her gentle, patient nature; of the mixture of innocence and thoughtfulness, of simplicity and wisdom, which rendered her character in my eyes at once so rare and so attractive.

I was concerned for the lad, and unhappy about his mother, for both of which reasons I was especially hard on Mrs. Trevor for always "looking at the worst side of everything," and "fancying Geoffrey a great deal more delicate than was really the case," to all of which she listened with a contented smile.

"You can say what you please now," she answered. "I am easy now Mr. Waldrum has seen my boy, and assures me he is not dangerously ill."

We were standing in the conservatory at that moment, she with her white fingers straying amongst the flowers of a great oleander tree, and something, I cannot tell what, prompted me to say:

"You have great faith in Mr. Waldrum, then, Mary?"

She lifted her eyes to mine—sweet, trustful eyes they were too—as she replied:

"Of course I have implicit faith."

"In that case do you not think you could manage to be a little more civil to him?"

"Civil!" she repeated. "Am I not civil to him?"

"No; and I fancy he feels your coolness when he is trying to do all in his power for your child."

She swept one look at me from under the shelter of her long lashes, and then there came such a sudden and vivid colour into her face, that for the moment her whole appearance was changed.

"I am very sorry," she said; "I did not mean to vex you or Mr. Waldrum. I have not been much in society, and I cannot help feeling shy with strangers."

"But Valentine ought to be no stranger," I argued; "to me he has always been just like a son."

"Ah! yes, but you have known him so much longer," she answered; and then she gathered one of the oleander buds and put it in her belt, and tripped out of my sight with a step as light as though she had been only nineteen instead of nine-and-twenty.

All that evening she did her best, in a timid, nervous kind of way, to be more sociable towards Mr. Waldrum; and she joined me most earnestly— but then this might not have been disinterested—in asking him to remain over Sunday.

As he positively, and, to my thinking, not very courteously, refused our invitation, all she could do was to order that the slaughtered goose should be cooked for an early dinner, so that her guest might partake of the delicacy before leaving for London.

Next morning came clear, crisp, sunshiny. Valentine and I had agreed over night we could have a long walk before breakfast, and by eight o'clock we were standing on an eminence commanding a view of Low Park, one of the very many residences of the Duke of Severn.

"I should think a man who owned a property like that must find dying a difficult business," remarked my companion.

"The present Duke is quite a young man," I replied; "I should not think he can be more than three or four and twenty. I know his aunt, Lady Mary Carey, and she has often referred to a long minority, during which the rents have been accumulating, and the young Duke growing older."

"I wonder how a man feels, who, looking over those woods and lands, feels they are all his own?"

"Very much as we do, only without the envy, I imagine," was my answer; and then we retraced our steps, talking of indifferent subjects as we did so.

After breakfast, which with me in the country as in London is, I regret to say, a mere formality, I retired to the library to write letters. One in especial occupied my attention. It was addressed to the secretary of a charitable institution, the managers of which wished to purchase Crow Hall, or, should I desire to retain the hall in my own possession, a certain number of acres, on which an asylum might be built, the remainder of the land to be converted into a model farm.

Caution having been the coach that has carried me through life, I answered:

"SIR,—Your proposal being one requiring serious consideration, I must request the delay of a month before giving a final answer.

"Your obedient servant,
"H. STAFFORD TREVOR."

This, and some other letters, I determined to post myself—a love of solitary and surreptitious walks being a peculiarity the country always develops in me; and accordingly, without asking anyone else in the house if he or she desired to send any confidential mission by the next day's mail, I started off to the nearest village all alone.

Just as I was emerging from the entrance gates, a groom in the Severn livery, driving a horse covered with foam, pulled up.

"Beg pardon, sir, but is Mr. Waldrum at your house?"

"I think he is in," I replied; "what do you want with him?"

Already the horse was trotting up the avenue as fast as he knew how, but the man shouted back:

"Duke! Sloane! Brains!"

"It will keep, whatever the matter may prove," thought I, and walked on to the office.

When I returned Mary met me in a pretty flutter. "What do you think?" she said, clasping her hands through my arm, "Mr. Waldrum has been sent for to Low Park."

"What is wrong there?"

"The Duke's gun exploded. He is dangerously injured."

"That is a chance at last for Val," I said.

"How worldly you are," she expostulated.

"Surely, my dear, if the Duke likes to meet with accidents, my friend may as well have the benefit of them as not."

"Of course," she agreed; "but what a dreadful thing to happen."

"What has happened?" I asked.

"Something to his eyes, and head, and hand," was the lucid reply.

"Clearly the goose is not roasting in vain."

"Oh, how can you!" she said, and went away, her handkerchief to her eyes, crying about the injuries of a man she had never seen.

It struck me then, as it has struck me since, that the feminine temperament is one which possesses much more of theoretical than of practical sympathy.

One o'clock chimed, two o'clock in due time followed suit, Valentine came not, and I was growing hungry.

"My dear," said I, "about that goose?"

"You imagine Mr. Waldrum will be detained," she remarked.

"Nothing more probable."

"Shall we wait a quarter of an hour longer?"

"An hour if you like"; which I consider was magnanimous, since hunger was gnawing at my vitals.

Ten minutes, twenty, thirty, forty minutes ticked their way onwards, and Mary was miserable. She had always considered me and me only, and now another guest claimed her courtesy and her patience.

"Oh!" at last she exclaimed, and that "oh" meant a whole thanksgiving service, as she heard the sound of wheels coming up the drive; "here he is."

"Softly, my dear," I remarked, and, arranging my double eye-glass comfortably on my nose, I beheld a phaeton drawn by a pair of ponies dashing over the gravel, containing not Mr. Waldrum, but certainly the very last person I desired to see at Fairy Water—Lady Mary Carey.

I am not often taken with a sudden tremor; it is not a usual thing with me to feel my head shaken down into my heart, and my heart shaken up into my head; but when I beheld that woman lolling back in the phaeton, scanning with her great eyes my cousin's modest home, my spirit sank within me.

She had thick wiry hair, wide nostrils, eager wondering eyes, and protuberant lips. Her skin was mottle-brown and yellow, her figure like nothing save a bundle of clothes tied up for the laundress; she was acquisitive beyond belief, and impertinent and insolent beyond description.

She could not be in the company of a stranger for an hour without giving utterance to some insult. She never knew a person for a week without soliciting some favour or demanding a present. She had divorced one husband, she had worried another into his grave, expecting he would leave her all his money.

In which expectation she was disappointed. As she told the story to everyone there can be no indiscretion in my repeating it.

Mr. Carey made a will, bequeathing to his dearly beloved wife the whole of his fortune, excepting such and such legacies to such and such people, and he placed this document in Lady Mary's hands.

A week subsequently he executed another will, which he left in the hands of his solicitors, leaving her ladyship a life annuity of only three thousand a year.

Upon the strength of this annuity of three thousand, and her own small fortune, Lady Mary led, as best she could, the life of a fashionable woman.

She had her receptions, her afternoons, her concerts, her evenings, her small dinners, and to them everyone who could obtain an invitation repaired. What did her plainness, her meanness, her insolence matter? Was she not the sister of one duke, the aunt of another? was it not rather an honour to be snubbed by her? whilst to be taken under her especial protection, and addressed by one's christian-name, were marks of distinction so great that they necessarily produced feelings of envy, hatred, and all uncharitableness in those less favoured by fortune.

To me Lady Mary had proved uniformly good-natured. I had been useful to her; I might be useful still. She called me "Stafford." She got me to dance with girls who knew no one, and girls whom men did not care to know. She commanded my attendance at a new piece, or to the opera. She took my arm as if she paid me a salary for its use; and she treated me like a friend of the house.

Once she conceived a fancy for my studs, and asked me to give them to her, as they were just what she thought she should like to fasten her cuffs; and within a week she decided some charms I had foolishly attached to my chain were the very things she had been seeking for without success.

After that time she searched my person in vain for any trifle to annex. Except for the benefit of her butler, she could not ask me to give her a coat; and he, indeed, was a gentleman of so corpulent a build, that it would have required three or four of my garments to encase his portly form.

It was not often Lady Mary met with a rebuff. People were too much afraid of her tongue and herself to adventure upon trying the experiment; but once I did see a daring shot between wind and water.

It was fired in this wise. Lady Mary had conceived a violent friendship for an authoress of some literary reputation, who was styled by those who admired her person less than her genius, "Rags and Bones." "Rags," because she never had a new gown on her back; "Bones," because whatever flesh might, in years gone by, have covered the framework of her body had long disappeared.

Accompanied by this eccentric person, my lady went out one evening to a party, where she met a fresh authoress who had not as yet forgotten how to put on her clothes, or ceased to recollect that men had once thought her pretty.

Said my lady, after the first amenities were over: "How strange to think you write! I always was led to believe literary ladies" (and her glance wandered to "Rags and Bones") "were perfectly indifferent to their personal appearance—indeed, held themselves superior to the adventitious aid of dress."

Said the authoress, without a change of countenance: "It is never safe to generalise upon a class from an individual; otherwise I might say no lady of quality was acquainted with the most ordinary rules of politeness."

A dead silence followed after this speech, which Lady Mary broke by a forced laugh.

"You will do, my dear," she said, patting the fair shoulder with a hand like that of a prize-fighter. "Heaven has given you a tongue, and the wit to use it."

Next day I beheld my lady and the new favourite driving in the Park, *vice* poor, clever, modest, unassuming "Rags and Bones," cashiered.

I met her afterwards.

"You know, dear Mr. Trevor," she said—and I could not help noticing her ill-fitting boots, her terrible bonnet, her gloves which wanted mending —"I can write much better than that woman; but she has a way of saying things, and Lady Mary has taken her up."

"Yes," I replied; "and, after a short time, Lady Mary will let her drop."

"Ah! Mr. Trevor; you are always so nice," said the elderly young lady; and she went home better satisfied.

There was one good thing, however, about Lady Mary. If she lashed other people, she never was nice about applying the whip to herself.

"I know what I am," she would say. "I have always known that. From my earliest youth I have never thought of myself as otherwise than plain— ugly if you will. I do not hate other women because they are pretty, fair, graceful, grateful to men's eyes. I hate them because they are such fools; because they are so petty, so jealous, so frivolous, so false; because if they are clever, they have no hearts; and if they have hearts, they are utterly destitute of head. Of course, I am obliged to know them, visit, receive them. No woman—not even a woman of my age, my rank, and my appearance—can afford to do without them. But I cannot love *le beau sexe*; and, as I am unable to do so, it is useless to affect the feeling."

With all her faults, Lady Mary was no hypocrite, no false friend, no plausible dissembler; and yet, as I said before, it made me turn almost sick to see her drive up to Fairy Water.

Under the circumstances, I would just as soon, or rather, have beheld Beelzebub—horns, tail, cloven hoof, blue flame, and all the other orthodox properties.

"Great Heaven!" I exclaimed. "It is Lady Mary Carey!"

"And who is she?" asked the other Mary, so different from the great woman who had come to invade our modest home.

"She is the Duke's aunt," I replied. Of course, in that primitive region, there was but one Duke known to fame. "You must not mind anything she may say, Mary. She means nothing by her random talk."

At that instant the door opened.

"How do, Stafford?" said my lady, walking across the room as unconcernedly as if she had been in the habit of visiting at Fairy Water all her life. "No, you need not introduce me, thank you. You, I am sure," she went on, addressing my cousin, "must be Mrs. Trevor; and I am Lady Mary Carey."

Having finished which sentence, she held out her hand for Mary to take if she liked. Mary did like; but, finding her ladyship made no attempt to shake hers, released the great hand with a promptitude which savoured of fear.

Lady Mary looked at her from the tips of her shoes to the widow's cap, which she had never laid aside—which I felt satisfied she never would—then turned to me and said:

"So I have found you out at last, sir! This is the meaning of those disappearances which have puzzled everyone; of those mysterious visits you were perpetually paying to vague male relatives. Well, it is said that still waters run deep, with a very undesirable gentleman lying at the bottom; but I would not have believed it of you, Stafford. I never could have credited you would turn out so shy and selfish as to keep your pretty cousin's existence a secret from all your friends."

"Lady Mary," I answered gravely, "my cousin, or indeed, I might almost say my daughter, has been so little in the world, that she is ignorant of the meaning of fashionable *badinage*, and I am sure you are too good-natured to vex her with it."

"I am a sweet, good-natured creature when I am not angry," said Lady Mary, "so I will not vex—your daughter," with a little ringing emphasis on the word; "Mrs. Trevor," she went on, "I have come to tell you that Mr. Waldrum cannot return to dinner, or any other meal here to-day. My precious nephew has somehow managed to rid himself of two fingers, one eye, and narrowly escaped lodging the remaining contents of his fowling-piece in that part of his anatomy which the surgeons politely term his brain. It is, therefore, necessary—at least so his mother thinks—that your friend should remain in attendance for the present. Such a house!" continued Lady Mary, lifting up her hands in horror at the memory. "All the guests who have any place to go, going; those who have not, trying to look unconscious that they are in the way. Miss Vinon, to whom my nephew is engaged, came tearing across country the moment she heard the news, on a great black horse, attended by a frightened groom. She has been crying at intervals, and taking Mr. Waldrum's hands, and imploring him to save Egerton, ever since her arrival. Of course it is a matter of importance to her, since it is in the last degree improbable she would ever again meet another duke so young, foolish, and desirable as my nephew. Now, Mrs. Trevor, if you will kindly ask me to dine with you, I shall accept the invitation with pleasure. A house of mourning is not, as you are doubtless aware, a house of feasting except to the servants; and I, for one, do not care for tears, swollen eyes, and red cheeks as accompaniments to a banquet."

Trembling as if she were going to execution, Mary invited her ladyship to stay for dinner, and to take off her bonnet.

When she came down again I considered it my duty to state the proposed repast was not likely to suit her taste. I reminded her the twenty-ninth of September was the feast of St. Michael and all angels.

"I think," she interrupted, "it is better known amongst modern heathens as quarter-day."

"When tenants no doubt formerly propitiated their landlords with a present of a young fat goose, fresh from the stubble-fields," I added, acknowledging her intervention with a bow. "And in the country, to this present day, a sacrifice of one of the birds which saved Rome is deemed propitious to those who assist at the rite, and calculated to ensure a certain amount of good fortune during the ensuing twelve months."

"Which means, in plain English, you have a goose for dinner, I suppose? What a tiresome prosy creature you are, Stafford. Have you not known me long enough to come to the point at once, without any nonsensical circumlocution? You have a goose, and I am delighted to hear it. I am weary of the orthodox *menu*, and shall be charmed to meet with a sensible *pièce de résistance* once more."

We three dined together. Mary had provided other good things besides that plump bird, of which I believed I should never hear the last; and I am bound to say our visitor did justice to all of them.

"That is where you middle-class people have the advantage over us," she said calmly, when I had helped her a second time to *the* dish of the dinner. "You can live as you like, eat as you like, sleep as you like, do what you like. I could not have a dinner such as this served up to me in my own house if I prayed for it. How very thankful you ought to feel, dear Mrs. Trevor, that you were not born in the shadow of the purple."

"I do feel very thankful," answered Mary, with a promptness which astonished me.

"I daresay the habits of our rank would seem irksome to you."

"My experience of any rank but my own has been extremely limited; but judging from that, I should say they would seem irksome in the extreme."

I looked at Mary imploringly, and our guest caught the look.

"Let her have her say, Stafford," she observed; "it delights me to listen to the untutored frankness of an unsophisticated mind. What a brute your husband must have been, my dear, to tie you to perpetual widowhood. You, so young, so *naïve*, so pretty."

"My husband did what he thought was best for me and his children," retorted Mary, tears filling her eyes, the colour coming up in her cheeks, and all her mind and body rising in battle array against the calm insolence of Lady Mary's style.

"That is a proposition the truth of which no one, I imagine, would dispute," answered her ladyship; and then she glanced at me, and laughed as one might at the babble of a child.

"She is very fresh and nice, is she not?" she remarked. "Who can tell what a day may bring forth? I had no idea this day would produce anything like Mrs. Trevor"; and then she changed the subject from personal to general topics, and Mary sat listening in amazement whilst she discussed the latest scandal; told me of the marriages which had been arranged or were to be; retailed the latest anecdote, which had generally something hidden in its point I trusted Mary would fail to understand; and then the wretched meal being over, and dessert placed on the table, she turned to my cousin, and said with that coolness which she always informed me was one of the attributes of good birth:

"I am sure, Mrs. Trevor, you must be longing to get back to your children. Do not let me detain you, not on any account, I beg. I want to have five minutes' private conversation with your—father before I go."

With a face which somehow combined the expressions of a criminal who has received a reprieve and a child who has been slapped, Mary left the room. Her ladyship waited till I had closed the door after her, and then drew her chair a little nearer to mine.

She lifted her hand, and brought it with no light weight down on my arm.

"Stafford Trevor," she said, "I never thought you were a fool before. I tell you you are one now."

I drew away my arm, and looked at her just—so she informed me subsequently—as though I had been a thief, and seen in her a policeman, armed with authority and provided with handcuffs, standing at my elbow.

"No, it is not that," she went on. "I do not quarrel with the affection you feel for that simple creature. There is no harm in it that I am aware of. Do not fear that I shall ever suggest there is. I can see no fun in putting serpents into dove's nests. But for you, Stafford—you whom I have always considered, if not a wise man, at least something better than a simpleton—to make the egregious mistake you have done, I feel ashamed of you. There!" and she pushed me away from her with a strength of muscle and freedom of its development which would not have been thought tender in a prize-fighter.

"What have I done, Lady Mary?" I inquired. "Into what mistake have I fallen?"

She brought her head round, and peered in my face curiously.

"You really have not an idea?" she said.

"Not the faintest idea, on my honour."

"Do you mean to say you don't know that handsome Waldrum is in love with your cousin?"

"Good God, no!" I exclaimed, appalled at the very suggestion.

"Such energy of expression is needless," she observed, in a tone of quiet banter which almost drove me to the verge of insanity. "Nor," she went on, "that your pretty cousin is in love with him?"

I covered my face with my hands, and groaned—actually groaned. Never had I known Lady Mary's intuition in such matters at fault.

"What makes you think this?" I asked at last.

She laughed outright.

"What makes me think the rivers flow to the sea, the sun shines, the rain falls, the wind blows? I see, feel, hear! When he said he wanted to get back to dinner, I noticed an inflection in his voice, a look in his face. When I spoke to her of him, I saw his look reflected in her expression. What have you to say now, sir, why you, a man who ought to know something of the world, have failed so signally in your charge of a young widow entrusted to you for safe keeping?"

"Nothing. If this be so, I have been worse than mad—criminal!"

"If! I tell you it is. What can be done?"

"Nothing."

"Cannot they marry?"

"No, it is impossible."

"Well, your young man had better not come here again."

"He came to see her sick boy."

"The boy must get well, then."

"Oh, Mary!" I cried, "I hoped this would never, never be."

If the aunts of fifty dukes had been present at the moment, I could not have helped that expression of feeling.

"Do you mean to say there is no loophole of escape out of the terms of that man's ridiculous will?"

"None whatever; and even if there were ——"

"Well, what is the other obstacle?"

"I began a sentence I cannot very well finish," I replied.

"Oh! you mean that story about Waldrum's father, I suppose? I heard something of it from the Conynghams; and now that brings me to the second object of my visit, or, I suppose I should say, my first, considering it concerns myself. You have got a quiet out-of-the-way sort of little place in Essex."

"Yes. But, Lady Mary, how does it happen you know everything about my cousin, and me, and the Waldrums?"

She broke into a fit of laughter.

"The explanation is very simple," she said, when she recovered her composure. "Excuse my laughing, but you look so astonished—so slow, in fact, that the temptation is irresistible. This morning my nephew went out very early with a shooting-party. I do not know whether he hit the animal at which he fired, but he certainly succeeded in maiming himself. We sent at once for Doctor Sloane, and telegraphed to London for a surgeon. Dr. Sloane came, and so did a reply to the telegram—'Mr. —— is in Switzerland.' Before the telegram reached us, however, Doctor Sloane had begged me to send for a Mr. Waldrum, who was staying at Fairy Water, Mrs. Trevor's place. The name struck me, and I asked for further information. In five minutes I had turned the poor doctor's mind inside out. I was acquainted with the contents of your cousin's will. I had listened to an earnest eulogy of Mrs. Trevor as wife, mother, woman. I heard you were guardian to the children. I knew all about the eldest boy's illness and Mr. Waldrum's visits, which he only paid because of his friendship towards you. Then the man himself appeared. After he had seen his patient, and done what he could for him; after he had quieted the Duchess, and released himself from Miss Vinor, who made a great deal more fuss over her grief with him than would have been the case had he been older and uglier, I secured Mr. Waldrum's ear for a few minutes. I reminded him we had met before, which we had at the Conynghams. I told him I had watched his rise with great interest; that, you know, is always a safe card to play, no matter what the suit may be. I assured him you were the oldest and dearest friend

I had in the world; that, in all the troubles and anxieties of my life, I felt I could depend upon you for advice and assistance. That touched him sensibly, I could see," added Lady Mary.

Of course, I knew her ladyship was now playing what she considered a good card to delude me; but I could only take her remark as a compliment, and bow in acknowledgment.

"Finally, I spoke of Mrs. Trevor, and then I knew what I have confided to your ear. That is the mystery of part one. As to part two: the Conynghams told me you had bought a place to which, when weary of the world, you had for years been in the habit of retiring to enjoy the company of bats, owls, and ghosts. So secret were you in the matter that no one suspected you were the actual owner, until quite recently."

"Yes," I said. It was a stupid expression, but I felt so dazed with her ladyship's flow of words; I felt so tired and harassed by the steady stare of her ladyship's black eyes; I was so utterly taken by surprise at the nature of her communications and extent of her information, that I could only sit still and listen, and say "Yes" like an idiot, when she paused to take breath.

"And now, Stafford, I want you to do something for me."

This was a formula with which I had good reason to be well acquainted, and accordingly it landed me on familiar ground at once; but before I could answer her black brows lowered, and she said:

"You are not going to refuse me, I hope."

"When did I ever refuse to do anything for you, Lady Mary, which it was in my power to accomplish?" I inquired, soothingly.

"Never," she agreed. "You were always a good kind soul, and I know you will not raise any ridiculous objections to the plan I am about to propose. In a word, I want you to let me rent that hermitage of yours in Essex for three months."

"What? Crow Hall!" I exclaimed.

"I do not know what the name of the place is, and I do not care. I know it will serve the purpose I have in view. Listen to me, Stafford. I do not mind telling you the whole secret. I have got into a scrape; I have lost a great deal of money. I am in debt to an extent I am afraid to contemplate. I sold my house in town—furniture and all—just as it stood, and came down here two days ago, intending to ask Egerton's assistance, and then reside abroad for a few years to retrench. Mr. Carey left what he did leave to me so tied up that I cannot sell or anticipate even a year's income."

I sat stunned. Mean though she was, Lady Mary had always borne the character of being extremely liberal to and extravagant on herself—further, she was very speculative; but still I had never dreamed she would get into a mess like this.

That she was ruined I understood perfectly; that the accident which had happened to her nephew precluded all hope of assistance from him for a considerable time to come was equally clear; but how she meant to get out of her difficulties was as great an enigma to me as the fancy she had taken for carrying her perplexities and herself to Crow Hall.

"I cannot imagine ——" I began, but she immediately interrupted me with:

"I know you cannot, you dear creature; but I will explain everything to you if you only remain quiet. It is clear Egerton is out of the question for a considerable period; so since there is nothing to be expected from that quarter, I have thought of another plan, which, however, I cannot perfect and carry out except in some lonely place like your Crow Hall; so name your rent, we shall not quarrel over a few pounds, and tell me when I can enter into possession."

"My dear Lady Mary," said I, fairly floated out of my usual depth by the torrent of her impetuosity, "if I thought you could possibly exist in Crow Hall, I should beg permission to place it at your disposal for any length of time you liked to name, but I am certain you could not."

"Why not?" she demanded.

"It is utterly removed from civilisation."

"So much the better for me."

"There is no furniture in the house suited to your requirements."

"You do not know what my requirements are, or whether I want any furniture," she retorted.

"Even if there were accommodation for servants, none of your people would remain at Crow Hall for three days."

"Andrews would, and I have discharged all the rest. Now, what other objection have you to urge?"

"Only one," I said. "The place is haunted."

"That decides the matter. When can I have possession?"

"I am serious," I persisted. "Indeed I am. Do you imagine, Lady Mary," I went on, noticing her incredulous smile, "that I would say such a thing in jest? I have never even mentioned my idea to anyone. Naturally, I do not wish to lose money by my purchase, and if it were known I attached any importance to the stories which have so long hung about the place, my chance of eventually disposing of it would be poor indeed. But there is something 'uncanny' about Crow Hall. I would not deceive you on that or any other subject."

Her smile had never departed.

"What have you seen?" she asked.

"Nothing," I replied.

"What have you heard?"

"The rustle of a woman's dress."

"What have you felt?"

"A sense of oppression as though someone were in the room with me."

After that she sat silent for a few moments. Then she said:

"We will strike a bargain, Stafford. I will exorcise your ghost, and you may refer anyone to me for the character of Crow Hall. Upon the other hand, I may inhabit it for twelve months free of rent. Is it agreed?"

I hesitated. I could not be blind to the advantages I might derive from Lady Mary's tenancy. I did not believe any phantom would trouble her repose, since late dinners, late hours, and a decided liking for good wines are not generally compatible with the seeing of ghosts and viewing of spectres. Nevertheless, I could not choose but hesitate.

"Suppose evil come of it," I thought; and that thought shows how thoroughly impressed I was with the weird legends circulated concerning Crow Hall.

"Well, is it decided?" said her ladyship.

"Lady Mary," I replied, "I wish you would not go to Crow Hall. If I had a dozen places they should all, as you know, be at your disposal. But I do not like your going to that house. You might see nothing to alarm you, but you might ——"

"What a goose you are, Stafford," she interrupted. "I shall see nothing half so bad as my debts and my duns, be sure of that. So write to the person in charge. He or she need not leave. Say you have let the place—it is unnecessary to mention my name—and that I may be expected next Thursday. Yes; Thursday will do very well indeed. And now I must go. Where is little Mrs. Trevor? I want to bid her good-bye."

My cousin came into the hall to see our visitor off.

"Thank you so much for your kindness," she said to Mary, carelessly; then moved, Heaven only knows by what feeling of pity or sympathy, or perhaps it might be by the sweet, sad repose of that patient face, my lady, stooping from her high estate, kissed her on both cheeks, and saying, "You are a dear little soul," hurried off to the phaeton, and was driven away.


## CHAPTER IX

### LADY MARY'S EXPERIENCES

Valentine came next day to Fairy Water to tell us all about his new patient, and to have a look at Geoffrey, who, to Mary's intense relief, was decidedly better.

Twenty-four hours' reflection had satisfied me that if I tried to put my oar into the difficulty presented on the previous afternoon, I should probably catch a crab, and I therefore decided to let matters proceed without my interference. Perhaps Lady Mary had been mistaken, perhaps she had not; in either case, what good could my interference effect? In the one, I might put lovelorn ideas into the heads of innocent people; in the other, I might, by precipitate speaking, crystallise a notion which would otherwise have remained permanently in solution.

No; if Val was in love with my cousin, he could not be considered otherwise than old enough and wise enough to keep away from Fairy Water. Thinking the matter over, it occurred to me he had done so as far as he could, and I determined to give him another opportunity.

"I shall be passing through town on Tuesday, Val," I said. "Can I do anything for you?"

"Thank you, no," he answered; "I must be in London to-morrow, and was just going to ask you the same question."

"You want further advice for the Duke?" I suggested; and he said:

"Yes; I think he ought to see someone more experienced than myself. As matters stand, it is a great responsibility."

"Doubtless," I remarked, but if he noticed the sneer he refrained from comment.

After all, Val Waldrum was a very nice sort of fellow. No matter how grievously out of sorts a man might be—no matter how rude he proved in consequence, Val took no notice; he talked on just as usual; he either did not or would not see that with all my heart I wished him at Low Park, or anywhere else, so long as it was beyond the gates of Fairy Water.

"Never mind," I thought; "he cannot, if he have any sense left, come here often in my absence, and by the time I return he will most probably be able to leave his patient to Sloane."

"Mary," I said out loud, "I want you to give me a pair of swans."

Both Mrs. Trevor and Valentine looked at me in amazement. "Swans!" repeated the latter; "where do you propose to keep them?"

"Not in my lodgings, you may be quite certain," I answered. "But I do not require them yet; I may not require them at all."

"He is thinking of being married, depend upon it," exclaimed Valentine.

Mary looked at me curiously.

"No," I said, "I am certainly not likely to walk into matrimony with my eyes open, and I do not think any man can be held excused who drifts into it."

"I am not quite certain of that," said Valentine; "many a good vessel has gone ashore merely because ignorant of the dangers of the coast."

"Perhaps so," I answered, "but matrimony is a coast from which I should think any prudent captain would keep at a safe distance."

A curious look came into Valentine's eyes. I had said the very thing I had purposed not to say, and he divined there was a second meaning underlying my words.

He rose and walked to one of the windows with a "Humph!" which was, I am sure, involuntary; and I heard him rattling the keys in his pockets, as I feel glad to remember I have often heard him since those days rattling sovereigns.

"Well," he said at last, "I suppose I must be riding back to my noble patient. I hope we shall save his eyesight after all."

"Oh! do; pray, pray do!" exclaimed Mary, whose sympathy was of course much exercised in those days in favour of the young man, with whom it was almost a toss-up, whether he would be blind for life or not.

At sight of the eager, pleading face, Valentine smiled, as he answered, "It does not rest with me, but you may be sure I shall do my best for him, if only for the sake of his *fiancée*, who is the sweetest and most beautiful girl I ever beheld."

He had spoken without the least thought of what a sweeping assertion his words implied, but I could see Mary's colour come and go, heighten and fade, at hearing such unqualified admiration expressed concerning another woman.

It *was* true then; it was. She had escaped all these years, and now, when her youth was fading away, when she might reasonably have been expected to go on living without other than the vaguest ideas of what love meant—through my instrumentality, through my folly and short-sightedness that knowledge had come to her, from which I had vainly hoped she would be kept for ever.

I went to the front door with Valentine. When I would have bid him good-bye, he laid his hand on my shoulder, and said:

"A wise man can take a hint; nevertheless you might have spoken plainly to me had you liked. Rest satisfied, when once my latest patient can dispense with my attendance, Fairy Water shall see me no more."

Next morning I departed for Crow Hall, and remained there until Lady Mary's arrival.

Although I had made preparations for her comfort and reception, I could not say I felt at all certain she would adhere to her resolution; and it was therefore with feelings of mingled relief and anxiety that I saw the solitary fly, which the nearest town boasted, turn into the drive.

"Now, Stafford, this is kind!" exclaimed her ladyship. "How sweet of you to come all this distance on my account. What a delicious old house!"

"I only hope," I said, in a low tone, "you will be able to remain in it."

She laughed in reply; and then, after grumbling a little because I refused to stay for dinner, allowed me to depart in the fly, which I had detained for the purpose.

"I wonder," I thought, as the wretched vehicle jogged and jolted along the road, "what the next chapter in the history of Crow Hall will bring forth?"

It was a cold, wet, blustering October evening when I returned to Fairy Water. As my movements were uncertain, I had told Mary not to send to the station to meet me; and, as no conveyance of any kind could, in that benighted region, be procured, there was nothing left for me to do except walk every step of the six miles that lay between the railway and my cousin's house.

Being on foot, it was not necessary for me to make my way through the entrance-gates and up the long avenue, and accordingly opening a door in the fence surrounding that part of the property which abutted on the road leading to the nearest town, I struck into the shrubbery paths, and soon reached Mary's own especial garden, a funny little place laid out in the Dutch style, which she kept in order herself, and of which she was, as I often told her, extravagantly proud. Keeping along the gravelled walk, with a thick hedge of yew low and close clipped, I came to what we called the water-side of the house, which brought me in a few seconds to the conservatory I have mentioned.

As usual, the door was unlocked; in that faraway region bolts and bars were at a discount, and turning the handle, I entered.

Cold as I was, and cheerless as had been my walk, the sight of the firelight dancing on the walls of the pleasant drawing-room, reflecting itself from mirrors, gleaming on the pictures, was very pleasant, and gave me a comfortable, home-like feeling; and advancing to the inner door, I pushed the heavy curtains, which were only partially drawn aside, and looked in.

I am not given to play the spy; eavesdropping is a thing repugnant both to my feelings and my principles. What I heard and saw when I thrust back those curtains deprived me of the power of speech and movement. On the hearthrug stood two people: the one Mary, the other Valentine.

"Then you will trust him to me," he said; and there was sadness as well as tenderness in his tone.

I could not catch her answer, if indeed she uttered one; but I did see her face uplifted for a moment to his; the next he held her in his arms, and her head dropped against his breast. It was only for an instant; then they parted as if by some mutual recoil.

"Forgive me, dear." I heard that. "For all the world could offer, I would not this had happened."

She did not speak a word, she only flitted away. She did not see me, she understood nothing save her joy and her sorrow—I grasped all that.

Straight up to Mr. Waldrum I went. "Do you think this right?" I asked.

"No," he answered.

"I trusted you."

"I think not," he said; "if you had foreseen this, you would have kept us asunder."

"That is true." I almost whispered the words.

"Not," he went on, "that for one moment I wish to throw the blame off my own shoulders and lay it on those of any other. I, and I only, am to blame. I have known what it all meant to me long before you suspected anything. I tried to fight the battle, and this is the result." He walked to the door.

"Stay a moment," I entreated.

"Not to-night; I will write to you and her. I will see you soon, but not here," and he was gone, the son of my heart and my adoption.

Next day the promised letters came—one for Mary, one for me. She took hers away to some safe sanctuary; I read mine where all the world might see. It was simple enough. The few lines it contained were to the effect that, feeling how dangerous his visits to Fairy Water were becoming to himself, how necessary it was to Geoffrey's recovery he should be under the eye of a surgeon who had made disease a speciality, he rode over to see

Mrs. Trevor, and obtain her consent to removing her son to his house in London.

"That is how it all came about," he finished. "I give you my word—I pledge you my honour."

"Poor Val!" I sighed, and put the letter in my pocket-book.

An hour afterwards Mary appeared. She was more than usually solicitous for my comfort, she was more than usually kind and gentle.

"Mary dear," I said, when we were quite alone.

Turning her face away, she answered, "Yes," and came close up to where I stood.

"You had a letter from Valentine Waldrum this morning," I began, leading her to a seat; "show it to me."

She hesitated, poor little soul; it was her first love-letter from a man she loved, and it seemed sacred in her eyes, as though she were still a girl, with the world's cares and the world's sorrows all before her.

"I want to see it, dear," I said, firmly, "in order to understand whether in the future he and I are to be friends or foes; whether I shall still be able to respect him, or feel for him a contempt no words can express."

Without another attempt at expostulation, she put the letter in my hand, and then she sat down beside me and watched the expression of my face, like a child or a dog.

When I had finished, she put her hand on my hand, laid her face on my arm, and broke out sobbing.

"Do not blame him or me," she said: "I did not know what it meant; I could not tell what it was. If I had, I should have stopped it long ago."

I let her cry—crying always does women good; it comforts them, and, in moderation, makes their eyes brighter. While she cried I endeavoured to solve a mental problem:

"Suppose Geoffrey had left her free, should I not have tried to win her?"

Emphatically yes. I understood that now—understood it when she was breaking her heart about a man young enough to be my son, and sobbing out her misery within about four inches of my heart.

Well, we cannot be young always; but the unfortunate thing is the right person for us seems to be born always so long after she ought to come into the world.

"You know what you have to do now, Mary," I suggested, after a few minutes devoted to sentiment on her part, and abstruse reflections on mine.

"Tell me," she whispered.

"I should prefer hearing it from you," I remarked.

She clasped her hands together, and said, like a child repeating some easy lesson:

"I must never see him again, or hear from him, or write to him, or think of him, if I can help doing so."

I drew her to me, lifted the fair, tear-stained face, and kissed it, Heaven be my witness, as a woman might kiss that of her sister, a father that of his child.

"God help you, Mary," I said; "you will get over this in time, but meanwhile it is hard to bear; your pain must be cruel."

She put up her hand and stroked my face, as though to assure me, although the pain might be cruel, she could endure.

"Never, my dear, never, have I known so womanly a woman as yourself—as truly feminine a nature as that possessed by you."

Well, well—I grow garrulous, perhaps. Let me hasten on to the end.

Shortly after that evening I left Fairy Water, Geoffrey in my charge. The easiest chariot from Low Park took him to the station. The Duke of Severn's footmen, directed and assisted by Valentine, carried the sick lad to the invalid carriage provided for him.

Twice a week I went to Valentine's house, and saw the invalid—twice a week I was, after a short time, able to send a good report of the boy back to Fairy Water.

By this time I was once more settled in London. With the exception of a few days at Christmas, I did not intend to leave my lodgings again for six months. The familiar fogs enveloped me, the gaslights which my soul loved tried vainly to dissipate the worse than Egyptian darkness of the deserted streets. Through the dull atmosphere the cries of "Walnuts!" "Muffins!" "Crumpets!" resounded with the effect of muffled drums; and there was a pervading feeling in the air, as if the sun had taken a fancy to remain in a state of perpetual eclipse, while the moon, femininely anxious to follow in the fashion and his wake, had decided to do likewise.

At that period of the year I usually dined with people who thought it somewhat of an honour to secure my company, and therefore, though I rarely spent an evening alone, I was generally bored in the evening.

After all, a man need not be a snob, if he says frankly he prefers the society of people who live west of Bond Street to that of the worthy individuals who keep up ponderous establishments in the central London squares.

From Lady Mary Carey I received letters by the dozen. She was so charmed with the place, the neighbourhood, the people—would I kindly call at so-and-so, and order such-and-such articles to be forwarded to her? She did not apologise; she did not ask pardon for the trouble she gave. How could she? Had she not tested the *depth*, and *breadth*, and *length* of my goodness (all in feminine italics) for a greater number of years than any woman *save myself* "would care to remember?"

I had told her it was my intention to send down a couple of swans, so as to lessen the weird desolation of the pine-circled pool; but shortly after taking possession of Crow Hall, she wrote, asking me to defer doing so till she discovered whether the water in the lake sunk much lower.

The summer had been unusually dry and warm; all through the country complaints were rife concerning the drying-up of springs and failing of streams; and it did not strike me as singular that the fated pool should suffer as she described.

It seemed, however, very singular to her—so singular, that she sent me bulletins on the subject twice a week, at all events.

"I am told," she wrote, "that for a century, at all events, the water in this little lake of yours has never been lower than the root of a certain pollard oak. It is now fully three feet lower than that point."

A day or two afterwards came another note: "Water is sinking rapidly."

Fast on the heels of this followed a long letter, crossed, in which italics vainly endeavoured to express her ladyship's astonishment at the phenomenon. "I wish you would come down and see for yourself," was one of her sentences—as if I suspected her of draining the pool; "it really is most extraordinary. The woman you left in charge here considers it a premonitory symptom of the Day of Judgment, and has begged my acceptance of two tracts. She says, I may take her word for it that, when that lake is empty, something will happen."

"Only thirty inches of water left," was the next report—then, "*The pool is dry.* But I am happy. I know where the water has gone, and so do the railway people, to their cost. Their line is flooded. They will have to make a fresh lake for themselves. Crow Hall is besieged. Even from beyond Latchford Common the population repair to see for themselves that the Black Pool has not a drop of water left in it. A variety of barrels and other curiosities appear to be sunk in the mud at the bottom. Some of the navvies and labourers have kindly offered to remove the rubbish, but, as we do not know of what it may consist, I am having the property watched by the sexton. Not another creature in the parish would consent to remain all night in your haunted grounds."

As may be imagined, I started off for Crow Hall at once, where I found Lady Mary in high spirits, the Black Pool dry, the barrels, whatever they may have contained originally, empty of everything but slime, the railway engineers in despair, and Mrs. Paul shaking her head ominously.

"It is all very well to talk of lower levels, and railway cuttings, and the like; but why should the lake dry up at this time, of all times? Will not the seventh of the next month, if any of us live to see it, be the night when Mr. Philip Waldrum's wife disappeared--Heaven be merciful to us sinners!"

Thus Mrs. Paul; whilst Mr. Dogsett looked wise, and delivered himself of oracular sentences.

"It had all been foretold," he explained to me: "but where, or when, or by whom, he could not just rightly remember."

"You will find it a good thing for you in the end," said Lady Mary to me. "Depend upon it, the railway people will have to buy the late site of the Black Pool."

"They will have to pay me well for it," I answered.

"And really you ought to make me a handsome present on the occasion," she remarked. "I am sure my taking Crow Hall has brought good fortune to it."

"You have seen nothing to shake your resolution then?" I asked.

"No; if there are ghosts here, they are not from another world," Lady

Mary answered. "I cannot say the house is one I should recommend to a nervous lady. The locks have a way of clicking, the woodwork of cracking, the floors of creaking, the windows of rattling, and the wind of howling in the chimneys, by no means pleasant to a light sleeper. If anyone were disposed to play tricks, it would be easy to frighten even so incredulous a person as myself; but I fancy Mrs. Paul would not like me to leave, and that if she ever has done any conjuring she repents now of her evil deeds."

"Do you really think then, Lady Mary, that Mrs. Paul had any hand in the appearances which have given the place so evil a repute?"

"Someone must—Mrs. Paul as probably as any other individual; but neither she nor her friends will try to make anything unpleasant for me, or I am greatly mistaken."

I never saw Lady Mary in better spirits than when we parted that day. Judge then of my consternation when a fortnight later I received the following note from Fairy Water:

"Lady Mary Carey is *here*. She arrived an hour since, very ill, and in a state of utter exhaustion, and entreated me to let her stay with me for a short time. She wishes to see you at once, and begs you will bring Mr. Waldrum with you. I suggested sending for Dr. Sloane, but she said 'No'; that Mr. Waldrum alone can treat her case, and that she has something important to say to both of you."

I did not fear taking Valentine with me to Fairy Water. I felt he and Mary could now be safely trusted with the keeping of their own peace, and that they were not likely voluntarily—she to give, he to seek—any opportunity of recurring to the one forbidden subject. Nevertheless, with all my heart and soul I wished Lady Mary had carried her ailments and herself anywhere except to my cousin's house. And further, I dreaded to hear what she might have to tell.

That her illness and her secret both had a common origin at Crow Hall I did not doubt in the least, and as Valentine and I journeyed down from London, I told him frankly the small deceit I had practised, and explained how it happened Lady Mary had taken a fancy to reside at Crow Hall.

He listened with merely slight interruptions to my story, almost in utter silence. When I had quite finished, he said, with a long-drawn sigh:

"If Lady Mary tells me she has seen that woman, it will be the happiest news I have heard since my father's death."

We found the invalid sitting in a great arm-chair in Mary's dressing-room, in a voluminous morning wrapper, her black coarse hair hanging straight down her back, her face destitute of any colour, save the dark hue conferred on it by nature, her nerves so shaken that the tears came into her eyes when she saw us, and the muscles round her mouth twitched when she answered our greeting. What did Lady Mary look like? At that moment she ought to have frightened away any number of ghosts.

Valentine wanted to prescribe for her first, and hear the story afterwards.

I entreated of him not to attempt to talk of anything disagreeable till her health was re-established.

"Sit down," she said, peremptorily. "If I do not speak to some one of what mine eyes have seen, I shall go mad, and I can only speak to you, or you," indicating each of us with a nod. "Stafford," she went on, "when I first went to your place, I suspected that woman Paul of complicity with the noises and repeated appearances. I beg to say I earnestly ask her pardon. Now, Mr. Waldrum, before I begin I wish to tell you distinctly that the thing I saw I beheld not in any dream, or while I was labouring under any delusion. It all happened as truly as you sit there. Listen.

"About ten days, Stafford, after you were last at Crow Hall, Mrs. Paul brought me a ring, which she said she had found somewhere about the house, and which she imagined to be one of mine.

"Of course I told her it was mine, and gave her five shillings for her trouble.

"But the ring was not mine; it was one the like of which I had never beheld before, cut, evidently, out of a solid lump of gold, with a good-sized piece of the same metal left solid in the middle like a stone. Into this piece of gold was let on the inner side a cross formed of *lapis lazuli*, and on the outside, carved most exquisitely, was an alto-relievo of the Crucifixion.

"It was the strangest ring, and about the smallest I ever beheld. I could not get it over the middle joint of my little finger, and so put it on the stand on my dressing-table, after I had thoroughly examined and puzzled my brains over it. In an old house strange things do sometimes however turn up, and I went to bed, thinking I would speak about the matter to you, Stafford, and beg you to allow me to retain the ring as a memorial of Crow Hall.

"About eleven o'clock I went to bed. I had been reading nothing sensational, thinking of nothing exciting. I had dined at seven in the anchorite style I have adopted since I left Low Park. Andrews undressed me, made up my fire, lit fresh candles—I always burn two candles at night—left me, and went to her own room, which adjoins mine. Everything was just as usual, everything with the exception of that strange ring, the very existence of which I had forgotten.

"After I had been asleep for perhaps a couple of hours, I woke suddenly, struggling for breath, bathed in perspiration, and with the strangest feeling—instinct I call it—of someone being in the room with me.

"I am not one of those people who can gather their wits together in a moment when roused out of slumber. I always feel more or less dazed when struggling back into real life from the land of dreams; and so I sat up in bed, and shook my mind into consciousness by degrees.

"The fire had burnt black and hollow, the candles were burning dim—as candles for some reason best known to themselves always do in a bedroom—and what made their light appear less bright even than ordinary was the fact that between the bed and the dressing-table stood a woman, searching about amongst the articles lying on the latter, as if for something she had lost.

" 'Andrews,' I said, 'what are you doing? what is the matter?' but no reply came.

"By this time I was wide awake, and had my senses about me. I jumped out of bed, and calling 'Andrews' at the top of my voice, put out a hand to seize the intruder.

"As I did so I saw her face reflected in the glass; then it faded away, and my hands, instead of meeting with any corporeal substance, grasped nothing but thin air.

"At that instant Andrews appeared. 'I have had a bad dream,' I explained. 'Make up a good fire, and sleep in the arm-chair, so that if I want anything you will be nearer at hand.' And then I crept back to bed, but not, you may be sure, to sleep."

"Can you describe the face you saw, Lady Mary?" Valentine asked, bending eagerly forward.

"Stop a little; let me tell you my story in my own way. Next morning the first thing I did was to look for the ring. *It was gone.*

"Now, as Andrews always bolted our door on the inside, it was quite clear no one could have entered the room except by some secret staircase. Further, the figure had not disappeared in any possible sort of way, supposing it to have been flesh and blood: it melted out of my sight, it faded into nothing in a second of time, and what was more to the purpose, my hand passed through the spectre as if it had been composed of nothing more tangible than a fog spray.

"I can tell you both I had plenty of food for thought that morning. It would not have suited my plans to leave Essex then, otherwise I should have packed up within the hour, and neither of you should have heard a word of the story.

"Well, we did not pack up, but I changed my room, and once again my doubts of Mrs. Paul were revived by hearing her remark to Andrews, 'Folks had never slept well in that oak room,' and further, 'that those who lived longest would see most.' However, I could not connect in my innermost heart the face I had seen in the glass with Mrs. Paul, or anyone belonging to her, and I grew so timid, I feared, actually feared, to go upstairs alone, either by day or night.

"I felt so miserable I asked the doctor and the curate to dine with me, and then when they were gone I relapsed into a state of greater wretchedness than ever.

"The next day I had arranged to spend at The Grange. Mr. Conyngham wished to show me all over the house, and Miss—well, Miss Conyngham thought it might be prudent to humour her brother's whim; at all events, I stood engaged to go to The Grange. There were several matters about which I wished to consult him, several subjects on which I desired his advice, and full of these worldly matters, and wishing to get rid of the remembrance of my nocturnal visitor, I drove off across Latchford Common, and in proper time arrived at your old home, Mr. Waldrum.

"I had a long chat with Mr. Conyngham while we walked about the grounds and wandered through the conservatories, and I may tell you, Stafford," added her ladyship, "in strict confidence, that he has, in the kindest manner, promised to arrange those difficulties I mentioned to you."

"Good heavens!" I thought, "she has secured a third husband, and that was why she wanted to go to Crow Hall."

"After luncheon Mr. Conyngham asked if I should not like to see the pictures. The dear good soul who owns The Grange has one craze—he fancies he understands art, and the consequence is he has been fleeced right and left, has purchased a large number of pictures at an exorbitant price, and honestly believes he has the finest collection, on a small scale, that can be found in England.

"Now if there is one thing more than another in which it shocks me to find a nice kind creature deficient, it is art; and if you believe me (I did believe her thoroughly) it went to my heart to see all that rubbish hung solemnly in the sight of day, and think of the money which must have been wasted upon it.

"Suddenly, however, I caught sight of something which arrested my attention.

" 'Where did you pick that up, Mr. Conyngham?' I inquired.

" 'That?' he repeated, following my glance; 'when Mr. Waldrum left here, my father bought that portrait, thinking that face a very beautiful one.'

" 'Did you say a portrait?' I asked; 'of whom is it a portrait?'

" 'Of the mysterious lady Philip Waldrum married, whose disappearance has never yet been accounted for.'

"By some means I got near an open window, on the plea of feeling faint. I obtained a moment's quiet, and then afterwards a glass of water.

"What was the matter with me, you want to know, Mr. Waldrum? This: the face I saw in the mirror was not merely like that which, limned on canvas, hung on the walls at The Grange; it was the original of that portrait. You may remember," she continued, speaking gently to Valentine, "that every trifling detail is carried out in the picture with almost painful minuteness. On the third finger of the left hand above her wedding-ring, that long-lost wife is shown in her picture as wearing another ring, as like that Mrs. Paul brought me as can well be imagined.

"I tell you as I looked my blood ran cold, but I kept the secret, Stafford; no one shall ever know from me that the Crow Hall Ghost is as far from being laid or explained as ever."

I thanked her ladyship very earnestly for the courage and kindness she had displayed, whilst Valentine, so agitated that he could scarcely frame an intelligible sentence, declared she had lifted a load off his heart which had been growing heavier day by day since his father's death.

I felt glad to hear him say this, but I did not like the expression I saw on his face as we walked together out of the room.

"One word, Val," I said; "remember that although your position may be different to what it was, Mrs. Trevor is just the same as ever. There are plenty of women in England you can marry now, but you can never marry her."

He shook my hands off, for the first time in my memory, with an impatient gesture, and stalked across the hall and opened the outer door himself, as though it were through any fault of mine Geoffrey had left his widow so powerless in the matter of a second marriage. Upon that step he turned, and said:

"You are guardian to the children; surely it rests with you; surely, if you liked, you could befriend us."

"My dear fellow," I answered, "believe me, I am powerless. I would help you if the will left me a chance of doing so."

"That is all very fine," he muttered.

"It is all very true," I replied.

He stood for a moment irresolute, then remarked: "I am going to Low Park."

"And I beg to suggest," I said, decidedly nettled, "that it will be better for you to stay there; or, at least, not return here."

"I must come here to see Lady Mary."

"If Lady Mary desires your attendance, she must remove to Low Park. I shall make that quite clear to her ladyship's comprehension."

"Do you mean that you would tell her ——?"

"I mean that she told me," I interrupted. "Come, Valentine, it is of no use your being either angry or sulky with me. Mrs. Trevor has suffered enough already, without having the additional trouble of a lover she can never marry hanging about the house. If it were a mere question of money, I should not raise an objection; but you know it is not, and that it is your duty to keep away from Fairy Water."

He did not answer a word. He either failed to see my outstretched hand, or declined to see it. He remained looking drearily about him for a few seconds; then pulling his hat down over his forehead, as most men do when trouble has for the nonce completely mastered them, he strode away along the drive; and, for the first time in his life, Valentine Waldrum parted from me in anger—his heart brimful of bitterness, and suspicion, and injustice.

# CHAPTER X

## THE SECRET OF CROW HALL

As I watched Valentine disappear in the windings of the avenue, I decided upon retracing my road to London without further delay.

If I remained in Fairy Water, I felt that, in his present mood, he would insist on coming to see me, and that it would not be in my power to prevent his doing so without a downright quarrel and open rupture supervening. Old though I might be, lover to his mother as I had been, friend and helper as I had tried to be to both him and Mary, I understood perfectly that for the time being he regarded me with a feeling of the keenest detestation; but I could make allowance for this.

If there be one feeling stronger than another which human beings and the brute creation have in common, it is that of jealousy; and when once a man becomes possessed by it, he is scarcely more responsible for his rudeness and his ill-temper than a cat is, when, seeing a dog patted, she scratches him till he screams again.

It was, of course, ridiculous for Valentine to be jealous, for a moment, of my presence or my influence; but I felt he was, and decided, as I have said, that I would leave Fairy Water forthwith. To Lady Mary I made no secret of my reason for going.

"Yes," she said, "it is absurd upon his part, no doubt; but still these fancies are beyond the power of rhyme or reason, and it is better to try to keep peace than come to open war. It seems to me an admirable idea altogether. You go to look after your Essex property, and I stay to prevent Mrs. Trevor feeling lonely. I will remain until after Christmas, and prove a very duenna over your pretty cousin."

"And when may your friends hope to see your ladyship in London?" I inquired.

"Whenever my nephew is sufficiently recovered to give me away," she answered. "As no man in his senses would dream of marrying me now, except for my position, it is only fair the kind good soul who gives so much in return for so little should have all the pleasure and *éclat* out of my relatives it is possible to extract from them."

Frequently there was a directness about Lady Mary's high breeding which savoured of simplicity, and produced somewhat the same effect upon unsophisticated people. I cannot say, however, it ever seemed to impress my cousin in that way. Natural and simple herself, she perhaps detected more rapidly than a less unaffected person might have done the false ring in Lady Mary's conversational coin.

I liked the counterfeit, I confess. It was bright, lively, a trifle sarcastic, never wearisome; and what a man has a weakness for is a woman who does not know how to be dull.

The art of vivacity may be acquired—I believe, indeed, it is never beheld in perfection save when acquired; but it is better than any genius or talent, for all that.

After a time, indeed, my cousin wrote to me that Lady Mary was a delightful companion, and made herself quite one of the household—which, indeed, I could readily credit. "The winter has never before seemed so pleasant at Fairy Water," continued Mrs. Trevor; "and I hope you will not be vexed, but Lady Mary has looked out several things here she would like to have in her new house, and I have begged her acceptance of them. She offered to buy them, but of course I told her I could not think of allowing anything of the kind. Ladies of fashion—if Lady Mary be a specimen of them—must be curious people to know, I think. Imagine our going to Low Park, and selecting various articles which happened to strike our fancy! And yet that is just what Lady Mary has done here. Do not think, please, that I object to it at all; only I cannot help saying how odd it seems to me."

When I went down to Fairy Water to partake of the Christmas dinner—which was always a great and wonderful display in that primitive household—I found Lady Mary installed as virtual mistress of the establishment, and my cousin—spite of her cheerful letters, and the fact that Geoffrey had been returned to his home cured of his complaint, if still generally delicate in health—looking thin, pale, and spiritless.

"I am afraid your guest bores you, Mary," I said.

"Ah! no. She is kindness itself."

"What, then, is the matter with you? Are you ill?"

"I am quite well, thank you," she said, shrinking away from me as I had never known her to do before.

Welladay! When Cupid rides, the oldest friend, the wisest man, the ablest scholar, the most profound philosopher, is nowhere in the race.

Said Lady Mary: "That *protégé* of yours is writing to her perpetually, I am afraid."

"I wash my hands of them and their affairs," I answered, with the determination and energy of a man who, dealing straightforwardly with other people himself, likes to be dealt by straightforwardly in return. But I repented me of this speech when, a day or two after, my cousin came to me and said—with the soft colour rising in her face, and her eyes downcast, and head a little drooped:

"Stafford, I am constantly receiving letters from Mr. Waldrum. I try to explain to him how I am situated; but either I cannot be explicit, or else he fails to comprehend. Will you tell him—will you—that I would not give up my children if I loved him a thousand times more than I do?"

"You set me a hard task, my dear," I answered.

"Is it too hard?" she inquired.

"Not when you ask me to do it," was my reply, and I left Fairy Water next day.

Before I wrote to Valentine, I furnished myself with a copy of Geoffrey's will. A perusal of it would, I considered, be more convincing than reams of argument or expostulation from me.

"You see she cannot have the children if she marry again," I wrote. "She says positively she will not give up the children. Is it manly to continue to importune a woman situated as Mary is? Of course this is a matter in which you must take your own way. I cannot and will not interfere further; so instead of hurling reproaches at your head, or stating that your letters must cease, when I have no power to prevent your sending or Mary receiving them, I simply repeat my question, and ask you if you consider it manly to increase a woman's troubles?"

To which I received this reply:

"I do not. She shall be troubled no more by me. Pray assure her of this, and believe, if you can, that I am still yours gratefully,
                                                    "V. WALDRUM."

My heart yearned over Valentine, but I did not mean to take him back into favour all at once. He had been ill-humoured, sulky, obstinate, defiant; and if I welcomed back the penitent at the first sign of contrition, who could tell what liberties he might not indulge in subsequently?

No, he should go his way and I would go mine; mine about that period taking me very frequently, and very much against my will, into Essex.

The fact is, Crow Hall had to my mind become a perfect *bête noire.* Sometimes, when ensconced in bed, the street noises in my ears, the objects familiar in a superior class of lodging-house meeting my eyes, a sudden memory of that dreary residence would cross my mind, and cause me to vow, incontinently, I would solve the difficulty connected with it by some means.

Already I had made my money out of it. The railway company were compelled to buy the Black Pool, and a very handsome sum they paid me for it.

Before, however, the lake was filled again with water, one of the navvies had discovered a curious fact.

At a place overgrown with brambles, ivy, and periwinkle, choked with weeds, wreathed over in the summer with convolvulus and wild briony, he had found an opening, and not merely an opening, but landing-steps.

"Used for smuggling purposes, doubtless, in years gone by," said a practical man in the London office of the company.

"No doubt," I answered, and went straight off to an architect I knew, who upon the strength of our plan contrived to keep a sickly wife and various unnecessary children.

To say he jumped at my proposal is a mild way of expressing his acquiescence. Ghosts! what did he care for ghosts? Ghosts meant bad air, bad drainage, bad water, and twenty other bad things besides. Only let him see the place, and I might rest assured means would be found of ridding Crow Hall of spectres.

"My good friend," said I, interposing; "there is only one way of laying the ghost. We must pull the old part of the house down, but I want your advice as to how that pulling down had best be accomplished."

We travelled into Essex together, and took up our quarters at Crow Hall. I did not put him in the "Guest Chamber"—that haunted oak room—neither did I occupy it myself, but directly after breakfast we repaired to that apartment.

He measured it within, he measured the house without. He then went upstairs once more, and sounded one wall that met the fireplace. He went over about three feet of that again and again.

"There is a space here," he remarked, "not accounted for."

"How shall we account for it?" I asked.

"Send for a bricklayer"; which I did.

In the most matter-of-fact way my friend told him to open a hole in the wall.

After he had been working for two hours the room was filled with rubbish, and we were able to put a candle and our heads through the aperture.

"Well?" inquired my friend triumphantly.

"There is a staircase, sure enough," I agreed.

"Shall we go down it?"

"I will not for any earthly consideration," was my prompt reply.

"Then I will presently," he remarked.

"Notwithstanding your wife and family?" I ventured to suggest.

"Notwithstanding twenty wives and twenty families," he replied, with a firmness born perhaps of his distance from the home atmosphere.

He explored the staircase, and came back baffled, but not despondent.

"We must examine the cellars," he said; "that way lies success."

"That way lies madness," I murmured.

"Eh? what did you say?" he exclaimed.

"I said nothing to the purpose," I replied, curtly.

We went down into the cellars, but nothing could there be discovered to help us in our difficulty.

"Part of the house," he remarked, "seems to have been built on the ground; but there is nothing unusual in that—nothing at least so unusual as to justify me in undermining the place to search for further cellarage. With your permission I will work from the staircase."

I gave permission, and for I suppose three mortal hours, that bricklayer, urged on by my friend, and stimulated with beer, for which his "mate" was being perpetually despatched, chipped away with his cold chisel upon mortar which was more, so he averred, like granite, than honest lime and sand.

By this time the winter's day had long closed; and the workman, intimating that his arms were a bit stiffish, and that it was tight working where there was no room to work, left us for the night, with the assurance that he would be back again after breakfast the next morning.

After this my friend, whose name was Tuft, and who is at the present moment distinguishing himself by designing various edifices each more ugly, and more uncomfortable, and more thoroughly according to the ethics of modern art than its predecessor, was, like many another busy man, taken with a notion that he must inspect once more the ghost's battle-field.

"Let the ghost rest for to-night, there's a good soul," I entreated; the idea of the ghost being, if I may say so, laid very considerably by the discovery of that secret staircase, but he would listen to no remonstrance.

"Stay here and rest, my dear sir," he entreated; "but let me, do let me examine once again the work accomplished to-day."

He repaired to the scene of his triumphs, and remained there for so long a time that I was thinking of seeing what had become of him, when he burst in upon me, pale but exultant.

"Come with me, come!" he cried; "the secret of Crow Hall is solved at last."

"Do you mean," said I, "that you want me to go down those steps to-night?"

"Yes, most decidedly."

"Then most decidedly I shall do nothing of the kind. To-morrow morning, if you have anything to show me, I will see it."

"How very odd you are," he remarked.

"Perhaps you might be odd if you had seen in Crow Hall the things that have appeared to me and others."

His enthusiasm died out a little after this.

On the whole, Crow Hall was not a nice house in which to be reminded of ghost-stories late at night.

Morning brought, however, fresh courage to Mr. Tuft; the presence of the bricklayer and his mate, who were already, ten minutes after breakfast, thirsting for beer, inspired me with such confidence that I agreed to descend those steps, the very sight of which filled me with dismay.

Mr. Tuft went first, carrying a dark lantern, the bricklayer followed him, bearing an ordinary lantern, with which he lit my steps, and last of all came the man whom he called mate.

What a smell of damp and mould greeted our nostrils as we descended the steps, and at last found ourselves standing in a space about three feet square, one side of which was occupied by a doorway through which I could see a space beyond black as Erebus.

"I 'spose it's all right, gov'nor?" said the bricklayer, addressing Mr. Tuft; "no foul air, nor nothing of that sort?"

"No foul nonsense," exclaimed Mr. Tuft; though that gentleman subsequently informed me the idea was not so preposterous as I might imagine from the tone of his reply.

"We began work at the wrong wall yesterday," he condescended to explain. "We could not tell, because all the sides were plastered over roughly to conceal the entrance, but no doubt the chipping and hammering loosened fastenings, or I might have failed to find and open the door last night. Now shall we go forward?"

"By all means," I agreed, and we passed into the yawning blackness beyond.

We found ourselves in a cellar, or dungeon, square, except for the little vestibule which had been taken out of one corner; behind us was the concealed door by which we had entered; facing it was another door, which stood open; this latter gave ingress to three other small chambers. Out of one of these opened an archway, leading to what seemed a subterraneous passage; out of another a steep flight of stone steps descended to unknown depths.

"I should say many a brave gentleman has lain *perdu* here, till he could escape to the coast, in the good old times, when no one could reckon how long he might be permitted to keep his head on his shoulders," said Mr. Tuft, waving his dark lantern above his head, and flashing the light now on the walls, the ground, the ceiling.

"I have always understood this was a smugglers' haunt," I remarked.

"The smuggling came after, doubtless," agreed Mr. Tuft, graciously.

"There does not seem much in these places to reward our search," I suggested, trying to speak carelessly, spite of a growing feeling of giddiness and nausea which made me glad to lay my hand on the bricklayer's shoulder as we moved from place to place.

"No," said Mr. Tuft, "dirt, dust, damp, mildew, are the usual tenants of concealed apartments nowadays. With the exception of a few empty barrels, there is nothing here to stimulate curiosity."

At this moment the bricklayer's mate, who had been lounging about the rooms with a sort of speculative stare, turned from a small heap of dust, which he first turned over with his foot, and then grubbed amongst with his hands, broke across Mr. Tuft's speech by saying:

"Show a light here, Bill."

Without troubling Bill, Mr. Tuft skipped across the floor, and threw a glance across the entrance of the subterranean passage.

"It's bones, ain't it?" asked the discoverer, looking up in Mr. Tuft's face, "and bits of glass."

Mr. Tuft pushed him aside, and kneeling down, took something from the ground and held it to the light.

"Come here, Trevor," he said, in a voice hoarse with excitement.

Still giddy and sick I staggered to his side.

"What is that?" he asked, putting something into my hand and flashing his bull's-eye on it.

"What is it? A diamond to be sure. For Heaven's sake," I went on, addressing the bricklayer, "help me into the air—I feel as if I were dying."

In an instant the men caught me—not too soon—for I almost reeled into their arms.

Though it was a cold winter's day I prayed them to take me into the open air, anywhere out of the atmosphere of that accursed house.

When I was a little better—when I had sat for awhile with the icy wind cooling my forehead, and swallowed some brandy which Mrs. Paul brought me of her own free will, though ordinarily she disapproved of what she called spiritual liquors, believing that tea was the only beverage "sinful creatures with immortal souls" should indulge in, when I had in a sentence, to quote Bill's mate, done what he styled, "come to hisself"—Mr. Tuft joined me.

"Shall I close the door again, Trevor," he said, "till you are well enough to go down with me again? There are jewels there worth a king's ransom."

"Collect them," I answered, "and then come back to me; never again will I set foot in any part of Crow Hall save Mrs. Paul's kitchen."

Leaning on his arm I made my way to that pleasant apartment. In it there was an old-fashioned sofa, upholstered in brown moreen, on which I stretched myself.

Mrs. Paul considerately placed a small table beside my couch, on which she left a Bible, hymnbook, Mr. Wesley's Discourses, and a few tracts before leaving me to repose.

Subsequently, I ascertained she assisted Mr. Tuft in picking up the bright stones that lay amongst the dust and bones, constituting the ghastly heap which had once, so we conjectured, been Philip Waldrum's wife.

I did not see the gems—I never saw them in fact. Mr. Tuft packed them away in my bag, and saw that and the rest of my luggage, together with my own person, *en route* for London during the course of the same afternoon.

I signed him a cheque for present expenses before I left, told him to raze Crow Hall with the ground, not to leave one stone of the old house on the other, begged him to send for the clergyman and the doctor, and the sexton and the undertaker, and let the dust and the bones be laid in the churchyard if possible.

Then I travelled back to town, reached Bishopsgate, hired a cab to take me to my lodgings; after which ensues a blank; a part of my life is blotted out of my memory—of the hours, days, weeks which ensued after I got out of the train and entered the cab, memory holds no record.

When I take up the thread of my recollection once again, I am lying in bed in my lodgings, and I have awakened wondering why it is broad daylight and why I feel so tired. I try to ring the bell, but my arm refuses to obey my wish. I see my hands—they are wasted—mere skin and bone, like those of a skeleton.

Someone, hearing me essay to move, comes and stands by my side.

"Mary!" I exclaim, but my voice is weak and hollow.

"Yes, dear."

"What is it—what does it mean?"

"You have been very ill, but you are better now, thank God."

And to her—His instrument—often and often since that day, has Valentine Waldrum told me her nursing saved my life.

"I tell you honestly," he said, "I did not think at one time you had a chance left."

"It was that house," I murmured.

"Yes, I know," was his reply; "you must not talk of it."

"But I must," I answered. "Ask for the black bag I brought back with me from Essex." He left the room, and returned with it in his hand.

"The key," I said wearily, "is on a bunch, which you will find in my pocket."

He looked for the keys and brought them to me.

"That unlocks the bag," I remarked, stopping him as he touched a small brass key.

"Shall I open it?" he inquired.

"No; take the bag home with you. For God's sake never let me see its contents again. You will find there that which will make you a rich man for life."

He thought I was wandering again, evidently, for he did not take the bag. It was not till I had grown almost well again that we recurred to the subject.

"I hope you got a good price for those diamonds, Val," I said.

"What diamonds?" he inquired.

"Those in the bag I told you to take away with you some time back."

"I did not take it. Were you in your right mind when you wished me to do so?" he asked.

"My good fellow," I answered, "so long as that bag is in the house I shall not get strong. Its contents caused my illness. Take them away."

And he did. About the same time Mary took me away to the seaside.

When next I saw Valentine Waldrum, I was well again, and leading the old life which I had decided years and years before was the life which suited me best. Crow Hall had meanwhile been levelled with the ground, the Charitable Society had bought the farm, and the railway company had purchased the ground formerly laid out as lawn, orchard, gardens, and drive.

"I shall go abroad," he said. "Thanks to you I am now rich enough to go where I please."

I did not answer. I knew it was the best thing he could do, and yet my heart sank within me at his words. In other lands he might forget, and win and woo someone free to return his love. In England he could not forget Mary, and alas! I knew Mary could not forget him.

I was leading my old life, as I have said. I was dining out more frequently than ever, when one night, or rather morning, when I was just about letting myself in with a latch-key, which was at once the pain and the pleasure of my landlady's life, a young fellow, in full evening dress, sprang out of a hansom, and addressing me said:

"Mr. Trevor, Lady Mary Conyngham wants to see you immediately."

"What, at this hour!" I exclaimed.

"On the instant," he replied.

"Is Mr. Conyngham dead or dying?" I inquired.

"Neither. She has bound me to secrecy, and the torture of the boot should not wring any admission from me."

We jumped into the cab, and drove to the great town house plebeian Mr. Conyngham had bought and furnished for his well-born bride.

Straight upstairs we went, without announcement, to the drawing-room, where, daylight already fighting its way through the Venetian blinds, Lady Mary, surrounded by a number of excited and expectant guests, stood holding a paper in her fingers.

Seeing me, she thrust it into my hands.

"Read, read," she said; and the guests, falling back, formed a semicircle round me.

I was so confused, that my glasses fell twice off my nose whilst I was trying to adjust them.

"In the name of Heaven, Stafford," cried her ladyship, "if you cannot see, why do you not wear spectacles?"

Which was an extremely unjust and cruel speech, inasmuch as her lady-ship knew I used glasses not to aid, but merely to preserve my eyesight.

When, however, I beheld the first statement set forth in the paper thrust upon me, I confess I felt like one blind.

"The last will and testament of Geoffrey Trevor, of Fairy Water, in the parish of so-and-so, situated in such-and-such county ——"

"Will someone read it aloud?" I entreated, whereupon a young man, with extremely red hair, at a sign from Lady Mary, took the document from me, and recited its contents aloud.

It was the missing will, the will of which my cousin Geoffrey had spoken to his wife, and that he had laid away in a secret corner of the cabinet he had pointed to in his last agony; that cabinet being one of the articles of furniture Lady Mary had fancied she should like when staying at Fairy Water.

Many and many a time I had examined the secret drawers of that cabinet in hopes of discovering something to Mary's advantage, but doubt-less judicious bumping about on the part of the railway company had loosened the false bottom underneath, on which some curious guest examining the relic had found the will and a letter sealed and directed to Mrs. Trevor.

"That dear little woman can marry Valentine Waldrum now, and be the happiest wife in England!" said Lady Mary, excitedly.

Ill-natured people declare her ladyship was so delighted about the dis-covery, that she put her arms round my neck and kissed me.

If this be so, I can state solemnly I retain no recollection of her conde-scension.

And for the rest ——

After reading the letter and perusing the will, Mrs. Trevor announced her intention of remaining a widow, and devoting herself to his children for the rest of her life; but after a time we talked her into a better and more rational frame of mind.

I told her it was her duty to marry Valentine Waldrum, and as for once in her life duty proved synonymous with pleasure, she promised to do as she was told.

The Duke of Severn wanted to give her away, but that being a privilege I meant to yield to no man, I asserted my prior claim, and accordingly he accompanied Valentine as best man, whilst Miss Vinon, all smiles and beauty, was sole bridesmaid at the quiet wedding.

I stood at the hall door looking after the newly-married pair as they drove away, and I alone saw Mary put her head out of the window and kiss her hand to me in token of farewell.

Then, my dear, that day, for the first time since I first beheld you, was my heart free from a dull, aching, remorseful pain.

Is there anything more to tell? Yes, Valentine and his wife live at Fairy Water, and we hope, when Geoffrey comes of age, to come to some arrangement by which they can continue to reside in the old place.

Valentine has made a name, but by his pen rather than his original profession.

He is wealthy, thanks to the jewels discovered at Crow Hall, and he is happy, thanks to the woman he once thought he should never be able to marry.

The ring which Lady Mary described so graphically, and which was eventually taken off a skeleton finger discovered in that ghastly heap of dust, Valentine offered for her ladyship's acceptance.

At first she recoiled from the mere mention of the trinket; then she expressed a desire to look at it again; then she remembered Crow Hall was no longer in existence, and that the original owner of the ring was lying in consecrated ground. Finally, she said it was the most curious piece of jewellery she had ever seen or heard of, and that it could be easily enlarged.

After which, she accepted the present. To this hour she wears it. I can honestly say, whenever my eye falls on that ring, I shiver. How she can endure it on her finger passes my comprehension. But then, as her ladyship sometimes is good enough to lucidly explain—

"Different ranks view different things differently."

In my opinion it is extremely fortunate that they do.

# THE
# LOST
# STRADIVARIUS

---

## by *J. Meade Falkner*

---

"A tale out of season is as
music in mourning."

—ECCLESIASTICUS xxii, 6

*LETTER* from Miss SOPHIA MALTRAVERS to her Nephew, Sir EDWARD MALTRAVERS, then a Student at Christ Church, Oxford.

*13 Pauncefort Buildings, Bath,*
*Oct. 21, 1867.*

"MY DEAR EDWARD,–It was your late father's dying request that certain events which occurred in his last years should be communicated to you on your coming of age. I have reduced them to writing partly from my own recollection, which is, alas! still too vivid, and partly with the aid of notes taken at the time of my brother's death. As you are now of full age, I submit the narrative to you. Much of it has necessarily been exceedingly painful to me to write, but at the same time I feel it is better that you should hear the truth from me than garbled stories from others who did not love your father as I did.

"Your loving Aunt,
"SOPHIA MALTRAVERS.

*"To Sir Edward Maltravers, Bart."*

# MISS SOPHIA
# MALTRAVER'S
# STORY

## CHAPTER I

Your father, John Maltravers, was born in 1820 at Worth, and succeeded his father and mine, who died when we were still young children. John was sent to Eton in due course, and in 1839, when he was nineteen years of age, it was determined that he should go to Oxford. It was intended at first to enter him at Christ Church; but Dr. Sarsdell, who visited us at Worth in the summer of 1839, persuaded Mr. Thoresby, our guardian, to send him instead to Magdalen Hall. Dr. Sarsdell was himself Principal of that institution, and represented that John, who then exhibited some symptoms of delicacy, would meet with more personal attention under his care than he could hope to do in so large a college as Christ Church. Mr. Thoresby, ever solicitious for his ward's welfare, readily waived other considerations in favour of an arrangement which he considered conducive to John's health, and he was accordingly matriculated at Magdalen Hall in the autumn of 1839.

Dr. Sarsdell had not been unmindful of his promise to look after my brother, and had secured him an excellent first-floor sitting-room, with a bedroom adjoining, having an aspect towards New College Lane.

I shall pass over the first two years of my brother's residence at Oxford, because they have nothing to do with the present story. They were spent, no doubt, in the ordinary routine of work and recreation common in Oxford at that period.

From his earliest boyhood he had been passionately devoted to music, and had attained a considerable proficiency on the violin. In the autumn term of 1841 he made the acquaintance of Mr. William Gaskell, a very talented student at New College, and also a more than tolerable musician. The practice of music was then very much less common at Oxford than it has since become, and there were none of those societies existing which now do so much to promote its study among undergraduates. It was therefore a cause of much gratification to the two young men, and it afterwards became a strong bond of friendship, to discover that one was as devoted to the pianoforte as was the other to the violin. Mr. Gaskell, though in easy circumstances, had not a pianoforte in his rooms, and was pleased to use a fine instrument by D'Almaine that John had that term received as a birthday present from his guardian.

From that time the two students were thrown much together, and in the autumn term of 1841 and Easter term of 1842 practised a variety of music in John's rooms, he taking the violin part and Mr. Gaskell that for the pianoforte.

It was, I think, in March, 1842, that John purchased for his rooms a piece of furniture which was destined afterwards to play no unimportant part in the story I am narrating. This was a very large and low wicker chair of a form then coming into fashion in Oxford, and since, I am told, become a familiar object of most college rooms. It was cushioned with a gaudy pattern of chintz, and bought for new of an upholsterer at the bottom of the High Street.

Mr. Gaskell was taken by his uncle to spend Easter in Rome, and obtaining special leave from his college to prolong his travels, did not return to Oxford till three weeks of the summer term were passed and May was well advanced. So impatient was he to see his friend that he would not let even the first evening of his return pass without coming round to John's rooms. The two young men sat without lights until the night was late; and Mr. Gaskell had much to narrate of his travels, and spoke specially of the beautiful music which he had heard at Easter in the Roman churches. He had also had lessons on the piano from a celebrated professor of the Italian style, but seemed to have been particularly delighted with the music of the seventeenth-century composers, of whose works he had brought back some specimens set for piano and violin.

It was past eleven o'clock when Mr. Gaskell left to return to New College; but the night was unusually warm, with a moon near the full, and John sat for some time in a cushioned window-seat before the open sash thinking over what he had heard about the music of Italy. Feeling still disinclined for sleep, he lit a single candle and began to turn over some of the musical works which Mr. Gaskell had left on the table. His attention was especially attracted to an oblong book, bound in soiled vellum, with a coat of arms stamped in gilt upon the side. It was a manuscript copy of some early suites by Graziani for violin and harpsichord, and was apparently written at Naples in the year 1744, many years after the death of that composer. Though the ink was yellow and faded, the transcript had been accurately made, and could be read with tolerable comfort by an advanced musician in spite of the antiquated notation.

Perhaps by accident, or perhaps by some mysterious direction which our minds are incapable of appreciating, his eye was arrested by a suite of four movements with a *basso continuo*, or figured bass, for the harpsichord. The other suites in the book were only distinguished by numbers, but this one the composer had dignified with the name of "l'Areopagita." Almost mechanically John put the book on his music-stand, took his violin from its case, and after a moment's turning stood up and played the first movement, a lively *Coranto*. The light of the single candle burning on the table was scarcely sufficient to illumine the page; the shadows hung in the creases of the leaves, which had grown into those wavy folds sometimes observable in books made of thick paper and remaining long shut; and it was with difficulty that he could read what he was playing. But he felt the strange impulse of the old-world music urging him forward, and did not even pause to light the candles which stood ready in their sconces on either side of the desk. The *Coranto* was followed by a *Sarabanda*, and the *Sarabanda* by a *Gagliarda*. My brother stood playing, with his face turned to the window, with the room and the large wicker chair of which I have spoken behind him. The *Gagliarda* began with a bold and lively air, and as he played the opening bars, he heard behind him a creaking of the wicker chair. The sound was a perfectly familiar one—as of some person placing a hand on either arm of the chair preparatory to lowering himself into it, followed by another as of the same person being leisurely seated. But for the tones of the violin, all was silent, and the creaking of the chair was strangely distinct. The illusion was so complete that my brother stopped playing suddenly, and turned round expecting that some late friend of his had slipped in unawares, being attracted by the sound of the violin, or that Mr. Gaskell himself had returned. With the cessation of the music an absolute stillness fell upon all; the light of the single candle scarcely reached the darker corners of the room, but fell directly on the wicker chair and showed it to be perfectly empty. Half amused, half vexed with himself at having without reason interrupted his music, my brother returned to the *Gagliarda*; but some impulse induced him to light the candles in the sconces, which gave an illumination more adequate to the occasion. The *Gagliarda* and the last movement, a *Minuetto*, were finished, and John closed the book, intending, as it was now late, to seek his bed. As he shut the pages a creaking of the wicker chair again attracted his attention, and he heard distinctly sounds such as would be made by a person raising himself from a sitting posture. This time, being less surprised, he could more aptly consider the probable causes of such a circumstance, and easily arrived at the conclusion that there must be in the wicker chair osiers responsive to certain notes of the violin, as panes of glass in church windows are observed to vibrate in sympathy with certain tones of the organ. But while this argument approved itself to his reason, his imagination was but half convinced; and he could not but be impressed with the fact that the second creaking of the chair had been coincident with his shutting the music-book; and, unconsciously, pictured to himself some strange visitor waiting until the termination of the music, and then taking his departure.

His conjectures did not, however, either rob him of sleep or even disturb it with dreams, and he woke the next morning with a cooler mind and one less inclined to fantastic imagination. If the strange episode of the previous evening had not entirely vanished from his mind, it seemed at least fully accounted for by the acoustic explanation to which I have alluded above. Although he saw Mr. Gaskell in the course of the morning, he did not think it necessary to mention to him so trivial a circumstance, but made with him an appointment to sup together in his own rooms that evening, and to amuse themselves afterwards by essaying some of the Italian music.

It was shortly after nine that night when, supper being finished, Mr. Gaskell seated himself at the piano and John tuned his violin. The evening was closing in; there had been heavy thunder-rain in the afternoon, and the moist air hung now heavy and steaming, while across it there throbbed the distant vibrations of the tenor bell at Christ Church. It was tolling the customary 101 strokes, which are rung every night in term-time as a signal for closing the college gates. The two young men enjoyed themselves for some while, playing first a suite by Cesti, and then two early sonatas by Buononcini. Both of them were sufficiently expert musicians to make reading at sight a pleasure rather than an effort; and Mr. Gaskell especially was well versed in the theory of music, and in the correct rendering of the *basso continuo*. After the Buononcini Mr. Gaskell took up the oblong copy of Graziani, and turning over its leaves, proposed that they should play the same suite which John had performed by himself the previous evening. His selection was apparently perfectly fortuitous, as my brother had purposely refrained from directing his attention in any way to that piece of music. They played the *Coranto* and the *Sarabanda*, and in the singular fascination of the music John had entirely forgotten the episode of the previous evening, when, as the bold air of the *Gagliarda* commenced, he suddenly became aware of the same strange creaking of the wicker chair that he had noticed on the first occasion. The sound was identical, and so exact was its resemblance to that of a person sitting down that he stared at the chair, almost wondering that it still appeared empty. Beyond turning his head sharply for a moment to look round, Mr. Gaskell took no notice of the sound; and my brother, ashamed to betray any foolish interest or excitement, continued the *Gagliarda*, with its repeat. At its conclusion Mr. Gaskell stopped before proceeding to the minuet, and turning the stool on which he was sitting round towards the room, observed, "How very strange, Johnnie,"—for these young men were on terms of sufficient intimacy to address each other in a familiar style—"How very strange! I thought I heard some one sit down in that chair when we began the *Gagliarda*. I looked round quite expecting to see some one had come in. Did you hear nothing?"

"It was only the chair creaking," my brother answered, feigning an indifference which he scarcely felt. "Certain parts of the wicker-work seem to be in accord with musical notes and respond to them; let us continue with the *Minuetto*."

Thus they finished the suite, Mr. Gaskell demanding a repetition of the *Gagliarda*, with the air of which he was much pleased. As the clocks had already struck eleven, they determined not to play more that night; and Mr. Gaskell rose, blew out the sconces, shut the piano, and put the music aside. My brother has often assured me that he was quite prepared for what followed, and had been almost expecting it; for as the books were put away, a creaking of the wicker chair was audible, exactly similar to that which he had heard when he stopped playing on the previous night. There was a moment's silence; the young men looked involuntarily at one another, and then Mr. Gaskell said, "I cannot understand the creaking of that chair; it has never done so before, with all the music we have played. I am perhaps imaginative and excited with the fine airs we have heard to-night, but I have an impression that I cannot dispel that something has been sitting listening to us all this time, and that now when the concert is ended it has got up and gone." There was a spirit of raillery in his words, but his tone was not so light as it would ordinarily have been, and he was evidently ill at ease.

"Let us try the *Gagliarda* again," said my brother; "it is the vibration of the opening notes which affects the wicker-work, and we shall see if the noise is repeated." But Mr. Gaskell excused himself from trying the experiment, and after some desultory conversation, to which it was evident that neither was giving any serious attention, he took his leave and returned to New College.

## CHAPTER II

I shall not weary you, my dear Edward, by recounting similar experiences which occurred on nearly every occasion that the young men met in the evenings for music. The repetition of the phenomenon had accustomed them to expect it. Both professed to be quite satisfied that it was to be attributed to acoustical affinities of vibration, between the wicker-work and certain of the piano wires, and indeed this seemed the only explanation possible. But, at the same time, the resemblance of the noises to those caused by a person sitting down in or rising from a chair was so marked, that even their frequent recurrence never failed to make a strong impression on them. They felt a reluctance to mention the matter to their friends, partly from a fear of being themselves laughed at, and partly to spare from ridicule a circumstance to which each perhaps, in spite of himself, attached some degree of importance. Experience soon convinced them that the first noise as of one sitting down never occurred unless the *Gagliarda* of the "Areopagita" was played, and that this first noise being once heard, the second only followed it when they ceased playing for the evening. They met every night, sitting later with the lengthening summer evenings, and every night, as by some tacit understanding, played the "Areopagita" suite before parting. At the opening bars of the *Gagliarda* the creaking of the chair occurred spontaneously with the utmost regularity. They seldom spoke even to one another of the subject; but one night, when John was putting away his violin after a long evening's music without having played the "Areopagita," Mr. Gaskell, who had risen from the pianoforte, sat down again as by a sudden impulse and said—

"Johnnie, do not put away your violin yet. It is near twelve o'clock and I shall get shut out, but I cannot stop to-night without playing the *Gagliarda*. Suppose that all our theories of vibration and affinity are wrong, suppose that there really comes here night by night some strange visitant to hear us, some poor creature whose heart is bound up in that tune; would it not be unkind to send him away without the hearing of that piece which he seems most to relish? Let us not be ill-mannered, but humour his whim; let us play the *Gagliarda*."

They played it with more vigour and precision than usual, and the now customary sound of one taking his seat at once ensued. It was that night that my brother, looking steadfastly at the chair, saw, or thought he saw, there some slight obscuration, some penumbra, mist, or subtle vapour which, as he gazed, seemed to struggle to take human form. He ceased playing for a moment and rubbed his eyes, but as he did so all dimness vanished and he saw the chair perfectly empty. The pianist stopped also at the cessation of the violin, and asked what ailed him.

"It is only that my eyes were dim," he answered.

"We have had enough for to-night," said Mr. Gaskell; "let us stop. I shall be locked out." He shut the piano, and as he did so the clock in New College tower struck twelve. He left the room running, but was late enough at his college door to be reported, admonished with a fine against such late hours, and confined for a week to college; for being out after midnight was considered, at that time at least, a somewhat serious offence.

Thus for some days the musical practice was compulsorily intermitted, but resumed on the first evening after Mr. Gaskell's term of confinement was expired. After they had performed several suites of Graziani, and finished as usual with the "Areopagita," Mr. Gaskell sat for a time silent at the instrument, as though thinking with himself, and then said—

"I cannot say how deeply this old-fashioned music affects me. Some would try to persuade us that these suites, of which the airs bear the names of different dances, were always written rather as a musical essay and for purposes of performance than for persons to dance to, as their names would more naturally imply. But I think these critics are wrong at least in some instances. It is to me impossible to believe that such a melody, for instance, as the *Giga* of Corelli which we have played, was not written for actual purposes of dancing. One can almost hear the beat of feet upon the floor, and I imagine that in the time of Corelli the practice of dancing, while not a whit inferior in grace, had more of the tripudistic or beating character than is now esteemed consistent with a correct ball-room performance. The *Gagliarda* too, which we play now so constantly, possesses a singular power of assisting the imagination to picture or repro-duce such scenes as those which it no doubt formerly enlivened. I know not why, but it is constantly identified in my mind with some revel which I have perhaps seen in a picture, where several couples are dancing a licentious measure in a long room lit by a number of silver sconces of the debased model common at the end of the seventeenth century. It is prob-ably a reminiscence of my late excursion that gives to these dancers in my fancy the olive skin, dark hair, and bright eyes of the Italian type; and they wear dresses of exceedingly rich fabric and elaborate design. Imagina-tion is whimsical enough to paint for me the character of the room itself, as having an arcade or arches running down one side alone, of the fantastic and paganised Gothic of the Renaissance. At the end is a gallery or bal-cony for the musicians, which on its coved front has a florid coat of arms of foreign heraldry. The shield bears, on a field *or*, a cherub's head blowing on three lilies—a blazon I have no doubt seen somewhere in my travels, though I cannot recollect where. This scene, I say, is so nearly connected in my brain with the *Gagliarda*, that scarcely are its first notes sounded ere it presents itself to my eyes with a vividness which increases every day. The couples advance, set, and recede, using free and licentious gestures which my imagination should be ashamed to recall. Amongst so many foreigners, fancy pictures, I know not in the least why, the presence of a young man of an English type of face, whose features, however, always elude my mind's attempt to fix them. I think that the opening subject of this *Gagliarda* is a superior composition to the rest of it, for it is only during the first sixteen bars that the vision of bygone revelry presents itself to me. With the last note of the sixteenth bar a veil is suddenly drawn across the scene, and with a sense almost of some catastrophe it vanishes. This I attribute to the fact that the second subject must be inferior in conception to the first, and by some sense of incongruity destroys the fabric which the fascination of the preceding one built up."

My brother, though he had listened with interest to what Mr. Gaskell had said, did not reply, and the subject was allowed to drop.

# CHAPTER III

It was in the same summer of 1842, and near the middle of June, that my brother John wrote inviting me to come to Oxford for the Commemora-tion festivities. I had been spending some weeks with Mrs. Temple, a distant cousin of ours, at their house of Royston in Derbyshire, and John was desirous that Mrs. Temple should come up to Oxford and chaperone her daughter Constance and myself at the balls and various other entertainments which take place at the close of the summer term. Owing to Royston being some two hundred miles from Worth Maltravers, our families had hitherto seen little of one another, but during my present visit I had learned to love Mrs. Temple, a lady of singular sweetness of disposition, and had contracted a devoted attachment to her daughter Constance. Constance Temple was then eighteen years of age, and to great beauty united such mental graces and excellent traits of character as must ever appear to reasoning persons more enduringly valuable than even the highest personal attractions. She was well read and witty, and had been trained in those principles of true religion which she afterwards followed with devoted consistency in the self-sacrifice and resigned piety of her too short life. In person, I may remind you, my dear Edward, since death removed her ere you were of years to appreciate either her appearance or her qualities, she was tall, with a somewhat long and oval face, with brown hair and eyes.

Mrs. Temple readily accepted Sir John Maltravers' invitation. She had never seen Oxford herself, and was pleased to afford us the pleasure of so delightful an excursion. John had secured convenient rooms for us above the shop of a well-known printseller in High Street, and we arrived in Oxford on Friday evening, June 18, 1842. I shall not dilate to you on the various Commemoration festivities, which have probably altered little since those days, and with which you are familiar. Suffice it to say that my brother had secured us admission to every entertainment, and that we enjoyed our visit as only youth with its keen sensibilities and uncloyed pleasures can. I could not help observing that John was very much struck by the attractions of Miss Constance Temple, and that she for her part, while exhibiting no unbecoming forwardness, certainly betrayed no aversion to him. I was greatly pleased both with my own powers of observation which had enabled me to discover so important a fact, and also with the circumstance itself. To a romantic girl of nineteen it appeared high time that a brother of twenty-two should be at least preparing some matrimonial project; and my friend was so good and beautiful that it seemed impossible that I should ever obtain a more lovable sister or my brother a better wife. Mrs. Temple could not refuse her sanction to such a scheme; for while their mental qualities seemed eminently compatible, John was in his own right master of Worth Maltravers, and her daughter sole heiress of the Royston estates.

The Commemoration festivities terminated on Wednesday night with a grand ball at the Music-Room in Holywell Street. This was given by a Lodge of University Freemasons, and John was there with Mr. Gaskell—whose acquaintance we had made with much gratification—both wearing blue silk scarves and small white aprons. They introduced us to many other of their friends similarly adorned, and these important and mysterious insignia sat not amiss with their youthful figures and boyish faces. After a long and pleasurable programme, it was decided that we should prolong our visit till the next evening, leaving Oxford at half-past ten o'clock at night and driving to Didcot, there to join the mail for the west. We rose late the next morning and spent the day rambling among the old colleges and gardens of the most beautiful of English cities. At seven o'clock we dined together for the last time at our lodgings in High Street, and my brother proposed that before parting we should enjoy the fine evening in the gardens of St. John's College. This was at once agreed to, and we proceeded thither, John walking on in front with Constance and Mrs. Temple, and I following with Mr. Gaskell. My companion explained that these gardens were esteemed the most beautiful in the University, but that under ordinary circumstances it was not permitted to strangers to walk there of an evening. Here he quoted some Latin about "aurum per medios ire satellites," which I smilingly made as if I understood, and did indeed gather from it that John had bribed the porter to admit us. It was a warm and very still night, without a moon, but with enough of fading light to show the outlines of the garden front. This long low line of buildings built in Charles I.'s reign looked so exquisitely beautiful that I shall never forget it, though I have not since seen its oriel windows and creeper-covered walls. There was a very heavy dew on the broad lawn, and we walked at first only on the paths. No one spoke, for we were oppressed by the very beauty of the scene, and by the sadness which an imminent parting from friends and from so sweet a place combined to cause. John had been silent and depressed the whole day, nor did Mr. Gaskell himself seem inclined to conversation. Constance and my brother fell a little way behind, and Mr. Gaskell asked me to cross the lawn if I was not afraid of the dew, that I might see the garden front to better advantage from the corner. Mrs. Temple waited for us on the path, not wishing to wet her feet. Mr. Gaskell pointed out the beauties of the perspective as seen from his vantage-point, and we were fortunate in hearing the sweet descant of nightingales for which this garden has ever been famous. As we stood silent and listening, a candle was lit in a small oriel at the end, and the light showing the tracery of the window added to the picturesqueness of the scene.

Within an hour we were in a landau driving through the still warm lanes to Didcot. I had seen that Constance's parting with my brother had been tender, and I am not sure that she was not in tears during some part at least of our drive; but I did not observe her closely, having my thoughts elsewhere.

Though we were thus being carried every moment further from the sleeping city, where I believe that both our hearts were busy, I feel as if I had been a personal witness of the incidents I am about to narrate, so often have I heard them from my brother's lips. The two young men, after parting with us in the High Street, returned to their respective colleges. John reached his rooms shortly before eleven o'clock. He was at once sad and happy—sad at our departure, but happy in a new-found world of delight which his admiration for Constance Temple opened to him. He was, in fact, deeply in love with her, and the full flood of a hitherto unknown passion filled him with an emotion so overwhelming that his ordinary life seemed transfigured. He moved, as it were, in an ether superior to our mortal atmosphere, and a new region of high resolves and noble possibilities spread itself before his eyes. He slammed his heavy outside door (called an "oak") to prevent any one entering and flung himself into the window-seat. Here he sat for a long time, the sash thrown up and his head outside, for he was excited and feverish. His mental exaltation was so great and his thoughts of so absorbing an interest that he took no notice of time, and only remembered afterwards that the scent of a syringa-bush was borne up to him from a little garden-patch opposite, and that a bat had circled slowly up and down the lane, until he heard the clocks striking three. At the same time the faint light of dawn made itself felt almost imperceptibly; the classic statues on the roof of the schools began to stand out against the white sky, and a faint glimmer to penetrate the darkened room. It glistened on the varnished top of his violin-case lying on the table, and on a jug of toast-and-water placed there by his college servant or scout every night before he left. He drank a glass of this mixture, and was moving towards his bedroom door when a sudden thought struck him. He turned back, took the violin from its case, tuned it, and began to play the "Areopagita" suite. He was conscious of that mental clearness and vigour which not unfrequently comes with the dawn to those who have sat watching or reading through the night: and his thoughts were exalted by the effect which the first consciousness of a deep passion causes in imaginative minds. He had never played the suite with more power; and the airs, even without the piano part, seemed fraught with a meaning hitherto unrealised. As he began the *Gagliarda* he heard the wicker chair creak; but he had his back towards it, and the sound was now too familiar to him to cause him even to look round. It was not till he was playing the repeat that he became aware of a new and overpowering sensation. At first it was a vague feeling, so often experienced by us all, of not being alone. He did not stop playing, and in a few seconds the impression of a presence in the room other than his own became so strong that he was actually afraid to look round. But in another moment he felt that at all hazards he must see what or who this presence was. Without stopping he partly turned and partly looked over his shoulder. The silver light of early morning was filling the room, making the various objects appear of less bright colour than usual, and giving to everything a pearl-grey neutral tint. In this cold but clear light he saw seated in the wicker chair the figure of a man.

In the first violent shock of so terrifying a discovery, he could not appreciate such details as those of features, dress, or appearance. He was merely conscious that with him, in a locked room of which he knew himself to be the only human inmate, there sat something which bore a human form. He looked at it for a moment with a hope, which he felt to be vain, that it might vanish and prove a phantom of his excited imagination, but still it sat there. Then my brother put down his violin, and he used to assure me that a horror overwhelmed him of an intensity which he had previously believed impossible. Whether the image which he saw was subjective or objective, I cannot pretend to say: you will be in a position to judge for yourself when you have finished this narrative. Our limited experience would lead us to believe that it was a phantom conjured up by some unusual condition of his own brain; but we are fain to confess that there certainly do exist in nature phenomena such as baffle human reason; and it is possible that, for some hidden purposes of Providence, permission may occasionally be granted to those who have passed from this life to assume again for a time the form of their earthly tabernacle. We must, I say, be content to suspend our judgment on such matters; but in this instance the subsequent course of events is very difficult to explain, except on the supposition that there was then presented to my brother's view the actual bodily form of one long deceased. The dread which took possession of him was due, he has more than once told me when analysing his feelings long afterwards, to two predominant causes. Firstly, he felt that mental dislocation which accompanies the sudden subversion of preconceived theories, the sudden alteration of long habit, or even the occurrence of any circumstance beyond the walk of our daily experience. This I have observed myself in the perturbing effect which a sudden death, a grievous accident, or in recent years the declaration of war, has exercised upon all except the most lethargic or the most determined minds. Secondly, he experienced the profound self-abasement or mental annihilation caused by the near conception of a being of a superior order. In the presence of an existence wearing, indeed, the human form, but of attributes widely different and superior to his own, he felt the combined reverence and revulsion which even the noblest wild animals exhibit when brought for the first time face to face with man. The shock was so great that I feel persuaded it exerted an effect on him from which he never wholly recovered.

After an interval which seemed to him interminable, though it was only of a second's duration, he turned his eyes again to the occupant of the wicker chair. His faculties had so far recovered from the first shock as to enable him to see that the figure was that of a man perhaps thirty-five years of age and still youthful in appearance. The face was long and oval, the hair brown, and brushed straight off an exceptionally high forehead. His complexion was very pale or bloodless. He was clean shaven, and his finely cut mouth, with compressed lips, wore something of a sneering smile. His general expression was unpleasing, and from the first my brother felt as by intuition that there was present some malign and wicked influence. His eyes were not visible, as he kept them cast down, resting his head on his hand in the attitude of one listening. His face and even his dress were impressed so vividly upon John's mind, that he never had any difficulty in recalling them to his imagination; and he and I had afterwards an opportunity of verifying them in a remarkable manner. He wore a long cut-away coat of green cloth with an edge of gold embroidery, and a white satin waistcoat figured with rose-sprigs, a full cravat of rich lace, knee-breeches of buff silk, and stockings of the same. His shoes were of polished black leather with heavy silver buckles, and his costume in general recalled that worn a century ago. As my brother gazed at him, he got up, putting his hands on the arms of the chair to raise himself, and causing the creaking so often heard before. The hands forced themselves on my brother's notice: they were very white, with the long delicate fingers of a musician. He showed a considerable height; and still keeping his eyes on the floor, walked with an ordinary gait towards the end of the bookcase at the side of the room farthest from the window. He reached the bookcase, and then John suddenly lost sight of him. The figure did not fade gradually, but went out, as it were, like the flame of a suddenly extinguished candle.

The room was now filled with the clear light of the summer morning: the whole vision had lasted but a few seconds, but my brother knew that there was no possibility of his having been mistaken, that the mystery of the creaking chair was solved, that he had seen the man who had come evening by evening for a month past to listen to the rhythm of the *Gagliarda*. Terribly disturbed, he sat for some time half dreading and half expecting a return of the figure; but all remained unchanged; he saw nothing, nor did he dare to challenge its reappearance by playing again the *Gagliarda*, which seemed to have so strange an attraction for it. At last, in the full sunlight of a late June morning at Oxford, he heard the steps of early pedestrians on the pavement below his windows, the cry of a milkman, and other sounds which showed the world was awake. It was after six o'clock, and going to his bedroom he flung himself on the outside of the bed for an hour's troubled slumber.

## CHAPTER IV

When his servant called him about eight o'clock my brother sent a note to Mr. Gaskell at New College, begging him to come round to Magdalen Hall as soon as might be in the course of the morning. His summons was at once obeyed, and Mr. Gaskell was with him before he had finished breakfast. My brother was still much agitated, and at once told him what had happened the night before, detailing the various circumstances with minuteness, and not even concealing from him the sentiments which he entertained towards Miss Constance Temple. In narrating the appearance which he had seen in the chair, his agitation was still so excessive that he had difficulty in controlling his voice.

Mr. Gaskell heard him with much attention, and did not at once reply when John had finished his narration. At length he said, "I suppose many friends would think it right to affect, even if they did not feel, an incredulity as to what you have just told me. They might consider it more prudent to attempt to allay your distress by persuading you that what you have seen has no objective reality, but is merely the phantasm of an excited imagination; that if you had not been in love, had not sat up all night, and had not thus overtaxed your physical powers, you would have seen no vision. I shall not argue thus, for I am as certainly convinced as of the fact that we sit here, that on all the nights when we have played this suite called the 'Areopagita' there has been some one listening to us, and that you have at length been fortunate or unfortunate enough to see him."

"Do not say fortunate," said my brother; "for I feel as though I shall never recover from last night's shock."

"That is likely enough," Mr. Gaskell answered, coolly; "for as in the history of the race or individual, increased culture and a finer mental susceptibility necessarily impair the brute courage and powers of endurance which we note in savages, so any supernatural vision such as you have seen must be purchased at the cost of physical reaction. From the first evening that we played this music, and heard the noises mimicking so closely the sitting down and rising up of some person, I have felt convinced that causes other than those which we usually call natural were at work, and that we were very near the manifestation of some extraordinary phenomenon."

"I do not quite apprehend your meaning."

"I mean this," he continued, "that this man or spirit of a man has been sitting here night after night, and that we have not been able to see him, because our minds are dull and obtuse. Last night the elevating force of a strong passion, such as that which you have confided to me, combined with the power of fine music, so exalted your mind that you became endowed, as it were, with a sixth sense, and suddenly were enabled to see that which had previously been invisible. To this sixth sense music gives, I believe, the key. We are at present only on the threshold of such a knowledge of that art as will enable us to use it eventually as the greatest of all humanising and educational agents. Music will prove a ladder to the loftier regions of thought; indeed I have long found for myself that I cannot attain to the highest range of my intellectual power except when hearing good music. All poets, and most writers of prose, will say that their thought is never so exalted, their sense of beauty and proportion never so just, as when they are listening either to the artificial music made by man, or to some of the grander tones of nature, such as the roar of a western ocean, or the sighing of wind in a clump of firs. Though I have often felt on such occasions on the very verge of some high mental discovery, and though a hand has been stretched forward as it were to rend the veil, yet it has never been vouchsafed me to see behind it. This you no doubt were allowed in a measure to do last night. You probably played the music with a deeper intuition than usual, and this, combined with the excitement under which you were already labouring, raised you for a moment to the required pitch of mental exaltation."

"It is true," John said, "that I never felt the melody so deeply as when I played it last night."

"Just so," answered his friend; "and there is probably some link between this air and the history of the man whom you saw last night; some fatal power in it which enables it to exert an attraction on him even after death. For we must remember that the influence of music, though always powerful, is not always for good. We can scarcely doubt that as certain forms of music tend to raise us above the sensuality of the animal, or the more degrading passion of material gain, and to transport us into the ether of higher thought, so other forms are directly calculated to awaken in us luxurious emotions, and to whet those sensual appetites which it is the business of a philosopher not indeed to annihilate or to be ashamed of, but to keep rigidly in check. This possibility of music to effect evil as well as good I have seen recognised, and very aptly expressed in some beautiful verses by Mr. Keble which I have just read: —

> "Cease, stranger, cease those witching notes,
>     The art of syren choirs;
> Hush the seductive voice that floats
>     Across the trembling wires.
>
> Music's ethereal power was given
>     Not to dissolve our clay,
> But draw Promethean beams from heaven
>     To purge the dross away."

"They are fine lines," said my brother, "but I do not see how you apply your argument to the present instance."

"I mean," Mr. Gaskell answered, "that I have little doubt that the melody of this *Gagliarda* has been connected in some manner with the life of the man you saw last night. It is not unlikely, either, that it was a favourite air of his whilst in the flesh, or even that it was played by himself or others at the moment of some crisis in his history. It is possible that such connection may be due merely to the innocent pleasure the melody gave him in life; but the nature of the music itself, and a peculiar effect it has upon my own thoughts, induce me to believe that it was associated with some occasion when he either fell into great sin or when some evil fate, perhaps even death itself, overtook him. You will remember I have told you that this air calls up to my mind a certain scene of Italian revelry in which an Englishman takes part. It is true that I have never been able to fix his features in my mind, nor even to say exactly how he was dressed. Yet now some instinct tells me that it is this very man whom you saw last night. It is not for us to attempt to pierce the mystery which veils from our eyes the secrets of an after-death existence; but I can scarcely suppose that a spirit entirely at rest would feel so deeply the power of a certain melody as to be called back by´ it to his old haunts like a dog by his master's whistle. It is more probable that there is some evil history connected with the matter, and this, I think, we ought to consider if it be possible to unravel."

My brother assenting, he continued, "When this man left you, Johnnie, did he walk to the door?"

"No; he made for the side wall, and when he reached the end of the bookcase I lost sight of him."

Mr. Gaskell went to the bookcase and looked for a moment at the titles of the books, as though expecting to see something in them to assist his inquiries; but finding apparently no clue, he said—

"This is the last time we shall meet for three months or more, let us play the *Gagliarda* and see if there be any response."

My brother at first would not hear of this, showing a lively dread of challenging any reappearance of the figure he had seen: indeed he felt that such an event would probably fling him into a state of serious physical disorder. Mr. Gaskell, however, continued to press him, assuring him that the fact of his now being no longer alone should largely allay any fear on his part, and urging that this would be the last opportunity they would have of playing together for some months.

At last, being overborne, my brother took his violin, and Mr. Gaskell seated himself at the pianoforte. John was very agitated, and as he commenced the *Gagliarda* his hands trembled so that he could scarcely play the air. Mr. Gaskell also exhibited some nervousness, not performing with his customary correctness. But for the first time the charm failed: no noise accompanied the music, nor did anything of an unusual character occur. They repeated the whole suite, but with a similar result.

Both were surprised, but neither had any explanation to offer. My brother, who at first dreaded intensely a repetition of the vision, was now almost disappointed that nothing had occurred; so quickly does the mood of man change.

After some further conversation the young men parted for the Long Vacation—John returning to Worth Maltravers and Mr. Gaskell going to London, where he was to pass a few days before he proceeded to his home in Westmoreland.


## CHAPTER V


John spent nearly the whole of this summer vacation at Worth Maltravers. He had been anxious to pay a visit to Royston; but the continued and serious illness of Mrs. Temple's sister had called her and Constance to Scotland, where they remained until the death of their relative allowed them to return to Derbyshire in the late autumn. John and I had been brought up together from childhood. When he was at Eton we had always spent the holidays at Worth, and after my dear mother's death, when we were left quite alone, the bonds of our love were naturally drawn still closer. Even after my brother went to Oxford, at a time when most young men are anxious to enjoy a new-found liberty, and to travel or to visit friends in their vacation, John's ardent affection for me and for Worth Maltravers kept him at home; and he was pleased on most occasions to make me the partner of his thoughts and of his pleasures. This long vacation of 1842 was, I think, the happiest of our lives. In my case I know it was so, and I think it was happy also for him; for none could guess that the small cloud seen in the distance like a man's hand was afterwards to rise and darken all his later days. It was a summer of brilliant and continued sunshine; many of the old people said that they could never recollect so fine a season, and both fruit and crops were alike abundant. John hired a small cutter-yacht, the *Palestine*, which he kept in our little harbour of Encombe, and in which he and I made many excursions, visiting Weymouth, Lyme Regis, and other places of interest on the south coast.

In this summer my brother confided to me two secrets,—his love for Constance Temple, which indeed was after all no secret, and the history of the apparition which he had seen. This last filled me with inexpressible dread and distress. It seemed cruel and unnatural that any influence so dark and mysterious should thus intrude on our bright life, and from the first I had an impression which I could not entirely shake off, that any such appearance or converse of a disembodied spirit must portend misfortune, if not worse, to him who saw or heard it. It never occurred to me to combat or to doubt the reality of the vision; he believed that he had seen it, and his conviction was enough to convince me. He had meant, he said, to tell no one, and had given a promise to Mr. Gaskell to that effect; but I think that he could not bear to keep such a matter in his own breast, and within the first week of his return he made me his confidant. I remember, my dear Edward, the look everything wore on that sad night when he first told me what afterwards proved so terrible a secret. We had dined quite alone, and he had been moody and depressed all the evening. It was a chilly night, with some fret blowing up from the sea. The moon showed that blunted and deformed appearance which she assumes a day or two past the full, and the moisture in the air encircled her with a stormy-looking halo. We had stepped out of the dining-room windows on to the little terrace looking down towards Smedmore and Encombe. The glaucous shrubs that grow in between the balusters were wet and dripping with the salt breath of the sea, and we could hear the waves coming into the cove from the west. After standing a minute I felt chill, and proposed that we should go back to the billiard-room, where a fire was lit on all except the warmest nights. "No," John said, "I want to tell you something, Sophy," and then we walked on to the old boat summer-house. There he told me everything. I cannot describe to you my feelings of anguish and horror when he told me of the appearance of the man. The interest of the tale was so absorbing to me that I took no note of time, nor of the cold night air, and it was only when it was all finished that I felt how deadly chill it had become. "Let us go in, John," I said; "I am cold and feel benumbed."

But youth is hopeful and strong, and in another week the impression had faded from our minds, and we were enjoying the full glory of midsummer weather, which I think only those know who have watched the blue sea come rippling in at the foot of the white chalk cliffs of Dorset.

I had felt a reluctance even so much as to hear the air of the *Gagliarda*, and though he had spoken to me of the subject on more than one occasion, my brother had never offered to play it to me. I knew that he had the copy of Graziani's suites with him at Worth Maltravers, because he had told me that he had brought it from Oxford; but I had never seen the book, and fancied that he kept it intentionally locked up. He did not, however, neglect the violin, and during the summer mornings, as I sat reading or working on the terrace, I often heard him playing to himself in the library. Though he had never even given me any description of the melody of the *Gagliarda*, yet I felt certain that he not unfrequently played it. I cannot say how it was; but from the moment that I heard him one morning in the library performing an air set in a curiously low key, it forced itself upon my attention, and I knew, as it were by instinct, that it must be the *Gagliarda* of the "Areopagita." He was using a *sordino* and playing it very softly; but I was not mistaken. One wet afternoon in October, only a week before the time of his leaving us to return to Oxford for the autumn term, he walked into the drawing-room where I was sitting, and proposed that we should play some music together. To this I readily agreed. Though but a mediocre performer, I have always taken much pleasure in the use of the pianoforte, and esteemed it an honour whenever he asked me to play with him, since my powers as a musician were so very much inferior to his. After we had played several pieces, he took up an oblong music-book bound in white vellum, placed it upon the desk of the pianoforte, and proposed that we should play a suite by Graziani. I knew that he meant the "Areopagita," and begged him at once not to ask me to play it. He rallied me lightly on my fears, and said it would much please him to play it, as he had not heard the pianoforte part since he had left Oxford three months ago. I saw that he was eager to perform it, and being loath to disoblige so kind a brother during the last week of his stay at home, I at length overcame my scruples and set out to play it. But I was so alarmed at the possibility of any evil consequences ensuing, that when we commenced the *Gagliarda* I could scarcely find my notes. Nothing in any way unusual, however, occurred; and being reassured by this, and feeling an irresistible charm in the music, I finished the suite with more appearance of ease. My brother, however, was, I fear, not satisfied with my performance, and compared it, very possibly, with that of Mr. Gaskell, to which it was necessarily much inferior, both through weakness of execution and from my insufficient knowledge of the principles of the *basso continuo*. We stopped playing, and John stood looking out of the window across the sea, where the sky was clearing low down under the clouds. The sun went down behind Portland in a fiery glow which cheered us after a long day's rain. I had taken the copy of Graziani's suites off the desk, and was holding it on my lap turning over the old foxed and yellow pages. As I closed it a streak of evening sunlight fell across the room and lighted up a coat of arms stamped in gilt on the cover. It was much faded and would ordinarily have been hard to make out; but the ray of strong light illumined it, and in an instant I recognised the same shield which Mr. Gaskell had pictured to himself as hanging on the musicians' gallery of his phantasmal dancing-room. My brother had often recounted to me this effort of his friend's imagination, and here I saw before me the same florid foreign blazon, a cherub's head blowing on three lilies on a gold field. This discovery was not only of interest, but afforded me much actual relief; for it accounted rationally for at least one item of the strange story. Mr. Gaskell had no doubt noticed at some time this shield stamped on the outside of the book, and bearing the impression of it unconsciously in his mind, had reproduced it in his imagined revels. I said as much to my brother, and he was greatly interested, and after examining the shield agreed that this was certainly a probable solution of that part of the mystery. On the 12th of October John returned to Oxford.

## CHAPTER VI

My brother told me afterwards that more than once during the summer vacation he had seriously considered with himself the propriety of changing his rooms at Magdalen Hall. He had thought that it might thus be possible for him to get rid at once of the memory of the apparition, and of the fear of any reappearance of it. He could either have moved into another set of rooms in the Hall itself, or else gone into lodgings in the town—a usual proceeding, I am told, for gentlemen near the end of their course at Oxford. Would to God that he had indeed done so! but with the supineness which has, I fear, my dear Edward, been too frequently a characteristic of our family, he shrank from the trouble such a course would involve, and the opening of the autumn term found him still in his old rooms. You will forgive me for entering here on a very brief description of your father's sitting-room. It is, I think, necessary for the proper understanding of the incidents that follow. It was not a large room, though probably the finest in the small buildings of Magdalen Hall, and panelled from floor to ceiling with oak which successive generations had obscured by numerous coats of paint. On one side were two windows having an aspect on to New College Lane, and fitted with deep cushioned seats in the recesses. Outside these windows there were boxes of flowers, the brightness of which formed in the summer term a pretty contrast to the grey and crumbling stone, and afforded pleasure at once to the inmate and to passers-by. Along nearly the whole length of the wall opposite to the windows, some tenant in years long past had had mahogany book-shelves placed, reaching to a height of perhaps five feet from the floor. They were handsomely made in the style of the eighteenth century and pleased my brother's taste. He had always exhibited a partiality for books, and the fine library at Worth Maltravers had no doubt contributed to foster his tastes in that direction. At the time of which I write he had formed a small collection for himself at Oxford, paying particular attention to the bindings, and acquiring many excellent specimens of that art, principally, I think, from Messrs. Payne & Foss, the celebrated London booksellers.

Towards the end of the autumn term, having occasion one cold day to take down a volume of Plato from its shelf, he found to his surprise that the book was quite warm. A closer examination easily explained to him the reason—namely, that the flue of a chimney, passing behind one end of the bookcase, sensibly heated not only the wall itself, but also the books in the shelves. Although he had been in his rooms now near three years, he had never before observed this fact; partly, no doubt, because the books in these shelves were seldom handled, being more for show as specimens of bindings than for practical use. He was somewhat annoyed at this discovery, fearing lest such a heat, which in moderation is beneficial to books, might through its excess warp the leather or otherwise injure the bindings. Mr. Gaskell was sitting with him at the time of the discovery, and indeed it was for his use that my brother had taken down the volume of Plato. He strongly advised that the bookcase should be moved, and suggested that it would be better to place it across that end of the room where the pianoforte then stood. They examined it and found that it would easily admit of removal, being, in fact, only the frame of a bookcase, and showing at the back the painted panelling of the wall. Mr. Gaskell noted it as curious that all the shelves were fixed and immovable except one at the end, which had been fitted with the ordinary arrangement allowing its position to be altered at will. My brother thought that the change would improve the appearance of his rooms, besides being advantageous for the books, and gave instructions to the college upholsterer to have the necessary work carried out at once.

The two young men had resumed their musical studies, and had often played the "Areopagita" and other music of Graziani since their return to Oxford in the autumn. They remarked, however, that the chair no longer creaked during the *Gagliarda*—and, in fact, that no unusual occurrence whatever attended its performance. At times they were almost tempted to doubt the accuracy of their own remembrances, and to consider as entirely mythical the mystery which had so much disturbed them in the summer term. My brother had also pointed out to Mr. Gaskell my discovery that the coat of arms on the outside of the music-book was identical with that which his fancy portrayed on the musicians' gallery. He readily admitted that he must at some time have noticed and afterwards forgotten the blazon on the book, and that an unconscious reminiscence of it had no doubt inspired his imagination in this instance. He rebuked my brother for having agitated me unnecessarily by telling me at all of so idle a tale; and was pleased to write a few lines to me at Worth Maltravers, felicitating me on my shrewdness of perception, but speaking banteringly of the whole matter.

On the evening of the 14th of November my brother and his friend were sitting talking in the former's room. The position of the bookcase had been changed on the morning of that day, and Mr. Gaskell had come round to see how the books looked when placed at the end instead of at the side of the room. He had applauded the new arrangement, and the young men sat long over the fire, with a bottle of college port and a dish of medlars which I had sent my brother from our famous tree in the Upper Croft at Worth Maltravers. Later on they fell to music, and played a variety of pieces, performing also the "Areopagita" suite. Mr. Gaskell before he left complimented John on the improvement which the alteration in the place of the bookcase had made in his room, saying, "Not only do the books in their present place very much enhance the general appearance of the room, but the change seems to me to have affected also a marked acoustical improvement. The oak panelling now exposed on the side of the room has given a resonant property to the wall which is peculiarly responsive to the tones of your violin. While you were playing the *Gagliarda* to-night, I could almost have imagined that some one in an adjacent room was playing the same air with a *sordino*, so distinct was the echo."

Shortly after this he left.

My brother partly undressed himself in his bedroom, which adjoined, and then returning to his sitting-room, pulled the large wicker chair in front of the fire, and sat there looking at the glowing coals, and thinking perhaps of Miss Constance Temple. The night promised to be very cold, and the wind whistled down the chimney, increasing the comfortable sensation of the clear fire. He sat watching the ruddy reflection of the firelight dancing on the panelled wall, when he noticed that a picture placed where the end of the bookcase formerly stood was not truly hung, and needed adjustment. A picture hung askew was particularly offensive to his eyes, and he got up at once to alter it. He remembered as he went up to it that at this precise spot four months ago he had lost sight of the man's figure which he saw rise from the wicker chair, and at the memory felt an involuntary shudder. This reminiscence probably influenced his fancy also in another direction, for it seemed to him that very faintly, as though played far off, and with the *sordino*, he could hear the air of the *Gagliarda*. He put one hand behind the picture to steady it, and as he did so his finger struck a very slight projection in the wall. He pulled the picture a little to one side, and saw that what he had touched was the back of a small hinge sunk in the wall, and almost obliterated with many coats of paint. His curiosity was excited, and he took a candle from the table and examined the wall carefully. Inspection soon showed him another hinge a little further up, and by degrees he perceived that one of the panels had been made at some time in the past to open, and serve probably as the door of a cupboard. At this point he assured me that a feverish anxiety to reopen this cupboard door took possession of him, and that the intense excitement filled his mind which we experience on the eve of a discovery which we fancy may produce important results. He loosened the paint in the cracks with a penknife, and attempted to press open the door; but his instrument was not adequate to such a purpose, and all his efforts remained ineffective. His excitement had now reached an overmastering pitch; for he anticipated, though he knew not why, some strange discovery to be made in this sealed cupboard. He looked round the room for some weapon with which to force the door, and at length with his penknife cut away sufficient wood at the joint to enable him to insert the end of the poker in the hole. The clock in the New College Tower struck one at the exact moment when with a sharp effort he thus forced open the door. It appeared never to have had a fastening, but merely to have been stuck fast by the accumulation of paint. As he bent it slowly back upon the rusted hinges his heart beat so fast that he could scarcely catch his breath, though he was conscious all the while of a ludicrous aspect of his position, knowing that it was most probable that the cavity within would be found empty. The cupboard was small but very deep, and in the obscure light seemed at first to contain nothing except a small heap of dust and cobwebs. His sense of disappointment was keen as he thrust his hand into it, but changed again in a moment to breathless interest on feeling something solid in what he had imagined to be only an accumulation of mould and dirt. He snatched up a candle, and holding this in one hand, with the other pulled out an object from the cupboard and put it on the table, covered as it was with the curious drapery of black and clinging cobwebs which I have seen adhering to bottles of old wine. It lay there between the dish of medlars and the decanter, veiled indeed with thick dust as with a mantle, but revealing beneath it the shape and contour of a violin.

## CHAPTER VII

John was excited at his discovery, and felt his thoughts confused in a manner that I have often experienced myself on the unexpected receipt of news interesting me deeply, whether for pleasure or pain. Yet at the same time he was half amused at his own excitement, feeling that it was childish to be moved over an event so simple as the finding of a violin in an old cupboard. He soon collected himself and took up the instrument, using great care, as he feared lest age should have rendered the wood brittle or rotten. With some vigorous puffs of breath and a little dusting with a handkerchief he removed the heavy outer coating of cobwebs, and began to see more clearly the delicate curves of the body and of the scroll. A few minutes' more gentle handling left the instrument sufficiently clean to enable him to appreciate its chief points. Its seclusion from the outer world, which the heavy accumulation of dust proved to have been for many years, did not seem to have damaged it in the least; and the fact of a chimney-flue passing through the wall at no great distance had no doubt conduced to maintain the air in the cupboard at an equable temperature. So far as he was able to judge, the wood was as sound as when it left the maker's hands; but the strings were of course broken, and curled up in little tangled knots. The body was of a light-red colour, with a varnish of peculiar lustre and softness. The neck seemed rather longer than ordinary, and the scroll was remarkably bold and free.

The violin which my brother was in the habit of using was a fine *Pressenda*, given to him on his fifteenth birthday by Mr. Thoresby, his guardian. It was of that maker's later and best period, and a copy of the Stradivarius model. John took this from its case and laid it side by side with his new discovery, meaning to compare them for size and form. He perceived at once that while the model of both was identical, the superiority of the older violin in every detail was so marked as to convince him that it was undoubtedly an instrument of exceptional value. The extreme beauty of its varnish impressed him vividly, and though he had never seen a genuine Stradivarius, he felt a conviction gradually gaining on him that he stood in the presence of a masterpiece of that great maker. On looking into the interior he found that surprisingly little dust had penetrated into it, and by blowing through the sound-holes he soon cleared it sufficiently to enable him to discern a label. He put the candle close to him, and held the violin up so that a little patch of light fell through the sound-hole on to the label. His heart leapt with a violent pulsation as he read the characters, "*Antonius Stradiuarius Cremonensis faciebat, 1704.*" Under ordinary circumstances it would naturally be concluded that such a label was a forgery, but the conditions were entirely altered in the case of a violin found in a forgotten cupboard, with proof so evident of its having remained there for a very long period.

He was not at that time as familiar with the history of the fiddles of the great maker as he, and indeed I also, afterwards became. Thus he was unable to decide how far the exact year of its manufacture would determine its value as compared with other specimens of Stradivarius. But although the Pressenda he had been used to play on was always considered a very fine instrument both in make and varnish, his new discovery so far excelled it in both points as to assure him that it must be one of the Cremonese master's greatest productions.

He examined the violin minutely, scrutinising each separate feature, and finding each in turn to be of the utmost perfection, so far as his knowledge of the instrument would enable him to judge. He lit more candles that he might be able better to see it, and holding it on his knees, sat still admiring it until the dying fire and increasing cold warned him that the night was now far advanced. At last, carrying it to his bedroom, he locked it carefully into a drawer and retired for the night.

He woke next morning with that pleasurable consciousness of there being some reason for gladness, which we feel on awaking in seasons of happiness, even before our reason, locating it, reminds us what the actual source of our joy may be. He was at first afraid lest his excitement, working on the imagination, should have led him on the previous night to overestimate the fineness of the instrument, and he took it from the drawer half expecting to be disappointed with its daylight appearance. But a glance sufficed to convince him of the unfounded nature of his suspicions. The various beauties which he had before observed were enhanced a hundred-fold by the light of day, and he realised more fully than ever that the instrument was one of altogether exceptional value.

And now, my dear Edward, I shall ask your forgiveness if in the history I have to relate any observation of mine should seem to reflect on the character of your late father, Sir John Maltravers. And I beg you to consider that your father was also my dear and only brother, and that it is inexpressibly painful to me to recount any actions of his which may not seem becoming to a noble gentleman, as he surely was. I only now proceed because, when very near his end, he most strictly enjoined me to narrate these circumstances to you fully when you should come of age. We must humbly remember that to God alone belongs judgment, and that it is not for poor mortals to decide what is right or wrong in certain instances for their fellows, but that each should strive most earnestly to do his own duty.

Your father entirely concealed from me the discovery he had made. It was not till long afterwards that I had it narrated to me, and I only obtained a knowledge of this and many other of the facts which I am now telling you at a date much subsequent to their actual occurrence.

He explained to his servant that he had discovered and opened an old cupboard in the panelling, without mentioning the fact of his having found anything in it, but merely asking him to give instructions for the paint to be mended and the cupboard put into a usable state. Before he had finished a very late breakfast Mr. Gaskell was with him, and it has been a source of lasting regret to me that my brother concealed also from his most intimate and trusted friend the discovery of the previous night. He did, indeed, tell him that he had found and opened an old cupboard in the panelling, but made no mention of there having been anything within. I cannot say what prompted him to this action; for the two young men had for long been on such intimate terms that the one shared almost as a matter of course with the other any pleasure or pain which might fall to his lot. Mr. Gaskell looked at the cupboard with some interest, saying afterwards, "I know now, Johnnie, why the one shelf of the bookcase which stood there was made movable when all the others were fixed. Some former occupant used the cupboard, no doubt, as a secret receptacle for his treasures, and masked it with the book-shelves in front. Who knows what he kept in here, or who he was! I should not be surprised if he were that very man who used to come here so often to hear us play the 'Areopagita,' and whom you saw that night last June. He had the one shelf made, you see, to move so as to give him access to this cavity on occasion: then when he left Oxford, or perhaps died, the mystery was forgotten, and with a few times of painting the cracks closed up."

Mr. Gaskell shortly afterwards took his leave as he had a lecture to attend, and my brother was left alone to the contemplation of his new-found treasure. After some consideration he determined that he would take the instrument to London, and obtain the opinion of an expert as to its authenticity and value. He was well acquainted with the late Mr. George Smart, the celebrated London dealer, from whom his guardian, Mr. Thoresby, had purchased the Pressenda violin which John commonly used. Besides being a dealer in valuable instruments, Mr. Smart was a famous collector of Stradivarius fiddles, esteemed one of the first authorities in Europe in that domain of art, and author of a valuable work of reference in connection with it. It was to him, therefore, that my brother decided to submit the violin, and he wrote a letter to Mr. Smart saying that he should give himself the pleasure of waiting on him the next day on a matter of business. He then called on his tutor, and with some excuse obtained leave to journey to London the next morning. He spent the rest of the day in very carefully cleaning the violin, and noon of the next saw him with it, securely packed, in Mr. Smart's establishment in Bond Street.

Mr. Smart received Sir John Maltravers with deference, demanded in what way he could serve him; and on hearing that his opinion was required on the authenticity of a violin, smiled somewhat dubiously and led the way into a back parlour.

"My dear Sir John," he said, "I hope you have not been led into buying any instrument by a faith in its antiquity. So many good copies of instruments by famous makers and bearing their labels are now afloat, that the chances of obtaining a genuine fiddle from an unrecognised source are quite remote; of hundreds of violins submitted to me for opinion, I find that scarce one in fifty is actually that which it represents itself to be. In fact the only safe rule," he added as a professional commentary, "is never to buy a violin unless you obtain it from a dealer with a reputation to lose, and are prepared to pay a reasonable price for it."

My brother had meanwhile unpacked the violin and laid it on the table. As he took from it the last leaf of silver paper he saw Mr. Smart's smile of condescension fade, and assuming a look of interest and excitement, he stepped forward, took the violin in his hands, and scrutinised it minutely. He turned it over in silence for some moments, looking narrowly at each feature, and even applying the test of a magnifying-glass. At last he said with an altered tone, "Sir John, I have had in my hands nearly all the finest productions of Stradivarius, and thought myself acquainted with every instrument of note that ever left his workshop; but I confess myself mistaken, and apologise to you for the doubt which I expressed as to the instrument you had brought me. This violin is of the great master's golden period, is incontestably genuine, and finer in some respects than any Stradivarius that I have ever seen, not even excepting the famous *Dolphin* itself. You need be under no apprehension as to its authenticity: no connoisseur could hold it in his hand for a second and entertain a doubt on the point."

My brother was greatly pleased at so favourable a verdict, and Mr. Smart continued—

"The varnish is of that rich red which Stradivarius used in his best period after he had abandoned the yellow tint copied by him at first from his master Amati. I have never seen a varnish thicker or more lustrous, and it shows on the back that peculiar shading to imitate wear which we term 'breaking up.' The purfling also is of an unsurpassable excellence. Its execution is so fine that I should recommend you to use a magnifying-glass for its examination."

So he ran on, finding from moment to moment some new beauties to admire.

My brother was at first anxious lest Mr. Smart should ask him whence so extraordinary an instrument came, but he saw that the expert had already jumped to a conclusion in the matter. He knew that John had recently come of age, and evidently supposed that he had found the violin among the heirlooms of Worth Maltravers. John allowed Mr. Smart to continue in this misconception, merely saying that he had discovered the instrument in an old cupboard, where he had reason to think it had remained hidden for many years.

"Are there no records attached to so splended an instrument?" asked Mr. Smart. "I suppose it has been with your family a number of years. Do you not know how it came into their possession?"

I believe this was the first occasion on which it had occurred to John to consider what right he had to the possession of the instrument. He had been so excited by its discovery that the question of ownership had never hitherto crossed his mind. The unwelcome suggestion that it was not his after all, that the College might rightfully prefer a claim to it, presented itself to him for a moment; but he set it instantly aside, quieting his conscience with the reflection that this at least was not the moment to make such a disclosure.

He fenced with Mr. Smart's inquiry as best he could, saying that he was ignorant of the history of the instrument, but not contradicting the assumption that it had been a long time in his family's possession.

"It is indeed singular," Mr. Smart continued, "that so magnificent an instrument should have lain buried so long; that even those best acquainted with such matters should be in perfect ignorance of its existence. I shall have to revise the list of famous instruments in the next edition of my 'History of the Violin,' and to write," he added smiling, "a special paragraph on the 'Worth Maltravers Stradivarius.'"

After much more, which I need not narrate, Mr. Smart suggested that the violin should be left with him that he might examine it more at leisure, and that my brother should return in a week's time, when he would have the instrument opened, an operation which would be in any case advisable.

"The interior," he added, "appears to be in a strictly original state, and this I shall be able to ascertain when opened. The label is perfect, but if I am not mistaken I can see something higher up on the back which appears like a second label. This excites my interest, as I know of no instance of an instrument bearing two labels."

To this proposal my brother readily assented, being anxious to enjoy alone the pleasure of so gratifying a discovery as that of the undoubted authenticity of the instrument.

As he thought over the matter more at leisure, he grew anxious as to what might be the import of the second label in the violin of which Mr. Smart had spoken. I blush to say that he feared lest it might bear some owner's name or other inscription proving that the instrument had not been so long in the Maltravers family as he had allowed Mr. Smart to suppose. So within so short a time it was possible that Sir John Maltravers of Worth should dread being detected, if not in an absolute falsehood, at least in having by his silence assented to one.

During the ensuing week John remained in an excited and anxious condition. He did little work, and neglected his friends, having his thoughts continually occupied with the strange discovery he had made. I know also that his sense of honour troubled him, and that he was not satisfied with the course he was pursuing. The evening of his return from London he went to Mr. Gaskell's rooms at New College, and spent an hour conversing with him on indifferent subjects. In the course of their talk he proposed to his friend as a moral problem the question of the course of action to be taken were one to find some article of value concealed in his room. Mr. Gaskell answered unhesitatingly that he should feel bound to disclose it to the authorities. He saw that my brother was ill at ease, and with a clearness of judgment which he always exhibited, guessed that he had actually made some discovery of this sort in the old cupboard in his rooms. He could not divine, of course, the exact nature of the object found, and thought it might probably relate to a hoard of gold; but insisted with much urgency on the obligation to at once disclose anything of this kind. My brother, however, misled, I fear, by that feeling of inalienable right which the treasure-hunter experiences over the treasure, paid no more attention to the advice of his friend than to the promptings of his own conscience, and went his way.

From that day, my dear Edward, he began to exhibit a spirit of secretiveness and reserve entirely alien to his own open and honourable disposition, and also saw less of Mr. Gaskell. His friend tried, indeed, to win his confidence and affection in every way in his power; but in spite of this the rift between them widened insensibly, and my brother lost the fellowship and counsel of a true friend at a time when he could ill afford to be without them.

He returned to London the ensuing week, and met Mr. George Smart by appointment in Bond Street. If the expert had been enthusiastic on a former occasion, he was ten times more so on this. He spoke in terms almost of rapture about the violin. He had compared it with two magnificent instruments in the collection of the late Mr. James Loding, then the finest in Europe; and it was admittedly superior to either, both in the delicate markings of its wood and singularly fine varnish. "Of its tone," he said, "we cannot, of course, yet pronounce with certainty, but I am very sure that its voice will not belie its splendid exterior. It has been carefully opened, and is in a strangely perfect condition. Several persons eminently qualified to judge unite with me in considering that it has been exceedingly little played upon, and admit that never has so intact an interior been seen. The scroll is exceptionally bold and original. Although undoubtedly from the hand of the great master, this is of a pattern entirely different and distinct from any that have ever come under my observation."

He then pointed out to my brother that the side lines of the scroll were unusually deeply cut, and that the front of it projected far more than is common with such instruments.

"The most remarkable feature," he concluded, "is that the instrument bears a double label. Besides the label which you have already seen bearing *'Antonius Stradiuarius Cremonensis faciebat,'* with the date of his most splendid period, 1704, so clearly that the ink seems scarcely dry, there is another smaller one higher up on the back which I will show you."

He took the violin apart and showed him a small label with characters written in faded ink. "That is the writing of Antonio Stradivarius himself, and is easily recognisable, though it is much firmer than a specimen which I once saw, written in extreme old age, and giving his name and the date 1736. He was then ninety-two, and died in the following year. But this, as you will see, does not give his name, but merely the two words *'Porphyrius philosophus.'* What this may refer to I cannot say: it is beyond my experience. My friend Mr. Calvert has suggested that Stradivarius may have dedicated this violin to the pagan philosopher, or named it after him; but this seems improbable. I have, indeed, heard of two famous violins being called 'Peter' and 'Paul,' but the instances of such naming are very rare; and I believe it to be altogether without precedent to find a name attached thus on a label.

"In any case, I must leave this matter to your ingenuity to decipher. Neither the sound-post nor the bass-bar have ever been moved, and you see here a Stradivarius violin wearing exactly the same appearance as it once wore in the great master's workshop, and in exactly the same condition; yet I think the belly is sufficiently strong to stand modern stringing. I should advise you to leave the instrument with me for some little while, that I may give it due care and attention and ensure its being properly strung."

My brother thanked him and left the violin with him, saying that he would instruct him later by letter to what address he wished it sent.

# CHAPTER VIII

Within a few days after this the autumn term came to an end, and in the second week of December John returned to Worth Maltravers for the Christmas vacation. His advent was always a very great pleasure to me, and on this occasion I had looked forward to his company with anticipation keener than usual, as I had been disappointed of the visit of a friend and had spent the last month alone. After the joy of our first meeting had somewhat sobered, it was not long before I remarked a change in his manner, which puzzled me. It was not that he was less kind to me, for I think he was even more tenderly forbearing and gentle than I had ever known him, but I had an uneasy feeling that some shadow had crept in between us. It was the small cloud rising in the distance that afterwards darkened his horizon and mine. I missed the old candour and open-hearted frankness that he had always shown; and there seemed to be always something in the background which he was trying to keep from me. It was obvious that his thoughts were constantly elsewhere, so much so that on more than one occasion he returned vague and incoherent answers to my questions. At times I was content to believe that he was in love, and that his thoughts were with Miss Constance Temple; but even so, I could not persuade myself that his altered manner was to be thus entirely accounted for. At other times a dazed air, entirely foreign to his bright disposition, which I observed particularly in the morning, raised in my mind the terrible suspicion that he was in the habit of taking some secret narcotic or other deleterious drug.

We had never spent a Christmas away from Worth Maltravers, and it had always been a season of quiet joy for both of us. But under these altered circumstances it was a great relief and cause of thankfulness for me to receive a letter from Mrs. Temple inviting us both to spend Christmas and New Year at Royston. This invitation had upon my brother precisely the effect that I had hoped for. It roused him from his moody condition, and he professed much pleasure in accepting it, especially as he had never hitherto been in Derbyshire.

There was a small but very agreeable party at Royston, and we passed a most enjoyable fortnight. My brother seemed thoroughly to have shaken off his indisposition; and I saw my fondest hopes realised in the warm attachment which was evidently springing up between him and Miss Constance Temple.

Our visit drew near its close, and it was within a week of John's return to Oxford. Mrs. Temple celebrated the termination of the Christmas festivities by giving a ball on Twelfth-night, at which a large party were present, including most of the county families. Royston was admirably adapted for such entertainments, from the number and great size of its reception rooms. Though Elizabethan in date and external appearance, succeeding generations had much modified and enlarged the house; and an ancestor in the middle of the last century had built at the back an enormous hall after the classic model, and covered it with a dome or cupola. In this room the dancing went forward. Supper was served in the older hall in the front, and it was while this was in progress that a thunderstorm began. The rarity of such a phenomenon in the depth of winter formed the subject of general remark; but though the lightning was extremely brilliant, being seen distinctly through the curtained windows, the storm appeared to be at some distance, and, except for one peal, the thunder was not loud. After supper dancing was resumed, and I was taking part in a polka (called, I remember, the "*King Pippin*"), when my partner pointed out that one of the footmen wished to speak with me. I begged him to lead me to one side, and the servant then informed me that my brother was ill. Sir John, he said, had been seized with a fainting fit, but had been got to bed, and was being attended by Dr. Empson, a physician who chanced to be present among the visitors.

I at once left the hall and hurried to my brother's room. On the way I met Mrs. Temple and Constance, the latter much agitated and in tears. Mrs. Temple assured me that Dr. Empson reported favourably of my brother's condition, attributing his faintness to over-exertion in the dancing-room. The medical man had got him to bed with the assistance of Sir John's valet, had given him a quieting draught, and ordered that he should not be disturbed for the present. It was better that I should not enter the room; she begged that I would kindly comfort and reassure Constance, who was much upset, while she herself returned to her guests.

I led Constance to my bedroom, where there was a bright fire burning, and calmed her as best I could. Her interest in my brother was evidently very real and unaffected, and while not admitting her partiality for him in words, she made no effort to conceal her sentiments from me. I kissed her tenderly, and bade her narrate the circumstances of John's attack.

It seemed that after supper they had gone upstairs into the music-room, and he had himself proposed that they should walk thence into the picture-gallery, where they would better be able to see the lightning, which was then particularly vivid. The picture-gallery at Royston is a very long, narrow, and rather low room, running the whole length of the south wing, and terminating in a large Tudor oriel or flat bay window looking east. In this oriel they had sat for some minutes watching the flashes, and the wintry landscape revealed for an instant and then plunged into outer blackness. The gallery itself was not illuminated, and the effect of the lightning was very fine.

There had been an unusually bright flash accompanied by that single reverberating peal of thunder which I had previously noticed. Constance had spoken to my brother, but he had not replied, and in a moment she saw that he had swooned. She summoned aid without delay, but it was some short time before consciousness had been restored to him.

She had concluded this narrative, and sat holding my hand in hers. We were speculating on the cause of my brother's illness, thinking it might be due to over-exertion, or to sitting in a chilly atmosphere as the picture-gallery was not warmed, when Mrs. Temple knocked at the door and said that John was now more composed and desired earnestly to see me.

On entering my brother's bedroom I found him sitting up in bed wearing a dressing-gown. Parnham, his valet, who was arranging the fire, left the room as I came in. A chair stood at the head of the bed and I sat down by him. He took my hand in his and without a word burst into tears. "Sophy," he said, "I am so unhappy, and I have sent for you to tell you of my trouble, because I know you will be forbearing to me. An hour ago all seemed so bright. I was sitting in the picture-gallery with Constance, whom I love dearly. We had been watching the lightning, till the thunder had grown gradually fainter and the storm seemed past. I was just about to ask her to become my wife when a brighter flash than all the rest burst on us, and I saw—I saw, Sophy, standing in the gallery as close to me as you are now—I saw—that man I told you about at Oxford; and then this faintness came on me."

"Whom do you mean?" I said, not understanding what he spoke of, and thinking for a moment he referred to some one else. "Did you see Mr. Gaskell?"

"No, it was not he; but that dead man whom I saw rising from my wicker chair the night you went away from Oxford."

You will perhaps smile at my weakness, my dear Edward, and indeed I had at that time no justification for it; but I assure you that I have not yet forgotten, and never shall forget, the impression of overwhelming horror which his words produced upon me. It seemed as though a fear which had hitherto stood vague and shadowy in the background, began now to advance towards me, gathering more distinctness as it approached. There was to me something morbidly terrible about the apparition of this man at such a momentous crisis in my brother's life, and I at once recognised that unknown form as being the shadow which was gradually stealing between John and myself. Though I feigned incredulity as best I might, and employed those arguments or platitudes which will always be used on such occasions, urging that such a phantom could only exist in a mind disordered by physical weakness, my brother was not deceived by my words, and perceived in a moment that I did not even believe in them myself.

"Dearest Sophy," he said, with a much calmer air, "let us put aside all dissimulation. I *know* that what I have to-night seen, and that what I saw last summer at Oxford, are *not* phantoms of my brain; and I believe that you too in your inmost soul are convinced of this truth. Do not, therefore, endeavour to persuade me to the contrary. If I am not to believe the evidence of my senses, it were better at once to admit my madness—and I know that I am not mad. Let us rather consider what such an appearance can portend, and who the man is who is thus presented. I cannot explain to you why this appearance inspires me with so great a revulsion. I can only say that in its presence I seem to be brought face to face with some abysmal and repellent wickedness. It is not that the form he wears is hideous. Last night I saw him exactly as I saw him at Oxford—his face waxen pale, with a sneering mouth, the same lofty forehead, and hair brushed straight up so as almost to appear standing on end. He wore the same long coat of green cloth and white waistcoat. He seemed as if he had been standing listening to what we said, though we had not seen him till this bright flash of lightning made him manifest. You will remember that when I saw him at Oxford his eyes were always cast down, so that I never knew their colour. This time they were wide open; indeed he was looking full at us, and they were a light brown and very brilliant."

I saw that my brother was exciting himself, and was still weak from his recent swoon. I knew, too, that any ordinary person of strong mind would say at once that his brain wandered, and yet I had a dreadful conviction all the while that what he told me was the truth. All I could do was to beg him to calm himself, and to reflect how vain such fancies must be. "We must trust, dear John," I said, "in God. I am sure that so long as we are not living in conscious sin, we shall never be given over to any evil power; and I know my brother too well to think that he is doing anything he knows to be evil. If there be evil spirits, as we are taught there are, we are taught also that there are good spirits stronger than they who will protect us."

So I spoke with him a little while, until he grew calmer; and then we talked of Constance and of his love for her. He was deeply pleased to hear from me how she had shown such obvious signs of interest in his illness, and sincere affection for him. In any case, he made me promise that I would never mention to her either what he had seen this night or last summer at Oxford.

It had grown late, and the undulating beat of the dances, which had been distinctly sensible in his room—even though we could not hear any definite noise—had now ceased. Mrs. Temple knocked at the door as she went to bed and inquired how he did, giving him at the same time a kind message of sympathy from Constance, which afforded him much gratification. After she had left I prepared also to retire; but before going he begged me to take a prayer-book lying on the table, and to read aloud a collect which he pointed out. It was that for the second Sunday in Lent, and evidently well known to him. As I read it the words seemed to bear a new and deeper significance, and my heart repeated with fervour the petition for protection from those "evil thoughts which may assault and hurt the soul." I bade him good night and went away very sorrowful. Parnham, at John's request, had arranged to sleep on a sofa in his master's bedroom.

I rose betimes the next morning and inquired at my brother's room how he was. Parnham reported that he had passed a restless night, and on entering a little later I found him in a high fever, slightly delirious, and evidently not so well as when I saw him last. Mrs. Temple, with much kindness and forethought, had begged Dr. Empson to remain at Royston for the night, and he was soon in attendance on his patient. His verdict was sufficiently grave: John was suffering from a sharp access of brain-fever; his condition afforded cause for alarm; he could not answer for any turn his sickness might take. You will easily imagine how much this intelligence affected me; and Mrs. Temple and Constance shared my anxiety and solicitude. Constance and I talked much with one another that morning. Unaffected anxiety had largely removed her reserve, and she spoke openly of her feelings towards my brother, not concealing her partiality for him. I on my part let her understand how welcome to me would be any union between her and John, and how sincerely I should value her as a sister.

It was a wild winter's morning, with some snow falling and a high wind. The house was in the disordered condition which is generally observable on the day following a ball or other important festivity. I roamed restlessly about, and at last found my way to the picture-gallery, which had formed the scene of John's adventure on the previous night. I had never been in this part of the house before, as it contained no facilities for heating, and so often remained shut in the winter months. I found a listless pleasure in admiring the pictures which lined the walls, most of them being portraits of former members of the family, including the famous picture of Sir Ralph Temple and his family, attributed to Holbein. I had reached the end of the gallery and sat down in the oriel watching the snow-flakes falling sparsely, and the evergreens below me waving wildly in the sudden rushes of the wind. My thoughts were busy with the events of the previous evening,—with John's illness, with the ball,—and I found myself humming the air of a waltz that had caught my fancy. At last I turned away from the garden scene towards the gallery, and as I did so my eyes fell on a remarkable picture just opposite to me.

It was a full-length portrait of a young man, life-size, and I had barely time to appreciate even its main features when I knew that I had before me the painted counterfeit of my brother's vision. The discovery caused me a violent shock, and it was with an infinite repulsion that I recognized at once the features and dress of the man whom John had seen rising from the chair at Oxford. So accurately had my brother's imagination described him to me, that it seemed as if I had myself seen him often before. I noted each feature, comparing them with my brother's description, and finding them all familiar and corresponding exactly. He was a man still in the prime of life. His features were regular and beautifully modelled; yet there was something in his face that inspired me with a deep aversion, though his brown eyes were open and brilliant. His mouth was sharply cut, with a slight sneer on the lips, and his complexion of that extreme pallor which had impressed itself deeply on my brother's imagination and my own.

After the first intense surprise had somewhat subsided, I experienced a feeling of great relief, for here was an extraordinary explanation of my brother's vision of last night. It was certain that the flash of lightning had lit up this ill-starred picture, and that to his predisposed fancy the painted figure had stood forth as an actual embodiment. That such an incident, however startling, should have been able to fling John into a brain-fever, showed that he must already have been in a very low and reduced state, on which excitement would act much more powerfully than on a more robust condition of health. A similar state of weakness, perturbed by the excitement of his passion for Constance Temple, might surely also have conjured up the vision which he thought he saw the night of our leaving Oxford in the summer. These thoughts, my dear Edward, gave me great relief; for it seemed a comparatively trivial matter that my brother should be ill, even seriously ill, if only his physical indisposition could explain away the supernatural dread which had haunted us for the past six months. The clouds were breaking up. It was evident that John had been seriously unwell for some months; his physical weakness had acted on his brain; and I had lent colour to his wandering fancies by being alarmed by them, instead of rejecting them at once or gently laughing them away as I should have done. But these glad thoughts took me too far, and I was suddenly brought up by a reflection that did not admit of so simple an explanation. If the man's form my brother saw at Oxford were merely an effort of disordered imagination, how was it that he had been able to describe it exactly like that represented in this picture? He had never in his life been to Royston, therefore he could have no image of the picture impressed unconsciously on or hidden away in his mind. Yet his description had never varied. It had been so close as to enable me to produce in my fancy a vivid representation of the man he had seen; and here I had before me the features and dress exactly reproduced. In the presence of a coincidence so extraordinary reason stood confounded, and I knew not what to think. I walked nearer to the picture and scrutinised it closely.

The dress corresponded in every detail with that which my brother had described the figure as wearing at Oxford: a long cut-away coat of green cloth with an edge of gold embroidery, a white satin waistcoat with sprigs of embroidered roses, gold lace at the pocket-holes, buff silk knee-breeches, and low down on the finely modelled neck a full cravat of rich lace. The figure was posed negligently against a fluted stone pedestal or short column on which the left elbow leant, and the right foot was crossed lightly over the left. His shoes were of polished black with heavy silver buckles, and the whole costume was very old-fashioned, and such as I had only seen worn at fancy balls. On the foot of the pedestal was the painter's name, "BATTONI pinxit, Romae, 1750." On the top of the pedestal, and under his left elbow, was a long roll apparently of music, of which one end, unfolded, hung over the edge.

For some minutes I stood still gazing at this portrait which so much astonished me, but turned on hearing footsteps in the gallery, and saw Constance, who had come to seek for me.

"Constance," I said, "whose portrait is this? it is a very striking picture, is it not?"

"Yes, it is a splendid painting, though of a very bad man. His name was Adrian Temple, and he once owned Royston. I do not know much about him, but I believe he was very wicked and very clever. My mother would be able to tell you more. It is a picture we none of us like, although so finely painted; and perhaps because he was always pointed out to me from childhood as a bad man, I have myself an aversion to it. It is singular that when the very bright flash of lightning came last night while your brother John and I were sitting here, it lit this picture with a dazzling glare that made the figure stand out so strangely as to seem almost alive. It was just after that I found that John had fainted."

The memory was not a pleasant one for either of us and we changed the subject. "Come," I said, "let us leave the gallery, it is very cold here."

Though I said nothing more at the time, her words had made a great impression on me. It was so strange that, even with the little she knew of this Adrian Temple, she should speak at once of his notoriously evil life, and of her personal dislike to the picture. Remembering what my brother had said on the previous night, that in the presence of this man he felt himself brought face to face with some indescribable wickedness, I could not but be surprised at the coincidence. The whole story seemed to me now to resemble one of those puzzle pictures or maps which I have played with as a child, where each bit fits into some other until the outline is complete. It was as if I were finding the pieces one by one of a bygone history, and fitting them to one another until some terrible whole should be gradually built up and stand out in its complete deformity.

Dr. Empson spoke gravely of John's illness, and entertained without reluctance the proposal of Mrs. Temple, that Dr. Dobie, a celebrated physician in Derby, should be summoned to a consultation. Dr. Dobie came more than once, and was at last able to report an amendment in John's condition, though both the doctors absolutely forbade any one to visit him, and said that under the most favourable circumstances a period of some weeks must elapse before he could be moved.

Mrs. Temple invited me to remain at Royston until my brother should be sufficiently convalescent to be moved; and both she and Constance, while regretting the cause, were good enough to express themselves pleased that accident should detain me so long with them.

As the reports of the doctors became gradually more favourable, and our minds were in consequence more free to turn to other subjects, I spoke to Mrs. Temple one day about the picture, saying that it interested me, and asking for some particulars as to the life of Adrian Temple.

"My dear child," she said, "I had rather that you should not exhibit any curiosity as to this man, whom I wish that we had not to call an ancestor. I know little of him myself, and indeed his life was of such a nature as no woman, much less a young girl, would desire to be well acquainted with. He was, I believe, a man of remarkable talent, and spent most of his time between Oxford and Italy, though he visited Royston occasionally, and built the large hall here, which we use as a dancing-room.

Before he was twenty wild stories were prevalent as to his licentious life, and by thirty his name was a by-word among sober and upright people. He had constantly with him at Oxford and on his travels a boon companion called Jocelyn, who aided him in his wickednesses, until on one of their Italian tours Jocelyn left him suddenly and became a Trappist monk. It was currently reported that some wild deed of Adrian Temple had shocked even him, and so outraged his surviving instincts of common humanity that he was snatched as a brand from the burning and enabled to turn back even in the full tide of his wickedness. However that may be, Adrian went on in his evil course without him, and about four years after disappeared. He was last heard of in Naples, and it is believed that he succumbed during a violent outbreak of the plague which took place in Italy in the autumn of 1752. That is all I shall tell you of him, and indeed I know little more myself. The only good trait that has been handed down concerning him is that he was a masterly musician, performing admirably upon the violin, which he had studied under the illustrious Tartini himself. Yet even his art of music, if tradition speaks the truth, was put by him to the basest of uses."

I apologised for my indiscretion in asking her about an unpleasant subject, and at the same time thanked her for what she had seen fit to tell me, professing myself much interested, as, indeed, I really was.

"Was he a handsome man?"

"That is a girl's question," she answered, smiling. "He is said to have been very handsome; and indeed his picture, painted after his first youth was past, would still lead one to suppose so. But his complexion was spoiled, it is said, and turned to deadly white by certain experiments, which it is neither possible nor seemly for us to understand. His face is of that long oval shape of which all the Temples are proud, and he had brown eyes: we sometimes tease Constance, saying she is like Adrian."

It was indeed true, as I remembered after Mrs. Temple had pointed it out, that Constance had a peculiarly long and oval face. It gave her, I think, an air of staid and placid beauty, which formed in my eyes, and perhaps in John's also, one of her greatest attractions.

"I do not like even his picture," Mrs. Temple continued, "and strange tales have been narrated of it by idle servants which are not worth repeating. I have sometimes thought of destroying it; but my late husband, being a Temple, would never hear of this, or even of removing it from its present place in the gallery; and I should be loath to do anything now contrary to his wishes, once so strongly expressed. It is, besides, very perfect from an artistic point of view, being painted by Battoni, and in his happiest manner."

I could never glean more from Mrs. Temple; but what she had told me interested me deeply. It seemed another link in the chain, though I could scarcely tell why, that Adrian Temple should be so great a musician and violinist. I had, I fancy, a dim idea of that malign and outlawed spirit sitting alone in darkness for a hundred years, until he was called back by the sweet tones of the Italian music, and the lilt of the "Areopagita" that he had loved so long ago.

# CHAPTER IX

John's recovery, though continuous and satisfactory, was but slow; and it was not until Easter, which fell early, that his health was pronounced to be entirely re-established. The last few weeks of his convalescence had proved to all of us a time of thankful and tranquil enjoyment. If I may judge from my own experience, there are few epochs in our life more favourable to the growth of sentiments of affection and piety, or more full of pleasurable content, than is the period of gradual recovery from serious illness. The chastening effect of our recent sickness has not yet passed away, and we are at once grateful to our Creator for preserving us, and to our friends for the countless acts of watchful kindness which it is the peculiar property of illness to evoke.

No mother ever nursed a son more tenderly than did Mrs. Temple nurse my brother, and before his restoration to health was complete the attachment between him and Constance had ripened into a formal betrothal. Such an alliance was, as I have before explained, particularly suitable, and its prospect afforded the most lively pleasure to all those concerned. The month of March had been unusually mild, and Royston being situated in a valley, as is the case with most houses of that date, was well sheltered from cold winds. It had, moreover, a south aspect, and as my brother gradually gathered strength, Constance and he and I would often sit out of doors in the soft spring mornings. We put an easy-chair with many cushions for him on the gravel by the front door, where the warmth of the sun was reflected from the red brick walls, and he would at times read aloud to us while we were engaged with our crochet-work. Mr. Tennyson had just published anonymously a first volume of poems, and the sober dignity of his verse well suited our frame of mind at that time. The memory of those pleasant spring mornings, my dear Edward, has not yet passed away, and I can still smell the sweet moist scent of the violets, and see the bright colours of the crocus-flowers in the parterres in front of us.

John's mind seemed to be gathering strength with his body. He had apparently flung off the cloud which had overshadowed him before his illness, and avoided entirely any reference to those unpleasant events which had been previously so constantly in his thoughts. I had, indeed, taken an early opportunity of telling him of my discovery of the picture of Adrian Temple, as I thought it would tend to show him that at least the last appearance of this ghostly form admitted of a rational explanation. He seemed glad to hear of this, but did not exhibit the same interest in the matter that I had expected, and allowed it at once to drop. Whether through lack of interest, or from a lingering dislike to revisit the spot where he was seized with illness, he did not, I believe, once enter the picture-gallery before he left Royston.

I cannot say as much for myself. The picture of Adrian Temple exerted a curious fascination over me, and I constantly took an opportunity of studying it. It was, indeed, a beautiful work; and perhaps because John's recovery gave a more cheerful tone to my thoughts, or perhaps from the power of custom to dull even the keenest antipathies, I gradually got to lose much of the feeling of aversion which it had at first inspired. In time the unpleasant look grew less unpleasing, and I noticed more the beautiful oval of the face, the brown eyes, and the fine chiselling of the features. Sometimes, too, I felt a deep pity for so clever a gentleman who had died young, and whose life, were it ever so wicked, must often have been also lonely and bitter. More than once I had been discovered by Mrs. Temple or Constance sitting looking at the picture, and they had gently laughed at me, saying that I had fallen in love with Adrian Temple.

One morning in early April, when the sun was streaming brightly through the oriel, and the picture received a fuller light than usual, it occurred to me to examine closely the scroll of music painted as hanging over the top of the pedestal on which the figure leant. I had hitherto thought that the signs depicted on it were merely such as painters might conventionally use to represent a piece of musical notation. This has generally been the case, I think, in such pictures as I have ever seen in which a piece of music has been introduced. I mean that while the painting gives a general representation of the musical staves, no attempt is ever made to paint any definite notes such as would enable an actual piece to be identified. Though, as I write this, I do remember that on the monument to Handel in Westminster Abbey there is represented a musical scroll similar to that in Adrian Temple's picture, but actually sculptured with the opening phrase of the majestic melody, "I know that my Redeemer liveth."

On this morning, then, at Royston I thought I perceived that there were painted on the scroll actual musical staves, bars, and notes; and my interest being excited, I stood upon a chair so as better to examine them. Though time had somewhat obscured this portion of the picture as with a veil or film, yet I made out that the painter had intended to depict some definite piece of music. In another moment I saw that the air represented consisted of the opening bars of the *Gagliarda* in the suite by Graziani with which my brother and I were so well acquainted. Though I believe that I had not seen the volume of music in which that piece was contained more than twice, yet the melody was very familiar to me, and I had no difficulty whatever in making myself sure that I had here before me the air of the *Gagliarda* and none other. It was true that it was only roughly painted, but to one who knew the tune there was no room left for doubt.

Here was a new cause, I will not say for surprise, but for reflection. It might, of course, have been merely a coincidence that the artist should have chosen to paint in this picture this particular piece of music; but it seemed more probable that it had actually been a favourite air of Adrian Temple, and that he had chosen deliberately to have it represented with him. This discovery I kept entirely to myself, not thinking it wise to communicate it to my brother, lest by doing so I might reawaken his interest in a subject which I hoped he had finally dismissed from his thoughts.

In the second week of April the happy party at Royston was dispersed, John returning to Oxford for the summer term, Mrs. Temple making a short visit to Scotland, and Constance coming to Worth Maltravers to keep me company for a time.

It was John's last term at Oxford. He expected to take his degree in June, and his marriage with Constance Temple had been provisionally arranged for the September following. He returned to Magdalen Hall in the best of spirits, and found his rooms looking cheerful with well-filled flower-boxes in the windows. I shall not detain you with any long narration of the events of the term, as they have no relation to the present history. I will only say that I believe my brother applied himself diligently to his studies, and took his amusement mostly on horseback, riding two horses which he had had sent to him from Worth Maltravers.

About the second week after his return he received a letter from Mr. George Smart to the effect that the Stradivarius violin was now in complete order. Subsequent examination, Mr. Smart wrote, and the unanimous verdict of connoisseurs whom he had consulted, had merely confirmed the views he had at first expressed—namely, that the violin was of the finest quality, and that my brother had in his possession a unique and intact example of Stradivarius's best period. He had had it properly strung; and as the bass-bar had never been moved, and was of a stronger nature than that usual at the period of its manufacture, he had considered it unnecessary to replace it. If any signs should become visible of its being inadequate to support the tension of modern stringing, another could be easily substituted for it at a later date. He had allowed a young German *virtuoso* to play on it, and though this gentleman was one of the first living performers, and had had an opportunity of handling many splendid instruments, he assured Mr. Smart that he had never performed on one that could in any way compare with this. My brother wrote in reply thanking him, and begging that the violin might be sent to Magdalen Hall.

The pleasant musical evenings, however, which John had formerly been used to spend in the company of Mr. Gaskell were now entirely praetermitted. For though there was no cause for any diminution of friendship between them, and though on Mr. Gaskell's part there was an ardent desire to maintain their former intimacy, yet the two young men saw less and less of one another, until their intercourse was confined to an accidental greeting in the street. I believe that during all this time my brother played very frequently on the Stradivarius violin, but always alone. Its very possession seemed to have engendered from the first in his mind a secretive tendency which, as I have already observed, was entirely alien to his real disposition. As he had concealed its discovery from his sister, so he had also from his friend, and Mr. Gaskell remained in complete ignorance of the existence of such an instrument.

On the evening of its arrival from London, John seems to have carefully unpacked the violin and tried it with a new bow of Tourte's make which he had purchased of Mr. Smart. He had shut the heavy outside door of his room before beginning to play, so that no one might enter unawares; and he told me afterwards that though he had naturally expected from the instrument a very fine tone, yet its actual merits so far exceeded his anticipations as entirely to overwhelm him. The sound issued from it in a volume of such depth and purity as to give an impression of the passages being chorded, or even of another violin being played at the same time. He had had, of course, no opportunity of practising during his illness, and so expected to find his skill with the bow somewhat diminished; but he perceived, on the contrary, that his performance was greatly improved, and that he was playing with a mastery and feeling of which he had never before been conscious. While attributing this improvement very largely to the beauty of the instrument on which he was performing, yet he could not but believe that by his illness, or in some other unexplained way, he had actually acquired a greater freedom of wrist and fluency of expression, with which reflection he was not a little elated. He had had a lock fixed on the cupboard in which he had originally found the violin, and here he carefully deposited it on each occasion after playing, before he opened the outer door of his room.

So the summer term passed away. The examinations had come in their due time, and were now over. Both the young men had submitted themselves to the ordeal, and while neither would of course have admitted as much to any one else, both felt secretly that they had no reason to be dissatisfied with their performance. The results would not be published for some weeks to come. The last night of the term had arrived, the last night too of John's Oxford career. It was near nine o'clock, but still quite light, and the rich orange glow of sunset had not yet left the sky. The air was warm and sultry, as on that eventful evening when just a year ago he had for the first time seen the figure or the illusion of the figure of Adrian Temple. Since that time he had played the "Areopagita" many, many times; but there had never been any reappearance of that form, nor even had the once familiar creaking of the wicker chair ever made itself heard. As he sat alone in his room, thinking with a natural melancholy that he had seen the sun set for the last time on his student life, and reflecting on the possibilities of the future and perhaps on opportunities wasted in the past, the memory of that evening last June recurred strongly to his imagination, and he felt an irresistible impulse to play once more the "Areopagita." He unlocked the now familiar cupboard and took out the violin, and never had the exquisite gradations of colour in its varnish appeared to greater advantage than in the soft mellow light of the fading day. As he began the *Gagliarda* he looked at the wicker chair, half expecting to see a form he well knew seated in it; but nothing of the kind ensued, and he concluded the "Areopagita" without the occurrence of any unusual phenomenon.

It was just at its close that he heard some one knocking at the outer door. He hurriedly locked away the violin and opened the "oak." It was Mr. Gaskell. He came in rather awkwardly, as though not sure whether he would be welcomed.

"Johnnie," he began, and stopped.

The force of ancient habit sometimes, dear nephew, leads us unwittingly to accost those who were once our friends by a familiar or nickname long after the intimacy that formerly justified it has vanished. But sometimes we intentionally revert to the use of such a name, not wishing to proclaim openly, as it were, by a more formal address that we are no longer the friends we once were. I think this latter was the case with Mr. Gaskell as he repeated the familiar name.

"Johnnie, I was passing down New College Lane, and heard the violin from your open windows. You were playing the 'Areopagita,' and it all sounded so familiar to me that I thought I must come up. I am not interrupting you, am I?"

"No, not at all," John answered.

"It is the last night of our undergraduate life, the last night we shall meet in Oxford as students. To-morrow we make our bow to youth and become men. We have not seen much of each other this term at any rate, and I daresay that is my fault. But at least let us part as friends. Surely our friends are not so many that we can afford to fling them lightly away."

He held out his hand frankly, and his voice trembled a little as he spoke—partly perhaps from real emotion, but more probably from the feeling of reluctance which I have noticed men always exhibit to discovering any sentiment deeper than those usually deemed conventional in correct society. My brother was moved by his obvious wish to renew their former friendship, and grasped the proffered hand.

There was a minute's pause, and then the conversation was resumed, a little stiffly at first, but more freely afterwards. They spoke on many indifferent subjects, and Mr. Gaskell congratulated John on the prospect of his marriage, of which he had heard. As he at length rose up to take his departure, he said, "You must have practised the violin diligently of late, for I never knew any one make so rapid progress with it as you have done. As I came along I was quite spellbound by your music. I never before heard you bring from the instrument so exquisite a tone: the chorded passages were so powerful that I believed there had been another person playing with you. Your Pressenda is certainly a finer instrument than I ever imagined."

My brother was pleased with Mr. Gaskell's compliment, and the latter continued, "Let me enjoy the pleasure of playing with you once more in Oxford; let us play the 'Areopagita.' "

And so saying he opened the pianoforte and sat down.

John was turning to take out the Stradivarius when he remembered that he had never even revealed its existence to Mr. Gaskell, and that if he now produced it an explanation must follow. In a moment his mood changed, and with less geniality he excused himself, somewhat awkwardly, from complying with the request, saying that he was fatigued.

Mr. Gaskell was evidently hurt at his friend's altered manner, and without renewing his petition rose at once from the pianoforte, and after a little forced conversation took his departure. On leaving he shook my brother by the hand, wished him all prosperity in his marriage and after-life, and said, "Do not entirely forget your old comrade, and remember that if at any time you should stand in need of a true friend, you know where to find him!"

John heard his footsteps echoing down the passage and made a half involuntary motion towards the door as if to call him back, but did not do so, though he thought over his last words then and on a subsequent occasion.

## CHAPTER X

The summer was spent by us in the company of Mrs. Temple and Constance, partly at Royston and partly at Worth Maltravers. John had again hired the cutter-yacht *Palestine*, and the whole party made several expeditions in her. Constance was entirely devoted to her lover; her life seemed wrapped up in his; she appeared to have no existence except in his presence.

I can scarcely enumerate the reasons which prompted such thoughts, but during these months I sometimes found myself wondering if John still returned her affection as ardently as I knew had once been the case. I can certainly call to mind no single circumstance which could justify me in such a suspicion. He performed punctiliously all those thousand little acts of devotion which are expected of an accepted lover; he seemed to take pleasure in perfecting any scheme of enjoyment to amuse her; and yet the impression grew in my mind that he no longer felt the same heart-whole love to her that she bore him, and that he had himself shown six months earlier. I cannot say, my dear Edward, how lively was the grief that even the suspicion of such a fact caused me, and I continually rebuked myself for entertaining for a moment a thought so unworthy, and dismissed it from my mind with reprobation. Alas! ere long it was sure again to make itself felt. We had all seen the Stradivarius violin; indeed it was impossible for my brother longer to conceal it from us, as he now played continually on it. He did not recount to us the story of its discovery, contenting himself with saying that he had become possessed of it at Oxford. We imagined naturally that he had purchased it; and for this I was sorry, as I feared Mr. Thoresby, his guardian, who had given him some years previously an excellent violin by Pressenda, might feel hurt at seeing his present so unceremoniously laid aside. None of us were at all intimately acquainted with the fancies of fiddle-collectors, and were consequently quite ignorant of the enormous value that fashion attached to so splendid an instrument. Even had we known, I do not think that we should have been surprised at John purchasing it; for he had recently come of age, and was in possession of so large a fortune as would amply justify him in such an indulgence had he wished to gratify it. No one, however, could remain unaware of the wonderful musical qualities of the instrument. Its rich and melodious tones would commend themselves even to the most unmusical ear, and formed a subject of constant remark. I noticed also that my brother's knowledge of the violin had improved in a very perceptible manner, for it was impossible to attribute the great beauty and power of his present performance entirely to the excellence of the instrument he was using. He appeared more than ever devoted to the art, and would shut himself up in his room alone for two or more hours together for the purpose of playing the violin—a habit which was a source of sorrow to Constance, for he would never allow her to sit with him on such occasions, as she naturally wished to do.

So the summer fled. I should have mentioned that in July, after going up to complete the *viva-voce* part of their examination, both Mr. Gaskell and John received information that they had obtained "first-classes." The young men had, it appears, done excellently well, and both had secured a place in that envied division of the first-class which was called "above the line." John's success proved a source of much pleasure to us all, and mutual congratulations were freely exchanged. We were pleased also at Mr. Gaskell's high place, remembering the kindness which he had shown us at Oxford in the previous year. I desired John to send him my compliments and felicitations when he should next be writing to him. I did not doubt that my brother would return Mr. Gaskell's congratulations, which he had already received: he said, however, that his friend had given no address to which he could write, and so the matter dropped.

On the 1st of September John and Constance Temple were married. The wedding took place at Royston, and by John's special desire (with which Constance fully agreed) the ceremony was of a strictly private and unpretentious nature. The newly married pair had determined to spend their honeymoon in Italy, and left for the Continent in the forenoon.

Mrs. Temple invited me to remain with her for the present at Royston, which I was very glad to do, feeling deeply the loss of a favourite brother, and looking forward with dismay to six weeks of loneliness which must elapse before I should again see him and my dearest Constance.

We received news of our travellers about a fortnight afterwards, and then heard from them at frequent intervals. Constance wrote in the best of spirits, and with the keenest appreciation. She had never travelled in Switzerland or Italy before, and all was enchantingly novel to her. They had journeyed through Basle to Lucerne, spending a few days in that delightful spot, and thence proceeding by the Simplon Pass to Lugano and the Italian lakes. Then we heard that they had gone further south than had at first been contemplated; they had reached Rome, and were intending to go on to Naples.

After the first few weeks we neither of us received any more letters from John. It was always Constance who wrote, and even her letters grew very much less frequent than had at first been the case. This was perhaps natural, as the business of travel no doubt engrossed their thoughts. But ere long we both perceived that the letters of our dear girl were more constrained and formal than before. It was as if she was writing now rather to comply with a sense of duty than to give vent to the light-hearted gaiety and naïve enjoyment which breathed in every line of her earlier communications. So at least it seemed to us, and again the old suspicion presented itself to my mind, and I feared that all was not as it should be.

Naples was to be the turning-point of their travels, and we expected them to return to England by the end of October. November had arrived, however, and we still had no intimation that their return journey had commenced or was even decided on. From John there was no word, and Constance wrote less often than ever. John, she said, was enraptured with Naples and its surroundings; he devoted himself much to the violin, and though she did not say so, this meant, I knew, that she was often left alone. For her own part, she did not think that a continued residence in Italy would suit her health; the sudden changes of temperature tried her, and people said that the airs rising in the evening from the bay were unwholesome.

Then we received a letter from her which much alarmed us. It was written from Naples and dated October 25. John, she said, had been ailing of late with nervousness and insomnia. On Wednesday, two days before the date of her letter, he had suffered all day from a strange restlessness, which increased after they had retired for the evening. He could not sleep and had dressed again, telling her he would walk a little in the night air to compose himself. He had not returned till near six in the morning, and then was so deadly pale and seemed so exhausted that she insisted on his keeping to his bed till she could get medical advice. The doctors feared that he had been attacked by some strange form of malarial fever, and said he needed much care. Our anxiety was, however, at least temporarily relieved by the receipt of later tidings which spoke of John's recovery; but November drew to a close without any definite mention of their return having reached us.

That month is always, I think, a dreary one in the country. It has neither the brilliant tints of October, nor the cosy jollity of mid-winter with its Christmas joys to alleviate it. This year it was more gloomy than usual. Incessant rain had marked its close, and the Roy, a little brook which skirted the gardens not far from the house, had swollen to unusual proportions. At last one wild night the flood rose so high as to completely cover the garden terraces, working havoc in the parterres, and covering the lawns with a thick coat of mud. Perhaps this gloominess of nature's outer face impressed itself in a sense of apprehension on our spirits, and it was with a feeling of more than ordinary pleasure and relief that early in December we received a letter dated from Laon, saying that our travellers were already well advanced on their return journey, and expected to be in England a week after the receipt by us of this advice. It was, as usual, Constance who wrote. John begged, she said, that Christmas might be spent at Worth Maltravers, and that we would at once proceed thither to see that all was in order against their return. They reached Worth about the middle of the month, and were, I need not say, received with the utmost affection by Mrs. Temple and myself.

In reply to our inquiries John professed that his health was completely restored; but though we could indeed discern no other signs of any special weakness, we were much shocked by his changed appearance. He had completely lost his old healthy and sun-burnt complexion, and his face, though not thin or sunken, was strangely pale. Constance assured us that though in other respects he had apparently recovered, he had never regained his old colour from the night of his attack of fever at Naples.

I soon perceived that her own spirits were not so bright as was ordinarily the case with her; and she exhibited none of the eagerness to narrate to others the incidents of travel which is generally observable in those who have recently returned from a journey. The cause of this depression was, alas! not difficult to discover, for John's former abstraction and moodiness seemed to have returned with an increased force. It was a source of infinite pain to Mrs. Temple, and perhaps even more so to me, to observe this sad state of things. Constance never complained, and her affection towards her husband seemed only to increase in the face of difficulties. Yet the matter was one which could not be hid from the anxious eyes of loving kinswomen, and I believe that it was the consciousness that these altered circumstances could not but force themselves upon our notice that added poignancy to my poor sister's grief. While not markedly neglecting her, my brother had evidently ceased to take that pleasure in her company which might reasonably have been expected in any case under the circumstances of a recent marriage, and a thousand times more so when his wife was so loving and beautiful a creature as Constance Temple. He appeared little except at meals, and not even always at lunch, shutting himself up for the most part in his morning-room or study and playing continually on the violin. It was in vain that we attempted even by means of his music to win him back to a sweeter mood. Again and again I begged him to allow me to accompany him on the pianoforte, but he would never do so, always putting me off with some excuse. Even when he sat with us in the evening, he spoke little, devoting himself for the most part to reading. His books were almost always Greek or Latin, so that I am ignorant of the subjects of his study; but he was content that either Constance or I should play on the pianoforte, saying that the melody, so far from distracting his attention, helped him rather to appreciate what he was reading. Constance always begged me to allow her to take her place at the instrument on these occasions, and would play to him sometimes for hours without receiving a word of thanks, being eager even in this unreciprocated manner to testify her love and devotion to him.

Christmas Day, usually so happy a season, brought no alleviation of our gloom. My brother's reserve continually increased, and even his longest-established habits appeared changed. He had been always most observant of his religious duties, attending divine service with the utmost regularity whatever the weather might be, and saying that it was a duty a landed proprietor owed as much to his tenantry as himself to set a good example in such matters. Ever since our earliest years he and I had gone morning and afternoon on Sundays to the little church of Worth, and there sat together in the Maltravers chapel where so many of our name had sat before us. Here their monuments and achievements stood about us on every side, and it had always seemed to me that with their name and property we had inherited also the obligation to continue those acts of piety, in the practice of which so many of them had lived and died. It was, therefore, a source of surprise and great grief to me when on the Sunday after his return my brother omitted all religious observances, and did not once attend the parish church. He was not present with us at breakfast, ordering coffee and a roll to be taken to his private sitting-room. At the hour at which we usually set out for church I went to his room to tell him that we were all dressed and waiting for him. I tapped at the door, but on trying to enter found it locked. In reply to my message he did not open the door, but merely begged us to go on to church, saying he would possibly follow us later. We went alone, and I sat anxiously in our seat with my eyes fixed on the door, hoping against hope that each late comer might be John, but he never came. Perhaps this will appear to you, Edward, a comparatively trivial circumstance (though I hope it may not), but I assure you that it brought tears to my eyes. When I sat in the Maltravers chapel and thought that for the first time my dear brother had preferred in an open way his convenience or his whim to his duty, and had of set purpose neglected to come to the house of God, I felt a bitter grief that seemed to rise up in my throat and choke me. I could not think of the meaning of the prayers nor join in the singing; and all the time that Mr. Butler, our clergyman, was preaching, a verse of a little piece of poetry which I learned as a girl was running in my head:

> How easy are the paths of ill;
>     How steep and hard the upward ways;
> A child can roll the stone down hill
>     That breaks a giant's arm to raise.

It seemed to me that our loved one had set his foot upon the downward slope, and that not all the efforts of those who would have given their lives to save him could now hold him back.

It was even worse on Christmas Day. Ever since we had been confirmed John and I had always taken the Sacrament on that happy morning, and after service he had distributed the Maltravers dole in our chapel. There are given, as you know, on that day to each of twelve old men £5 and a green coat, and a like sum of money with a blue cloth dress to as many old women. These articles of dress are placed on the altar-tomb of Sir Esmoun de Maltravers, and have been thence distributed from days immemorial by the head of our house. Ever since he was twelve years old it had been my pride to watch my handsome brother doing this deed of noble charity, and to hear the kindly words he added with each gift.

Alas! alas! it was all different this Christmas. Even on this holy day my brother did not approach either the altar or the house of God. Till then Christmas had always seemed to me to be a day given us from above, that we might see even while on earth a faint glimpse of that serenity and peaceful love which will hereafter gild all days in heaven. Then covetous men lay aside their greed and enemies their rancour, then warm hearts grow warmer, and Christians feel their common brotherhood. I can scarcely imagine any man so lost or guilty as not to experience on that day some desire to turn back to the good once more, as not to recognise some far-off possibility of better things. It was thoughts free and happy such as these that had previously come into my heart in the service of Christmas Day, and been particularly associated with the familiar words that we all love so much. But that morning the harmonies were all jangled: it seemed as though some evil spirit was pouring wicked thoughts into my ear; and even while children sang "Hark the herald angels," I thought I could hear through it all a melody which I had learnt to loathe, the *Gagliarda* of the "Areopagita."

Poor Constance! Though her veil was down, I could see her tears, and knew her thoughts must be sadder even than mine: I drew her hand towards me, and held it as I would a child's. After the service was over a new trial awaited us. John had made no arrangement for the distribution of the dole. The coats and dresses were all piled ready on Sir Esmoun's tomb, and there lay the little leather pouches of money, but there was no one to give them away. Mr. Butler looked puzzled, and approaching us, said he feared Sir John was ill—had he made no provision for the distribution? Pride kept back the tears which were rising fast, and I said my brother was indeed unwell, that it would be better for Mr. Butler to give away the dole, and that Sir John would himself visit the recipients during the week. Then we hurried away, not daring to watch the distribution of the dole, lest we should no longer be able to master our feelings, and should openly betray our agitation.

From one another we no longer attempted to conceal our grief. It seemed as though we had all at once resolved to abandon the farce of pretending not to notice John's estrangement from his wife, or of explaining away his neglectful and unaccountable treatment of her.

I do not think that three poor women were ever so sad on Christmas Day before as were we on our return from church that morning. None of us had seen my brother, but about five in the afternoon Constance went to his room, and through the locked door begged piteously to see him. After a few minutes he complied with her request and opened the door. The exact circumstances of that interview she never revealed to me, but I knew from her manner when she returned that something she had seen or heard had both grieved and frightened her. She told me only that she had flung herself in an agony of tears at his feet, and kneeling there, weary and broken-hearted, had begged him to tell her if she had done aught amiss, had prayed him to give her back his love. To all this he answered little, but her entreaties had at least such an effect as to induce him to take his dinner with us that evening. At that meal we tried to put aside our gloom, and with feigned smiles and cheerful voices, from which the tears were hardly banished, sustained a weary show of conversation and tried to wile away his evil mood. But he spoke little; and when Foster, my father's butler, put on the table the three-handled Maltravers' loving-cup that he had brought up Christmas by Christmas for thirty years, my brother merely passed it by without a taste. I saw by Foster's face that the master's malady was no longer a secret even from the servants.

I shall not harass my own feelings nor yours, my dear Edward, by entering into further details of your father's illness, for such it was obvious his indisposition had become. It was the only consolation, and that a sorry one, that we could use with Constance, to persuade her that John's estrangement from her was merely the result or manifestation of some physical infirmity. He obviously grew worse from week to week, and his treatment of his wife became colder and more callous. We had used all efforts to persuade him to take a change of air—to go to Royston for a month, and place himself under the care of Dr. Dobie. Mrs. Temple had even gone so far as to write privately to this physician, telling him as much of the case as was prudent, and asking his advice. Not being aware of the darker sides of my brother's ailment, Dr. Dobie replied in a less serious strain than seemed to us convenient, but recommended in any case a complete change of air and scene.

It was, therefore, with no ordinary pleasure and relief that we heard my brother announce quite unexpectedly one morning in March that he had made up his mind to seek change, and was going to leave almost immediately for the Continent. He took his valet Parnham with him, and quitted Worth one morning before lunch, bidding us an unceremonious adieu, though he kissed Constance with some apparent tenderness. It was the first time for three months, she confessed to me afterwards, that he had shown her even so ordinary a mark of affection; and her wounded heart treasured up what she hoped would prove a token of returning love. He had not proposed to take her with him, and even had he done so, we should have been reluctant to assent, as signs were not wanting that it might have been imprudent for her to undertake foreign travel at that period.

For nearly a month we had no word of him. Then he wrote a short note to Constance from Naples, giving no news, and indeed, scarce speaking of himself at all, but mentioning as an address to which she might write if she wished, the Villa de Angelis at Posilipo. Though his letter was cold and empty, yet Constance was delighted to get it, and wrote henceforth herself nearly every day, pouring out her heart to him, and retailing such news as she thought would cheer him.

## CHAPTER XI

A month later Mrs. Temple wrote to John warning him of the state in which Constance now found herself, and begging him to return at least for a few weeks in order that he might be present at the time of her confinement. Though it would have been in the last degree unkind, or even inhuman, that a request of this sort should have been refused, yet I will confess to you that my brother's recent strangeness had prepared me for any behaviour on his part however wild; and it was with a feeling of extreme relief that I heard from Mrs. Temple a little later that she had received a short note from John to say that he was already on his return journey. I believe Mrs. Temple herself felt as I did in the matter, though she said nothing.

When he returned we were all at Royston, whither Mrs. Temple had taken Constance to be under Dr. Dobie's care. We found John's physical appearance changed for the worse. His pallor was as remarkable as before, but he was visibly thinner; and his strange mental abstraction and moodiness seemed little if any abated. At first, indeed, he greeted Constance kindly or even affectionately. She had been in a terrible state of anxiety as to the attitude he would assume towards her, and this mental strain affected prejudicially her very delicate bodily condition. His kindness, of an ordinary enough nature indeed, seemed to her yearning heart a miracle of condescending love, and she was transported with the idea that his affection to her, once so sincere, was indeed returning. But I grieve to say that his manner thawed only for a very short time, and ere long he relapsed into an attitude of complete indifference. It was as if his real, true, honest, and loving character had made one more vigorous effort to assert itself—as though it had for a moment broken through the hard and selfish crust that was forming around him; but the blighting influence which was at work proved seemingly too strong for him to struggle against, and riveted its chains again upon him with a weight heavier than before. That there was some malefic influence, mental or physical, thus working on him, no one who had known him before could for a moment doubt. But while Mrs. Temple and I readily admitted this much, we were entirely unable even to form a conjecture as to its nature. It is true that Mrs. Temple's fancy suggested that Constance had some rival in his affections; but we rejected such a theory almost before it was proposed, feeling that it was inherently improbable, and that, had it been true, we could not have remained entirely unaware of the circumstances which had conduced to such a state of things. It was this inexplicable nature of my brother's affliction that added immeasurably to our grief. If we could only have ascertained its cause we might have combated it; but as it was, we were fighting in the dark, as against some enemy who was assaulting us from an obscurity so thick that we could not see his form. Of any mental trouble we thus knew nothing, nor could we say that my brother was suffering from any definite physical ailment, except that he was certainly growing thinner.

Your birth, my dear Edward, followed very shortly. Your poor mother rallied in an unusually short time, and was filled with rapture at the new treasure which was thus given as a solace to her afflictions. Your father exhibited little interest at the event, though he sat nearly half an hour with her one evening, and allowed her even to stroke his hair and caress him as in time long past. Although it was now the height of summer he seldom left the house, sitting much and sleeping in his own room, where he had a field-bed provided for him, and continually devoting himself to the violin.

One evening near the end of July we were sitting after dinner in the drawing-room at Royston, having the French windows looking on to the lawn open, as the air was still oppressively warm. Though things were proceeding as indifferently as before, we were perhaps less cast down than usual, for John had taken his dinner with us that evening. This was a circumstance now, alas! sufficiently uncommon, for he had nearly all his meals served for him in his own rooms. Constance, who was once more downstairs, sat playing at the pianoforte, performing chiefly melodies by Scarlatti or Bach, of which old-fashioned music she knew her husband to be most fond. A later fashion, as you know, has revived the cultivation of these composers, but at the time of which I write their works were much less commonly known. Though she was more than a passable musician, he would not allow her to accompany him; indeed he never now performed at all on the violin before us, reserving his practice entirely for his own chamber. There was a pause in the music while coffee was served. My brother had been sitting in an easy-chair apart reading some classical work during his wife's performance, and taking little notice of us. But after a while he put down his book and said, "Constance, if you will accompany me, I will get my violin and play a little while." I cannot say how much his words astonished us. It was so simple a matter for him to say, and yet it filled us all with an unspeakable joy. We concealed our emotion till he had left the room to get his instrument, then Constance showed how deeply she was gratified by kissing first her mother and then me, squeezing my hand but saying nothing. In a minute he returned, bringing his violin and a music-book. By the soiled vellum cover and the shape I perceived instantly that it was the book containing the "Areopagita." I had not seen it for near two years, and was not even aware that it was in the house, but I knew at once that he intended to play that suite. I entertained an unreasoning but profound aversion to its melodies, but at that moment I would have welcomed warmly that or any other music, so that he would only choose once more to show some thought for his neglected wife. He put the book open at the "Areopagita" on the desk of the pianoforte, and asked her to play it with him. She had never seen the music before, though I believe she was not unacquainted with the melody, as she had heard him playing it by himself, and once heard, it was not easily forgotten.

They began the "Areopagita" suite, and at first all went well. The tone of the violin, and also, I may say with no undue partiality, my brother's performance, were so marvellously fine that though our thoughts were elsewhere when the music commenced, in a few seconds they were wholly engrossed in the melody, and we sat spellbound. It was as if the violin had become suddenly endowed with life, and was singing to us in a mystical language more deep and awful than any human words. Constance was comparatively unused to the figuring of the *basso continuo*, and found some trouble in reading it accurately, especially in manuscript; but she was able to mask any difficulty she may have had until she came to the *Gagliarda*. Here she confessed to me her thoughts seemed against her will to wander, and her attention became too deeply riveted on her husband's performance to allow her to watch her own. She made first one slight fault, and then growing nervous, another, and another. Suddenly John stopped and said brusquely, "Let Sophy play, I cannot keep time with you." Poor Constance! The tears came swiftly to my own eyes when I heard him speak so thoughtlessly to her, and I was almost provoked to rebuke him openly. She was still weak from her recent illness; her nerves were excited by the unusual pleasure she felt in playing once more with her husband, and this sudden shattering of her hopes of a renewed tenderness proved more than she could bear: she put her head between her hands upon the keyboard and broke into a paroxysm of tears.

We both ran to her; but while we were attempting to assuage her grief, John shut his violin into its case, took the music-book under his arm, and left the room without saying a word to any of us, not even to the weeping girl, whose sobs seemed as though they would break her heart.

We got her put to bed at once, but it was some hours before her convulsive sobbing ceased. Mrs. Temple had administered to her a soothing draught of proved efficacy, and after sitting with her till after one o'clock I left her at last dozing off to sleep, and myself sought repose. I was quite wearied out with the weight of my anxiety, and with the crushing bitterness of seeing my dearest Constance's feelings so wounded. Yet in spite, or rather perhaps on account of my trouble, my head had scarcely touched my pillow ere I fell into a deep sleep.

A room in the south wing had been converted for the nonce into a nursery, and for the convenience of being near her infant Constance now slept in a room adjoining. As this portion of the house was somewhat isolated, Mrs. Temple had suggested that I should keep her daughter company, and occupy a room in the same passage, only removed a few doors, and this I had accordingly done. I was aroused from my sleep that night by some one knocking gently on the door of my bedroom; but it was some seconds before my thoughts became sufficiently awake to allow me to remember where I was. There was some moonlight, but I lighted a candle, and looking at my watch saw that it was two o'clock. I concluded that either Constance or her baby was unwell, and that the nurse needed my assistance. So I left my bed, and moving to the door, asked softly who was there. It was, to my surprise, the voice of Constance that replied, "O Sophy, let me in."

In a second I had opened the door, and found my poor sister wearing only her night-dress, and standing in the moonlight before me.

She looked frightened and unusually pale in her white dress and with the cold gleam of the moon upon her. At first I thought she was walking in her sleep, and perhaps rehearsing again in her dreams the troubles which dogged her waking footsteps. I took her gently by the arm, saying, "Dearest Constance, come back at once to bed; you will take cold."

She was not asleep, however, but made a motion of silence, and said in a terrified whisper, "Hush; do you hear nothing?" There was something so vague and yet so mysterious in the question and in her evident perturbation that I was infected too by her alarm. I felt myself shiver, as I strained my ear to catch if possible the slightest sound. But a complete silence pervaded everything: I could hear nothing.

"Can you hear it?" she said again. All sorts of images of ill presented themselves to my imagination: I thought the baby must be ill with croup, and that she was listening for some stertorous breath of anguish; and then the dread came over me that perhaps her sorrows had been too much for her, and that reason had left her seat. At that thought the marrow froze in my bones.

"Hush," she said again; and just at that moment, as I strained my ears, I thought I caught upon the sleeping air a distant and very faint murmur.

"Oh, what is it, Constance?" I said. "You will drive me mad"; and while I spoke the murmur seemed to resolve itself into the vibration, felt almost rather than heard, of some distant musical instrument. I stepped past her into the passage. All was deadly still, but I could perceive that music was being played somewhere far away; and almost at the same minute my ears recognised faintly but unmistakably the *Gagliarda* of the "Areopagita."

I have already mentioned that for some reason which I can scarcely explain, this melody was very repugnant to me. It seemed associated in some strange and intimate way with my brother's indisposition and moral decline. Almost at the moment that I had heard it first two years ago, peace seemed to have risen up and left our house, gathering her skirts about her, as we read that the angels left the Temple at the siege of Jerusalem. And now it was even more detestable to my ears, recalling as it did too vividly the cruel events of the preceding evening.

"John must be sitting up playing," I said.

"Yes," she answered; "but why is he in this part of the house, and why does he always play *that* tune?"

It was as if some irresistible attraction drew us towards the music. Constance took my hand in hers and we moved together slowly down the passage. The wind had risen, and though there was a bright moon, her beams were constantly eclipsed by driving clouds. Still there was light enough to guide us, and I extinguished the candle. As we reached the end of the passage the air of the *Gagliarda* grew more and more distinct.

Our passage opened on to a broad landing with a balustrade, and from one side of it ran out the picture-gallery which you know.

I looked at Constance significantly. It was evident that John was playing in this gallery. We crossed the landing, treading carefully and making no noise with our naked feet, for both of us had been too excited even to think of putting on shoes.

We could now see the whole length of the gallery. My poor brother sat in the oriel window of which I have before spoken. He was sitting so as to face the picture of Adrian Temple, and the great windows of the oriel flung a strong light on him. At times a cloud hid the moon, and all was plunged in darkness; but in a moment the cold light fell full on him again, and we could trace every feature as in a picture. He had evidently not been to bed, for he was fully dressed, exactly as he had left us in the drawing-room five hours earlier when Constance was weeping over his thoughtless words. He was playing the violin, playing with a passion and reckless energy which I had never seen, and hope never to see again. Perhaps he remembered that this spot was far removed from the rest of the house, or perhaps he was careless whether any were awake and listening to him or not; but it seemed to me that he was playing with a sonorous strength greater than I had thought possible for a single violin. There came from his instrument such a volume and torrent of melody as to fill the gallery so full, as it were, of sound that it throbbed and vibrated again. He kept his eyes fixed on something at the opposite side of the gallery; we could not indeed see on what, but I have no doubt at all that it was the portrait of Adrian Temple. His gaze was eager and expectant, as though he were waiting for something to occur which did not.

I knew that he had been growing thin of late, but this was the first time I had realised how sunk were the hollows of his eyes and how haggard his features had become. It may have been some effect of moonlight which I do not well understand, but his fine-cut face, once so handsome, looked on this night worn and thin like that of an old man. He never for a moment ceased playing. It was always one same dreadful melody, the *Gagliarda* of the "Areopagita," and he repeated it time after time with the perseverance and apparent aimlessness of an automaton.

He did not see us, and we made no sign, standing afar off in silent horror at that nocturnal sight. Constance clutched me by the arm: she was so pale that I perceived it even in the moonlight. "Sophy," she said, "he is sitting in the same place as on the first night when he told me how he loved me." I could answer nothing, my voice was frozen in me. I could only stare at my brother's poor withered face, realising then for the first time that he must be mad, and that it was the haunting of the *Gagliarda* that had made him so.

We stood there I believe for half an hour without speech or motion, and all the time that sad figure at the end of the gallery continued its performance. Suddenly he stopped, and an expression of frantic despair came over his face as he laid down the violin and buried his head in his hands. I could bear it no longer. "Constance," I said, "come back to bed. We can do nothing." So we turned and crept away silently as we had come. Only as we crossed the landing Constance stopped, and looked back for a minute with a heartbroken yearning at the man she loved. He had taken his hands from his head, and she saw the profile of his face clear cut and hard in the white moonlight.

It was the last time her eyes ever looked upon it.

She made for a moment as if she would turn back and go to him, but her courage failed her, and we went on. Before we reached her room we heard in the distance, faintly but distinctly, the burden of the *Gagliarda.*

## CHAPTER XII

The next morning my maid brought me a hurried note written in pencil by my brother. It contained only a few lines, saying that he found that his continued sojourn at Royston was not beneficial to his health, and had determined to return to Italy. If we wished to write, letters would reach him at the Villa de Angelis: his valet Parnham was to follow him thither with his baggage as soon as it could be got together. This was all; there was no word of adieu even to his wife.

We found that he had never gone to bed that night. But in the early morning he had himself saddled his horse *Sentinel* and ridden in to Derby, taking the early mail thence to London. His resolve to leave Royston had apparently been arrived at very suddenly, for so far as we could discover, he had carried no luggage of any kind. I could not help looking somewhat carefully round his room to see if he had taken the Stradivarius violin. No trace of it or even of its case was to be seen, though it was difficult to imagine how he could have carried it with him on horseback. There was, indeed, a locked travelling-trunk which Parnham was to bring with him later, and the instrument might, of course, have been in that; but I felt convinced that he had actually taken it with him in some way or other, and this proved afterwards to have been the case.

I shall draw a veil, my dear Edward, over the events which immediately followed your father's departure. Even at this distance of time the memory is too inexpressibly bitter to allow me to do more than briefly allude to them.

A fortnight after John's departure, we left Royston and removed to Worth, wishing to get some sea-air, and to enjoy the late summer of the south coast. Your mother seemed entirely to have recovered from her confinement, and to be enjoying as good health as could be reasonably expected under the circumstances of her husband's indisposition. But suddenly one of those insidious maladies which are incidental to women in her condition seized upon her. We had hoped and believed that all such period of danger was already happily past; but, alas! it was not so, and within a few hours of her first seizure all realised how serious was her case. Everything that human skill can do under such conditions was done, but without avail. Symptoms of blood-poisoning showed themselves, accompanied with high fever, and within a week she was in her coffin.

Though her delirium was terrible to watch, yet I thank God to this day, that if she was to die, it pleased him to take her while in an unconscious condition. For two days before her death she recognised no one, and was thus spared at least the sadness of passing from life without one word of kindness or even of reconciliation from her unhappy husband.

The communication with a place so distant as Naples was not then to be made under fifteen or twenty days, and all was over before we could hope that the intelligence even of his wife's illness had reached John. Both Mrs. Temple and I remained at Worth in a state of complete prostration, awaiting his return. When more than a month had passed without his arrival, or even a letter to say that he was on his way, our anxiety took a new turn, as we feared that some accident had befallen him, or that the news of his wife's death, which would then be in his hands, had so seriously affected him as to render him incapable of taking any action. To repeated subsequent communications we received no answer; but at last, to a letter which I wrote to Parnham, the servant replied, stating that his master was still at the Villa de Angelis, and in a condition of health little differing from that in which he left Royston, except that he was now slightly paler if possible and thinner. It was not till the end of November that any word came from him, and then he wrote only one page of a sheet of note-paper to me in pencil, making no reference whatever to his wife's death, but saying that he should not return for Christmas, and instructing me to draw on his bankers for any moneys that I might require for household purposes at Worth.

I need not tell you the effect that such conduct produced on Mrs. Temple and myself; you can easily imagine what would have been your own feelings in such a case. Nor will I relate any other circumstances which occurred at this period, as they would have no direct bearing upon my narrative. Though I still wrote to my brother at frequent intervals, as not wishing to neglect a duty, no word from him ever came in reply.

About the end of March, indeed, Parnham returned to Worth Maltravers, saying that his master had paid him a half-year's wages in advance, and then dispensed with his services. He had always been an excellent servant, and attached to the family, and I was glad to be able to offer him a suitable position with us at Worth until his master should return. He brought disquieting reports of John's health, saying that he was growing visibly weaker. Though I was sorely tempted to ask him many questions as to his master's habits and way of life, my pride forbade me to do so. But I heard incidentally from my maid that Parnham had told her Sir John was spending money freely in alterations at the Villa de Angelis, and had engaged Italians to attend him, with which his English valet was naturally much dissatisfied.

So the spring passed and the summer was well advanced.

On the last morning of July I found waiting for me on the breakfast-table an envelope addressed in my brother's hand. I opened it hastily. It only contained a few words, which I have before me as I write now. The ink is a little faded and yellow, but the impression it made is yet vivid as on that summer morning.

"MY DEAREST SOPHY," it began,—"Come to me here at once, if possible, or it may be too late. I want to see you. They say that I am ill, and too weak to travel to England.
                    "Your loving brother,
                              "JOHN."

There was a great change in the style, from the cold and conventional notes that he had hitherto sent at such long intervals; from the stiff "Dear Sophia" and "Sincerely yours" to which, I grieve to say, I had grown accustomed. Even the writing itself was altered. It was more the bold boyish hand he wrote when first he went to Oxford, than the smaller cramped and classic character of his later years. Though it was a little matter enough, God knows, in comparison with his grievous conduct, yet it touched me much that he should use again the once familiar "Dearest Sophy," and sign himself "my loving brother." I felt my heart go out towards him; and so strong is woman's affection for her own kin, that I had already forgotten any resentment and reprobation in my great pity for the poor wanderer, lying sick perhaps unto death and alone in a foreign land.

I took his note at once to Mrs. Temple. She read it twice or thrice, trying to take in the meaning of it. Then she drew me to her and, kissing me, said, "Go to him at once, Sophy. Bring him back to Worth; try to bring him back to the right way."

I ordered my things to be packed, determining to drive to Southampton and take train thence to London; and at the same time Mrs. Temple gave instructions that all should be prepared for her own return to Royston within a few days. I knew she did not dare to see John after her daughter's death.

I took my maid with me, and Parnham to act as courier. At London we hired a carriage for the whole journey, and from Calais posted direct to Naples. We took the short route by Marseilles and Genoa, and travelled for seventeen days without intermission, as my brother's note made me desirous of losing no time on the way. I had never been in Italy before; but my anxiety was such that my mind was unable to appreciate either the beauty of the scenery or the incidents of travel. I can, in fact, remember nothing of our journey now, except the wearisome and interminable jolting over bad roads and the insufferable heat. It was the middle of August in an exceptionally warm summer, and after passing Genoa the heat became almost tropical. There was no relief even at night, for the warm air hung stagnant and suffocating, and the inside of my travelling coach was often like a furnace.

We were at last approaching the conclusion of our journey, and had left Rome behind us. The day that we set out from Aversa was the hottest that I have ever felt, the sun beating down with an astonishing power even in the early hours, and the road being thick with a white and blinding dust. It was soon after midnight that our carriage began rattling over the great stone blocks with which the streets of Naples are paved. The suburbs that we at first passed through were, I remember, in darkness and perfect quiet; but after traversing the heart of the city and reaching the western side, we suddenly found ourselves in the midst of an enormous and very dense crowd. There were lanterns everywhere, and interminable lanes of booths, whose proprietors were praising their wares with loud shouts; and here acrobats, jugglers, minstrels, black-vested priests, and blue-coated soldiers mingled with a vast crowd whose number at once arrested the progress of the carriage. Though it was so late of a Sunday night, all seemed here awake and busy as at noonday. Oil-lamps with reeking fumes of black smoke flung a glare over the scene, and the discordant cries and chattering conversation united in so deafening a noise as to make me turn faint and giddy, wearied as I already was with long travelling. Though I felt that intense eagerness and expectation which the approaching termination of a tedious journey inspires, and was desirous of pushing forward with all imaginable despatch, yet here our course was sadly delayed. The horses could only proceed at the slowest of foot-paces, and we were constantly brought to a complete stop for some minutes before the post-boy could force a passage through the unwilling crowd. This produced a feeling of irritation, and despair of ever reaching my destination; and the mirth and careless hilarity of the people round us chafed with bitter contrast on my depressed spirits. I inquired from the post-boy what was the origin of so great a commotion, and understood him to say in reply that it was a religious festival held annually in honour of "Our Lady of the Grotto." I cannot, however, conceive of any truly religious person countenancing such a gathering, which seemed to me rather like the unclean orgies of a heathen deity than an act of faith of Christian people. This disturbance occasioned us so serious a delay, that as we were climbing the steep slope leading up to Posilipo it was already three in the morning and the dawn was at hand.

After mounting steadily for a long time we began to rapidly descend, and just as the sun came up over the sea we arrived at the Villa de Angelis. I sprang from the carriage, and passing through a trellis of vines, reached the house. A man-servant was in waiting, and held the door open for me; but he was an Italian, and did not understand me when I asked in English where Sir John Maltravers was. He had evidently, however, received instructions to take me at once to my brother, and led the way to an inner part of the house. As we proceeded I heard the sound of a rich alto voice singing very sweetly to a mandoline some soothing or religious melody. The servant pulled aside a heavy curtain and I found myself in my brother's room. An Italian youth sat on a stool near the door, and it was he who had been singing. At a few words from John, addressed to him in his own language, he set down his mandoline and left the room, pulling to the curtain and shutting a door behind it.

The room looked directly on to the sea: the villa was, in fact, built upon rocks at the foot of which the waves lapped. Through two folding windows which opened on to a balcony the early light of the summer morning streamed in with a rosy flush. My brother sat on a low couch or sofa, propped up against a heap of pillows, with a rug of brilliant colours flung across his feet and legs. He held out his arms to me, and I ran to him; but even in so brief an interval I had perceived that he was terribly weak and wasted.

All my memories of his past faults had vanished and were dead in that sad aspect of his worn features, and in the conviction which I felt, even from the first moment, that he had but little time longer to remain with us. I knelt by him on the floor, and with my arms round his neck, embraced him tenderly, not finding any place for words, but only sobbing in great anguish. Neither of us spoke, and my weariness from long travel and the strangeness of the situation caused me to feel that paralysing sensation of doubt as to the reality of the scene, and even of my own existence, which all, I believe, have experienced at times of severe mental tension. That I, a plain English girl, should be kneeling here beside my brother in the Italian dawn; that I should read, as I believed, on his young face the unmistakable image and superscription of death; and reflect that within so few months he had married, had wrecked his home, that my poor Constance was no more;—these things seemed so unrealisable that for a minute I felt that it must all be a nightmare, that I should immediately wake with the fresh salt air of the Channel blowing through my bedroom window at Worth, and find I had been dreaming. But it was not so; the light of day grew stronger and brighter, and even in my sorrow the panorama of the most beautiful spot on earth, the Bay of Naples, with Vesuvius lying on the far side, as seen then from these windows, stamped itself for ever on my mind. It was unreal as a scene in some brilliant dramatic spectacle, but, alas! no unreality was here. The flames of the candles in their silver sconces waxed paler and paler, the lines and shadows on my brother's face grew darker, and the pallor of his wasted features showed more striking in the bright rays of the morning sun.

# CHAPTER XIII

I had spent near a week at the Villa de Angelis. John's manner to me was most tender and affectionate; but he showed no wish to refer to the tragedy of his wife's death and the sad events which had preceded it, or to attempt to explain in any way his own conduct in the past. Nor did I ever lead the conversation to these topics; for I felt that even if there were no other reason, his great weakness rendered it unadvisable to introduce such subjects at present, or even to lead him to speak at all more than was actually necessary. I was content to minister to him in quiet, and infinitely happy in his restored affection. He seemed desirous of banishing from his mind all thoughts of the last few months, but spoke much of the years before he had gone to Oxford, and of happy days which we had spent together in our childhood at Worth Maltravers. His weakness was extreme, but he complained of no particular malady except a short cough which troubled him at night.

I had spoken to him of his health, for I could see that his state was such as to inspire anxiety, and begged that he would allow me to see if there was an English doctor at Naples who could visit him. This he would not assent to, saying that he was quite content with the care of an Italian doctor who visited him almost daily, and that he hoped to be able, under my escort, to return within a very short time to England.

"I shall never be much better, dear Sophy," he said one day. "The doctor tells me that I am suffering from some sort of consumption, and that I must not expect to live long. Yet I yearn to see Worth once more, and to feel again the west wind blowing in the evening across from Portland, and smell the thyme on the Dorset downs. In a few days I hope perhaps to be a little stronger, and I then wish to show you a discovery which I have made in Naples. After that you may order them to harness the horses, and carry me back to Worth Maltravers."

I endeavoured to ascertain from Signor Baravelli, the doctor, something as to the actual state of his patient; but my knowledge of Italian was so slight that I could neither make him understand what I would be at, nor comprehend in turn what he replied, so that this attempt was relinquished. From my brother himself I gathered that he had begun to feel his health much impaired as far back as the early spring, but though his strength had since then gradually failed him, he had not been confined to the house until a month past. He spent the day and often the night reclining on his sofa and speaking little. He had apparently lost that taste for the violin which had once absorbed so much of his attention; indeed I think the bodily strength necessary for its performance had probably now failed him. The Stradivarius instrument lay near his couch in its case; but I only saw the latter open on one occasion, I think, and was deeply thankful that John no longer took the same delight as heretofore in the practice of this art,—not only because the mere sound of his violin was now fraught to me with such bitter memories, but also because I felt sure that its performance had in some way which I could not explain a deleterious effect upon himself. He exhibited that absence of vitality which is so often noticeable in those who have not long to live, and on some days lay in a state of semi-lethargy from which it was difficult to rouse him. But at other times he suffered from a distressing restlessness which forbade him to sit still even for a few minutes, and which was more painful to watch than his lethargic stupor. The Italian boy, of whom I have already spoken, ex-hibited an untiring devotion to his master which won my heart. His name was Raffaelle Carotenuto, and he often sang to us in the evening, accom-panying himself on the mandoline. At nights, too, when John could not sleep, Raffaelle would read for hours till at last his master dozed off. He was well educated, and though I could not understand the subject he read, I often sat by and listened, being charmed with his evident attachment to my brother and with the melodious intonation of a sweet voice.

My brother was nervous apparently in some respects, and would never be left alone even for a few minutes; but in the intervals while Raffaelle was with him I had ample opportunities to examine and appreciate the beauties of the Villa de Angelis. It was built, as I have said, on some rocks jutting into the sea, just before coming to the Capo di Posilipo as you proceed from Naples. The earlier foundations were, I believe, originally Roman, and upon them a modern villa had been constructed in the eighteenth century, and to this again John had made important additions in the past two years. Looking down upon the sea from the windows of the villa, one could on calm days easily discern the remains of Roman piers and moles lying below the surface of the transparent water; and the tufa-rock on which the house was built was burrowed with those unintelligible excavations of a classic date so common in the neighbourhood. These subterraneous rooms and passages, while they aroused my curiosity, seemed at the same time so gloomy and repellent that I never explored them. But on one sunny morning, as I walked at the foot of the rocks by the sea, I ventured into one of the larger of these chambers, and saw that it had at the far end an opening leading apparently to another inner room. I had walking with me an old Italian female servant who took a motherly interest in my proceedings, and who, relying principally upon a very slight knowledge of English, had constituted herself my body-guard. Encouraged by her presence, I penetrated this inner room and found that it again opened in turn into another, and so on until we had passed through no less than four chambers.

They were all lighted after a fashion through vent-holes which some-where or other reached the outer air, but the fourth room opened into a fifth which was unlighted. My companion who had been showing signs of alarm and an evident reluctance to proceed further, now stopped abruptly and begged me to return. It may have been that her fear communicated itself to me also, for on attempting to cross the threshold and explore the darkness of the fifth cell, I was seized by an unreasoning panic and by the feeling of undefined horror experienced in a nightmare. I hesitated for an instant, but my fear became suddenly more intense, and springing back, I followed my companion, who had set out to run back to the outer air. We never paused until we stood panting in the full sunlight by the sea. As soon as the maid had found her breath, she begged me never to go there again, explaining in broken English that the caves were known in the neighbour-hood as the "Cells of Isis," and were reputed to be haunted by demons. This episode, trifling as it may appear, had so great an effect upon me that I never again ventured on to the lower walk which ran at the foot of the rocks by the sea.

In the house above, my brother had built a large hall after the ancient Roman style, and this, with a dining-room and many other chambers, were decorated in the fashion of those discovered at Pompeii. They had been furnished with the utmost luxury, and the beauty of the painting, furni-ture, carpets, and hangings was enhanced by statues in bronze and marble. The villa, indeed, and its fittings were of a kind to which I was little used, and at the same time of such beauty that I never ceased to regard all as a creation of an enchanter's wand, or as the drop-scene to some drama which might suddenly be raised and disappear from my sight. The house, in short, together with its furniture, was, I believe, intended to be a reproduction of an ancient Roman villa, and had something about it re-pellent to my rustic and insular ideas. In the contemplation of its per-fection I experienced a curious mental sensation, which I can only compare to the physical oppression produced on some persons by the heavy and cloying perfume of a bouquet of gardenias or other too highly-scented exotics.

In my brother's room was a medieval reproduction in mellow alabaster of a classic group of a dolphin encircling a Cupid. It was, I think, the fairest work of art I ever saw, but it jarred upon my sense of propriety that close by it should hang an ivory crucifix. I would rather, I think, have seen all things material and pagan entirely, with every view of the future life shut out, than have found a medley of things sacred and profane, where the emblems of our highest hopes and aspirations were placed in insulting indifference side by side with the embodied forms of sensuality. Here, in this scene of magical beauty, it seemed to me for a moment that the years had rolled back, that Christianity had still to fight with a *living* Paganism, and that the battle was not yet won. It was the same all through the house; and there were many other matters which filled me with regret, mingled with vague and apprehensive surmises which I shall not here repeat.

At one end of the house was a small library, but it contained few works except Latin and Greek classics. I had gone thither one day to look for a book that John had asked for, when in turning out some drawers I found a number of letters written from Worth by my lost Constance to her husband. The shock of being brought suddenly face to face with a handwriting that evoked memories at once so dear and sad was in itself a sharp one; but its bitterness was immeasurably increased by the discovery that not one of these envelopes had ever been opened. While that dear heart, now at rest, was pouring forth her love and sorrow to the ears that should have been above all others ready to receive them, her letters, as they arrived, were flung uncared for, unread, even unopened, into any haphazard receptacle.

The days passed one by one at the Villa de Angelis with but little incident, nor did my brother's health either visibly improve or decline. Though the weather was still more than usually warm, a grateful breeze came morning and evening from the sea and tempered the heat so much as to render it always supportable. John would sometimes in the evening sit propped up with cushions on the trellised balcony looking towards Baia, and watch the fishermen setting their nets. We could hear the melody of their deep-voiced songs carried up on the night air. "It was here, Sophy," my brother said, as we sat one evening looking on a scene like this—"It was here that the great epicure Pollio built himself a famous house, and called it by two Greek words meaning a 'truce to care,' from which our name of Posilipo is derived. It was his *sans-souci*, and here he cast aside his vexations; but they were lighter than mine. Posilipo has brought no cessation of care to me. I do not think I shall find any truce this side the grave; and beyond, who knows?"

This was the first time John had spoken in this strain, and he seemed stirred to an unusual activity, as though his own words had suddenly reminded him how frail was his state. He called Raffaelle to him and despatched him on an errand to Naples. The next morning he sent for me earlier than usual, and begged that a carriage might be ready by six in the evening, as he desired to drive into the city. I tried at first to dissuade him from this project, urging him to consider his weak state of health. He replied that he felt somewhat stronger, and had something that he particularly wished me to see in Naples. This done, it would be better to return at once to England; he could, he thought, bear the journey if we travelled by very short stages.

## CHAPTER XIV

Shortly after six o'clock in the evening we left the Villa de Angelis. The day had been as usual cloudlessly serene; but a gentle sea-breeze, of which I have spoken, rose in the afternoon and brought with it a refreshing coolness. We had arranged a sort of couch in the landau with many cushions for my brother, and he mounted into the carriage with more ease than I had expected. I sat beside him, with Raffaelle facing me on the opposite seat. We drove down the hill of Posilipo through the ilex-trees and tamarisk-bushes that then skirted the sea, and so into the town. John spoke little except to remark that the carriage was an easy one. As we were passing through one of the principal streets he bent over to me and said, "You must not be alarmed if I show you to-day a strange sight. Some women might perhaps be frightened at what we are going to see; but my poor sister has known already so much of trouble that a light thing like this will not affect her." In spite of his encomiums upon my supposed courage, I felt alarmed and agitated by his words. There was a vagueness in them which frightened me, and bred that indefinite apprehension which is often infinitely more terrifying than the actual object which inspires it. To my inquiries he would give no further response than to say that he had whilst at Posilipo made some investigations in Naples leading to a strange discovery, which he was anxious to communicate to me. After traversing a considerable distance, we had penetrated apparently into the heart of the town. The streets grew narrower and more densely thronged; the houses were more dirty and tumble-down, and the appearance of the people themselves suggested that we had reached some of the lower quarters of the city. Here we passed through a further network of small streets of the name of which I took no note, and found ourselves at last in a very dark and narrow lane called the *Via del Giardino*. Although my brother had, so far as I had observed, given no orders to the coachman, the latter seemed to have no difficulty in finding his way, driving rapidly in the Neapolitan fashion, and proceeding direct as to a place with which he was already familiar.

In the Via del Giardino the houses were of great height, and overhung the street so as nearly to touch one another. It seemed that this quarter had been formerly inhabited, if not by the aristocracy, at least by a class very much superior to that which now lived there; and many of the houses were large and dignified, though long since parcelled out into smaller tenements. It was before such a house that we at last brought up. Here must have been at one time a house or palace of some person of distinction, having a long and fine façade adorned with delicate pilasters, and much florid ornamentation of the Renaissance period. The ground-floor was divided into a series of small shops, and its upper storeys were evidently peopled by sordid families of the lowest class. Before one of these little shops, now closed and having its windows carefully blocked with boards, our carriage stopped. Raffaelle alighted, and taking a key from his pocket unlocked the door, and assisted John to leave the carriage. I followed, and directly we had crossed the threshold, the boy locked the door behind us, and I heard the carriage drive away.

We found ourselves in a narrow and dark passage, and as soon as my eyes grew accustomed to the gloom I perceived there was at the end of it a low staircase leading to some upper room, and on the right a door which opened into the closed shop. My brother moved slowly along the passage, and began to ascend the stairs. He leant with one hand on Raffaelle's arm, taking hold of the balusters with the other. But I could see that to mount the stairs cost him considerable effort, and he paused frequently to cough and get his breath again. So we reached a landing at the top, and found ourselves in a small chamber or magazine directly over the shop. It was quite empty except for a few broken chairs, and appeared to be a small loft formed by dividing what had once been a high room into two storeys, of which the shop formed the lower. A long window, which had no doubt once formed one of several in the walls of this large room, was now divided across its width by the flooring, and with its upper part served to light the loft, while its lower panes opened into the shop. The ceiling was, in consequence of these alterations, comparatively low, but though much mutilated, retained evident traces of having been at one time richly decorated, with the raised mouldings and pendants common in the sixteenth century. At one end of the loft was a species of coved and elaborately carved dado, of which the former use was not obvious; but the large original room had without doubt been divided in length as well as in height, as the lath-and-plaster walls at either end of the loft had evidently been no part of the ancient structure.

My brother sat down in one of the old chairs, and seemed to be collecting his strength before speaking. My anxiety was momentarily increasing, and it was a great relief when he began talking in a low voice as one that had much to say and wished to husband his strength.

"I do not know whether you will recollect my having told you of something Mr. Gaskell once said about the music of Graziani's 'Areopagita' suite. It had always, he used to say, a curious effect upon his imagination, and the melody of the *Gagliarda* especially called up to his thoughts in some strange way a picture of a certain hall where people were dancing. He even went so far as to describe the general appearance of the room itself, and of the persons who were dancing there."

"Yes," I answered, "I remember your telling me of this"; and indeed my memory had in times past so often rehearsed Mr. Gaskell's description, that although I had not recently thought of it, its chief features immediately returned to my mind.

"He described it," my brother continued, "as a long hall with an arcade of arches running down one side, of the fantastic Gothic of the Renaissance. At the end was a gallery or balcony for the musicians, which on its front carried a coat of arms."

I remembered this perfectly and told John so, adding that the shield bore a cherub's head fanning three lilies on a golden field.

"It is strange," John went on, "that the description of a scene which our friend thought a mere effort of his own imagination has impressed itself so deeply on both our minds. But the picture which he drew was more than a fancy, for we are at this minute in the very hall of his dream."

I could not gather what my brother meant, and thought his reason was failing him; but he continued, "This miserable floor on which we stand has of course been afterwards built in; but you may see above you the old ceiling, and here at the end was the musicians' gallery with the shield upon its front."

He pointed to the carved and whitewashed dado which had hitherto so puzzled me. I stepped up to it, and although the lath-and-plaster partition wall was now built around it, it was clear that its curved outline might very easily, as John said, have formed part of the front of a coved gallery. I looked closely at the relief-work which had adorned it. Though the edges were all rubbed off, and the mouldings in some cases entirely removed, I could trace without difficulty a shield in the midst; and a more narrow inspection revealed underneath the whitewash, which had partly peeled away, enough remnants of colour to show that it had certainly been once painted gold and borne a cherub's head with three lilies.

"That is the shield of the old Neapolitan house of Domacavalli," my brother continued; "they bore a cherub's head fanning three lilies on a shield *or*. It was in the balcony behind this shield, long since blocked up as you see, that the musicians sat on that ball night of which Gaskell dreamt. From it they looked down on the hall below where dancing was going forward, and I will now take you downstairs that you may see if the description tallies."

So saying, he raised himself, and descending the stairs with much less difficulty than he had shown in mounting them, flung open the door which I had seen in the passage and ushered us into the shop on the ground-floor. The evening light had now faded so much that we could scarcely see even in the passage, and the shop having its windows barricaded with shutters, was in complete darkness. Raffaelle, however, struck a match and lit three half-burnt candles in a tarnished sconce upon the wall.

The shop had evidently been lately in the occupation of a wine-seller, and there were still several empty wooden wine-butts, and some broken flasks on shelves. In one corner I noticed that the earth which formed the floor had been turned up with spades. There was a small heap of mould, and a large flat stone was thus exposed below the surface. This stone had an iron ring attached to it, and seemed to cover the aperture of a well, or perhaps a vault. At the back of the shop, and furthest from the street, were two lofty arches separated by a column in the middle, from which the outside casing had been stripped.

To these arches John pointed and said, "That is a part of the arcade which once ran down the whole length of the hall. Only these two arches are now left, and the fine marbles which doubtless coated the outside of this dividing pillar have been stripped off. On a summer's night about one hundred years ago dancing was going on in this hall. There were a dozen couples dancing a wild step such as is never seen now. The tune that the musicians were playing in the gallery above was taken from the 'Areopagita' suite of Graziani. Gaskell has often told me that when he played it the music brought with it to his mind a sense of some impending catastrophe, which culminated at the end of the first movement of the *Gagliarda*. It was just at that moment, Sophy, that an Englishman who was dancing here was stabbed in the back and foully murdered."

I had scarcely heard all that John had said, and had certainly not been able to take in its import; but without waiting to hear if I should say anything, he moved across to the uncovered stone with the ring in it. Exerting a strength which I should have believed entirely impossible in his weak condition, he applied to the stone a lever which lay ready at hand. Raffaelle at the same time seized the ring, and so they were able between them to move the covering to one side sufficiently to allow access to a small staircase which thus appeared to view. The stair was a winding one, and once led no doubt to some vaults below the ground-floor. Raffaelle descended first, taking in his hand the sconce of three candles, which he held above his head so as to fling a light down the steps. John went next, and then I followed, trying to support my brother if possible with my hand. The stairs were very dry, and on the walls there was none of the damp or mould which fancy usually associates with a subterraneous vault. I do not know what it was I expected to see, but I had an uneasy feeling that I was on the brink of some evil and distressing discovery. After we had descended about twenty steps we could see the entry to some vault or underground room, and it was just at the foot of the stairs that I saw something lying, as the light from the candles fell on it from above. At first I thought it was a heap of dust or refuse, but on looking closer it seemed rather a bundle of rags. As my eyes penetrated the gloom, I saw there was about it some tattered cloth of a faded green tint, and almost at the same minute I seemed to trace under the clothes the lines or dimensions of a human figure. For a moment I imagined it was some poor man lying face downward and bent up against the wall. The idea of a man or of a dead body being there shocked me violently, and I cried to my brother, "Tell me, what is it?" At that instant the light from Raffaelle's candles fell in a somewhat different direction. It lighted up the white bowl of a human skull, and I saw that what I had taken for a man's form was instead that of a clothed skeleton. I turned faint and sick for an instant, and should have fallen had it not been for John, who put his arm about me and sustained me with an unexpected strength.

"God help us!" I exclaimed, "let us go. I cannot bear this; there are foul vapours here; let us get back to the outer air."

He took me by the arm, and pointing at the huddled heap, said, "Do you know whose bones those are? That is Adrian Temple. After it was all over, they flung his body down the steps dressed in the clothes he wore."

At that name, uttered in so ill-omened a place, I felt a fresh access of terror. It seemed as though the soul of that wicked man must be still hovering over his unburied remains, and boding evil to us all. A chill crept over me, the light, the walls, my brother, and Raffaelle all swam round, and I sank swooning on the stairs.

When I returned fully to my senses we were in the landau again making our way back to the Villa de Angelis.

## CHAPTER XV

The next morning my health and strength were entirely restored to me, but my brother, on the contrary, seemed weak and exhausted from his efforts of the previous night. Our return journey to the Villa de Angelis had passed in complete silence. I had been too much perturbed to question him on the many points relating to the strange events as to which I was still completely in the dark, and he on his side had shown no desire to afford me any further information. When I saw him the next morning he exhibited signs of great weakness, and in response to an effort on my part to obtain some explanation of the discovery of Adrian Temple's body, avoided an immediate reply, promising to tell me all he knew after our return to Worth Maltravers.

I pondered over the last terrifying episode very frequently in my own mind, and as I thought more deeply of it all, it seemed to me that the outlines of some evil history were piece by piece developing themselves, that I had almost within my grasp the clue that would make all plain, and that had eluded me so long. In that dim story Adrian Temple, the music of the *Gagliarda*, my brother's fatal passion for the violin, all seemed to have some mysterious connection, and to have conspired in working John's mental and physical ruin. Even the Stradivarius violin bore a part in the tragedy, becoming, as it were, an actively malignant spirit, though I could not explain how, and was yet entirely unaware of the manner in which it had come into my brother's possession.

I found that John was still resolved on an immediate return to England. His weakness, it is true, led me to entertain doubts as to how he would support so long a journey; but at the same time I did not feel justified in using any strong efforts to dissuade him from his purpose. I reflected that the more wholesome air and associations of England would certainly re-invigorate both body and mind, and that any extra strain brought about by the journey would soon be repaired by the comforts and watchful care with which we could surround him at Worth Maltravers.

So the first week in October saw us once more with our faces set towards England. A very comfortable swinging-bed or hammock had been arranged for John in the travelling carriage, and we determined to avoid fatigue as much as possible by dividing our journey into very short stages. My brother seemed to have no intention of giving up the Villa de Angelis. It was left complete with its luxurious furniture, and with all his servants, under the care of an Italian *maggior-duomo*. I felt that as John's state of health forbade his entertaining any hope of an immediate return thither, it would have been much better to close entirely his Italian house. But his great weakness made it impossible for him to undertake the effort such a course would involve, and even if my own ignorance of the Italian tongue had not stood in the way, I was far too eager to get my invalid back to Worth to feel inclined to import any further delay, while I should myself adjust matters which were after all comparatively trifling. As Parnham was now ready to discharge his usual duties of valet, and my brother seemed quite content that he should do so, Raffaelle was of course to be left behind. The boy had quite won my heart by his sweet manners, combined with his evident affection to his master, and in making him understand that he was now to leave us, I offered him a present of a few pounds as a token of my esteem. He refused, however, to touch this money, and shed tears when he learnt that he was to be left in Italy, and begged with many protestations of devotion that he might be allowed to accompany us to England. My heart was not proof against his entreaties, supported by so many signs of attachment, and it was agreed, therefore, that he should at least attend us as far as Worth Maltravers. John showed no surprise at the boy being with us, indeed I never thought it necessary to explain that I had originally purposed to leave him behind.

Our journey, though necessarily prolonged by the shortness of its stages, was safely accomplished. John bore it as well as I could have hoped, and though his body showed no signs of increased vigour, his mind, I think, improved in tone, at any rate for a time. From the evening on which he had shown me the terrible discovery in the Via del Giardino he seemed to have laid aside something of his care and depression. He now exhibited little trace of the moroseness and selfishness which had of late so marred his character; and though he naturally felt severely at times the fatigue of travel, yet we had no longer to dread any relapse into that state of lethargy or stupor which had so often baffled every effort to counteract it at Posilipo. Some feeling of superstitious aversion had prompted me to give orders that the Stradivarius violin should be left behind at Posilipo. But before parting my brother asked for it, and insisted that it should be brought with him, though I had never heard him play a note on it for many weeks. He took an interest in all the petty episodes of travel, and certainly appeared to derive more entertainment from the journey than was to have been anticipated in his feeble state of health.

To the incidents of the evening spent in the Via del Giardino he made no allusion of any kind, nor did I for my part wish to renew memories of so unpleasant a nature. His only reference occurred one Sunday evening as we were passing a small graveyard near Genoa. The scene apparently turned his thoughts to that subject, and he told me that he had taken measures before leaving Naples to ensure that the remains of Adrian Temple should be decently interred in the cemetery of Santa Bibiana. His words set me thinking again, and unsatisfied curiosity prompted me strongly to inquire of him how he had convinced himself that the skeleton at the foot of the stairs was indeed that of Adrian Temple. But I restrained myself, partly from a reliance on his promise that he would one day explain the whole story to me, and partly being very reluctant to mar the enjoyment of the peaceful scenes through which we were passing, by the introduction of any subjects so jarring and painful as those to which I have alluded.

We reached London at last, and here we stopped a few days to make some necessary arrangements before going down to Worth Maltravers. I had urged upon John during the journey that immediately on his arrival in London he should obtain the best English medical advice as to his own health. Though he at first demurred, saying that nothing more was to be done, and that he was perfectly satisfied with the medicine given him by Dr. Baravelli, which he continued to take, yet by constant entreaty I prevailed upon him to accede to so reasonable a request. Dr. Frobisher, considered at that time the first living authority on diseases of the brain and nerves, saw him on the morning after our arrival. He was good enough to speak with me at some length after seeing my brother, and to give me many hints and recipes whereby I might be better enabled to nurse the invalid.

Sir John's condition, he said, was such as to excite serious anxiety. There was, indeed, no brain mischief of any kind to be discovered, but his lungs were in a state of advanced disease, and there were signs of grave heart affection. Yet he did not bid me to despair, but said that with careful nursing life might certainly be prolonged, and even some measure of health in time restored. He asked me more than once if I knew of any trouble or worry that preyed upon Sir John's mind. Were there financial difficulties; had he been subjected to any mental shock; had he received any severe fright? To all this I could only reply in the negative. At the same time I told Dr. Frobisher as much of John's history as I considered pertinent to the question. He shook his head gravely, and recommended that Sir John should remain for the present in London, under his own constant supervision. To this course my brother would by no means consent. He was eager to proceed at once to his own house, saying that if necessary we could return again to London for Christmas. It was therefore agreed that we should go down to Worth Maltravers at the end of the week.

Parnham had already left us for Worth in order that he might have everything ready against his master's return, and when we arrived we found all in perfect order for our reception. A small morning-room next to the library, with a pleasant south aspect and opening on to the terrace, had been prepared for my brother's use, so that he might avoid the fatigue of mounting stairs, which Dr. Frobisher considered very prejudicial in his present condition. We had also purchased in London a chair fitted with wheels, which enabled him to be moved, or, if he were feeling equal to the exertion, to move himself, without difficulty, from room to room.

His health, I think, improved; very gradually, it is true, but still sufficiently to inspire me with hope that he might yet be spared to us. Of the state of his mind or thoughts I knew little, but I could see that he was at times a prey to nervous anxiety. This showed itself in the harassed look which his pale face often wore, and in his marked dislike to being left alone. He derived, I think, a certain pleasure from the quietude and monotony of his life at Worth, and perhaps also from the consciousness that he had about him loving and devoted hearts. I say hearts, for every servant at Worth was attached to him, remembering the great consideration and courtesy of his earlier years, and grieving to see his youthful and once vigorous frame reduced to so sad a strait. Books he never read himself, and even the charm of Raffaelle's reading seemed to have lost its power; though he never tired of hearing the boy sing, and liked to have him sit by his chair even when his eyes were shut and he was apparently asleep. His general health seemed to me to change but little either for better or worse. Dr. Frobisher had led me to expect some such a sequel. I had not concealed from him that I had at times entertained suspicions as to my brother's sanity; but he had assured me that they were totally unfounded, that Sir John's brain was as clear as his own. At the same time he confessed that he could not account for the exhausted vitality of his patient—a condition which he would under ordinary circumstances have attributed to excessive study or severe trouble. He had urged upon me the pressing necessity for complete rest, and for much sleep. My brother never even incidentally referred to his wife, his child, or to Mrs. Temple, who constantly wrote to me from Royston, sending kind messages to John, and asking how he did. These messages I never dared to give him, fearing to agitate him, or retard his recovery by diverting his thoughts into channels which must necessarily be of a painful character. That he should never even mention her name, or that of Lady Maltravers, led me to wonder sometimes if one of those curious freaks of memory which occasionally accompany a severe illness had not entirely blotted out from his mind the recollection of his marriage and of his wife's death. He was unable to consider any affairs of business, and the management of the estate remained as it had done for the last two years in the hands of our excellent agent, Mr. Baker.

But one evening in the early part of December he sent Raffaelle about nine o'clock, saying he wished to speak to me. I went to his room, and without any warning he began at once, "You never show me my boy now, Sophy; he must be grown a big child, and I should like to see him." Much startled by so unexpected a remark, I replied that the child was at Royston under the care of Mrs. Temple, but that I knew that if it pleased him to see Edward she would be glad to bring him down to Worth. He seemed gratified with this idea, and begged me to ask her to do so, desiring that his respects should be at the same time conveyed to her. I almost ventured at that moment to recall his lost wife to his thoughts, by saying that his child resembled her strongly; for your likeness at that time, and even now, my dear Edward, to your poor mother was very marked. But my courage failed me, and his talk soon reverted to an earlier period, comparing the mildness of the month to that of the first winter which he spent at Eton. His thoughts, however, must, I fancy, have returned for a moment to the days when he first met your mother, for he suddenly asked, "Where is Gaskell? Why does he never come to see me?" This brought quite a new idea to my mind. I fancied it might do my brother much good to have by him so sensible and true a friend as I knew Mr. Gaskell to be. The latter's address had fortunately not slipped from my memory, and I put all scruples aside and wrote by the next mail to him, setting forth my brother's sad condition, saying that I had heard John mention his name, and begging him on my own account to be so good as to help us if possible and come to us in this hour of trial. Though he was so far off as Westmoreland, Mr. Gaskell's generosity brought him at once to our aid, and within a week he was installed at Worth Maltravers, sleeping in the library, where we had arranged a bed at his own desire, so that he might be near his sick friend.

His presence was of the utmost assistance to us all. He treated John at once with the tenderness of a woman and the firmness of a clever and strong man. They sat constantly together in the mornings, and Mr. Gaskell told me John had not shown with him the same reluctance to talk freely of his married life as he had discovered with me. The tenor of his communications I cannot guess, nor did I ever ask; but I knew that Mr. Gaskell was much affected by them.

John even amused himself now at times by having Mr. Baker into his rooms of a morning, that the management of the estate might be discussed with his friend; and he also expressed his wish to see the family solicitor, as he desired to draw his will. Thinking that any diversion of this nature could not but be beneficial to him, we sent to Dorchester for our solicitor, Mr. Jeffreys, who together with his clerk spent three nights at Worth, and drew up a testament for my brother. So time went on, and the year was drawing to a close.

It was Christmas Eve, and I had gone to bed shortly after twelve o'clock, having an hour earlier bid good night to John and Mr. Gaskell. The long habit of watching with, or being in charge of an invalid at night, had made my ears extraordinarily quick to apprehend even the slightest murmur. It must have been, I think, near three in the morning when I found myself awake and conscious of some unusual sound. It was low and far off, but I knew instantly what it was, and felt a choking sensation of fear and horror, as if an icy hand had gripped my throat, on recognising the air of the *Gagliarda*. It was being played on the violin, and a long way off, but I knew that tune too well to permit of my having any doubt on the subject.

Any trouble or fear becomes, as you will some day learn, my dear nephew, immensely intensified and exaggerated at night. It is so, I suppose, because our nerves are in an excited condition, and our brain not sufficiently awake to give a due account of our foolish imaginations. I have myself many times lain awake wrestling in thought with difficulties which

in the hours of darkness seemed insurmountable, but with the dawn resolved themselves into merely trivial inconveniences. So on this night, as I
sat up in bed looking into the dark, with the sound of that melody in my
ears, it seemed as if something too terrible for words had happened; as
though the evil spirit, which we had hoped was exorcised, had returned
with others sevenfold more wicked than himself, and taken up his abode
again with my lost brother. The memory of another night rushed to my
mind when Constance had called me from my bed at Royston, and we had
stolen together down the moonlit passages with the lilt of that wicked
music vibrating on the still summer air. Poor Constance! She was in her
grave now; yet *her* troubles at least were over, but here, as by some bitter
irony, instead of carol or sweet symphony, it was the *Gagliarda* that woke
me from my sleep on Christmas morning.

I flung my dressing-gown about me, and hurried through the corridor
and down the stairs which led to the lower storey and my brother's room.
As I opened my bedroom door the violin ceased suddenly in the middle of
a bar. Its last sound was not a musical note, but rather a horrible scream,
such as I pray I may never hear again. It was a sound such as a wounded
beast might utter. There is a picture I have seen of Blake's, showing the
soul of a strong wicked man leaving his body at death. The spirit is flying
out through the window with awful staring eyes, aghast at the desolation
into which it is going. If in the agony of dissolution such a lost soul could
utter a cry, it would, I think, sound like the wail which I heard from the
violin that night.

Instantly all was in absolute stillness. The passages were silent and
ghostly in the faint light of my candle; but as I reached the bottom of the
stairs I heard the sound of other footsteps, and Mr. Gaskell met me. He
was fully dressed, and had evidently not been to bed. He took me kindly
by the hand and said, "I feared you might be alarmed by the sound of
music. John has been walking in his sleep; he had taken out his violin and
was playing on it in a trance. Just as I reached him something in it gave
way, and the discord caused by the slackened strings roused him at once.
He is awake now and has returned to bed. Control your alarm for his sake
and your own. It is better that he should not know you have been awakened."

He pressed my hand and spoke a few more reassuring words, and I went
back to my room still much agitated, and yet feeling half ashamed for
having shown so much anxiety with so little reason.

That Christmas morning was one of the most beautiful that I ever
remember. It seemed as though summer was so loath to leave our sunny
Dorset coast that she came back on this day to bid us adieu before her
final departure. I had risen early and had partaken of the Sacrament at our
little church. Dr. Butler had recently introduced this early service, and
though any alteration of time-honoured customs in such matters might not
otherwise have met with my approval, I was glad to avail myself of the
privilege on this occasion, as I wished in any case to spend the later

morning with my brother. The singular beauty of the early hours, and the tranquillising effect of the solemn service brought back serenity to my mind, and effectually banished from it all memories of the preceding night. Mr. Gaskell met me in the hall on my return, and after greeting me kindly with the established compliments of the day, inquired after my health, and hoped that the disturbance of my slumber on the previous night had not affected me injuriously. He had good news for me: John seemed decidedly better, was already dressed, and desired, as it was Christmas morning, that we would take our breakfast with him in his room.

To this, as you may imagine, I readily assented. Our breakfast party passed off with much content, and even with some quiet humour, John sitting in his easy-chair at the head of the table and wishing us the compliments of the season. I found laid in my place a letter from Mrs. Temple greeting us all (for she knew Mr. Gaskell was at Worth), and saying that she hoped to bring little Edward to us at the New Year. My brother seemed much pleased at the prospect of seeing his son, and though perhaps it was only imagination, I fancied he was particularly gratified that Mrs. Temple herself was to pay us a visit. She had not been to Worth since the death of Lady Maltravers.

Before we had finished breakfast the sun beat on the panes with an unusual strength and brightness. His rays cheered us all, and it was so warm that John first opened the windows, and then wheeled his chair on to the walk outside. Mr. Gaskell brought him a hat and mufflers, and we sat with him on the terrace basking in the sun. The sea was still and glassy as a mirror, and the Channel lay stretched before us like a floor of moving gold. A rose or two still hung against the house, and the sun's rays reflected from the red sandstone gave us a December morning more mild and genial than many June days that I have known in the north. We sat for some minutes without speaking, immersed in our own reflections and in the exquisite beauty of the scene.

The stillness was broken by the bells of the parish church ringing for the morning service. There were two of them, and their sound, familiar to us from childhood, seemed like the voices of old friends. John looked at me and said with a sigh, "I should like to go to church. It is long since I was there. You and I have always been on Christmas mornings, Sophy, and Constance would have wished it had she been with us."

His words, so unexpected and tender, filled my eyes with tears; not tears of grief, but of deep thankfulness to see my loved one turning once more to the old ways. It was the first time I had heard him speak of Constance, and that sweet name, with the infinite pathos of her death, and of the spectacle of my brother's weakness, so overcame me that I could not speak. I only pressed his hand and nodded. Mr. Gaskell, who had turned away for a minute, said he thought John would take no harm in attending the morning service provided the church were warm. On this point I could reassure him, having found it properly heated even in the early morning.

Mr. Gaskell was to push John's chair, and I ran off to put on my cloak, with my heart full of profound thankfulness for the signs of returning grace so mercifully vouchsafed to our dear sufferer on this happy day. I was ready dressed and had just entered the library when Mr. Gaskell stepped hurriedly through the window from the terrace. "John has fainted!" he said. "Run for some smelling salts and call Parnham!"

There was a scene of hurried alarm, giving place ere long to terrified despair. Parnham mounted a horse and set off at a wild gallop to Swanage to fetch Dr. Bruton; but an hour before he returned we knew the worst. My brother was beyond the aid of the physician: his wrecked life had reached a sudden term!

I have now, dear Edward, completed the brief narrative of some of the facts attending the latter years of your father's life. The motive which has induced me to commit them to writing has been a double one. I am anxious to give effect as far as may be to the desire expressed most strongly to Mr. Gaskell by your father, that you should be put in possession of these facts on your coming of age. And for my own part I think it better that you should thus hear the plain truth from me, lest you should be at the mercy of haphazard reports, which might at any time reach you from ignorant or interested sources. Some of the circumstances were so remarkable that it is scarcely possible to suppose that they were not known, and most probably frequently discussed, in so large an establishment as that of Worth Maltravers. I even have reason to believe that exaggerated and absurd stories were current at the time of Sir John's death, and I should be grieved to think that such foolish tales might by any chance reach your ear without your having any sure means of discovering where the truth lay. God knows how grievous it has been to me to set down on paper some of the facts that I have here narrated. You as a dutiful son will reverence the name even of a father whom you never knew; but you must remember that his sister did more: she loved him with a single-hearted devotion, and it still grieves her to the quick to write anything which may seem to detract from his memory. Only, above all things, let us speak the truth. Much of what I have told you needs, I feel, further explanation, but this I cannot give, for I do not understand the circumstances. Mr. Gaskell, your guardian, will, I believe, add to this account a few notes of his own, which may tend to elucidate some points, as he is in possession of certain facts of which I am still ignorant.

## MR. GASKELL'S NOTE

I have read what Miss Maltravers has written, and have but little to add to it. I can give no explanation that will tally with all the facts or meet all the difficulties involved in her narrative. The most obvious solution of some points would be, of course, to suppose that Sir John Maltravers was insane. But to any one who knew him as intimately as I did, such an hypothesis is untenable; nor, if admitted, would it explain some of the strangest incidents. Moreover, it was strongly negatived by Dr. Frobisher, from whose verdict in such matters there was at the time no appeal, by Dr. Dobie, and by Dr. Bruton, who had known Sir John from his infancy. It is possible that towards the close of his life he suffered occasionally from hallucination, though I could not positively affirm even so much; but this was only when his health had been completely undermined by causes which are very difficult to analyse.

When I first knew him at Oxford he was a strong man physically as well as mentally; open-hearted, and of a merry and genial temperament. At the same time he was, like most cultured persons—and especially musicians,—highly strung and excitable. But at a certain point in his career his very nature seemed to change; he became reserved, secretive, and saturnine. On this moral metamorphosis followed an equally startling physical change. His robust health began to fail him, and although there was no definite malady which doctors could combat, he went gradually from bad to worse until the end came.

The commencement of this extraordinary change coincided, I believe, almost exactly with his discovery of the Stradivarius violin; and whether this was, after all, a mere coincidence or something more it is not easy to say. Until a very short time before his death neither Miss Maltravers nor I had any idea how that instrument had come into his possession, or I think something might perhaps have been done to save him.

Though towards the end of his life he spoke freely to his sister of the finding of the violin, he only told her half the story, for he concealed from her entirely that there was any thing else in the hidden cupboard at Oxford. But as a matter of fact, he found there also two manuscript books containing an elaborate diary of some years of a man's life. That man was Adrian Temple, and I believe that in the perusal of this diary must be sought the origin of John Maltravers's ruin. The manuscript was beautifully written in a clear but cramped eighteenth century hand, and gave the idea of a man writing with deliberation, and wishing to transcribe his impressions with accuracy for further reference. The style was excellent, and the minute details given were often of high antiquarian interest; but the record throughout was marred by gross license. Adrian Temple's life had undoubtedly so definite an influence on Sir John's that a brief outline of it, as gathered from his diaries, is necessary for the understanding of what followed.

Temple went up to Oxford in 1737. He was seventeen years old, without parents, brothers, or sisters; and he possessed the Royston estates in Derbyshire, which were then, as now, a most valuable property. With the year 1738 his diaries begin, and though then little more than a boy, he had tasted every illicit pleasure that Oxford had to offer. His temptations were no doubt great; for besides being wealthy he was handsome, and had probably never known any proper control, as both his parents had died when he was still very young. But in spite of other failings, he was a brilliant scholar, and on taking his degree, was made at once a fellow of St. John's. He took up his abode in that College in a fine set of rooms looking on to the gardens, and from this period seems to have used Royston but little, living always either at Oxford, or on the Continent. He formed at this time the acquaintance of one Jocelyn, whom he engaged as companion and amanuensis. Jocelyn was a man of talent, but of irregular life, and was no doubt an accomplice in many of Temple's excesses. In 1743 they both undertook the so-called "grand tour," and though it was not his first visit, it was then probably that Temple first felt the fascination of pagan Italy,—a fascination which increased with every year of his after-life.

On his return from foreign travel he found himself among the stirring events of 1745. He was an ardent supporter of the Pretender, and made no attempt to conceal his views. Jacobite tendencies were indeed generally prevalent in the College at the time, and had this been the sum of his offending, it is probable that little notice would have been taken by the College authorities. But his notoriously wild life told against the young man, and certain dark suspicions were not easily passed over. After the *fiasco* of the Rebellion Dr. Holmes, then President of the College, seems to have made a scapegoat of Temple. He was deprived of his fellowship, and though not formally expelled, such pressure was put upon him as resulted in his leaving St. John's and removing to Magdalen Hall. There his great wealth evidently secured him consideration, and he was given the best rooms in the Hall, that very set looking on to New College Lane which Sir John Maltravers afterwards occupied.

In the first half of the eighteenth century the romance of the middle ages, though dying, was not dead, and the occult sciences still found followers among the Oxford towers. From his early years Temple's mind seems to have been set strongly towards mysticism of all kinds, and he and Jocelyn were versed in the jargon of the alchemist and astrologer, and practised according to the ancient rules. It was his reputation as a necromancer, and the stories current of illicit rites performed in the garden-rooms at St. John's, that contributed largely to his being dismissed from that College. He had also become acquainted with Francis Dashwood, the notorious Lord le Despencer, and many a winter's night saw him riding through the misty Thames meadows to the door of the sham Franciscan abbey. In his diaries were more notices than one of the "Franciscans" and the nameless orgies of Medmenham.

He was devoted to music. It was a rare enough accomplishment then, and a rarer thing still to find a wealthy landowner performing on the violin. Yet so he did, though he kept his passion very much to himself, as fiddling was thought lightly of in those days. His musical skill was altogether exceptional, and he was the first possessor of the Stradivarius violin which afterwards fell so unfortunately into Sir John's hands. This violin Temple bought in the autumn of 1738, on the occasion of a first visit to Italy. In that year died the nonagenarian Antonius Stradivarius, the greatest violin-maker the world has ever seen. After Stradivarius's death the stock of fiddles in his shop was sold by auction. Temple happened to be travelling in Cremona at the time with a tutor, and at the auction he bought that very instrument which we afterwards had cause to know so well. A note in his diary gave its cost at four louis, and said that a curious history attached to it. Though it was of his golden period, and probably the finest instrument he ever made, Stradivarius would never sell it, and it had hung for more than thirty years in his shop. It was said that from some whim as he lay dying he had given orders that it should be burnt; but if that were so, the instructions were neglected, and after his death it came under the hammer. Adrian Temple from the first recognised the great value of the instrument. His notes show that he only used it on certain special occasions, and it was no doubt for its better protection that he devised the hidden cupboard where Sir John eventually found it.

The later years of Temple's life were spent for the most part in Italy. On the Scoglio di Venere, near Naples, he built the Villa de Angelis, and there henceforth passed all except the hottest months of the year. Shortly after the completion of the villa Jocelyn left him suddenly, and became a Carthusian monk. A caustic note in the diary hinted that even this foul parasite was shocked into the austerest form of religion by something he had seen going forward. At Naples Temple's dark life became still darker. He dallied, it is true, with Neo-Platonism, and boasts that he, like Plotinus, had twice passed the circle of the *nous* and enjoyed the fruition of the deity; but the ideals of even that easy doctrine grew in his evil life still more miserably debased. More than once in the manuscript he made mention by name of the *Gagliarda* of Graziani as having been played at pagan mysteries which these enthusiasts revived at Naples, and the air had evidently impressed itself deeply on his memory. The last entry in his diary is made on the 16th of December, 1752. He was then in Oxford for a few days, but shortly afterwards returned to Naples. The accident of his having just completed a second volume, induced him, no doubt, to leave it behind him in the secret cupboard. It is probable that he commenced a third, but if so it was never found.

In reading the manuscript I was struck with the author's clear and easy style, and found the interest of the narrative increase rather than diminish.

At the same time its study was inexpressibly painful to me. Nothing could have supported me in my determination to thoroughly master it but the conviction that if I was to be of any real assistance to my poor friend Maltravers, I must know as far as possible every circumstance connected with his malady. As it was I felt myself breathing an atmosphere of moral contagion during the perusal of the manuscript, and certain passages have since returned at times to haunt me in spite of all efforts to dislodge them from my memory. When I came to Worth at Miss Maltravers's urgent invitation, I found my friend Sir John terribly altered. It was not only that he was ill and physically weak, but he had entirely lost the manner of youth, which, though indefinable, is yet so appreciable, and draws so sharp a distinction between the first period of life and middle age. But the most striking feature of his illness was the extraordinary pallor of his complexion, which made his face resemble a subtle counterfeit of white wax rather than that of a living man. He welcomed me undemonstratively, but with evident sincerity; and there was an entire absence of the constraint which often accompanies the meeting again of friends whose cordial relations have suffered interruption. From the time of my arrival at Worth until his death we were constantly together; indeed I was much struck by the almost childish dislike which he showed to be left alone even for a few moments. As night approached this feeling became intensified. Parnham slept always in his master's room; but if anything called the servant away even for a minute, he would send for Carotenuto or myself to be with him until his return. His nerves were weak; he started violently at any unexpected noise, and, above all, he dreaded being in the dark. When night fell he had additional lamps brought into his room, and even when he composed himself to sleep, insisted on a strong light being kept by his bedside.

I had often read in books of people wearing a "hunted" expression, and had laughed at the phrase as conventional and unmeaning. But when I came to Worth I knew its truth; for if any face ever wore a hunted—I had almost written a haunted—look, it was the white face of Sir John Maltravers. His air seemed that of a man who was constantly expecting the arrival of some evil tidings, and at times reminded me painfully of the guilty expectation of a felon who knows that a warrant is issued for his arrest.

During my visit he spoke to me frequently about his past life, and instead of showing any reluctance to discuss the subject, seemed glad of the opportunity of disburdening his mind. I gathered from him that the reading of Adrian Temple's memoirs had made a deep impression on his mind, which was no doubt intensified by the vision which he thought he saw in his rooms at Oxford, and by the discovery of the portrait at Royston. Of those singular phenomena I have no explanation to offer.

The romantic element in his disposition rendered him peculiarly susceptible to the fascination of that mysticism which breathed through Temple's narrative. He told me that almost from the first time he read it he was filled with a longing to visit the places and to revive the strange life of which it spoke. This inclination he kept at first in check, but by degrees it gathered strength enough to master him.

There is no doubt in my mind that the music of the *Gagliarda* of Graziani helped materially in this process of mental degradation. It is curious that Michael Praetorius in the "Syntagma musicum" should speak of the Galliard generally as an "invention of the devil, full of shameful and licentious gestures and immodest movements," and the singular melody of the *Gagliarda* in the "Areopagita" suite certainly exercised from the first a strange influence over me. I shall not do more than touch on the question here, because I see Miss Maltravers has spoken of it at length, and will only say, that though since the day of Sir John's death I have never heard a note of it, the air is still fresh in my mind, and has at times presented itself to me unexpectedly and always with an unwholesome effect. This I have found happen generally in times of physical depression, and the same air no doubt exerted a similar influence on Sir John, which his impressionable nature rendered from the first more deleterious to him.

I say this advisedly, because I am sure that if some music is good for man and elevates him, other melodies are equally bad and enervating. An experience far wider than any we yet possess is necessary to enable us to say how far this influence is capable of extension. How far, that is, the mind may be directed on the one hand to ascetic abnegation by the systematic use of certain music, or on the other to illicit and dangerous pleasures by melodies of an opposite tendency. But this much is, I think, certain, that after a comparatively advanced standard of culture has once been attained, music is the readiest if not the only key which admits to the yet narrower circle of the highest imaginative thought.

On the occasion for travel afforded him by his honeymoon, an impulse which he could not at the time explain, but which after-events have convinced me was the haunting suggestion of the *Gagliarda*, drove him to visit the scenes mentioned so often in Temple's diary. He had always been an excellent scholar, and a classic of more than ordinary ability. Rome and Southern Italy filled him with a strange delight. His education enabled him to appreciate to the full what he saw; he peopled the stage with the figures of the original actors, and tried to assimilate his thought to theirs. He began reading classical literature widely, no longer from the scholarly but the literary standpoint. In Rome he spent much time in the librarians' shops, and there met with copies of the numerous authors of the later empire and of those Alexandrine philosphers which are rarely seen in England. In these he found a new delight and fresh food for his mysticism.

Such study, if carried to any extent, is probably dangerous to the English character, and certainly was to a man of Maltravers's romantic sympathies. This reading produced in time so real an effect upon his mind that if he did not definitely abandon Christianity, as I fear he did, he at least adulterated it with other doctrines till it became to him Neo-Platonism. That most seductive of philosophies, which has enthralled so many minds from Proclus and Julian to Augustine and the Renaissancists, found an easy convert in John Maltravers. Its passionate longing for the vague and undefined good, its tolerance of aesthetic impressions, the pleasant superstitions of its dynamic pantheism, all touched responsive chords in his nature. His mind, he told me, became filled with a measureless yearning for the old culture of pagan philosophy, and as the past became clearer and more real, so the present grew dimmer, and his thoughts were gradually weaned entirely from all the natural objects of affection and interest which should otherwise have occupied them. To what a terrible extent this process went on, Miss Maltravers's narrative shows. Soon after reaching Naples he visited the Villa de Angelis, which Temple had built on the ruins of a sea-house of Pomponius. The later building had in its turn become dismantled and ruinous, and Sir John found no difficulty in buying the site outright. He afterwards rebuilt it on an elaborate scale, endeavouring to reproduce in its equipment the luxury of the later empire. I had occasion to visit the house more than once in my capacity of executor, and found it full of priceless works of art, which though neither so difficult to procure at that time nor so costly as they would be now, were yet sufficiently valuable to have necessitated an unjustifiable outlay.

The situation of the building fostered his infatuation for the past. It lay between the Bay of Naples and the Bay of Baia, and from its windows commanded the same exquisite views which had charmed Cicero and Lucullus, Severus and the Antonines. Hard by stood Baia, the princely seaside resort of the empire. That most luxurious and wanton of all cities of antiquity survived the cataclysms of ages, and only lost its civic continuity and became the ruined village of to-day in the sack of the fifteenth century. But a continuity of wickedness is not so easily broken, and those who know the spot best say that it is still instinct with memories of a shameful past.

For miles along that haunted coast the foot cannot be put down except on the ruins of some splendid villa, and over all there broods a spirit of corruption and debasement actually sensible and oppressive. Of the dawns and sunsets, of the noonday sun tempered by the sea-breeze and the shade of scented groves, those who have been there know the charm, and to those who have not no words can describe it. But there are malefic vapours rising from the corpse of a past not altogether buried, and most cultivated Englishmen who tarry there long feel their influence as did John Maltravers. Like so many *decepti deceptores* of the Neo-Platonic school, he did not practise the abnegation enjoined by the very cult he professed to follow. Though his nature was far too refined, I believe, ever to sink into the sensualism revealed in Temple's diaries, yet it was through the gratification of corporeal tastes that he endeavoured to achieve the divine *extasis*; and there were constantly lavish and sumptuous entertainments at the villa, at which strange guests were present.

In such a nightmare of a life it was not to be expected that any mind would find repose, and Maltravers certainly found none. All those cares which usually occupy men's minds, all thoughts of wife, child, and home, were, it is true, abandoned; but a wild unrest had hold of him, and never suffered him to be at ease. Though he never told me as much, yet I believe he was under the impression that the form which he had seen at Oxford and Royston had reappeared to him on more than one subsequent occasion. It must have been, I fancy, with a vague hope of "laying" this spectre that he now set himself with eagerness to discover where or how Temple had died. He remembered that Royston tradition said he had succumbed at Naples in the plague of 1752, but an idea seized him that this was not the case; indeed I half suspect his fancy unconsciously pictured that evil man as still alive. The methods by which he eventually discovered the skeleton, or learnt the episodes which preceded Temple's death, I do not know. He promised to tell me some day at length, but a sudden death prevented his ever doing so. The facts as he narrated them, and as I have little doubt they actually occurred, were these. Adrian Temple, after Jocelyn's departure, had made a confidant of one Palamede Domacavalli, a scion of a splendid Parthenopean family of that name. Palamede had a palace in the heart of Naples, and was Temple's equal in age and also in his great wealth. The two men became boon companions, associating in all kinds of wickedness and excess. At length Palamede married a beautiful girl named Olimpia Aldobrandini, who was also of the noblest lineage; but the intimacy between him and Temple was not interrupted. About a year subsequent to this marriage dancing was going on after a splendid banquet in the great hall of the Palazzo Domacavalli. Adrian, who was a favoured guest, called to the musicians in the gallery to play the "Areopagita" suite, and danced it with Olimpia, the wife of his host. The *Gagliarda* was reached but never finished, for near the end of the second movement Palamede from behind drove a stiletto into his friend's heart. He had found out that day that Adrian had not spared even Olimpia's honour.

I have endeavoured to condense into a connected story the facts learnt piecemeal from Sir John in conversation. To a certain extent they supplied, if not an explanation, at least an account of the change that had come over my friend. But only to a certain extent; there the explanation broke down and I was left baffled. I could imagine that a life of unwholesome surroundings and disordered studies might in time produce such a loss of mental tone as would lead in turn to moral *acolasia*, sensual excess, and physical ruin. But in Sir John's case the cause was not adequate; he had, so far as I know, never wholly given the reins to sensuality, and the change was too abrupt and the break-down of body and mind too complete to be accounted for by such events as those of which he had spoken.

I had, too, an uneasy feeling which grew upon me the more I saw of him, that while he spoke freely enough on certain topics, and obviously meant to give a complete history of his past life, there was in reality something in the background which he always kept from my view. He was, it seemed, like a young man asked by an indulgent father to disclose his debts in order that they may be discharged, who although he knows his parent's leniency, and that any debt not now disclosed will be afterwards but a weight upon his own neck, yet hesitates for very shame to tell the full amount, and keeps some items back. So poor Sir John kept something back from me his friend, whose only aim was to afford him consolation and relief, and whose compassion would have made me listen without rebuke to the narration of the blackest crimes. I cannot say how much this conviction grieved me. I would most willingly have given my all, my very life, to save my friend and Miss Maltravers's brother; but my efforts were paralysed by the feeling that I did not know what I had to combat, that some evil influence was at work on him which continually evaded my grasp. Once or twice it seemed as though he were within an ace of telling me all; once or twice, I believe, he had definitely made up his mind to do so; but then the mood changed, or more probably his courage failed him.

It was on one of these occasions that he asked me, somewhat suddenly, whether I thought that a man could by any conscious act committed in the flesh take away from himself all possibility of repentance and ultimate salvation. Though, I trust, a sincere Christian, I am nothing of a theologian, and the question touching on a topic which had not occurred to my mind since childhood, and which seemed to savour rather of medieval romance than of practical religion, took me for a moment aback. I hesitated for an instant, and then replied that the means of salvation offered man were undoubtedly so sufficient as to remove from one truly penitent the guilt of any crime however dark. My hesitation had been but momentary; but Sir John seemed to have noticed it, and sealed his lips to any confession, if he had indeed intended to make any, by changing the subject abruptly. This question naturally gave me food for serious reflection and anxiety. It was the first occasion on which he appeared to me to be undoubtedly suffering from definite hallucination, and I was aware that any illusions connected with religion are generally most difficult to remove. At the same time, anything of this sort was the more remarkable in Sir John's case, as he had, so far as I knew, for a considerable time entirely abandoned the Christian belief.

Unable to elicit any further information from him, and being thus thrown entirely upon my own resources, I determined that I would read through again the whole of Temple's diaries. The task was a very distasteful one, as I have already explained, but I hoped that a second reading might perhaps throw some light on the dark misgiving that was troubling Sir John. I read the manuscript again with the closest attention. Nothing, however, of any importance seemed to have escaped me on the former occasions, and I had reached nearly the end of the second volume when a comparatively slight matter arrested my attention. I have said that the pages were all carefully numbered, and the events of each day recorded separately; even where Temple had found nothing of moment to notice on a given day, he had still inserted the date with the word *nil* written against it. But as I sat one evening in the library at Worth after Sir John had gone to bed, and was finally glancing through the days of the months in Temple's diary to make sure that all were complete, I found one day was missing. It was towards the end of the second volume, and the day was the 23d of October in the year 1752. A glance at the numbering of the pages revealed the fact that three leaves had been entirely removed, and that the pages numbered 349 to 354 were not to be found. Again I ran through the diaries to see whether there were any leaves removed in other places, but found no other single page missing. All was complete except at this one place, the manuscript beautifully written, with scarcely an error or erasure throughout. A closer examination showed that these three leaves had been cut out close to the back, and the cut edges of the paper appeared too fresh to admit of this being done a century ago. A very short reflection convinced me, in fact, that the excision was not likely to have been Temple's, and that it must have been made by Sir John.

My first intention was to ask him at once what the lost pages had contained, and why they had been cut out. The matter might be a mere triviality which he could explain in a moment. But on softly opening his bedroom door I found him sleeping, and Parnham (whom the strong light always burnt in the room rendered more wakeful) informed me that his master had been in a deep sleep for more than an hour. I knew how sorely his wasted energies needed such repose and stepped back to the library without awaking him. A few minutes before, I had been feeling sleepy at the conclusion of my task, but now all wish for sleep was suddenly banished and a painful wakefulness took its place. I was under a species of mental excitement which reminded me of my feelings some years before at Oxford on the first occasion of our ever playing the *Gagliarda* together, and an idea struck me with the force of intuition that in these three lost leaves lay the secret of my friend's ruin.

I turned to the context to see whether there was anything in the entries preceding or following the lacuna that would afford a clue to the missing passage. The record of the few days immediately preceding the 23d of October was short and contained nothing of any moment whatever. Adrian and Jocelyn were alone together at the Villa de Angelis. The entry on the 22d was very unimportant and apparently quite complete, ending at the bottom of page 348. Of the 23d there was, as I have said, no record at all, and the entry for the 24th began at the top of page 355. This last memorandum was also brief, and written when the author was annoyed by Jocelyn leaving him.

The defection of his companion had been apparently entirely unexpected. There was at least no previous hint of any such intention. Temple wrote that Jocelyn had left the Villa de Angelis that day and taken up his abode with the Carthusians of San Martino. No reason for such an extraordinary change was given; but there was a hint that Jocelyn had professed himself shocked at something that had happened. The entry concluded with a few bitter remarks: *"So farewell to my holy anchoret; and if I cannot speed him with a leprosie as one Elisha did his servant, yet at least he went out from my presence with a face white as snow."*

I had read this sentence more than once before without its attracting other than a passing attention. The curious expression, that Jocelyn had gone out from his presence with a face white as snow, had hitherto seemed to me to mean nothing more than that the two men had parted in violent anger, and that Temple had abused or bullied his companion. But as I sat alone that night in the library the words seemed to assume an entirely new force, and a strange suspicion began to creep over me.

I have said that one of the most remarkable features of Sir John's illness was his deadly pallor. Though I had now spent some time at Worth, and had been daily struck by this lack of colour, I had never before remembered in this connection that a strange paleness had also been an attribute of Adrian Temple, and was indeed very clearly marked in the picture painted of him by Battoni. In Sir John's account, moreover, of the vision which he thought he had seen in his rooms at Oxford, he had always spoken of the white and waxen face of his spectral visitant. The family tradition of Royston said that Temple had lost his colour in some deadly magical experiment, and a conviction now flashed upon me that Jocelyn's face "as white as snow" could refer only to this same unnatural pallor, and that he too had been smitten with it as with the mark of the beast.

In a drawer of my despatch-box I kept by me all the letters which the late Lady Maltravers had written home during her ill-fated honeymoon. Miss Maltravers had placed them in my hands in order that I might be acquainted with every fact that could at all elucidate the progress of Sir John's malady. I remembered that in one of these letters mention was made of a sharp attack of fever in Naples, and of her noticing in him for the first time this singular pallor. I found the letter again without difficulty and read it with a new light. Every line breathed of surprise and alarm. Lady Maltravers feared that her husband was very seriously ill. On the Wednesday, two days before she wrote, he had suffered all day from a strange restlessness, which had increased after they had retired in the evening. He could not sleep and had dressed again, saying he would walk a little in the night air to compose himself. He had not returned till near six in the morning, and then seemed so exhausted that he had since been confined to his bed. He was terribly pale, and the doctors feared he had been attacked by some strange fever.

The date of the letter was the 25th of October, fixing the night of the 23d as the time of Sir John's first attack. The coincidence of the date with that of the day missing in Temple's diary was significant, but it was not needed now to convince me that Sir John's ruin was due to something that occurred on that fatal night at Naples.

The question that Dr. Frobisher had asked Miss Maltravers when he was first called to see her brother in London returned to my memory with an overwhelming force. "Had Sir John been subjected to any mental shock; had he received any severe fright?" I knew now that the question should have been answered in the affirmative, for I felt as certain as if Sir John had told me himself that he *had* received a violent shock, probably some terrible fright, on the night of the 23d of October. What the nature of that shock could have been my imagination was powerless to conceive, only I knew that whatever Sir John had done or seen, Adrian Temple and Jocelyn had done or seen also a century before and at the same place. That horror which had blanched the face of all three men for life had perhaps fallen with a less overwhelming force on Temple's seasoned wickedness, but had driven the worthless Jocelyn to the cloister, and was driving Sir John to the grave.

These thoughts as they passed through my mind filled me with a vague alarm. The lateness of the hour, the stillness and the subdued light, made the library in which I sat seem so vast and lonely that I began to feel the same dread of being alone that I had observed so often in my friend. Though only a door separated me from his bedroom, and I could hear his deep and regular breathing, I felt as though I must go in and waken him or Parnham to keep me company and save me from my own reflections. By a strong effort I restrained myself, and sat down to think the matter over and endeavour to frame some hypothesis that might explain the mystery. But it was all to no purpose. I merely wearied myself without being able to arrive at even a plausible conjecture, except that it seemed as though the strange coincidence of date might point to some ghastly charm or incantation which could only be carried out on one certain night of the year.

It must have been near morning when, quite exhausted, I fell into an uneasy slumber in the arm-chair where I sat. My sleep, however brief, was peopled with a succession of fantastic visions, in which I continually saw Sir John, not ill and wasted as now, but vigorous and handsome as I had known him at Oxford, standing beside a glowing brazier and reciting words I could not understand, while another man with a sneering white face sat in a corner playing the air of the *Gagliarda* on a violin. Parnham woke me in my chair at seven o'clock; his master, he said, was still sleeping easily.

I had made up my mind that as soon as he awoke I would inquire of Sir John as to the pages missing from the diary; but though my expectation and excitement were at a high pitch, I was forced to restrain my curiosity, for Sir John's slumber continued late into the day. Dr. Bruton called in the morning, and said that this sleep was what the patient's condition most required and was a distinctly favourable symptom; he was on no account to be disturbed. Sir John did not leave his bed, but continued dozing all day till the evening. When at last he shook off his drowsiness, the hour was already so late that, in spite of my anxiety, I hesitated to talk with him about the diaries lest I should unduly excite him before the night.

As the evening advanced he became very uneasy, and rose more than once from his bed. This restlessness following on the repose of the day, ought perhaps to have made me anxious, for I have since observed that when death is very near an apprehensive unrest often sets in both with men and animals. It seems as if they dreaded to resign themselves to sleep, lest as they slumber the last enemy should seize them unawares. They try to fling off the bedclothes, they sometimes must leave their beds and walk. So it was with poor John Maltravers on his last Christmas Eve. I had sat with him grieving for his disquiet until he seemed to grow more tranquil, and at length fell asleep. I was sleeping that night in his room instead of Parnham, and tired with sitting up through the previous night, I flung myself, dressed as I was, upon the bed. I had scarcely dozed off, I think, before the sound of his violin awoke me. I found he had risen from his bed, had taken his favourite instrument, and was playing in his sleep. The air was the *Gagliarda* of the "Areopagita" suite, which I had not heard since we had played it last together at Oxford, and it brought back with it a crowd of far-off memories and infinite regrets. I cursed the sleepiness which had overcome me at my watchman's post, and allowed Sir John to play once more that melody which had always been fraught with such evil for him; and I was about to wake him gently when he was startled from sleep by a strange accident. As I walked towards him the violin seemed entirely to collapse in his hands, and, as a matter of fact, the belly then gave way and broke under the strain of the strings. As the strings slackened, the last note became an unearthly discord. If I were superstitious I should say that some evil spirit then went out of the violin, and broke in his parting throes the wooden tabernacle which had so long sheltered him. It was the last time the instrument was ever used, and that hideous chord was the last that Maltravers ever played.

I had feared that the shock of waking thus suddenly from sleep would have a very prejudicial effect upon the sleepwalker, but this seemed not to be the case. I persuaded him to go back at once to bed, and in a few minutes he fell asleep again. In the morning he seemed for the first time distinctly better; there was indeed something of his old self in his manner. It seemed as though the breaking of the violin had been an actual relief to him; and I believe that on that Christmas morning his better instincts woke, and that his old religious training and the associations of his boyhood then made their last appeal. I was pleased at such a change, however temporary it might prove. He wished to go to church, and I determined that again I would subdue my curiosity and defer the questions I was burning to put till after our return from the morning service. Miss Maltravers had gone indoors to make some preparation, Sir John was in his wheelchair on the terrace, and I was sitting by him in the sun. For a few moments he appeared immersed in silent thought, and then bent over towards me till his head was close to mine and said, "Dear William, there is something I must tell you. I feel I cannot even go to church till I have told you all." His manner shocked me beyond expression. I knew that he was going to tell me the secret of the lost pages, but instead of wishing any longer to have my curiosity satisfied, I felt a horrible dread of what he might say next. He took my hand in his and held it tightly, as a man who was about to undergo severe physical pain and sought the consolation of a friend's support. Then he went on, "You will be shocked at what I am going to tell you; but listen, and do not give me up. You must stand by me and comfort me and help me to turn again." He paused for a moment and continued, "It was one night in October, when Constance and I were at

Naples. I took that violin and went by myself to the ruined villa on the Scoglio di Venere." He had been speaking with difficulty. His hand clutched mine convulsively, but still I felt it trembling, and I could see the moisture standing thick on his forehead. At this point the effort seemed too much for him and he broke off. "I cannot go on, I cannot tell you, but you can read it for yourself. In that diary which I gave you there are some pages missing." The suspense was becoming intolerable to me, and I broke in, "Yes, yes, I know, you cut them out. Tell me where they are." He went on, "Yes, I cut them out lest they should possibly fall into any one's hands unaware. But before you read them you must swear, as you hope for salvation, that you will never try to do what is written in them. Swear this to me now or I never can let you see them." My eagerness was too great to stop now to discuss trifles, and to humour him I swore as desired. He had been speaking with a continual increasing effort; he cast a hurried and fearful glance round as though he expected to see some one listening, and it was almost in a whisper that he went on, "You will find them in ——" His agitation had become most painful to watch, and as he spoke the last words a convulsion passed over his face, and speech failing him, he sank back on his pillow. A strange fear took hold of me. For a moment I thought there were others on the terrace beside myself, and turned round expecting to see Miss Maltravers returned; but we were still alone. I even fancied that just as Sir John spoke his last words I felt something brush swiftly by me. He put up his hands, beating the air with a most painful gesture as though he were trying to keep off an antagonist who had gripped him by the throat, and made a final struggle to speak. But the spasm was too strong for him; a dreadful stillness followed, and he was gone.

There is little more to add; for Sir John's guilty secret perished with him. Though I was sure from his manner that the missing leaves were concealed somewhere at Worth, and though as executor I caused the most diligent search to be made, no trace of them was afterwards found; nor did any circumstance ever transpire to fling further light upon the matter. I must confess that I should have felt the discovery of these pages as a relief; for though I dreaded what I might have had to read, yet I was more anxious lest, being found at a later period and falling into other hands, they should cause a recrudescence of that plague which had blighted Sir John's life.

Of the nature of the events which took place on that night at Naples I can form no conjecture. But as certain physical sights have ere now proved so revolting as to unhinge the intellect, so I can imagine that the mind may in a state of extreme tension conjure up to itself some forms of moral evil so hideous as metaphysically to sear it: and this, I believe, happened in the case both of Adrian Temple and of Sir John Maltravers.

It is difficult to imagine the accessories used to produce the mental excitation in which alone such a presentment of evil could become imaginable. Fancy and legend, which have combined to represent as possible appearances of the supernatural, agree also in considering them as more likely to occur at certain times and places than at others; and it is possible that the missing pages of the diary contained an account of the time, place, and other conditions chosen by Temple for some deadly experiment. Sir John most probably re-enacted the scene under precisely similar conditions, and the effect on his overwrought imagination was so vivid as to upset the balance of his mind. The time chosen was no doubt the night of the 23d of October, and I cannot help thinking that the place was one of those evil-looking and ruinous sea-rooms which had so terrifying an effect on Miss Maltravers. Temple may have used on that night one of the medieval incantations, or possibly the more ancient invocation of the Isiac rite with which a man of his knowledge and proclivities would certainly be familiar. The accessories of either are suffiently hideous to weaken the mind by terror, and so prepare it for a belief in some frightful apparition. But whatever was done, I feel sure that the music of the *Gagliarda* formed part of the ceremonial.

Medieval philosophers and theologians held that evil is in its essence so horrible that the human mind, if it could realise it, must perish at its contemplation. Such realisation was by mercy ordinarily withheld, but its possibility was hinted in the legend of the *Visio malefica*. The *Visio Beatifica* was, as is well known, that vision of the Deity or realisation of the perfect Good which was to form the happiness of heaven, and the reward of the sanctified in the next world. Tradition says that this vision was accorded also to some specially elect spirits even in this life, as to Enoch, Elijah, Stephen, and Jerome. But there was a converse to the Beatific Vision in the *Visio malefica*, or presentation of absolute Evil, which was to be the chief torture of the damned, and which, like the Beatific Vision, had been made visible in life to certain desperate men. It visited Esau, as was said, when he found no place for repentance, and Judas, whom it drove to suicide. Cain saw it when he murdered his brother, and legend relates that in his case, and in that of others, it left a physical brand to be borne by the body to the grave. It was supposed that the Malefic Vision, besides being thus spontaneously presented to typically abandoned men, had actually been purposely called up by some few great adepts, and used by them to blast their enemies. But to do so was considered equivalent to a conscious surrender to the powers of evil, as the vision once seen took away all hope of final salvation.

Adrian Temple would undoubtedly be cognisant of this legend, and the lost experiment may have been an attempt to call up the Malefic Vision. It is but a vague conjecture at the best, for the tree of the knowledge of Evil bears many sorts of poisonous fruit, and no one can give full account of the extravagances of a wayward fancy.

Conjointly with Miss Sophia, Sir John appointed me his executor and guardian of his only son. Two months later we had lit a great fire in the library at Worth. In it, after the servants were gone to bed, we burnt the book containing the "Areopagita" of Graziani, and the Stradivarius fiddle.

The diaries of Temple I had already destroyed, and wish that I could as easily blot out their foul and debasing memories from my mind. I shall probably be blamed by those who would exalt art at the expense of everything else, for burning a unique violin. This reproach I am content to bear. Though I am not unreasonably superstitious, and have no sympathy for that potential pantheism to which Sir John Maltravers surrendered his intellect, yet I felt so great an aversion to this violin that I would neither suffer it to remain at Worth, nor pass into other hands. Miss Sophia was entirely at one with me on this point. It was the same feeling which restrains any except fools or braggarts from wishing to sleep in "haunted" rooms, or to live in houses polluted with the memory of a revolting crime. No sane mind believes in foolish apparitions, but fancy may at times bewitch the best of us. So the Stradivarius was burnt. It was, after all, perhaps not so serious a matter, for, as I have said, the bass-bar had given way. There had always been a question whether it was strong enough to resist the strain of modern stringing. Experience showed at last that it was not. With the failure of the bass-bar the belly collapsed, and the wood broke across the grain in so extraordinary a manner as to put the fiddle beyond repair, except as a curiosity. Its loss, therefore, is not to be so much regretted. Sir Edward has been brought up to think more of a cricket-bat than of a violin-bow; but if he wishes at any time to buy a Stradivarius, the fortunes of Worth and Royston, nursed through two long minorities, will certainly justify his doing so.

Miss Sophia and I stood by and watched the holocaust. My heart misgave me for a moment when I saw the mellow red varnish blistering off the back, but I put my regret resolutely aside. As the bright flames jumped up and lapped it round, they flung a red glow on the scroll. It was wonderfully wrought, and differed, as I think Miss Maltravers has already said, from any known example of Stradivarius. As we watched it, the scroll took form, and we saw what we had never seen before, that it was cut so that the deep lines in a certain light showed as the profile of a man. It was a wizened little paganish face, with sharp-cut features and a bald head. As I looked at it I knew at once (and a cameo has since confirmed the fact) that it was a head of Porpyhry. Thus the second label found in the violin was explained and Sir John's view confirmed, that Stradivarius had made the instrument for some Neo-Platonist enthusiast who had dedicated it to his master Porphyrius.

A year after Sir John's death I went with Miss Maltravers to Worth church to see a plain slab of slate which we had placed over her brother's grave. We stood in bright sunlight in the Maltravers chapel, with the monuments of that splendid family about us. Among them were the altar-tomb of Sir Esmoun, and the effigies of more than one Crusader. As I looked on their knightly forms, with their heads resting on their tilted helms, their faces set firm, and their hands joined in prayer, I could not help envying them that full and unwavering faith for which they had fought and died. It seemed to stand out in such sharp contrast with our latter-day sciolism and half-believed creeds, and to be flung into higher relief by the Dark Shadow of John Maltravers's ruined life. At our feet was the great brass of one Sir Roger de Maltravers. I pointed out the end of the inscription to my companion—"CVJVS ANIMAE, ATQVE ANIMABVS OMNIVM FIDELIVM DEFVNCTORVM, ATQVE NOSTRIS ANIMABVS QVVM EX HAC LVCE TRANSIVERIMVS, PROPITIETVR DEVS." Though no Catholic, I could not refuse to add a sincere Amen. Miss Sophia, who is not ignorant of Latin, read the inscription after me. "Ex hac luce," she said, as though speaking to herself, "out of this light; alas! alas! for some the light is darkness."

A CATALOGUE OF SELECTED DOVER BOOKS
IN ALL FIELDS OF INTEREST

# A CATALOGUE OF SELECTED DOVER BOOKS
## IN ALL FIELDS OF INTEREST

AMERICA'S OLD MASTERS, James T. Flexner. Four men emerged unexpectedly from provincial 18th century America to leadership in European art: Benjamin West, J. S. Copley, C. R. Peale, Gilbert Stuart. Brilliant coverage of lives and contributions. Revised, 1967 edition. 69 plates. 365pp. of text.
21806-6 Paperbound $3.00

FIRST FLOWERS OF OUR WILDERNESS: AMERICAN PAINTING, THE COLONIAL PERIOD, James T. Flexner. Painters, and regional painting traditions from earliest Colonial times up to the emergence of Copley, West and Peale Sr., Foster, Gustavus Hesselius, Feke, John Smibert and many anonymous painters in the primitive manner. Engaging presentation, with 162 illustrations. xxii + 368pp.
22180-6 Paperbound $3.50

THE LIGHT OF DISTANT SKIES: AMERICAN PAINTING, 1760-1835, James T. Flexner. The great generation of early American painters goes to Europe to learn and to teach: West, Copley, Gilbert Stuart and others. Allston, Trumbull, Morse; also contemporary American painters—primitives, derivatives, academics—who remained in America. 102 illustrations. xiii + 306pp.
22179-2 Paperbound $3.50

A HISTORY OF THE RISE AND PROGRESS OF THE ARTS OF DESIGN IN THE UNITED STATES, William Dunlap. Much the richest mine of information on early American painters, sculptors, architects, engravers, miniaturists, etc. The only source of information for scores of artists, the major primary source for many others. Unabridged reprint of rare original 1834 edition, with new introduction by James T. Flexner, and 394 new illustrations. Edited by Rita Weiss. 6⅝ x 9⅝.
21695-0, 21696-9, 21697-7 Three volumes, Paperbound $15.00

EPOCHS OF CHINESE AND JAPANESE ART, Ernest F. Fenollosa. From primitive Chinese art to the 20th century, thorough history, explanation of every important art period and form, including Japanese woodcuts; main stress on China and Japan, but Tibet, Korea also included. Still unexcelled for its detailed, rich coverage of cultural background, aesthetic elements, diffusion studies, particularly of the historical period. 2nd, 1913 edition. 242 illustrations. lii + 439pp. of text.
20364-6, 20365-4 Two volumes, Paperbound $6.00

THE GENTLE ART OF MAKING ENEMIES, James A. M. Whistler. Greatest wit of his day deflates Oscar Wilde, Ruskin, Swinburne; strikes back at inane critics, exhibitions, art journalism; aesthetics of impressionist revolution in most striking form. Highly readable classic by great painter. Reproduction of edition designed by Whistler. Introduction by Alfred Werner. xxxvi + 334pp.
21875-9 Paperbound $3.00

VISUAL ILLUSIONS: THEIR CAUSES, CHARACTERISTICS, AND APPLICATIONS, Matthew Luckiesh. Thorough description and discussion of optical illusion, geometric and perspective, particularly; size and shape distortions, illusions of color, of motion; natural illusions; use of illusion in art and magic, industry, etc. Most useful today with op art, also for classical art. Scores of effects illustrated. Introduction by William H. Ittleson. 100 illustrations. xxi + 252pp.

21530-X Paperbound $2.00

A HANDBOOK OF ANATOMY FOR ART STUDENTS, Arthur Thomson. Thorough, virtually exhaustive coverage of skeletal structure, musculature, etc. Full text, supplemented by anatomical diagrams and drawings and by photographs of undraped figures. Unique in its comparison of male and female forms, pointing out differences of contour, texture, form. 211 figures, 40 drawings, 86 photographs. xx + 459pp. 5⅜ x 8⅜.

21163-0 Paperbound $3.50

150 MASTERPIECES OF DRAWING, Selected by Anthony Toney. Full page reproductions of drawings from the early 16th to the end of the 18th century, all beautifully reproduced: Rembrandt, Michelangelo, Dürer, Fragonard, Urs, Graf, Wouwerman, many others. First-rate browsing book, model book for artists. xviii + 150pp. 8⅜ x 11¼.

21032-4 Paperbound $3.50

THE LATER WORK OF AUBREY BEARDSLEY, Aubrey Beardsley. Exotic, erotic, ironic masterpieces in full maturity: Comedy Ballet, Venus and Tannhauser, Pierrot, Lysistrata, Rape of the Lock, Savoy material, Ali Baba, Volpone, etc. This material revolutionized the art world, and is still powerful, fresh, brilliant. With *The Early Work,* all Beardsley's finest work. 174 plates, 2 in color. xiv + 176pp. 8⅛ x 11.

21817-1 Paperbound $3.75

DRAWINGS OF REMBRANDT, Rembrandt van Rijn. Complete reproduction of fabulously rare edition by Lippmann and Hofstede de Groot, completely reedited, updated, improved by Prof. Seymour Slive, Fogg Museum. Portraits, Biblical sketches, landscapes, Oriental types, nudes, episodes from classical mythology—All Rembrandt's fertile genius. Also selection of drawings by his pupils and followers. "Stunning volumes," *Saturday Review.* 550 illustrations. lxxviii + 552pp. 9⅛ x 12¼.

21485-0, 21486-9 Two volumes, Paperbound $10.00

THE DISASTERS OF WAR, Francisco Goya. One of the masterpieces of Western civilization—83 etchings that record Goya's shattering, bitter reaction to the Napoleonic war that swept through Spain after the insurrection of 1808 and to war in general. Reprint of the first edition, with three additional plates from Boston's Museum of Fine Arts. All plates facsimile size. Introduction by Philip Hofer, Fogg Museum. v + 97pp. 9⅜ x 8¼.

21872-4 Paperbound $2.50

GRAPHIC WORKS OF ODILON REDON. Largest collection of Redon's graphic works ever assembled: 172 lithographs, 28 etchings and engravings, 9 drawings. These include some of his most famous works. All the plates from *Odilon Redon: oeuvre graphique complet,* plus additional plates. New introduction and caption translations by Alfred Werner. 209 illustrations. xxvii + 209pp. 9⅛ x 12¼.

21966-8 Paperbound $5.00

DESIGN BY ACCIDENT; A BOOK OF "ACCIDENTAL EFFECTS" FOR ARTISTS AND DESIGNERS, James F. O'Brien. Create your own unique, striking, imaginative effects by "controlled accident" interaction of materials: paints and lacquers, oil and water based paints, splatter, crackling materials, shatter, similar items. Everything you do will be different; first book on this limitless art, so useful to both fine artist and commercial artist. Full instructions. 192 plates showing "accidents," 8 in color. viii + 215pp. 8⅜ x 11¼.                    21942-9 Paperbound $3.75

THE BOOK OF SIGNS, Rudolf Koch. Famed German type designer draws 493 beautiful symbols: religious, mystical, alchemical, imperial, property marks, runes, etc. Remarkable fusion of traditional and modern. Good for suggestions of timelessness, smartness, modernity. Text. vi + 104pp. 6⅛ x 9¼.
                                        20162-7 Paperbound $1.25

HISTORY OF INDIAN AND INDONESIAN ART, Ananda K. Coomaraswamy. An unabridged republication of one of the finest books by a great scholar in Eastern art. Rich in descriptive material, history, social backgrounds; Sunga reliefs, Rajput paintings, Gupta temples, Burmese frescoes, textiles, jewelry, sculpture, etc. 400 photos. viii + 423pp. 6⅜ x 9¾.                    21436-2 Paperbound $5.00

PRIMITIVE ART, Franz Boas. America's foremost anthropologist surveys textiles, ceramics, woodcarving, basketry, metalwork, etc.; patterns, technology, creation of symbols, style origins. All areas of world, but very full on Northwest Coast Indians. More than 350 illustrations of baskets, boxes, totem poles, weapons, etc. 378 pp.
                                        20025-6 Paperbound $3.00

THE GENTLEMAN AND CABINET MAKER'S DIRECTOR, Thomas Chippendale. Full reprint (third edition, 1762) of most influential furniture book of all time, by master cabinetmaker. 200 plates, illustrating chairs, sofas, mirrors, tables, cabinets, plus 24 photographs of surviving pieces. Biographical introduction by N. Bienenstock. vi + 249pp. 9⅞ x 12¾.                    21601-2 Paperbound $4.00

AMERICAN ANTIQUE FURNITURE, Edgar G. Miller, Jr. The basic coverage of all American furniture before 1840. Individual chapters cover type of furniture— clocks, tables, sideboards, etc.—chronologically, with inexhaustible wealth of data. More than 2100 photographs, all identified, commented on. Essential to all early American collectors. Introduction by H. E. Keyes. vi + 1106pp. 7⅞ x 10¾.
                    21599-7, 21600-4 Two volumes, Paperbound $11.00

PENNSYLVANIA DUTCH AMERICAN FOLK ART, Henry J. Kauffman. 279 photos, 28 drawings of tulipware, Fraktur script, painted tinware, toys, flowered furniture, quilts, samplers, hex signs, house interiors, etc. Full descriptive text. Excellent for tourist, rewarding for designer, collector. Map. 146pp. 7⅞ x 10¾.
                                        21205-X Paperbound $2.50

EARLY NEW ENGLAND GRAVESTONE RUBBINGS, Edmund V. Gillon, Jr. 43 photographs, 226 carefully reproduced rubbings show heavily symbolic, sometimes macabre early gravestones, up to early 19th century. Remarkable early American primitive art, occasionally strikingly beautiful; always powerful. Text. xxvi + 207pp. 8⅜ x 11¼.                    21380-3 Paperbound $3.50

ALPHABETS AND ORNAMENTS, Ernst Lehner. Well-known pictorial source for decorative alphabets, script examples, cartouches, frames, decorative title pages, calligraphic initials, borders, similar material. 14th to 19th century, mostly European. Useful in almost any graphic arts designing, varied styles. 750 illustrations. 256pp. 7 x 10.                                    21905-4 Paperbound $4.00

PAINTING: A CREATIVE APPROACH, Norman Colquhoun. For the beginner simple guide provides an instructive approach to painting: major stumbling blocks for beginner; overcoming them, technical points; paints and pigments; oil painting; watercolor and other media and color. New section on "plastic" paints. Glossary. Formerly *Paint Your Own Pictures*. 221pp.        22000-1 Paperbound $1.75

THE ENJOYMENT AND USE OF COLOR, Walter Sargent. Explanation of the relations between colors themselves and between colors in nature and art, including hundreds of little-known facts about color values, intensities, effects of high and low illumination, complementary colors. Many practical hints for painters, references to great masters. 7 color plates, 29 illustrations. x + 274pp.
20944-X Paperbound $2.75

THE NOTEBOOKS OF LEONARDO DA VINCI, compiled and edited by Jean Paul Richter. 1566 extracts from original manuscripts reveal the full range of Leonardo's versatile genius: all his writings on painting, sculpture, architecture, anatomy, astronomy, geography, topography, physiology, mining, music, etc., in both Italian and English, with 186 plates of manuscript pages and more than 500 additional drawings. Includes studies for the Last Supper, the lost Sforza monument, and other works. Total of xlvii + 866pp. $7\frac{7}{8}$ x $10\frac{3}{4}$.
22572-0, 22573-9 Two volumes, Paperbound $11.00

MONTGOMERY WARD CATALOGUE OF 1895. Tea gowns, yards of flannel and pillow-case lace, stereoscopes, books of gospel hymns, the New Improved Singer Sewing Machine, side saddles, milk skimmers, straight-edged razors, high-button shoes, spittoons, and on and on . . . listing some 25,000 items, practically all illustrated. Essential to the shoppers of the 1890's, it is our truest record of the spirit of the period. Unaltered reprint of Issue No. 57, Spring and Summer 1895. Introduction by Boris Emmet. Innumerable illustrations. xiii + 624pp. $8\frac{1}{2}$ x $11\frac{5}{8}$.
22377-9 Paperbound $6.95

THE CRYSTAL PALACE EXHIBITION ILLUSTRATED CATALOGUE (LONDON, 1851). One of the wonders of the modern world—the Crystal Palace Exhibition in which all the nations of the civilized world exhibited their achievements in the arts and sciences—presented in an equally important illustrated catalogue. More than 1700 items pictured with accompanying text—ceramics, textiles, cast-iron work, carpets, pianos, sleds, razors, wall-papers, billiard tables, beehives, silverware and hundreds of other artifacts—represent the focal point of Victorian culture in the Western World. Probably the largest collection of Victorian decorative art ever assembled—indispensable for antiquarians and designers. Unabridged republication of the Art-Journal Catalogue of the Great Exhibition of 1851, with all terminal essays. New introduction by John Gloag, F.S.A. xxxiv + 426pp. 9 x 12.
22503-8 Paperbound $5.00

A HISTORY OF COSTUME, Carl Köhler. Definitive history, based on surviving pieces of clothing primarily, and paintings, statues, etc. secondarily. Highly readable text, supplemented by 594 illustrations of costumes of the ancient Mediterranean peoples, Greece and Rome, the Teutonic prehistoric period; costumes of the Middle Ages, Renaissance, Baroque, 18th and 19th centuries. Clear, measured patterns are provided for many clothing articles. Approach is practical throughout. Enlarged by Emma von Sichart. 464pp.        21030-8 Paperbound $3.50

ORIENTAL RUGS, ANTIQUE AND MODERN, Walter A. Hawley. A complete and authoritative treatise on the Oriental rug—where they are made, by whom and how, designs and symbols, characteristics in detail of the six major groups, how to distinguish them and how to buy them. Detailed technical data is provided on periods, weaves, warps, wefts, textures, sides, ends and knots, although no technical background is required for an understanding. 11 color plates, 80 halftones, 4 maps. vi + 320pp. $6\frac{1}{8}$ x $9\frac{1}{8}$.        22366-3 Paperbound $5.00

TEN BOOKS ON ARCHITECTURE, Vitruvius. By any standards the most important book on architecture ever written. Early Roman discussion of aesthetics of building, construction methods, orders, sites, and every other aspect of architecture has inspired, instructed architecture for about 2,000 years. Stands behind Palladio, Michelangelo, Bramante, Wren, countless others. Definitive Morris H. Morgan translation. 68 illustrations. xii + 331pp.        20645-9 Paperbound $3.00

THE FOUR BOOKS OF ARCHITECTURE, Andrea Palladio. Translated into every major Western European language in the two centuries following its publication in 1570, this has been one of the most influential books in the history of architecture. Complete reprint of the 1738 Isaac Ware edition. New introduction by Adolf Placzek, Columbia Univ. 216 plates. xxii + 110pp. of text. $9\frac{1}{2}$ x $12\frac{3}{4}$.
       21308-0 Clothbound $12.50

STICKS AND STONES: A STUDY OF AMERICAN ARCHITECTURE AND CIVILIZATION, Lewis Mumford. One of the great classics of American cultural history. American architecture from the medieval-inspired earliest forms to the early 20th century; evolution of structure and style, and reciprocal influences on environment. 21 photographic illustrations. 238pp.        20202-X Paperbound $2.00

THE AMERICAN BUILDER'S COMPANION, Asher Benjamin. The most widely used early 19th century architectural style and source book, for colonial up into Greek Revival periods. Extensive development of geometry of carpentering, construction of sashes, frames, doors, stairs; plans and elevations of domestic and other buildings. Hundreds of thousands of houses were built according to this book, now invaluable to historians, architects, restorers, etc. 1827 edition. 59 plates. 114pp. $7\frac{7}{8}$ x $10\frac{3}{4}$.
       22236-5 Paperbound $3.50

DUTCH HOUSES IN THE HUDSON VALLEY BEFORE 1776, Helen Wilkinson Reynolds. The standard survey of the Dutch colonial house and outbuildings, with constructional features, decoration, and local history associated with individual homesteads. Introduction by Franklin D. Roosevelt. Map. 150 illustrations. 469pp. $6\frac{5}{8}$ x $9\frac{1}{4}$.        21469-9 Paperbound $5.00

THE ARCHITECTURE OF COUNTRY HOUSES, Andrew J. Downing. Together with Vaux's *Villas and Cottages* this is the basic book for Hudson River Gothic architecture of the middle Victorian period. Full, sound discussions of general aspects of housing, architecture, style, decoration, furnishing, together with scores of detailed house plans, illustrations of specific buildings, accompanied by full text. Perhaps the most influential single American architectural book. 1850 edition. Introduction by J. Stewart Johnson. 321 figures, 34 architectural designs. xvi + 560pp.

22003-6 Paperbound $4.00

LOST EXAMPLES OF COLONIAL ARCHITECTURE, John Mead Howells. Full-page photographs of buildings that have disappeared or been so altered as to be denatured, including many designed by major early American architects. 245 plates. xvii + 248pp. 7⅞ x 10¾.

21143-6 Paperbound $3.50

DOMESTIC ARCHITECTURE OF THE AMERICAN COLONIES AND OF THE EARLY REPUBLIC, Fiske Kimball. Foremost architect and restorer of Williamsburg and Monticello covers nearly 200 homes between 1620-1825. Architectural details, construction, style features, special fixtures, floor plans, etc. Generally considered finest work in its area. 219 illustrations of houses, doorways, windows, capital mantels. xx + 314pp. 7⅞ x 10¾.

21743-4 Paperbound $4.00

EARLY AMERICAN ROOMS: 1650-1858, edited by Russell Hawes Kettell. Tour of 12 rooms, each representative of a different era in American history and each furnished, decorated, designed and occupied in the style of the era. 72 plans and elevations, 8-page color section, etc., show fabrics, wall papers, arrangements, etc. Full descriptive text. xvii + 200pp. of text. 8⅜ x 11¼.

21633-0 Paperbound $5.00

THE FITZWILLIAM VIRGINAL BOOK, edited by J. Fuller Maitland and W. B. Squire. Full modern printing of famous early 17th-century ms. volume of 300 works by Morley, Byrd, Bull, Gibbons, etc. For piano or other modern keyboard instrument; easy to read format. xxxvi + 938pp. 8⅜ x 11.

21068-5, 21069-3 Two volumes, Paperbound $10.00

KEYBOARD MUSIC, Johann Sebastian Bach. Bach Gesellschaft edition. A rich selection of Bach's masterpieces for the harpsichord: the six English Suites, six French Suites, the six Partitas (Clavierübung part I), the Goldberg Variations (Clavierübung part IV), the fifteen Two-Part Inventions and the fifteen Three-Part Sinfonias. Clearly reproduced on large sheets with ample margins; eminently playable. vi + 312pp. 8⅛ x 11.

22360-4 Paperbound $5.00

THE MUSIC OF BACH: AN INTRODUCTION, Charles Sanford Terry. A fine, nontechnical introduction to Bach's music, both instrumental and vocal. Covers organ music, chamber music, passion music, other types. Analyzes themes, developments, innovations. x + 114pp.

21075-8 Paperbound $1.50

BEETHOVEN AND HIS NINE SYMPHONIES, Sir George Grove. Noted British musicologist provides best history, analysis, commentary on symphonies. Very thorough, rigorously accurate; necessary to both advanced student and amateur music lover. 436 musical passages. vii + 407 pp.

20334-4 Paperbound $2.75

JOHANN SEBASTIAN BACH, Philipp Spitta. One of the great classics of musicology, this definitive analysis of Bach's music (and life) has never been surpassed. Lucid, nontechnical analyses of hundreds of pieces (30 pages devoted to St. Matthew Passion, 26 to B Minor Mass). Also includes major analysis of 18th-century music. 450 musical examples. 40-page musical supplement. Total of xx + 1799pp.

(EUK) 22278-0, 22279-9 Two volumes, Clothbound $17.50

MOZART AND HIS PIANO CONCERTOS, Cuthbert Girdlestone. The only full-length study of an important area of Mozart's creativity. Provides detailed analyses of all 23 concertos, traces inspirational sources. 417 musical examples. Second edition. 509pp.　　　　　　　　　　　　　　　　　　　　21271-8 Paperbound $3.50

THE PERFECT WAGNERITE: A COMMENTARY ON THE NIBLUNG'S RING, George Bernard Shaw. Brilliant and still relevant criticism in remarkable essays on Wagner's Ring cycle, Shaw's ideas on political and social ideology behind the plots, role of Leitmotifs, vocal requisites, etc. Prefaces. xxi + 136pp.

(USO) 21707-8 Paperbound $1.75

DON GIOVANNI, W. A. Mozart. Complete libretto, modern English translation; biographies of composer and librettist; accounts of early performances and critical reaction. Lavishly illustrated. All the material you need to understand and appreciate this great work. Dover Opera Guide and Libretto Series; translated and introduced by Ellen Bleiler. 92 illustrations. 209pp.

21134-7 Paperbound $2.00

BASIC ELECTRICITY, U. S. Bureau of Naval Personel. Originally a training course, best non-technical coverage of basic theory of electricity and its applications. Fundamental concepts, batteries, circuits, conductors and wiring techniques, AC and DC, inductance and capacitance, generators, motors, transformers, magnetic amplifiers, synchros, servomechanisms, etc. Also covers blue-prints, electrical diagrams, etc. Many questions, with answers. 349 illustrations. x + 448pp. 6½ x 9¼.

20973-3 Paperbound $3.50

REPRODUCTION OF SOUND, Edgar Villchur. Thorough coverage for laymen of high fidelity systems, reproducing systems in general, needles, amplifiers, preamps, loudspeakers, feedback, explaining physical background. "A rare talent for making technicalities vividly comprehensible," R. Darrell, *High Fidelity*. 69 figures. iv + 92pp.　　　　　　　　　　　　　　　　　　　21515-6 Paperbound $1.35

HEAR ME TALKIN' TO YA: THE STORY OF JAZZ AS TOLD BY THE MEN WHO MADE IT, Nat Shapiro and Nat Hentoff. Louis Armstrong, Fats Waller, Jo Jones, Clarence Williams, Billy Holiday, Duke Ellington, Jelly Roll Morton and dozens of other jazz greats tell how it was in Chicago's South Side, New Orleans, depression Harlem and the modern West Coast as jazz was born and grew. xvi + 429pp.

21726-4 Paperbound $3.00

FABLES OF AESOP, translated by Sir Roger L'Estrange. A reproduction of the very rare 1931 Paris edition; a selection of the most interesting fables, together with 50 imaginative drawings by Alexander Calder. v + 128pp. 6½x9¼.

21780-9 Paperbound $1.50

AGAINST THE GRAIN (A REBOURS), Joris K. Huysmans. Filled with weird images, evidences of a bizarre imagination, exotic experiments with hallucinatory drugs, rich tastes and smells and the diversions of its sybarite hero Duc Jean des Esseintes, this classic novel pushed 19th-century literary decadence to its limits. Full unabridged edition. Do not confuse this with abridged editions generally sold. Introduction by Havelock Ellis. xlix + 206pp. 22190-3 Paperbound $2.50

VARIORUM SHAKESPEARE: HAMLET. Edited by Horace H. Furness; a landmark of American scholarship. Exhaustive footnotes and appendices treat all doubtful words and phrases, as well as suggested critical emendations throughout the play's history. First volume contains editor's own text, collated with all Quartos and Folios. Second volume contains full first Quarto, translations of Shakespeare's sources (Belleforest, and Saxo Grammaticus), Der Bestrafte Brudermord, and many essays on critical and historical points of interest by major authorities of past and present. Includes details of staging and costuming over the years. By far the best edition available for serious students of Shakespeare. Total of xx + 905pp.
21004-9, 21005-7, 2 volumes, Paperbound $7.00

A LIFE OF WILLIAM SHAKESPEARE, Sir Sidney Lee. This is the standard life of Shakespeare, summarizing everything known about Shakespeare and his plays. Incredibly rich in material, broad in coverage, clear and judicious, it has served thousands as the best introduction to Shakespeare. 1931 edition. 9 plates. xxix + 792pp. 21967-4 Paperbound $4.50

MASTERS OF THE DRAMA, John Gassner. Most comprehensive history of the drama in print, covering every tradition from Greeks to modern Europe and America, including India, Far East, etc. Covers more than 800 dramatists, 2000 plays, with biographical material, plot summaries, theatre history, criticism, etc. "Best of its kind in English," New Republic. 77 illustrations. xxii + 890pp.
20100-7 Clothbound $10.00

THE EVOLUTION OF THE ENGLISH LANGUAGE, George McKnight. The growth of English, from the 14th century to the present. Unusual, non-technical account presents basic information in very interesting form: sound shifts, change in grammar and syntax, vocabulary growth, similar topics. Abundantly illustrated with quotations. Formerly Modern English in the Making. xii + 590pp.
21932-1 Paperbound $4.00

AN ETYMOLOGICAL DICTIONARY OF MODERN ENGLISH, Ernest Weekley. Fullest, richest work of its sort, by foremost British lexicographer. Detailed word histories, including many colloquial and archaic words; extensive quotations. Do not confuse this with the Concise Etymological Dictionary, which is much abridged. Total of xxvii + 830pp. 6½ x 9¼.
21873-2, 21874-0 Two volumes, Paperbound $7.90

FLATLAND: A ROMANCE OF MANY DIMENSIONS, E. A. Abbott. Classic of science-fiction explores ramifications of life in a two-dimensional world, and what happens when a three-dimensional being intrudes. Amusing reading, but also useful as introduction to thought about hyperspace. Introduction by Banesh Hoffmann. 16 illustrations. xx + 103pp. 20001-9 Paperbound $1.25

POEMS OF ANNE BRADSTREET, edited with an introduction by Robert Hutchinson. A new selection of poems by America's first poet and perhaps the first significant woman poet in the English language. 48 poems display her development in works of considerable variety—love poems, domestic poems, religious meditations, formal elegies, "quaternions," etc. Notes, bibliography. viii + 222pp.

22160-1 Paperbound $2.50

THREE GOTHIC NOVELS: THE CASTLE OF OTRANTO BY HORACE WALPOLE; VATHEK BY WILLIAM BECKFORD; THE VAMPYRE BY JOHN POLIDORI, WITH FRAGMENT OF A NOVEL BY LORD BYRON, edited by E. F. Bleiler. The first Gothic novel, by Walpole; the finest Oriental tale in English, by Beckford; powerful Romantic supernatural story in versions by Polidori and Byron. All extremely important in history of literature; all still exciting, packed with supernatural thrills, ghosts, haunted castles, magic, etc. xl + 291pp.

21232-7 Paperbound $2.50

THE BEST TALES OF HOFFMANN, E. T. A. Hoffmann. 10 of Hoffmann's most important stories, in modern re-editings of standard translations: Nutcracker and the King of Mice, Signor Formica, Automata, The Sandman, Rath Krespel, The Golden Flowerpot, Master Martin the Cooper, The Mines of Falun, The King's Betrothed, A New Year's Eve Adventure. 7 illustrations by Hoffmann. Edited by E. F. Bleiler. xxxix + 419pp. 21793-0 Paperbound $3.00

GHOST AND HORROR STORIES OF AMBROSE BIERCE, Ambrose Bierce. 23 strikingly modern stories of the horrors latent in the human mind: The Eyes of the Panther, The Damned Thing, An Occurrence at Owl Creek Bridge, An Inhabitant of Carcosa, etc., plus the dream-essay, Visions of the Night. Edited by E. F. Bleiler. xxii + 199pp. 20767-6 Paperbound $1.50

BEST GHOST STORIES OF J. S. LEFANU, J. Sheridan LeFanu. Finest stories by Victorian master often considered greatest supernatural writer of all. Carmilla, Green Tea, The Haunted Baronet, The Familiar, and 12 others. Most never before available in the U. S. A. Edited by E. F. Bleiler. 8 illustrations from Victorian publications. xvii + 467pp. 20415-4 Paperbound $3.00

MATHEMATICAL FOUNDATIONS OF INFORMATION THEORY, A. I. Khinchin. Comprehensive introduction to work of Shannon, McMillan, Feinstein and Khinchin, placing these investigations on a rigorous mathematical basis. Covers entropy concept in probability theory, uniqueness theorem, Shannon's inequality, ergodic sources, the E property, martingale concept, noise, Feinstein's fundamental lemma, Shanon's first and second theorems. Translated by R. A. Silverman and M. D. Friedman. iii + 120pp. 60434-9 Paperbound $2.00

SEVEN SCIENCE FICTION NOVELS, H. G. Wells. The standard collection of the great novels. Complete, unabridged. *First Men in the Moon, Island of Dr. Moreau, War of the Worlds, Food of the Gods, Invisible Man, Time Machine, In the Days of the Comet.* Not only science fiction fans, but every educated person owes it to himself to read these novels. 1015pp. (USO) 20264-X Clothbound $6.00

LAST AND FIRST MEN AND STAR MAKER, TWO SCIENCE FICTION NOVELS, Olaf Stapledon. Greatest future histories in science fiction. In the first, human intelligence is the "hero," through strange paths of evolution, interplanetary invasions, incredible technologies, near extinctions and reemergences. Star Maker describes the quest of a band of star rovers for intelligence itself, through time and space: weird inhuman civilizations, crustacean minds, symbiotic worlds, etc. Complete, unabridged. v + 438pp. (USO) 21962-3 Paperbound $2.50

THREE PROPHETIC NOVELS, H. G. WELLS. Stages of a consistently planned future for mankind. *When the Sleeper Wakes,* and *A Story of the Days to Come,* anticipate *Brave New World* and *1984,* in the 21st Century; *The Time Machine,* only complete version in print, shows farther future and the end of mankind. All show Wells's greatest gifts as storyteller and novelist. Edited by E. F. Bleiler. x + 335pp. (USO) 20605-X Paperbound $2.50

THE DEVIL'S DICTIONARY, Ambrose Bierce. America's own Oscar Wilde—Ambrose Bierce—offers his barbed iconoclastic wisdom in over 1,000 definitions hailed by H. L. Mencken as "some of the most gorgeous witticisms in the English language." 145pp. 20487-1 Paperbound $1.25

MAX AND MORITZ, Wilhelm Busch. Great children's classic, father of comic strip, of two bad boys, Max and Moritz. Also Ker and Plunk (Plisch und Plumm), Cat and Mouse, Deceitful Henry, Ice-Peter, The Boy and the Pipe, and five other pieces. Original German, with English translation. Edited by H. Arthur Klein; translations by various hands and H. Arthur Klein. vi + 216pp. 20181-3 Paperbound $2.00

PIGS IS PIGS AND OTHER FAVORITES, Ellis Parker Butler. The title story is one of the best humor short stories, as Mike Flannery obfuscates biology and English. Also included, That Pup of Murchison's, The Great American Pie Company, and Perkins of Portland. 14 illustrations. v + 109pp. 21532-6 Paperbound $1.25

THE PETERKIN PAPERS, Lucretia P. Hale. It takes genius to be as stupidly mad as the Peterkins, as they decide to become wise, celebrate the "Fourth," keep a cow, and otherwise strain the resources of the Lady from Philadelphia. Basic book of American humor. 153 illustrations. 219pp. 20794-3 Paperbound $2.00

PERRAULT'S FAIRY TALES, translated by A. E. Johnson and S. R. Littlewood, with 34 full-page illustrations by Gustave Doré. All the original Perrault stories—Cinderella, Sleeping Beauty, Bluebeard, Little Red Riding Hood, Puss in Boots, Tom Thumb, etc.—with their witty verse morals and the magnificent illustrations of Doré. One of the five or six great books of European fairy tales. viii + 117pp. 8⅛ x 11. 22311-6 Paperbound $2.00

OLD HUNGARIAN FAIRY TALES, Baroness Orczy. Favorites translated and adapted by author of the *Scarlet Pimpernel.* Eight fairy tales include "The Suitors of Princess Fire-Fly," "The Twin Hunchbacks," "Mr. Cuttlefish's Love Story," and "The Enchanted Cat." This little volume of magic and adventure will captivate children as it has for generations. 90 drawings by Montagu Barstow. 96pp. (USO) 22293-4 Paperbound $1.95

THE RED FAIRY BOOK, Andrew Lang. Lang's color fairy books have long been children's favorites. This volume includes Rapunzel, Jack and the Bean-stalk and 35 other stories, familiar and unfamiliar. 4 plates, 93 illustrations x + 367pp.
21673-X Paperbound $2.50

THE BLUE FAIRY BOOK, Andrew Lang. Lang's tales come from all countries and all times. Here are 37 tales from Grimm, the Arabian Nights, Greek Mythology, and other fascinating sources. 8 plates, 130 illustrations. xi + 390pp.
21437-0 Paperbound $2.75

HOUSEHOLD STORIES BY THE BROTHERS GRIMM. Classic English-language edition of the well-known tales — Rumpelstiltskin, Snow White, Hansel and Gretel, The Twelve Brothers, Faithful John, Rapunzel, Tom Thumb (52 stories in all). Translated into simple, straightforward English by Lucy Crane. Ornamented with headpieces, vignettes, elaborate decorative initials and a dozen full-page illustrations by Walter Crane. x + 269pp.
21080-4 Paperbound **$2.00**

THE MERRY ADVENTURES OF ROBIN HOOD, Howard Pyle. The finest modern versions of the traditional ballads and tales about the great English outlaw. Howard Pyle's complete prose version, with every word, every illustration of the first edition. Do not confuse this facsimile of the original (1883) with modern editions that change text or illustrations. 23 plates plus many page decorations. xxii + 296pp.
22043-5 Paperbound $2.75

THE STORY OF KING ARTHUR AND HIS KNIGHTS, Howard Pyle. The finest children's version of the life of King Arthur; brilliantly retold by Pyle, with 48 of his most imaginative illustrations. xviii + 313pp. 6⅛ x 9¼.
21445-1 Paperbound $2.50

THE WONDERFUL WIZARD OF OZ, L. Frank Baum. America's finest children's book in facsimile of first edition with all Denslow illustrations in full color. The edition a child should have. Introduction by Martin Gardner. 23 color plates, scores of drawings. iv + 267pp.
20691-2 Paperbound $2.50

THE MARVELOUS LAND OF OZ, L. Frank Baum. The second Oz book, every bit as imaginative as the Wizard. The hero is a boy named Tip, but the Scarecrow and the Tin Woodman are back, as is the Oz magic. 16 color plates, 120 drawings by John R. Neill. 287pp.
20692-0 Paperbound $2.50

THE MAGICAL MONARCH OF MO, L. Frank Baum. Remarkable adventures in a land even stranger than Oz. The best of Baum's books not in the Oz series. 15 color plates and dozens of drawings by Frank Verbeck. xviii + 237pp.
21892-9 Paperbound $2.25

THE BAD CHILD'S BOOK OF BEASTS, MORE BEASTS FOR WORSE CHILDREN, A MORAL ALPHABET, Hilaire Belloc. Three complete humor classics in one volume. Be kind to the frog, and do not call him names . . . and 28 other whimsical animals. Familiar favorites and some not so well known. Illustrated by Basil Blackwell. 156pp.
(USO) 20749-8 Paperbound $1.50

EAST O' THE SUN AND WEST O' THE MOON, George W. Dasent. Considered the best of all translations of these Norwegian folk tales, this collection has been enjoyed by generations of children (and folklorists too). Includes True and Untrue, Why the Sea is Salt, East O' the Sun and West O' the Moon, Why the Bear is Stumpy-Tailed, Boots and the Troll, The Cock and the Hen, Rich Peter the Pedlar, and 52 more. The only edition with all 59 tales. 77 illustrations by Erik Werenskiold and Theodor Kittelsen. xv + 418pp.      22521-6 Paperbound $3.50

GOOPS AND HOW TO BE THEM, Gelett Burgess. Classic of tongue-in-cheek humor, masquerading as etiquette book. 87 verses, twice as many cartoons, show mischievous Goops as they demonstrate to children virtues of table manners, neatness, courtesy, etc. Favorite for generations. viii + 88pp. 6½ x 9¼.     22233-0 Paperbound $1.50

ALICE'S ADVENTURES UNDER GROUND, Lewis Carroll. The first version, quite different from the final *Alice in Wonderland,* printed out by Carroll himself with his own illustrations. Complete facsimile of the "million dollar" manuscript Carroll gave to Alice Liddell in 1864. Introduction by Martin Gardner. viii + 96pp. Title and dedication pages in color.     21482-6 Paperbound $1.25

THE BROWNIES, THEIR BOOK, Palmer Cox. Small as mice, cunning as foxes, exuberant and full of mischief, the Brownies go to the zoo, toy shop, seashore, circus, etc., in 24 verse adventures and 266 illustrations. Long a favorite, since their first appearance in St. Nicholas Magazine. xi + 144pp. 6⅝ x 9¼.     21265-3 Paperbound $1.75

SONGS OF CHILDHOOD, Walter De La Mare. Published (under the pseudonym Walter Ramal) when De La Mare was only 29, this charming collection has long been a favorite children's book. A facsimile of the first edition in paper, the 47 poems capture the simplicity of the nursery rhyme and the ballad, including such lyrics as I Met Eve, Tartary, The Silver Penny. vii + 106pp. (USO) 21972-0 Paperbound $2.00

THE COMPLETE NONSENSE OF EDWARD LEAR, Edward Lear. The finest 19th-century humorist-cartoonist in full: all nonsense limericks, zany alphabets, Owl and Pussycat, songs, nonsense botany, and more than 500 illustrations by Lear himself. Edited by Holbrook Jackson. xxix + 287pp.     (USO) 20167-8 Paperbound $2.00

BILLY WHISKERS: THE AUTOBIOGRAPHY OF A GOAT, Frances Trego Montgomery. A favorite of children since the early 20th century, here are the escapades of that rambunctious, irresistible and mischievous goat—Billy Whiskers. Much in the spirit of *Peck's Bad Boy,* this is a book that children never tire of reading or hearing. All the original familiar illustrations by W. H. Fry are included: 6 color plates, 18 black and white drawings. 159pp.     22345-0 Paperbound $2.00

MOTHER GOOSE MELODIES. Faithful republication of the fabulously rare Munroe and Francis "copyright 1833" Boston edition—the most important Mother Goose collection, usually referred to as the "original." Familiar rhymes plus many rare ones, with wonderful old woodcut illustrations. Edited by E. F. Bleiler. 128pp. 4½ x 6⅜.     22577-1 Paperbound $1.00

Two Little Savages; Being the Adventures of Two Boys Who Lived as Indians and What They Learned, Ernest Thompson Seton. Great classic of nature and boyhood provides a vast range of woodlore in most palatable form, a genuinely entertaining story. Two farm boys build a teepee in woods and live in it for a month, working out Indian solutions to living problems, star lore, birds and animals, plants, etc. 293 illustrations. vii + 286pp.

20985-7 Paperbound $2.50

Peter Piper's Practical Principles of Plain & Perfect Pronunciation. Alliterative jingles and tongue-twisters of surprising charm, that made their first appearance in America about 1830. Republished in full with the spirited woodcut illustrations from this earliest American edition. 32pp. 4½ x 6⅜.

22560-7 Paperbound $1.00

Science Experiments and Amusements for Children, Charles Vivian. 73 easy experiments, requiring only materials found at home or easily available, such as candles, coins, steel wool, etc.; illustrate basic phenomena like vacuum, simple chemical reaction, etc. All safe. Modern, well-planned. Formerly *Science Games for Children*. 102 photos, numerous drawings. 96pp. 6⅛ x 9¼.

21856-2 Paperbound $1.25

An Introduction to Chess Moves and Tactics Simply Explained, Leonard Barden. Informal intermediate introduction, quite strong in explaining reasons for moves. Covers basic material, tactics, important openings, traps, positional play in middle game, end game. Attempts to isolate patterns and recurrent configurations. Formerly *Chess*. 58 figures. 102pp. (USO) 21210-6 Paperbound $1.25

Lasker's Manual of Chess, Dr. Emanuel Lasker. Lasker was not only one of the five great World Champions, he was also one of the ablest expositors, theorists, and analysts. In many ways, his Manual, permeated with his philosophy of battle, filled with keen insights, is one of the greatest works ever written on chess. Filled with analyzed games by the great players. A single-volume library that will profit almost any chess player, beginner or master. 308 diagrams. xli x 349pp.

20640-8 Paperbound $2.75

The Master Book of Mathematical Recreations, Fred Schuh. In opinion of many the finest work ever prepared on mathematical puzzles, stunts, recreations; exhaustively thorough explanations of mathematics involved, analysis of effects, citation of puzzles and games. Mathematics involved is elementary. Translated by F. Göbel. 194 figures. xxiv + 430pp.

22134-2 Paperbound $3.50

Mathematics, Magic and Mystery, Martin Gardner. Puzzle editor for Scientific American explains mathematics behind various mystifying tricks: card tricks, stage "mind reading," coin and match tricks, counting out games, geometric dissections, etc. Probability sets, theory of numbers clearly explained. Also provides more than 400 tricks, guaranteed to work, that you can do. 135 illustrations. xii + 176pp.

20335-2 Paperbound $1.75

MATHEMATICAL PUZZLES FOR BEGINNERS AND ENTHUSIASTS, Geoffrey Mott-Smith. 189 puzzles from easy to difficult—involving arithmetic, logic, algebra, properties of digits, probability, etc.—for enjoyment and mental stimulus. Explanation of mathematical principles behind the puzzles. 135 illustrations. viii + 248pp.

20198-8 Paperbound $1.75

PAPER FOLDING FOR BEGINNERS, William D. Murray and Francis J. Rigney. Easiest book on the market, clearest instructions on making interesting, beautiful origami. Sail boats, cups, roosters, frogs that move legs, bonbon boxes, standing birds, etc. 40 projects; more than 275 diagrams and photographs. 94pp.

20713-7 Paperbound $1.00

TRICKS AND GAMES ON THE POOL TABLE, Fred Herrmann. 79 tricks and games— some solitaires, some for two or more players, some competitive games—to entertain you between formal games. Mystifying shots and throws, unusual caroms, tricks involving such props as cork, coins, a hat, etc. Formerly *Fun on the Pool Table*. 77 figures. 95pp.

21814-7 Paperbound $1.25

HAND SHADOWS TO BE THROWN UPON THE WALL: A SERIES OF NOVEL AND AMUSING FIGURES FORMED BY THE HAND, Henry Bursill. Delightful picturebook from great-grandfather's day shows how to make 18 different hand shadows: a bird that flies, duck that quacks, dog that wags his tail, camel, goose, deer, boy, turtle, etc. Only book of its sort. vi + 33pp. 6½ x 9¼. 21779-5 Paperbound $1.00

WHITTLING AND WOODCARVING, E. J. Tangerman. 18th printing of best book on market. "If you can cut a potato you can carve" toys and puzzles, chains, chessmen, caricatures, masks, frames, woodcut blocks, surface patterns, much more. Information on tools, woods, techniques. Also goes into serious wood sculpture from Middle Ages to present, East and West. 464 photos, figures. x + 293pp.

20965-2 Paperbound $2.00

HISTORY OF PHILOSOPHY, Julián Marías. Possibly the clearest, most easily followed, best planned, most useful one-volume history of philosophy on the market; neither skimpy nor overfull. Full details on system of every major philosopher and dozens of less important thinkers from pre-Socratics up to Existentialism and later. Strong on many European figures usually omitted. Has gone through dozens of editions in Europe. 1966 edition, translated by Stanley Appelbaum and Clarence Strowbridge. xviii + 505pp. 21739-6 Paperbound $3.50

YOGA: A SCIENTIFIC EVALUATION, Kovoor T. Behanan. Scientific but non-technical study of physiological results of yoga exercises; done under auspices of Yale U. Relations to Indian thought, to psychoanalysis, etc. 16 photos. xxiii + 270pp.

20505-3 Paperbound $2.50

*Prices subject to change without notice.*
Available at your book dealer or write for free catalogue to Dept. GI, Dover Publications, Inc., 180 Varick St., N. Y., N. Y. 10014. Dover publishes more than 150 books each year on science, elementary and advanced mathematics, biology, music, art, literary history, social sciences and other areas.